GRANITE
HARBOR

Also by Peter Nichols

The Rocks

Oil and Ice

Evolution's Captain

A Voyage for Madmen

Voyage to the North Star

Sea Change

GRANITE HARBOR

Peter Nichols

CELADON
BOOKS

NEW YORK

GRANITE HARBOR. Copyright © 2024 by Peter Nichols. All rights reserved.
Printed in the United States of America. For information,
address Celadon Books, a division of Macmillan Publishers,
120 Broadway, New York, NY 10271.

www.celadonbooks.com

Library of Congress Cataloging-in-Publication Data

Names: Nichols, Peter, 1950– author.
Title: Granite harbor / Peter Nichols.
Description: First edition. | New York : Celadon Books, 2024.
Identifiers: LCCN 2023028773 | ISBN 9781250894816 (hardcover) |
    ISBN 9781250894830 (ebook)
Subjects: LCGFT: Detective and mystery fiction. | Novels.
Classification: LCC PS3564.I19844 G73 2024 | DDC 813/.54—dc23/
    eng/20230626
LC record available at https://lccn.loc.gov/2023028773

Our books may be purchased in bulk for promotional, educational,
or business use. Please contact your local bookseller or the Macmillan
Corporate and Premium Sales Department at 1-800-221-7945, extension 5442,
or by email at MacmillanSpecialMarkets@macmillan.com.

First Edition: 2024

10 9 8 7 6 5 4 3 2 1

For my son, Gus Nichols,
David Nichols, Liz Sharp, Matt deGarmo, Ann Caswell,
Peter Selgin, Annie Nichols, Roger Salloch,
Richard Podolsky, Bridget Conway, Bill and Jan Conrad,
and Emily Fletcher.

When the crowd caught sight of the murderers, with their escort of blue-coated highway patrolmen, it fell silent, as though amazed to find them humanly shaped.

—Truman Capote, *In Cold Blood*

. . .

The three boys rode their skateboards down Chestnut Street until long after dark. Streetlights glowed faintly in the depthless shadow that draped Granite Harbor below the rim of Mount Meguntic. Channel buoys winked green and red out in the blackness of Penobscot Bay.

The boys whooped and shrieked as their boards flew over unseen bumps and hollows. These hours were the buffer between school and home, when time became elastic and they didn't think of their changing lives, school pressures, disapproving parents, the looming end of childhood.

The evening's cool fall mist was turning to a cold rain. The backs and hoods of the boys' sweatshirts were dark. Tramping back up Chestnut Street, Jared said, "Man, I'm getting soaked. Let's go to my house."

"I'm hungry," said Ethan.

"We've got Hot Pockets at my place," said Jared.

"Let's stay out a little longer," said Shane. He jumped on his board and drifted away from the other two at the intersection of Limerock Street.

They'd been born within days of each other. Their mothers, who met on the Midcoast Medical Center maternity ward, drifted apart over the years as they went through divorce, widowhood, a move to a distant neighborhood, but the boys remained inseparable growing up. Now, in their teenage years, their characters were evolving. They were not always in sync.

These days, Shane wanted to stay out later.

"It's more fun in the dark," he said. "Let's go down Elm Street, then we'll go to your place."

"Bro, c'mon . . ." Ethan called, "it's—"

His words were blown away. A fierce gust of wind tore into the large oak at the corner of Chestnut and Limerock, shaking it with a sound like breaking surf, scattering spray down the street.

"Shane . . ."

They could hardly see him through the filmy air. When the gust dropped he had disappeared into the gloom beneath the black outline of Mount Meguntic. But they could still hear his skateboard clattering away.

Then through the rain they saw a flame. A brief smeary glimpse of Shane's face as he lit a cigarette. "Dude . . . I'm staying out," his voice came back after a moment. "It's too beautiful a day."

The other two boys laughed. Ethan called louder, "We'll be at Jared's."

As Ethan and Jared turned, headlights swept them. They lowered their eyes and moved to the side of the road to let the vehicle pass.

The pickup truck's high beams raked the two boys' faces as it slowed and turned onto Limerock Street. The driver saw them squint, avert their eyes, and turn away as he passed.

He passed the third boy halfway down the block.

Two had stepped off their boards, stopped at the corner. The third floated slowly away.

They were separating.

The driver lifted his foot off the accelerator and coasted. . . .

His truck, a slightly battered Ford, dark blue, was like many others in every town in Maine. In winter, he hitched a snowplow to the front. He drove around at all hours. He parked and ate sandwiches, sipped coffee, and watched the people who passed. He learned their routines, who they spent time with.

At the next stop sign, he was no longer in the cab of his truck. He was squatting beside the dog shaking and groaning above the muddy brown Florida canal. The pictures shifted. . . . He was beneath the small blond girl riding him like a rocking horse. . . . He was pinned to the ground as boys and girls spread their legs above him. . . . In the woods with Ivan, the Master . . .

The hanging coyote was speaking his name. . . . In his mouth he tasted the bitter pus. . . .

Chemical neurotransmitters leaped in his brain.

Then the rain was drumming again on the roof. The wipers slashed back and forth.

He turned right onto Union Street. Sped up, touching forty as the road sloped downhill, then slowed and turned right again on Elm. A block of six tall captains' houses returned him to the intersection at the bottom of Chestnut Street.

He stopped and looked around. There was no traffic. On such a night, everyone in town was at home, making supper, watching TV.

He turned right and drove slowly up the hill again.

The two boys appeared ahead on their skateboards. His headlights lit them up through the rain, forcing their eyes down and away as they clattered past.

He knew the headlights were all they would see of him. They wouldn't remember the truck.

He turned once more onto Limerock Street. Before the stop sign, he reached the third boy.

Part One

I

The air was frigid, condensing Isabel's breath into plumes above her face. It was October and she was no closer to being able to pay for a new furnace than when it had died in August. She had to throw the thought aside like the down comforter as she jumped out of bed, turned on the space heater in her bathroom, and went downstairs to let the dog out.

Back upstairs, with no hot water, she used a washcloth at the sink. Then she began to dress.

She'd laid out her costume the night before. Roger Priestly had given her a photocopied illustration showing the name and arrangement of each particular layer: linen shift (over her own cotton underpants and L.L. Bean sports bra), large-weave woolen hose stockings, petticoat, free-hanging pock-ets of some rugged burlap material fastened around the waist like empty udders beneath outer layers, front-lacing bodice, thick homespun woolen dress, apron, cape, and the linen "coif," shaped like a loose-fitting bathing cap. Finally, those awful shoes, like black orthopedic clogs with a large orna-mental buckle—pirate shoes from some Disney cartoon. All of it purchased for her from a theatrical costume house in Boston.

Good lord, Isabel thought, looking at Goodwife Swaine in the tall bedroom mirror. *You poor woman! You milk cows, chop wood, nurse infants, churn butter, slaughter pigs, chickens, God knows what else, cook over an open fire, and* entertain *your husband . . . in this getup?*

At least she felt warm.

Ethan was still asleep as she passed his bedroom door and negotiated the narrow staircase with her voluminous layers, making a noise as if she were dragging a canvas tent down the stairs.

When she opened the door to let the dog back in, Flynn barked at her and stepped backward.

"Quiet, Flynn! Come inside."

Warily, the dog edged in, giving her a wide berth. He looked at her and growled.

"Oh shush. It's just me. Now lie down in your bed." Isabel pointed.

A high-strung Australian shepherd, Flynn had difficulty with change, surprises. He slunk to his bed in a corner of the kitchen and lay down.

Now the house was still. No noise—not even the rumbling of a furnace in the basement. She'd never noticed the sound until it had stopped. No shouting—one of the mercies of the new regime of Ethan's "unschooling." Her doubts at pulling him out of school allayed for now by the extraordinary peace in the house every morning. Ethan had stopped throwing up from stress before slouching off to the bus with that insanely overloaded backpack. She should have done this five years ago. Or maybe from the beginning. He knew everything anyway. And he had his ships to build.

She grabbed her mug and pushed herself and her outfit out the kitchen door.

The girl at the Granite Deli & Bagel drive-through window didn't bat an eye at the cape, the bodice, the voluminous dress and apron bunched under the steering wheel. Isabel felt like someone on her way to a Halloween party.

She sipped her latte and let out a long heartfelt sigh. Again, she was awash with relief that Ethan was no longer in school. Better now they were both out. As a high school teacher, she'd grown sick of pushing her students through the prescribed mass of facts, dates, summaries, training them for tests, abetting the notion that education consisted of the rote repetition of curricula. Trying to get Ethan to do his homework, repeating all the tired and tedious rationales, had only made him angry, frustrated, and, in recent months, physically ill. Almost every kid she knew in school was anxious, bored, heading for or already suffering deep depression. Half of them were on the standard prescriptive response: Zoloft or Ritalin.

They should all be outdoors! she'd screamed inside her head a hundred times, watching them bent over their phones at school, on the way to school, after school, at home. *They should be in the woods! On the water! Making things, breaking things! Digging holes! Climbing and falling out of trees!*

A few other teachers and parents agreed with her. Others told her kindly that the problem was hers: she was burning out. She needed to take up yoga, qigong, cut out gluten. Quit mourning and get a relationship. She'd tried that.

It was a relief when the high school fired her. Afterward, four years of copyediting on the *Penobscot Bay Journal* had been peaceful, dull, but it paid the bills, until the magazine had folded. Then an additional year of getting up in the icy predawn to prepare the sourdough had made it easy to quit the Red Barn Bakery and, at Nancy's urging, join the crew at the Granite Harbor Settlement.

The Settlement paid even less than the bakery, but "it'll be fun!" Nancy promised. "Dressing up! Gardening! Making fires! Physical things! Educating people who *want* to know everything you can tell them! And you'll go back in time!"

She sipped her latte, still warm—the new commute was not far. Two miles north of town, she slowed as she approached the sign and turn for the GRANITE HARBOR LIVING HISTORY SETTLEMENT.

Roger had filled her in on the history of the place, ancient and modern. Sometime in the 1970s, picnickers had found a half-buried scattering of old tools, broken ceramic pieces, and colored glass in the gravel bank of the stream that ran through the marshes to the rocky beach two miles north of Granite Harbor. The archaeology department at the University of Maine dated them from the early seventeenth century. Subsequent investigation of the site unearthed rusted pieces of flintlock mechanisms, stones arranged in the shape of a crude forge, rotting half-buried timbers roughly the size of the cabins erected by early European settlers in what was then still part of the Massachusetts Bay Colony.

A single paragraph among the many histories of the colonization of this part of the Maine coast mentioned the landing, in 1643, of a ship from Wareham, England. Here, a band of English colonists founded and later, for reasons unknown, abandoned a small settlement.

After it gave up its small, buried artifacts, the dig was also abandoned in the 1980s. A group of investors decided to erect over the scrabble of unfilled holes an imagined re-creation of the original settlement. They built four small shingle-roofed log cabins, a blacksmith's forge, laid out a split-rail stockade fence perimeter, installed a gift shop, a parking lot, and charged an entrance fee. Local "players"—retirees, history buffs, burned-out schoolteachers—were hired to inhabit the roles of the settlers. They dressed in seventeenth-century clothing and interacted with visitors. Operating as a 501(c)(3) nonprofit enterprise, Granite Harbor Living History Settlement became a popular midcoast attraction. Tourists, schoolchildren in buses, came and chatted with the "settlers," asking them about their daily lives.

Isabel had been trying to imagine Goodwife Hannah Swaine, the settler she had been assigned to represent. A scant record, listing the owners of cattle in 1649, recorded her age as thirty-two, and her husband, Samuel Swaine, thirty-six.

Nothing more was known about Hannah—whether she and Samuel had children, if she loved her husband, was a cheerful soul or a bitter, complaining shrew. Nor why they had left England for the sketchy perils of the New World. They were simply two names in the aspic of history. They lived and struggled here, at the mouth of this river, before, at some unknown date, the settlement had been abandoned.

At forty-two, Isabel Dorr was ten years older than Hannah. She had grown anxious, broker, and finally, despite fighting it with all the usual remedies—drugs, alcohol, yoga, Buddhism—deeply depressed since her husband, Joshua Dorr, had disappeared on a yacht race to England eleven years earlier. Without a body, a funeral, or witnesses, she'd had a problem with *closure*. She hadn't passed through the predicted five stages of grief but gotten stuck in an unending rut between denial and anger.

She suffered from trichotillomania—a childhood tic that became a full-blown disorder after Joshua's disappearance—and couldn't stop pulling out the hair on both sides of her head with fingers like tweezers. More recently, coinciding with Ethan's adolescence, it had gotten worse, resulting in bare patches over her ears. Finally she'd cut it all off, an eighth of an inch all over, too short to get a purchase on it with her fingers, maintaining a Sinéad O'Connor buzz cut that her friends insisted made her look sexy and awesome. She'd adopted chemo headwear fashions, fleece cloches, beanies, watch caps, or a scarf knotted at the top of her head, and sometimes she wore no covering at all on the rare occasions when she felt she could carry off sexy and awesome, or when she was at home. She was five foot nine, and with her height and slim hips she looked "awesome in jeans!" her friends told her. She practiced yoga with Kathy McKinnon at Mountain Hall when she could find the time, walked the two miles out and back to Calderwood Point with Flynn most mornings around dawn. She'd become aware of incipient vertical lines above her lips and the suggestion of gathering flesh beneath her jaw, but on good days she felt she was still holding her own—whatever that might still be.

But she was probably doing better than Hannah. From what she'd read, the early colonial settlers had been worn to nubs and early death by hardship. There was no knowing when Hannah had died, but at thirty-two, she'd reached what would have then been considered solid middle age, or older. Isabel imagined her: weather-beaten, with scarred, chapped, thickened hands, dirty, broken nails. Her hair, if she wasn't pulling it out, was no doubt thinning from stress and poor nutrition, lank with unwashing, beginning to streak with gray. Her face reddened and broken-veined, vertical lines, worse than Isabel's, furrowing lips habitually pursed with worry and resignation.

But this didn't allow for character: a woman who might have been warm, humorous, feisty, shy or assertive, strong or weak, forgiving, tender, meek or mean. As a person, Hannah was a blank.

But a voice—Hannah's—started in her head. A kind of earworm that suggested a character with a tongue in her, who began to make unsolicited comments. *Look at the state of this place!* the voice scolded inside Isabel's house. *Have you no shame, woman?* And, on seeing the closed door to Ethan's room: *That lad of yours—idler! Lie-abed!—why isn't he up helping you?*

Hannah or not, Isabel got a sense of someone there. She began to like her.

• • •

The road ended in a gravel parking lot beside the gift shop: a modest National Park–style building that also housed a small office and naturally composting toilets.

And today, a police car, its roof light flashing.

2

Once upon a time, Alex would have said:

"Sophie, we've got to get going or you'll be late for school. What do you want for breakfast? I've got eggs, nice crunchy seedy toast, or porridge, or—"

"Lucky Charms."

"I don't have Lucky Charms."

Sophie would make a disappointed frown. "I want Lucky Charms."

"They're just sugar, sweetheart. They're not good for you."

"Mommy lets me have Lucky Charms."

And Alex would say evenly, "Yes, well, we don't have Lucky Charms here."

At six months, when Sophie began to eat solid foods, Alex boiled organic squash, steamed organic spinach, puréed organic fruit and other high-nutrient, pure-as-angels foodstuffs for his little girl, and stored tubs of it in the freezer. This gave him profound satisfaction. *Fatherhood? I'm all over this,* he'd thought, and been sure of it. One of the many things he hadn't anticipated before becoming a father was how much he would love feeding his daughter—how much he would *need* to. He became possessed, recognizing it for what it was: an evolutionary imperative. The image came to him of a mother bird, as he hovered, spoon in hand, over Sophie's gaping mouth, his entire focus and life force intent on filling it.

But when she turned three, Sophie's tastes abruptly contracted. This coincided with Alex's divorce from her mother, another thing he hadn't anticipated, and the beginning of her eating in two different households. Soon she refused to eat anything but white mishmash food. Alex suspected it was because Morgana had begun to feed her crap.

"I feed my daughter only the finest food!" Morgana said confidently when he mentioned it.

This happened to all kids, other parents told him. At seven, all Sophie wanted was sweet or salty mushy food, like mac 'n' cheese. Or Lucky Charms.

But at seven she still spoke to him, hugged him, laughed with him.

Nine years later, she barely ate or spoke, with him anyway, and she appeared to be suffering from chronic fatigue. Morgana pooh-poohed his concern. "It's called being a teenager," she told Alex.

Really? He hadn't been that way. Nor had any of his friends. They hadn't shuffled through life like zombies, groaning when they spoke, hard of hearing, flaking out on their beds, working only the muscles used to operate their phones. He'd insisted that Sophie be tested for chronic fatigue, or whatever torpor-inducing neurasthenic disorder had sapped all the vitality out of her. But she was found to be healthy and normal. "See?" Morgana said. "Normal."

"Sophie?" He knocked on her door. "Five minutes . . . I want you to eat something, please."

Five minutes later he knocked again: "Sophie, time to go—"

"*St-o-o-op, D-a-a-a-d . . .*" she groaned from behind the door.

Finally she came out of her room, pale, exhausted, stumbling forward as if sleepwalking.

"There's a piece of toast on the table. You can eat it in the car."

"I don't want anything."

"Just take the toast."

"*Stop*, Da-a-a-d. . . ."

Dragging her backpack—he was worried it was giving her scoliosis—she moped out the door. She dumped the backpack in the front passenger seat and plopped herself in the back.

. . .

When she was seven and he'd buckled her into her car seat in the back, Sophie would often say, with a note of tragic longing in her voice, "Daddy, when will I see you again?"

"Next Monday, sweetie. I'll pick you up after school. Like always. Mummy will pick you up this afternoon and you'll be with her this week and next weekend, and then I'll pick you up from school next Monday. Right? You know how it works."

"It's *Mom*, Daddy! M-O-M! *Mommy!* Not M-U-M! You always say it wrong."

"Well, that's because Daddy's an alien."

"You are not an *alien!*"

"Haven't I shown you my flying saucer? It's a folding model, it's in the garage."

"*Daddy!*" Sophie shrieked happily.

They both knew the court-mandated schedule. That was how Alex and Morgana exchanged her: picked her up from school on alternating Monday afternoons. That way, in theory, neither parent had to come to the home of the other.

So why was she asking? Except when Morgana traveled on her antique-buying trips to Europe, this had been the custody arrangement since Sophie was two. Was she rubbing in the failure of her parents' marriage? *Calm down,* he told himself. *She's still in the bliss of childhood. She's not putting you on trial. That's your doing.* She just wants reassurance. She wants to hear you say: *I will pick you up next Monday after school, sweetheart. As always.*

"I'll pick you up next Monday after school, sweetheart. As always."

The arrangement had relaxed in recent years. It was now mostly determined by Sophie: which parent's house best provided for her activities, plans with friends, and the current state of her relationship with her mother.

"We have to pick up Kendra," Sophie said now from the backseat.

When they drew up outside Kendra's house, Kendra opened the back door and got in beside Sophie.

"Good morning," she said politely to Alex.

"Hi, Kendra," he said.

As he drove up West Street to Granite Harbor High School, the girls didn't talk. Strangled, snorting sounds came from the backseat. He glanced once in the mirror, under cover of looking both ways when he stopped and crossed Rockland Street. Sitting close together, they were looking at their phones, their own, each other's.

From first to fifth grade Sophie had gone to the Yellow House Waldorf. In those days, he didn't just drop her off. He'd park, get out, unbuckle her from the backseat, and Sophie would climb out, hug him hard, and say, "Bye, Daddy, I love you."

"I love you too, sweetie. I'll see you next Monday."

She would grab her little backpack and run away from him without looking back, through the white wooden gate, like a portal in a magical story, until she reached Erin and Kendra. Sometimes Alex stood outside the gate, smiling his besotted father's smile, watching her with her friends as they laughed and squealed, struck poses, made faces at each other.

Now, at the high school, Sophie opened the front passenger door and hauled her backpack out, pushing the door behind her with insufficient effort to close it, walking away. Still without looking back, but it felt different now.

He reached over and pulled the door shut. He watched Sophie and Kendra join the other girls moving hypnotically forward, staring into their phones. These girls—he still saw them as children—wore sprayed-on tight stretch jeans (Sophie today) or black yoga pants. Short jean jackets over long torn flannel shirts worn studiously askew, hair gel-punked or hanging in wild lustrous strands, makeup, lip gloss.

He wanted to call out "Bye, sweetheart! I love you," but she would be mortified.

3

Alex parked in front of Brown & Cord and went in for his second cup of coffee. The thermos on the left, labeled BIOHAZARD, dispensed a blend that brought in firefighters from the fire station across Mechanic Street, lobstermen headed for sea before dawn, prison guards starting eight-hour shifts at the Supermax. Alex found most publicly brewed coffee in the United States insipid, but Biohazard, formulated by Gary, B & C's walrus-mustachioed, suspender-wearing owner and roaster, was bracing.

Cup in holder, he drove up Union Street and parked a few hundred yards below the large, turreted, sea captain's house that was now home to the Granite Harbor Historical Society. He was seven minutes early.

Glenn Bell, the society's director, had called two days ago and asked if he'd be interested in authoring a history of Granite Harbor, an illustrated book being commissioned by the Historical Society, and if he thought he could fit it in with his day job. Alex was one of several local authors who were being approached by the Historical Society, Glenn told him. The fee would be $50,000, the work to be completed in a year.

Glenn didn't tell him who the other contenders were, but Alex could guess: Hud Stradling, whose Alewives and Elderberry Wine series of historical novels about four sisters, wives of Maine fishermen, set around Penobscot Bay during the Great Depression, had to be a favorite. The consummate local author, Hud had actually hung a shingle that read: HUDSON STRADLING, NEW YORK

TIMES REVIEWED MAINE AUTHOR outside his barn writing studio on Bayview Street, where fans and summer tourists stopped in and bought boxed sets of his books and took selfies with Hud.

Mary Louise Ralston had published a genuine *New York Times* bestseller, *Monhegan Summer*, about a badly divorced Boston plein air painter who discovers love with a traumatized Vietnam veteran ornithologist counting ospreys on an offshore island. Mary Louise had subsequently published two more novels, *Isleboro Fall* and *Isle au Haut Equinox*, all *New York Times* bestsellers, and Alex doubted she'd be interested.

Hatch Stornaway, who wore a thick rim of whiskers around an otherwise shaved face in the manner of the old whaleship captains, had written twenty or thirty slim books, monographs, on maritime mysteries and shipwrecks. His "hearty as lobstah chowdah" style might not be what the Historical Society was hoping for, but his research skills and local knowledge were unquestionable.

Alex's own slender literary efforts were dwarfed by all of them in sales and output and bore no relation to Maine: two novels set in a working-class suburb of Manchester, England, where he'd grown up, during the early years of the millennium. But one of them, *Swallow Street*, had been shortlisted for the Booker Prize, and he had once been numbered among the Best British Novelists Under 30 by *Granta* magazine.

He finished his coffee, drove down Union Street, and parked in front of the Historical Society.

"Hey, Alex." Glenn Bell himself opened the front door. He smiled, crushed Alex's hand, and led him into a large entrance hall lined with maps and oil paintings.

Glenn and his wife, Tinker, who used her maiden name, Fox, though everyone still called her Tinker Bell, were *the* Granite Harbor power couple. They were funded by Tinker's money, which provided endowments to the library, the literary and art festivals, got her onto the town council, made Glenn an active member of the Rotary Club, the Meguntic Watershed Association, director of the Historical Society, and paid for their cosmetic surgeries. Both gazed out through the smooth, bright-eyed masks of face-lifts, and this morning Glenn's thin hair glinted with fresh chestnut highlights, his clearly visible scalp still tinted from recent dyeing.

"Been in here before?"

"Yes."

Glenn didn't seem to hear him. "It's quite a place. Come take a look."

He led Alex through magnificently curated rooms: floor-to-ceiling shelves of jacket-less leather and green and blue cloth-bound books; the wall spaces between the shelves covered with early nautical charts, old photographs, venerable paintings of the coast of Maine, limpid in dusk or frothing with sea spray breaking upon the unyielding granite.

The tour finished in Glenn's office.

"Given the job some thought?"

Alex's phone began to vibrate audibly in his jacket pocket.

"You want to get that?" Glenn asked.

"No, that's okay," said Alex. "Yes, I have thought about it. I'm certainly interested."

"How does it square with the day job?"

"I think I can do both. I'd find the time." He'd be writing, at least, and getting paid for it.

His phone stopped vibrating.

"Well, we've considered the competition. . . . We've got a lot of talented authors in this town," Glenn beamed, drawing out the suspense, ". . . and you're our choice, Alex. We've all read your book. We're all agreed. I mean, you're a *real* writer. Not to cast aspersions on any other candidate, but that Bookman prize, that's impressive."

"I didn't win it." Alex was surprised Glenn knew about that, and even had the name half right. "I was just shortlisted."

"That means you made the cut. You're way ahead of anyone else here. And we like the cut of your jib."

Alex was sure that his jib—for Glenn, Tinker, and the town's social and political movers and shakers—had been partly tailored by Morgana, and her postdivorce purchase of Belleport, in the Chestnut Street Historic District. The house, designed by the famous firm of McKim, Mead, & White, was a National Historic Landmark, which Morgana had renovated to a degree that earned it a feature spread in *Architectural Digest*. Her garden parties filling the gazebo, spreading out on the terraced lawn overlooking Penobscot Bay, had established her as a patroness of the first rank, and brought an invitation to the board of the Historical Society. While amusing her few friends with vicious stories about Alex, she publicly talked up her daughter's father, and she had no doubt been a factor in his being awarded the job. She would rub it in forever.

"Well, I'm very glad to hear it, Glenn. Thank you."

"Great! Then we're all happy! Betsy—our Betsy Plourde—you know Betsy, I'm sure—she's here most days. She knows our library. She'll be a great resource to you."

Alex's phone began vibrating again.

"Go ahead and take a look," said Glenn, leaning back grandly in his leather chair.

"Okay, thanks." Alex pulled his phone out and looked at it. "The day job. I'd better answer it."

Alex looked away from Glenn's beady eyes as he listened to his caller. He tried to compose his face. "I'm on my way," he said, then pocketed his phone. "Glenn, I'm sorry. I have to go."

"I guess you'd better—when they need you, they need you, right? We can talk about it all later. Just wanted you to know you're our man, and we're very happy."

"Great," said Alex, standing up. "Me too. Thank you."

He drove a hundred yards down Union Street before turning on the blue police strobe lights hardwired into his Subaru Outback and picked up speed.

4

Alex saw Patrolman Mark Beltz beyond the yellow crime scene tape he'd run across the path from the gift shop. A big man, top-heavy, he was standing beside a bed of herbs and flowers, weight on one leg, a relaxed posture, his stomach hanging over his bulky duty belt. Mark had taken his hat off and was holding it beside his thigh with one hand. He was staring into the flower bed like a man struck with wonder at nature.

Alex ducked under the tape and walked toward him. Mark looked up as he approached. His eyes found Alex's. "Good morning, Detective."

He'd known Mark for seven years. They'd been patrolmen together before Alex had made detective, and had called each other "Mark" and "Alex." Mark was at least ten years younger than Alex, but he'd been a policeman since his early twenties and he was an old hand by the time Alex joined the department. He'd been a generous mentor to the older recruit during Alex's first two years on the job.

Yet Mark now called him "Detective" when they spoke.

His eyes skittered away as he put on his hat. "Over here." He began to lumber across the center of the re-created village, past the log cabins, outbuildings, the forge, facing an open space of grass, gravel paths, small crop beds. Alex followed.

Mark stopped beside several rows of pumpkins, squashes, and other leafy things where the tilled ground gave way to cordgrass and ferns that sloped up to the trees that marked the edge of the Settlement, the beginning of the woods.

"There," said Mark. He pointed, to the trees and upward, but Alex had already seen the naked body, male, hanging from the odd structure: a rectangle the size of a doorframe, built of two-by-fours bolted together, mounted on a simple plywood box. The body hung by the bound wrists, arms raised, from a short crossbeam in the "doorway" space between vertical posts. It almost looked like an art installation: a crude, shocking statement, framed for presentation.

Why the structure? There was a stout oak tree with good hanging limbs just behind it.

Before he noticed anything else, Alex's eyes were drawn to the body's most prominent, lurid feature: the long, clean, vertical incision stretching from the sternum through the center of the belly button, stopping above the pubic bone. The edges of the wound were half an inch apart. A long row of stitches would have pulled them neatly together.

Alex looked down at the ground, mostly ferns and marsh grass, between where he stood and the body hanging from the frame. No blood.

"Did you approach the body, Mark?"

"No closer than you are now."

"And the person who found it?"

"That was Jeff Block. One of the people here. I don't think he got any closer. He said he backed away once he saw it."

Alex walked slowly forward, aiming to reach the body by a side-circling route, watching where he placed each foot, looking for any sign of disturbed vegetation, or footprints. But he also looked up continually at the body as he drew closer to it. Long bangs of brown hair obscured the face; the head hung forward over the chest, as if staring down at the foot-long wound. The body, male, was full grown, long, skinny, sinewy, and, he could easily see, young.

Alex had seen only four other dead bodies since he'd become a police officer seven years ago. Granite Harbor's troubles were mostly traffic violations, unruly summer residents, domestic troubles, the occasional stolen bicycle. The deaths he'd been forced to examine were one teenage gunshot suicide in a bedroom on John Street, considerably done so that the result-

ing mess had been mostly contained in a thick wool blanket emblazoned
L.L. BEAN, and three bodies that were the result of accidents: a drowning, a
rock-climbing fall, and a woman, alcoholic according to her family, frozen in
her own backyard within yards of an open door.

He had never seen a murdered corpse.

As he got within a few feet, he felt a lurch in his chest as he realized he
knew this boy.

He heard Mark approach and stop just behind him. Mark took off his
hat again and peered upward. "That's Shane Carter."

Sophie knew a Shane at school.

"Doreen Wisner's boy," Mark went on. "He's in the eleventh grade with
my boys, Jack and David. Judy at the station knows them."

"His name's Carter but his mother's called Wisner?"

"Carter's his father's name. Doreen remarried, to Dennis Wisner." Mark's
thick Maine accent was evident. *His fahtha's name. Dawreen Wisner.*

Watching where he planted his feet, Alex walked around the other side
of the frame with the hanging boy. From here, because of the way the head
was tilted, he had a better view of the face. He could have been any boy in
Granite Harbor, boys he'd seen for years, a mess of open jackets, untucked
shirts and untied shoelaces, crowding into and out of school, hanging out
in the library, his own house even. The eyelids were half open, suggesting an
impression that he was still only half asleep.

There was no sign of blood on the leaves around the frame base, no footprints, no sign of disturbance. This was not the kill site. The body had been
brought here dead. Maybe the forensic team would find—

"Oh my!" Mark said suddenly.

Alex looked over his shoulder at Mark and then, following the direction
of his gaze, back at the body. His eyes involuntarily caught at the wound.

The clean line of the incision undulated. Something was moving beneath
it. Inside Shane's belly.

As both men stared, a tiny hand, almost humanlike, dark red with gore,
protruded from the wound.

"Oh my Lord!" Mark said, louder.

A second hand thrust itself out of the wound.

Mark stepped back, lost his footing on a tree root beneath the leaves and fell backward. He got to his feet. He was breathing hard. "What in the good Lord . . ."

They both watched the hands waving, reaching out of the wound just above the belly button, and now the edges of the incision distended . . . pushed from inside . . .

"Oh . . . my . . ."

A small head, wide, flat, smeared with clotted blood, emerged. A protuberant golden eye closed and opened in a slow blink.

"What the—"

"It's a frog," said Alex.

"What the hell's it doing in there?"

"That's a good question."

The frog's arm reached farther along the incision, gripping the edge with the bulb-tipped fingers of both hands. The head quivered. A leg emerged—

It leaped, plopping onto the leaves between the two men.

"We need to get it, Mark!"

It jumped again, away from them, behind the frame, toward the trees.

As they stepped after it, the frog sprang again, away from Mark's heavier footfall, clanking bulk—to land in front of Alex. He dropped onto his knees, fell forward onto his elbows, and closed both hands around the frog.

"Get a bag! And gloves."

Mark was breathing fast. "Okay." He ran off heavily, panting audibly, his belt jangling.

The frog squirmed. Alex kept his hands closed over it. He felt the wet thick blood on the cold reptilian skin.

5

Isabel slowed at the sight of the police car. Mark Beltz, one of Granite Harbor's patrolmen, was standing near the yellow tape talking with Detective Alex Brangwen. Both turned to look in her direction as she came to a stop in the middle of the parking lot.

A second patrol car pulled up close behind her. Its flashing roof light strobed into her eyes through the mirror.

Crazy thoughts flooded her—Are they waiting for me? What have I done? Has something happened to Ethan? No, he was home in bed . . . she was sure.

Mark Beltz came forward and directed her to a parking space. She pulled in, and the other police car moved past and parked near the tape.

"Good morning, Mrs. Dorr," said Mark as she got out of her car. "We'll ask you to wait in the gift shop for now, please."

"What's going on? Why are you here?"

"We've got a situation. We'll just ask you to wait in the gift shop, please." He raised a hand toward the gift shop, as if directing traffic.

Isabel looked past him at the detective. He was talking with the stocky young patrolwoman, Becky Watrous, in a too-tight uniform, who had arrived in the second police car.

"Mrs. Dorr, please."

"Yes. Sorry."

As she entered the gift shop, a tiny, crone-like woman came swiftly forward and gripped her arm.

"Oh Isabel! Your first day." Nancy Keeler peered up at her through crooked wire-rim spectacles.

Isabel hardly recognized her friend. Framed beneath the linen coif, the wizened face appeared almost a small accessory at the top of her voluminous Goodwife outfit. Nancy and her husband, Graham, had owned the Belvedere Inn, a bed-and-breakfast with water views on Bayview Street. After Graham's sudden death at sixty-eight from cancer, Nancy sold the inn. But a year later, bored in retirement inside the small Cape she'd purchased on Sea Street, she joined the roster of players at the Granite Harbor Settlement. Nancy was Goodwife Howe. Her usual twenty-first-century appearance—thin, a white-haired bob, large round tortoiseshell glasses, black blazer, slim fashion jeans—was dramatically altered by her seventeenth-century threads, which emphasized her four-foot-eleven-inch height.

Isabel looked beyond Nancy at the other people in the room.

"Isabel," said Chester Coffey, standing beside Nancy. Chester—Goodman Denham, the Settlement's blacksmith—looked more like a forest creature than a Pilgrim father, with a dense beard that grew high into his red cheeks and down his throat, wispy hair beneath a shapeless felt hat pierced with a pheasant feather. His barrel chest was accentuated by a dark leather jerkin with many pockets that fell to shapeless woolen knee britches.

"Goody Swaine," Monte Glover—Goodman Clews, magistrate—greeted her gravely in a deep baritone that was the heart and ballast of the small but dedicated Granite Harbor Gay Men's Chorus. "Roger's made coffee."

Roger Priestly—Goodman Bowles, the Settlement's apothecary—slim, fortyish, close-cropped salt-and-pepper whiskers, held up a pot of fresh coffee behind the counter. The Settlement's historian, Roger had determined the appropriate outfits and advised the players on the seventeenth-century details they shared with visitors. A fourth man, Jeff Block—Goodman Swaine, fisherman-boatbuilder, Hannah's historical husband—sat in a chair in the back.

They were all looking at Isabel.

"Why are the police here?" she asked. "What's going on?"

"Jeff found a body near the vegetable patch," said Monte Glover. His deep voice sounded like an amplified theatrical announcement.

"Oh my God." Isabel looked at Jeff and then quickly at the others in the shop. "Who?"

"A boy," said Roger. "Probably one of the high school kids. About that age."

"Oh my God! *Who?*"

"They haven't told us."

Ethan's at home in bed, asleep, she told herself, again. He was always there in the morning now. But she hadn't *seen* him since last night. She turned her back to the room, pulled her phone from the dangling pocket beneath the many layers of clothing, and tapped his number. It went to voicemail. "Ethan, call me when you wake up. It's *very important.* Call me first thing. I mean it. *Call me.*" She sent the same message to him as a text.

"A kid," said Jeff, shaking his head.

"Oh, Jeff." Nancy walked quickly to the back of the room. She knelt before Jeff and took the hand that wasn't holding the coffee mug. "Are you all right?"

Jeff shrugged. "I'm okay. . . . Thanks."

They heard vehicles out on the gravel.

"More police," said Chester at the window.

Isabel looked out to see two unmarked white windowless vans pulling into the parking lot. Men and women got out, pulled on white Tyvek suits and bootees and rubber gloves. Mark Beltz conferred with them.

Isabel saw Detective Alex Brangwen walking toward the gift shop. She backed away from the window.

The door hissed open again and Alex entered. He closed it behind him and turned to face the people in the gift shop.

"Morning." He recognized Nancy. "Hello, Nancy."

"Hello, Alex."

He nodded at Isabel. "Isabel," he said.

"Hello," she said.

He looked at the four men. "Morning. I'm Detective Brangwen. I think we all know one another, by sight anyway."

"Good morning, Detective. Roger Priestly," said Roger.

The other three men identified themselves.

"Jeff, you found the body and called it in?"

"Yes, sir."

Deep inside her costume, Isabel's phone beeped. It was loud, they could all hear it.

"Do you want to get that?" Alex asked.

She was already digging it out. "Yes. I'm sorry."

"It's fine," Alex said.

What? Ethan had texted. He was safe. Her chest expanded, her legs felt weak with relief. But she could hear, in the single word and question mark, his tone of annoyance.

I'll be home early. Stay there! she texted back.

The phone beeped immediately in response. *Mom, chill.*

Alex addressed them without looking at her again. "Our crew will probably be here most of the day. We have to close the place for now, today anyway. And I'll need to interview all of you—is this everyone who works here?"

"Bill and Jan Conrad aren't here yet," said Roger. "And Sylvia Grinnell. She runs the gift shop. She comes in a little before ten."

"All right. I have to leave now. Patrolman Beltz will come in here and talk with you. He'll get your phone numbers and tell you when you can go home. I'll call each of you later and set up a time, today preferably, when I can come and see you. So please don't go anywhere. Don't leave town."

He pulled business cards from his jacket and placed them on the gift shop counter. "This is my phone number and email. Please take one before you go."

"Do you know who it is?" Isabel asked.

He looked at her briefly and then around the room. "We don't have any information on that yet."

He turned. The door hissed open again and he pulled it shut after him.

6

Outside, Alex called Morgana. As usual, his call went straight to voicemail. *"Hi! This is Morgana Claymore. I'm so sorry to miss your call."* The friendly, lilting tone of a Texan Realtor, or the secretary of a prosperity gospel church. *"Please leave me a message and I'll be sure to call you back."*

"Morgana, please call me. It's urgent. You have to pick up Sophie from school, now. Take her home and don't let her go out. Something's happened that involves the local kids, her friends. It's important that you call me as soon as possible."

Alex turned to Mark Beltz, who was standing nearby, waiting for him. "Where's the frog, Mark?"

"I put it in a bag. I put air holes in it. It's in my car."

"Give it to the medical examiner. Apart from him and the forensic team, no mention of it to anyone else. Nobody else knows about it except the killer."

"Right. I took photographs of Shane's face and sent them to Judy. She's known Doreen and the family since grade school. She's calling Cathy Fremont, Doreen's cousin, to go out to Doreen's house and tell her. She'll text Cathy the photos, so Doreen can identify him."

"I'm going there now."

• • •

In the car, he called Judy Waite, the department dispatcher.

"Yes, dear God, that's Shane, Doreen's boy."

"Can you text me the address, please, Judy? I'm going out there now."

"They're out on Cobb Road, I'll text you the address now. That poor woman."

He tried Morgana again—voicemail. He couldn't shake the image of Sophie, strung up, a frog inside her. But he'd dropped her at school. He summoned the memory of her getting out of the car with Kendra at school. *She's safe—for now.* Security at the high school had been beefed up in recent years in the wake of the cascade of school shootings they'd all seen on television. *It could happen here*, people said.

This too, apparently.

They had to keep Sophie at home, safe—after school anyway—until he caught the killer.

Good luck with that. In the last year, Sophie had discovered that she could do as she pleased. The final frontier of parental enforcement—coercion with threats, bribes, offers of special considerations—had crumbled when Sophie had discovered the power of "no." And its equally dismaying sidekick—"I don't care"—when threatened with grounding, loss of allowance.

How had this happened? Her friends, from what he could tell talking with other parents, were the same. They assumed an independence from parental authority unimaginable when Alex was a boy. His father would have thumped his ear if he'd talked back to his parents the way Sophie did to him. Alex had no control at all over his daughter now. When he tried laying down the law with what sounded to him like implacable authority, she demolished it with her own impregnable logic, or sheer refusal. Morgana was tougher—she was the bad cop. Through some mother-daughter connection or alchemy she appeared to have more sway with Sophie.

But they had to keep her close, for now. Home early. Monitor her as much as possible. He had to impress that upon Morgana. Death, horrible butchery, could be the consequence of misbehavior. No grounding would fix that.

His phone vibrated—Shane's mother's address from Judy. He tapped and it opened in maps.

• • •

Cobb Road ran uphill through woods away from the sea. It had been routed and laid to transport lumber and granite from inland forests and quarries to the midcoast, to be loaded aboard the great four- and five-masted schooners that once filled Granite Harbor.

Descending out of the woods, he drove through another Maine. Far from the vacationland of summer people, the leaf peepers, or winter's cross-country skiers. Most of the older wooden farmhouses had been torn down and replaced with charmless, efficiently heated, vinyl-clad ranch designs, or double-wide manufactured homes.

Shane's home was a white vinyl-sided raised ranch. It sat on the edge of the road in front of a small field hacked out of spindly woods. Parts of old cars, tractors, rusty snowplows, barrels, and two fiberglass boats growing gray mold lay scattered in the unmown grass. A sagging string of holiday lights was nailed above the front door.

"Mrs. Wisner," Alex said when the door opened. "Detective Brangwen, Granite Harbor Police. Has your cousin—"

"Yes, she's here. I've heard. Come in." Doreen Wisner met his eyes briefly. Her face was impassive, her mouth a pinched, downturned slit. Though she was stooped, shoulders hunched forward, she might have once been tall, five eight or nine. She was thin, almost emaciated inside a too-large PATRIOTS sweatshirt above loose jeans. Lank hair beginning to gray. *Fifties*, Alex thought. But then he realized Shane, her oldest child, was only sixteen. . . . Forties, late thirties? She was already adrift in the wilderness of her middle years.

She wore slippers and dragged them as she walked. He followed her into the open kitchen.

"My cousin Cathy," she said.

Another PATS sweatshirt, also gray, but this one XXL, over a pillow mound of breast and stomach. Cathy's eyes ranged sullenly over him as if to say, *What are you going to do about it?*

Doreen sat down at the table and lit a cigarette. Cathy was already smoking. Stale cigarette air filled the room. The kitchen was decorated on the same principle as the rest of the property: nothing once used could be discarded. Shelves and countertop crammed with old birthday and Christmas cards, small plastic animals, more than a few Bob's Big Boy figurine piggy banks, catalogs, Uncle Henry's classifieds.

"Mrs. Wisner, I'm so sorry for your loss." The words were perfunctory, but he had no others. And he meant them. "Have you seen the photo we sent over?" He glanced at Cathy.

"It's him," said Doreen.

"If you don't mind, I have to ask you a few questions."

"Go ahead." Doreen pulled on her cigarette and looked dully out the kitchen window at a backyard that reminded Alex of the swap-shop section of the town's landfill. Shane's mother looked bored. Or drugged. She'd moved slowly, like sleepwalking, through the kitchen. Maybe she'd already arrived at some extremity that this latest tragedy couldn't dent further.

"Okay if I sit here?" He indicated a chair.

"Help yourself."

Alex pulled that chair away from the table, sat down, pulled out a pad and pen. "When did you last see Shane?"

"Couple of days ago. Tuesday, I think."

"Two days ago? He was missing for two days?"

"He wasn't missing. I just didn't see him. He must've been over to friends' houses. He stays with them sometimes."

"What friends?"

"Ethan—Ethan Dorr. Jared McKinnon."

"Did you call over there? The Dorrs or the McKinnons?"

"No."

"Why not?"

"Like I said, I thought he must've been there. He's always with them."

"You weren't worried about him?"

"Nope."

"How many of you are in the household here, Mrs. Wisner?"

"Five. Me, my husband, Dennis—that's my second husband, he's not Shane's father—so there's us, and Dennis's son Brian, and Dennis's and my little girl, Skye—she's sleeping."

"Where is Shane's father?"

"Somewhere in upstate New York last I heard."

"Have you been in touch with him yet?"

"No."

"Do you have his contact information?"

"Somewhere."

"What is his name, please?"

"Derek Carter."

"Are he and Shane close?"

"No. His father hasn't been in touch for a while."

"What's a while?"

"Ten years, maybe."

"He hasn't seen his father in ten years?"

"Nope."

"Do you ever look at Shane's phone?"

"No."

Alex wrote in one of the small pads he bought in bundles of ten from Renys. Apart from getting down the basic and usually irrelevant details, writing notes gave him something to do with his eyes as he asked people questions. He could look up and down, from his pad to the face of the person he was talking to, and look away, as if thinking, and take in everything he saw around him. People expected him to take notes and to look thoughtful. They looked away too, eyes settling on things around them, or they looked at him when they thought he wasn't looking, and he saw when they did that.

At the other end of the table, Cathy sat gazing at him with unconscious curiosity, like a child, as if waiting to hear what he would ask next. Her eyes shifting from Alex when he asked his questions, to Doreen when she answered, as if watching a tennis match.

Alex had a sense of life here already blasted into pieces, long ago. A crater full of knickknacks to fill a bottomless emptiness.

"Are there any other adults he's had particular contact with, now or in the past?"

"Just the teachers at school. His friends' parents."

"How about older friends? Someone not in school he might have hung out with?"

"Nope."

"Have you found anything in his room that looks unusual?"

"No."

"Can I see his room, please?"

"What for?"

"It's routine, Mrs. Wisner. I'd like to see what interests him, what he might have been reading, looking at."

Doreen exhaled a stream of smoke and stabbed the butt out in a full ashtray. She rose and scuffed her slippers into a hall off the kitchen and opened a door onto a staircase leading downward. She switched on a light, and they descended to the basement. Damp. Cinder block walls. Rusty washing machine and dryer, furnace, steel shelves loaded with toolboxes, piles of damp sagging cardboard boxes. Two narrow windows in the top of the walls at ground level showed weedy vegetation that dimmed the daylight.

One corner of the basement was walled off with two-by-fours, enclosing a space eight-by-eight feet, Sheetrocked on the inner side, the studs bare to the rest of the basement. Doreen pushed open an unpainted hollow-core door between the studs and turned on a light. Inside the "room," a single bed, shelves with books, a table—you couldn't call it a desk—clothes hung on hooks, heaped in corners of the floor. A poster of a skeleton wearing a beanie—skeletal fingers clutching a skateboard above the words: SKATE OR DIE—was pinned to the unpainted gray Sheetrock walls beside dark patches of mold. There were no windows in the room—which would only have opened into the basement. The Sheetrock didn't go all the way up, leaving a gap of an inch or two below the joists—ventilation at least between the room and the basement.

"This is Shane's room?"

"Yuh. Dennis fixed it up for him when our daughter, Skye, was born three years ago."

Let's go hang at my place was something Alex didn't imagine Shane had often said to his friends. But he asked: "Did he have much company down here? Friends after school?"

"Never."

"Can I look around for a few minutes?"

"Suit yourself."

Doreen turned and headed to the stairs. Alex walked into the room. He heard the stairs creaking.

He looked through the wardrobe, the clothes on the floor—bundles you might see in bins at Goodwill—under the bed—a scattering of empty Juul pods—through the shelves, which mostly held school textbooks, a few YA novels, *Percy Jackson & the Olympians*, Harry Potters, *I Am Malala*. The place was a repository for Shane's most basic needs. Nothing, apart from the skateboard poster, indicating this particular boy's interests, passions, desires—except the wish to be elsewhere. This was where Shane came to crash, change, leave again. Not where he lived.

Alex sat on Shane's bed. He looked up at the gap between the Sheetrock and the joists.

You poor boy.

He took photos with his iPhone.

Upstairs, he found the two women smoking at the kitchen table. "Mrs. Wisner, could I get Shane's father's contact information from you, please?"

"If I can find it." Doreen rose and ambled listlessly across the kitchen to a bookshelf crammed with magazines, baskets, bottles, a few books.

She pulled out a basket, rooted through it.

Her cousin Cathy looked at Alex unblinkingly.

"Here," Doreen finally said. She held up an old-looking address book, open to a page.

"How old is that address?"

"I dunno. That's where he was last."

Alex raised his phone and photographed the page.

"Thank you," he said, nodding to both women. "Again, I'm very sorry for your loss."

In his car, he found himself breathing as if he'd climbed a flight of stairs very fast.

7

The ship was in trouble. It lay tilted up at the stern, the pack ice heaped around it in jagged shapes. The topmasts had broken and fallen to the deck in a tangle of rigging. Sails were shredded. A whale was breaching in the cold water nearby. Men holding spears stood on the shore, looking at the scene.

Before getting started on it, Ethan brought his space heater—one of two Isabel bought after the furnace died—down into the basement workshop, turned it on, and climbed back upstairs to the kitchen to make coffee.

He looked at the clock on the wall over the door: 11:40. Social studies, with Mrs. Davito. *Yes!* Ethan felt a savage pleasure. He made a fist and jabbed it upward. He'd been awake for half an hour, all of her class so far, lying in bed, scrolling through Snapchat before coming downstairs. Fuck you, Mrs. Davito!

Down in the workshop—it had been his father's—he put a CD in the boom box—his father's boom box, his father's CD collection: The Bothy Band, Irish music his father loved and now Ethan loved too—and sat at the broad pine worktable. He sipped his coffee, then set the mug down well away to one side. He picked up the bottle, clamped it in the small padded vise, and peered into it from different angles.

The thick wavy glass made the ship, the sea, the men, and the whale ripple as Ethan moved his head. Along one edge of the Prussian blue sea where it met the glass rose a strip of brown material speckled with black and white paint: a distant shore. The other edge was marked with jagged white lumps: icebergs. The ship sat apparently sinking at the center of this rippling diorama, stuck in time and space.

Both the ship and the bottle were crude. Thick matchsticks substituted for some of the wooden booms and spars. The bottle, fashioned for a gallon of some ancient grog, was an equally makeshift fabrication—but the roughness was part of its charm, its originality, and, Ethan hoped, its eventual value. Modern ship-in-a-bottle makers usually put their models inside commercially produced, readily available, clear liquor bottles. Most of the new model ships, ships-in-bottles, easily available online, were made in China from uniform, machine-punched parts, as alike as the parts of model airplanes. By those standards, this one was all wrong: an imperfect piece of glassblowing, its contours irregular, its shape asymmetrical, small air bubbles trapped in the glass. But the modeler who had made the ship, imagined its dire situation, got it into the bottle surrounded by windblown seas, the surfacing whale, the imperiled men, the pack ice, could not have found a more complementary theater for his drama. Definitely old, Ethan knew—maybe nineteenth century? Contemporary with the scene it depicted? That would increase its value.

Ethan was sure that the modeler who had created this ship-in-a-bottle was a real whaleman, who had known the sea, witnessed such scenes, or was depicting a particular event. But he was also an artist. To peer at the scene through the bottle was like seeing it through a storm.

He'd found it at a yard sale: a three-masted whaleship, two masts broken, lying on its side amid the ice floes made of putty and linseed oil. The ship's name, *Concordia*, was painted in tiny faded gold letters on the ship's transom. Ethan knew that a whaleship named *Concordia* had been one of the fleet of New Bedford ships lost in the Arctic off the coast of Alaska in 1871—was this *the Concordia?*

At some point, the bottle had been dropped or jarred sharply, breaking the ship's rig. Now Ethan would get in there, inside the bottle, fix or replace the broken topmast and other spars, pull out and repair the "torn" sails—their threads frayed from years of lying creased beneath the broken rig—and reset the gale-lashed strips of rust-colored cotton. If he made a good repair, he thought he might be able to sell it to someplace like the Salem Maritime Museum, or the New Bedford Whaling Museum. Those people would appreciate this ship-and-scene-in-a-bottle and see, he hoped, the authenticity of its creator and his work. Maybe they'd even recognize it, know the maker—know this *Concordia*. And pay him for it.

Like they'd paid his father. Joshua Dorr had disappeared when Ethan was five. He'd been in a yacht race, sailing alone across the Atlantic in his thirty-six-foot wooden boat from Marblehead, Massachusetts, to Falmouth, England. He was an experienced sailor; he'd sailed from Maine to the Caribbean and back many times, and crossed the Atlantic alone twice before that race.

He never arrived in England. He was missing, his mother told him. *When will they find him?* he'd asked her. One day she told him his father probably wasn't coming back. He was lost at sea.

Gathering dust on shelves around the workshop sat the ship models his father had not finished or remained unsold. Joshua Dorr had crafted scale replicas of large yachts for their owners; and between such paying commissions, models to his own taste: older commercial sailing craft, whale ships, Gloucester fishing schooners. Ethan had an album containing photographs of every model his father had made and sold. Unless there was something in the photographs to show their scale, they looked like real ships. Ethan knew he could sell some of the completed, unsold models for more than enough money to buy a new furnace for the house, but he and his mother had both agreed to hold on to his father's work.

When he turned ten, Ethan's mother finally let him use his father's tools—some of them were very sharp. His father had books on ship models and how to make them. Ethan sold his first model, a simple sailboat ten inches long with one mast, when he was twelve, to Star Bright, one of the tourist gift stores in Granite Harbor, for twenty dollars. He'd been amazed to later stand outside the store on Bayview Street and see his model in the store window with a price tag of forty dollars hanging off it. That meant his model was worth forty dollars—that *he* should be able to get forty dollars for it. He made more models. As quickly as he made them, the store sold them. He told the store's buyer he wanted more money for them. The buyer smiled at him and said he thought thirty dollars was a lot of money for a twelve-year-old boy. Ethan never took another model back to the store.

Instead, he started his own website and promptly sold a model of the *Ger-trude L. Thebaud*, the famous Gloucester fishing and racing schooner, for $250. He bought his mother a new beanie and a large bag of dog food for Flynn. He also located on eBay and bought for himself a really outstanding Bathing Ape shark head hoodie that glowed in the dark. But it had taken him four months, between school and other distractions, to build the model, and he realized it would take him years to make money building models as his father had.

One of his father's books was about making ships in bottles. It recom-mended looking for old bottles at yard sales. It showed how to make the rough wavy "sea" inside the bottle with linseed oil putty mixed with Prussian blue oil paint—Ethan learned to get that oozy paste into the bottles and push it into wavy shapes with long wooden spatulas that he whittled to tool-size and shape, then touch the blue wavetops with white paint on a small brush. He made the ship's hull narrow enough to fit through the neck of the bottle, with masts that hinged flat on small loops of wire. He slipped that into the bottle and sat it in glue on top of the sea, and when it was dry he pulled on a string attached to the rigging to raise the masts, and finally sealed the bottle with red sealing wax. He sold the first one on his website for $150.

Once Ethan started selling his models, it was all he wanted to do. School was a total waste of time. His grades got worse. He failed classes. He fought with his mother, and they were both unhappy—until, amazingly, she'd given in and let him stay home. They agreed he would practice "unschooling," a version of homeschooling that allowed him to pursue his own interests. They stopped fighting. The house was peaceful. Now he spent most of his days—school hours, anyway—downstairs in the workshop making models and ships-in-bottles—or playing video games upstairs in his room. He liked being home alone. He made long late breakfasts for himself in the kitchen. He loved his new independence.

And he was making money—not a lot, but he'd been able to tell his mother to stop giving him an allowance.

When he went upstairs to make another cup of coffee, his phone dinged and he saw his mother's text: *Call me when you wake up. It's very important. Call me first thing. I mean it. Call me.* He didn't feel like calling her, hearing whatever was so important, breaking his peaceful mood and space. *What?* he responded.

I'll be home early. Stay there!

Mom, chill, he thumbed back.

Downstairs, he passed an hour pulling the broken pieces of the *Concordia* from the bottle with the long surgical tweezers before he heard his mother coming into the kitchen upstairs. WTF? What was she doing home so early?

She called down the stairs. "Ethan? Are you home?"

There was an edge to her voice. Like he'd done something wrong.

"Wha-ut?" he answered, slightly annoyed.

He heard her clomping down the stairs in her crazy witch's shoes.

8

It was one of the little Craftsman-style, Sears, Roebuck houses, bought by catalog, shipped in prefabricated sections by railroad in the 1920s. There were four on Jacobs Avenue. Three had been nicely renovated. Isabel's was the one that needed paint, with a gutter askew, and bushes at the side of the house choked by weeds. But it was still pretty, with a low, over-hanging hip roof, small dormer upstairs, porches with tapered rectangular posts, double-hung windows with separated lights on the upper sashes.

Alex had liked the inside too. The cozy living room, the fireplace, the accommodating old sofa.

He parked in the driveway and came, as always, to the kitchen door. The dog, new since he'd last been there, barked furiously when he knocked.

"Flynn, stop!" her voice barked back, followed by the sound of the back door to the deck opening and closing again. Then he saw her coming toward him through the glass. She still wore her costume, but she'd removed the linen headwear. Her shaven head was new since his time too. He'd seen her around town in her beanies. He'd worried she might be going through chemo, but a mutual friend had told him no, it was just the way she wore her hair now.

"Come in," said Isabel, opening the door. The wan midday light plain on her face.

There is no excellent beauty that hath not some strangeness in the proportion, Francis Bacon, Viscount St. Alban, philosopher and statesman, had written sometime in the seventeenth century. Ian Fleming had always given James Bond's women some errant blemish: a broken nose, a limp, a flaw in the pupil of one eye. They were the more beautiful for it. Isabel's "strangeness" was the asymmetry of her face. One eyebrow arched upward, the eyes on a subtly different plane, giving the other eye, the one beneath the lower brow, a cool, acute regard. He'd loved her face.

Grief had collapsed it. Five years had deepened the hollows in her cheeks.

She led him through the mudroom into the kitchen. The air inside the house was colder than outside.

"I'm sorry it's cold. The furnace is broken."

Ethan stood beside the kitchen table. He was almost fully grown now. He'd elongated with a teenage spurt. Tall, skinny, mass of tousled long hair, baggy jeans, sweatshirt beneath a fleece bathrobe, worn sheepskin slippers. He was pale and shaking.

Alex had told her on the phone it was Shane.

She's told him.

"Hi, Ethan."

"What happened to Shane?" he croaked.

"Can we sit down?" Alex asked them.

They sat beside each other. Alex faced them across the table.

"What happened to Shane?" Ethan repeated, his brown eyes huge, boring into Alex.

What words would he use to tell Sophie? "Someone killed him, Ethan."

"I know that. Who? How?"

"We don't know who. Or even how yet. There's still a lot we don't know. That's why I need to ask you some questions."

"Why me?"

"Because you and Shane were best friends. You and Jared. I'm going to talk with him too. I need to talk with everyone who knew Shane. Who spent time with him. That will help us figure out what happened. When did you last see him?"

"Tuesday night."

"What were you doing?"

"Just hanging out. Skateboarding."

"Where?" Alex had his notebook out.

"Just around. Like, Chestnut Street. Limerock Street."

"Until what time?"

"Like, seven, maybe?"

"Did you see anyone else around?"

"No."

"Any cars?"

"A few, I guess."

"No one stopped and spoke with you?"

"No."

He went slowly, pressed for details, scribbled answers, steering toward the question he most needed to ask.

Alex looked down, as if reading his notes. Then he looked up, across the table at Ethan. "Was Shane into anything weird? Like, I don't know, witch-craft? Rituals? Funny stuff with animals?"

Ethan's face scrunched into confusion. "No. Why?"

"It's just some—"

"Because of how he was killed? What *was it*?"

"We just have to look—"

"What *happened*?" He was furious, quivering. "Was he shot? Or . . . what?"

"Honestly, Ethan, until there's an autopsy, we won't—"

"*Bullshit!* Fuck!" Ethan brought both fists down on the table in front of him. Then his face collapsed and he began to cry. His mother put her arm around him and pulled him close.

"I'm sorry," Alex said.

Ethan abruptly pulled away from his mother, stood, and ran to the door to the basement, opened it and disappeared, slamming the door. Thumping down the stairs.

"I'm sorry," he said again, to Isabel.

She was looking studiously at the door to the basement.

"How come he's not in school?"

"We're doing homeschooling now."

She stood up.

His cue. He stood and put away his notepad. "How's that working?"

"We're figuring it out." Not a sharing tone. She walked toward the mud-room.

"I'll probably need to talk with him again. You'll have to be present."

"I understand. Just let me know."

She paused at the door. "You can't tell me how he was killed?"

"I honestly don't know yet."

"What was the witchcraft stuff?"

"Isabel, I can't talk about it."

She opened the door, and he walked past her. Before he could turn on the granite step outside to face her, he heard the door shut behind him.

In his car, he looked at his phone and tried to focus his thoughts. Mark had texted Kathy McKinnon's number. Jared would be in school, but the kids would be getting out early. He'd spoken with Jodie Decker, the principal. He called Kathy. No answer, he left a message.

He looked up at Isabel's house through the windshield. A stab of self-loathing.

He pushed it aside as he drove back to the station.

The TV vans were already there.

9

Billie Raintree was the first local Alex got to know by sight in Granite Harbor, years ago, just after they'd moved from London, stamping his initial impressions of the town, the state of Maine, and its inhabitants. One of the tough natives, he presumed, whose ancestors had adapted to granite moraines, impenetrable forests, icy waterways, a climate more brutal than now, and bent all these to their will to arrive at their own notion of home.

A short, powerful-looking woman of indeterminate middle age, tanned, deeply creased face, thick salt-and-pepper hair cut short, sprouting straight up and back from an off-center cowlick. Already coming down the trail in the predawn dark, a chocolate Lab in front of her, as he passed her going up Mount Meguntic on his first early morning runs. She and the dog would step aside as Alex jogged past.

She always gave him a firm "Good morning." The verbal equivalent of a strong handshake.

"Good morning," Alex replied.

Occasionally, he saw her bench-pressing a sandwich of weights—more than he'd dream of trying—at the Y: a squat LEGO physique in shorts and T-shirt. If their eyes met, they acknowledged each other with nods.

They were not formally introduced until his interview at the police department, when Granite Harbor Police Chief Belinda—"Billie"—Raintree sat behind her desk wearing a creased uniform shirt and badge. Citations, diplomas, awards hung on the wall behind her. She looked bulletproof. Alex sat facing her across the desk.

"You're a book writer," said Chief Raintree.

"Yes, Chief. I've been a professor of creative writing here and there. But those were temporary positions. I'm not writing much now."

"You going to jump ship when the inspiration hits?"

With piercing accuracy, Chief Raintree had shot straight to the heart of his career plan. This, he hoped, would be a day job to tide him over until writing could support him again.

"Writing's really a part-time thing for me. So's the teaching. I want a full-time job." Alex wondered if the chief heard the lie.

"Why policeman? You want to write mysteries?"

Because it's the only job I can find in this small town for an otherwise unskilled creative type? He had prepared a better answer, most of it true. "I have a child, I need a more reliable income. I want to do what I can here in Granite Harbor, be a more active member of the community. Perhaps make a difference to the place where my daughter is growing up."

"Fair enough. You're certainly a different kind of applicant." Raintree glanced down at Alex's application on the desk in front of her. "Oxford University—that'll take care of the high school diploma or equivalent requirement." She looked back across the desk at Alex. "Book writing. I'm not sure what's needed for that, but I'd guess some kind of thoughtfulness. Observation. Different frame of reference, maybe. Could be useful around here. Granite Harbor's a broad mix. Local folk, people from away, creative types—people like you—techies, entrepreneurs. You could be a good fit. Glad to have you aboard." The chief reached her hand across the desk. "Good luck, Alex."

He went back to school: the eighteen-week police training course at the Maine Criminal Justice Academy in Vassalboro. He'd been apprehensive about Firearms Training and Tactics—he'd never fired a gun—and he thought he'd be bored by the five-hour Note Taking and Report Writing class, for which he didn't believe he needed any further instruction. But he'd been surprised to find himself engaged by the program.

"Details," said Officer Evans, the Note Taking instructor. A man with a blinking tic, as if he were doing a double take at everything. "You don't know what you're looking at when you get to a crime scene, when you talk to a witness, so make a note of everything. Not just what people say. What's right in front of your eyes? What jumps out? What are your impressions of the people you're talking to?"

As if for emphasis, Officer Evans blinked twice and stared at the recruits in the front row of the lecture hall. "Write it all down. Go over it later. You might start putting things together. *Details tell a story.*"

Alex couldn't have put it better in a fiction writing class. Many of the courses of the Basic Law Enforcement Training Curriculum might have been creative writing seminars: Ethics, Moral Issues, and Discretion; Dealing with the Vulnerable; Family Dynamics; Admissions and Confessions.

He was riveted.

Police training depicted a panoply of human misbehavior, malfeasance, perversion, tawdriness, and pathos that suggested stories he would never have imagined—a world he would supposedly be introduced to at the end of his training program.

Could any of this, he wondered, really be going on beneath the surface of genteel and pretty Granite Harbor? He'd been unaware of wrongdoing around town. His divorce from Morgana and the time spent with his lawyer had brought him into the Calder County Courthouse, where he'd glimpsed some unhappy and bruised people sitting on benches waiting to be called into a courtroom, cases involving traffic violations or domestic abuse. He couldn't imagine worse behind the facade of attractive houses, the harbor full of expensive yachts, well-heeled summer visitors, cheerful college students waiting tables at the Wharf Bar & Grill.

Two years of car theft, bike theft, boat theft, breaking-and-entering, drunk-and-disorderlies, auto crashes, noise complaints, minor drug arrests, missing children (all of whom had turned up), one suspected explosive device (a misplaced high school robotic experiment), had only confirmed the relatively benign personality of the town.

When Jack Yatsevitch, the department's only detective investigator, was about to retire, Chief Raintree asked Alex if he'd like to apply for the position.

"I've read your books, Alex," said Chief Raintree. "I think it might suit you."

He couldn't quite believe this—Billie Raintree reading about the Cargills and the Alkers of Salford? What had she made of Granddad, naughty Sheila, Bent Ben, and the Corporation Street bomb?

"Really? You read one of them?"

"I read both of them. You think I'd hire you without reading your books? Barbara gave them to me."

"Barbara?"

"My wife, Barbara. I think you know her. Body and Soul."

"Oh . . . yes." Of course he knew Barbara Goldman. The thin, egret-like woman was the owner of Body and Soul Bookstore, the town's time-warp emporium of secondhand books on Bayview Street. A labyrinthine establishment on two floors, half a block deep. Barbara knew his tastes, had met Sophie, had steered him through the dark bookcases built by shipwrights on the upper floor where he'd found many cloth-bound treasures.

Then Alex remembered he'd seen Chief Raintree and Barbara standing together at the store's table during library book sales. And sitting together in the Grand movie theater.

All this in a second as Chief Raintree continued over his embarrassment: "Yes, Barbara and I like to say that between us we take care of the town's body and soul, law enforcement and literature. She made me aware of your books and reputation. If Mark Beltz and Frank Duggan and young Becky Watrous wrote books, you can believe I'd read them. I want to know who I've got working for me. You've got an understanding of life and characters, and that's why I think you might be good in the job."

"Thank you, Chief. What about the others for detective? Like Mark?"

"They're not interested. Or I'm not interested. And I don't want to look outside the department. I want someone who knows the town, someone I know."

So Alex had returned to the Academy for further training in Police Investigative Procedures. He took and passed the LEIE, the Law Enforcement Investigator Examination. He was happier back in his own rumpled clothes. He'd felt like an imposter in his blue-black police uniform. He'd almost forgotten the eager young man from Manchester, who'd made it to Oxford, the promising novelist, as if, in a *Twilight Zone* episode, those identities were a dream from which he'd awoken into his true identity: small-town American lawman. He would no more have imagined himself an astronaut on Mars.

But he felt more himself back in jeans and a Gore-Tex jacket, Blundstone boots. He stopped shaving daily. He exchanged the too big .45 caliber department-issue Heckler & Koch HK45 pistol he'd carried on his belt as a uniformed cop for a slimmer, subcompact Glock 26 9mm that weighed almost half a pound less and was more concealable in the shoulder holster he adopted after getting back into his own clothes. The little Glock almost disappeared beneath a down vest or his old tweed jacket. Except for mandatory shooting practice at various indoor and outdoor ranges, and regular cleaning, he never touched his pistol. Except to keep it in a safe when at home, whether Sophie was there or not—she might drop in. It was only noticeable if someone—Sophie, say—hugged him. But no one had for years.

"Maybe your storyteller instincts will be of use to you as a detective," Chief Billie Raintree said at the conclusion of his LEIE training, when she presented Alex with his Granite Harbor Police Detective badge, which he would carry with him but tucked away out of sight like his gun. "There's no such thing as random, senseless crime. Behind every sad, sorry, dumbass crime is a story."

"A frog?" Chief Raintree said now, looking up when Alex came into her office. His first printed report lay on her desk. With photographs from the site, the Settlement, Shane hanging from the makeshift frame.

Through the chief's closed window he heard the whine of generators. MPBN and the Bangor and Portland network television news crews were setting up in front of the William P. Merrill Station, the single-story complex of two modern brick buildings that housed the town's fire station and police department. Alex and Chief Raintree would be giving a short news conference at noon.

"Yes. I'm planning to look up any local connection to witchcraft—"

"I doubt it," said Chief Raintree, shaking her head dismissively. "This isn't witchcraft, or Wicca, goblin worship, anything like that. That's all women with candles, the *Witches of Eastwick*, herbs and elderberry wine. They're like book groups. This is not that. What about Shane's friends?"

Alex explained what he'd learned of the relationship between Shane Carter, Ethan Dorr, and Jared McKinnon. All three boys had been born in the same week at Midcoast Medical Center. They'd grown up together. Isabel Dorr and Kathy McKinnon were now single parents. Doreen Wisner's situation, the location of the family's house way out on Cobb Road, and Shane's room in the basement, meant that he had spent a lot of time in the Dorr and McKinnon households. Isabel now worked at the Settlement, Kathy taught yoga. He'd interviewed Ethan and Isabel. He was trying to get ahold of Kathy—

"Alex, I've requested FBI assistance from Boston. They're sending up one of their agents tomorrow."

"Oh. Because this is my first murder?"

"Not at all. I'm not enthusiastic about bringing in the Bureau. They're into profiling, which is no better than astrology in my book. But this is not a local argument, petty theft, burglary. The MO"—she tapped the photographs—"suggests the killer may have acted before, maybe outside of Maine, so it could be a federal crime, in which case we would have to call in the FBI. They've got a big database, they'll turn up anything similar. So you'll work with their agent, Harris, who's coming up today or tomorrow, but you report to me. It's your case, the agent cooperates with our department."

"I understand."

"Have you talked to Kevin Regis?"

Kevin Regis was a software developer and computer technician who ran a computer repair service out on West Street. An independent civilian contractor, Kevin, who looked more like a sandy-haired high school football coach, was the Granite Harbor Police IT department.

"Yes. He's looking for information on Derek Carter, the boy's biological father. And we're exploring all locally registered pedophiles and sex offenders—there was no sign of interference or violation, but I'm waiting for the autopsy, and that's tomorrow morning. Somebody took Shane somewhere. What they did required private space, a kill location, so I'm thinking probably someone local."

"Agreed. Someone everyone knows, who does a good job of blending in. Maybe someone Shane knew. Someone he was happy to get into a car with."

Judy Waite, short, round, gray-blond, knocked at the open doorway. "Chief, they're ready for you both outside. They're broadcasting live."

"Thank you, Judy." Chief Raintree stood up behind her desk. "We'll keep it short. I'll start. Our thoughts are with the family, and hand it over to you. No frog, no details, of course."

"Right."

He followed Chief Raintree outside into the press of reporters, an eruption of questions, cameras, flashes—

Eye of newt and toe of frog—half-remembered fragments tumbled into Alex's brain. *Never hung poison on a fouler toad . . . poisonous bunch-backed toad . . .* Shakespeare was full of such invocations—late sixteenth, early seventeenth century—the time when the settlers sailed from England to the now abandoned site north of Granite Harbor. What did those people who rejected home, family, the whole of the known world, for a chance simply not to perish on a wild and distant shore—what did they believe of frogs and newts and toads?

"Thank you for coming," Chief Billie Raintree announced to the small crowd waving microphones, cameras, cell phones. "Our thoughts go first to the family. . . ."

10

Morgana Claymore didn't like waiting in line at school. It wasn't her thing, taking her daughter to school, or the pickup crawl, sitting in her truck behind other parents' cars, going nowhere. Sophie took the school bus. It picked her up on Bayview Street, a block from Belleport, Morgana's house on Chestnut. After school, she got the bus back into town, or rides with friends, went to the library to do her homework, or to a friend's house, and came home before supper. An arrangement that suited them both: they had their afternoons to themselves. Or she went home to her father's house.

On the few occasions when she *had* driven to school for 3:30 P.M. pickup—some project, sports equipment, whatever, that Sophie needed to bring home—she didn't remember it being this crowded. But the news was out. Morgana saw it in the shocked faces of the other parents, mostly mothers, in the other cars, looking at one another in collective dismay, wide-eyed, shaking heads. All of them had rushed to school to physically lay their hands on their children as soon as possible.

The car in front of her rolled ahead a few feet. Morgana didn't move, allowing the space between the vehicles to open up. In the door's side mirror she saw the car behind her trying to nudge her forward, all but disappearing from view under the tailgate of her truck. *Go ahead, make my day.* At over nineteen feet, Morgana's Crew Cab Ford F-150 King Ranch truck was five feet longer than a Subaru Outback and half again as high. She had an urge to get out of this ridiculous crawl, drive forward, and double-park near the buses, but it was more fun to take her time and let the fleet of muddy Subarus and Toyotas try to maneuver around her.

Don't fence me in.

She switched from Willie's Roadhouse on Sirius to Maine Public Radio, and caught the crunchy station's latest report update on the story:

"—learned that the identity of the victim is Granite Harbor High School student Shane Carter, sixteen years of age. The body was discovered this morning at the historic Granite Harbor Settlement site. No further details are being released at this time, according to Granite Harbor Police Detective Alex Brangwen, who spoke with Maine Public's reporter Kelly Jones a little while ago—"

Morgana barked involuntarily. *Alex Brangwen, Detective.* Another invention! She long ago realized that she'd invented the man she married. She'd imagined the great writer. But it had been there in front of her all along—if she'd bothered to look: the self-indulgent melancholy, the narcissism. So wrapped up in his tortured self-involved writing, unhappy, frustrated, complaining, like some baby trying to open a package that was beyond him. How could she not have seen it? She'd thought he was going to be a major writer—*and make some money.* She'd read his novel, the one he was known for, and accepted that it must be good from all the rave blurbs on the back, but it took her a while to realize she hadn't liked it *at all.* That claustrophobic street of depressed, complaining characters. What had impressed her were the newspaper articles about Alex Brangwen: *The books on my bedside table* for the *Sunday Times.* Shortlisted for a prize. The fancy dinner in some famous library, with his publisher, who looked like a middle-aged Harry Potter, and all those clever literary people. They all loved him! How smart and clever her husband was!

She'd imagined them together. The house with her beautiful antiques and paintings. The great writer, the smart, beautiful people they would know. It still embarrassed her when she thought about how she'd fallen for all that literary horseshit.

As soon as she learned she was pregnant, the scales fell from her eyes. The idea of being saddled with this narcissistic baby-man—*for life.* And London—so dark and dreary. She couldn't get out of England fast enough.

Back home in the States, she *really* saw him. That English charm and humor didn't travel well.

Granite Harbor Police Detective Alex Brangwen. What a joke! As if he were a real detective!

Then Alex's voice came through on her radio: "Our thoughts are with Shane's family and friends. We've begun our investigation but have no details to release at this time. We would like to hear from anyone in the community who saw Shane recently and has any information they'd like to tell us."

"That was Detective Alex Brangwen, of the Granite Harbor Police Department. This is Kelly Jones in Granite Harbor for Maine Public Radio."

Morgana looked up at the cars ahead of her in the line, her face still creased with her wonderfully amused smirk. A woman in another car was staring at her, her own face hanging with grief and confusion.

"Oh, go fuck yourself," said Morgana, sorry the window was rolled up. She pushed at the radio and returned to Willie's Roadhouse.

Sophie was not waiting for her when she finally pulled up to the front of the drop-off zone. Morgana had texted her: *Picking you up now. Be there.* There had been no reply, but she hadn't expected or needed one.

Morgana put the gear in park and looked around. Other kids piled into their parents' cars, which pulled out behind Morgana and drove away. Principal Jodie Decker was hugging the kids as they climbed into the cars, looking sincerely at each parent with a tight smile that said, *Thank you for coming. Somehow we will get through this together. God bless you.*

There was a knuckle rap on the window beside Morgana's face. A man with a yellow nylon vest over a brown security uniform stood beside her car, squinting up at her through the tinted glass. "Ma'am, could you please move your vehicle."

She lowered the window sufficiently to say, "I'm picking up my daughter. She'll be right out."

"You're blocking traffic here. You can park over there"—he pointed way over to the staff parking area—"or go around in the pickup line again."

"I've been in the line for twenty minutes. She'll be out any moment."

"We need this space to get the vans and other vehicles by. Please move your vehicle."

The security man walked away.

Jodie Decker, now visible through the passenger window, nodded and looked straight at Morgana with an expression that said all of the above, plus: *Hi, Morgana. It's good to see you at the school, since we don't see you here often. It's a difficult day. So appreciate your help with the parking and traffic flow.*

"Gah!" She pulled the gearshift, waited for a Subaru to pass, and drove off toward the staff parking area.

She waited another fifteen minutes, craning her head over her shoulder for more than half of that time. She grew furious. She wasn't worried about Sophie, she knew she had simply ignored her text.

The traffic line thinned out.

Morgana got out and walked to the pickup spot. Jodie Decker was still there, now talking to some teacher, while she shook hands with a student getting into a car and gazed at the parent behind the wheel with that pained, profound, moment-defining expression.

"Have you seen my daughter, Sophie?"

"I haven't, Morgana," said Jodie Decker. "Marion, have you seen Sophie come out?"

"I think she came out a while ago?" said the teacher, squinting into her memory while peering at Morgana at the same time.

"Thank you." Morgana fastened the center button of her hacking jacket, turned, and strode back to her truck.

As she pulled the door shut, she became aware of . . . what was it? A sensation . . . something unusual beneath her irritation. She reached for it . . . then she had it.

Fear.

So where was Sophie?

11

"Hey," said Jared when the door to Aerie Ink opened, and Ashley stood there and looked briefly at him and then over his shoulder. "Hey," said Ashley.

Behind Jared stood Mrs. Dorr's son, Ethan. She knew him because Mrs. Dorr had been friends with her grandmother Wendy when they'd both taught at Granite Harbor High.

And behind the boys stood a chestnut-haired girl. Ashley knew her too. The policeman's daughter.

Jared hadn't remembered Ashley from high school—later he figured out she'd been a senior when he was a sophomore—but he'd become aware of her around town. The crazy long black hair, pale skin. And the ink. She was remote and weird and unearthly, like a girl in a horror movie. He'd once stood behind her in the Shed and tried to think of something to say to her, but then she got her coffee and was gone. He imagined scenarios where she would be in danger—attacked by a dog, or almost run over by a car, or hit on by one of those bearded lobsterman types who hung out at Captain Smithy's, and he would save her, or get beaten up trying, and then she'd be grateful and want to know him. But these were daydreams and she was a few years older than he was and he knew she'd never notice him.

Then one evening in August, as he was skating in the park above the harbor, someone called his name. He stepped off his board and looked around. It was Ashley.

"Hey, Jared."

"Oh, hey"—his mind totally blown—"what's up?"

"You've got a van, right?"

"Uh, yes." He and Ethan had bought an old Econoline van, rusty but mechanically sound, for $500 two months ago. They each had a key and kept it parked in the public lot behind Calder Mill. Over the last few summers, Jared had worked on several of the town's windjammer schooners that took guests out for cruises, and now he used the van to transport marine supplies and make some extra money. Ethan used it to cruise yard sales. She must have seen him in the van. How did she know his name?

"Could you give me a ride down to Rockland and help me pick up a chair? It's big, so I need a van. I'll pay you."

"Yeah, sure. You don't have to pay me."

"No, I'll pay you."

She'd bought a La-Z-Boy recliner on the Rockland Facebook Marketplace. In the van he asked her how she knew him.

"Jared, I've known you for years," she said, like he was an idiot. "My grandmother Wendy practiced yoga with your mom at Mountain Hall."

"Oh, right," said Jared, reeling.

After that, whenever he could, which was increasingly like all the time, he climbed the stairs to Aerie Ink, Ashley's third-floor studio, to watch her work and draw her designs. To stare at the tattoos on her neck and arms. She told him about the designs, some of which were in Chinese squiggles, what each one meant. She pulled her T-shirt up over her back and stuck her thumb in her pants and pulled them down a bit to show him. Jared had never seen anything more beautiful than the milky whiteness of her skin set off by the dark blue tats. And he noticed the slenderness of her back, and her small waist, and what he could see of the swelling around the sides of her chest. He asked if she had any more tattoos on her. It was a few weeks before she showed him.

Ashley liked being on top. Jared would lie beneath her on the futon, his eyes fixed on the pale blue orchid blossoms that seemed to be growing up across her pale belly from the point where their bodies met. *Wow,* he thought as he perceived the artistry in the intended effect. Orchids sprouting from down there when she had sex with someone.

Even as he watched the swaying orchids, Jared wondered at Ashley's grown-up world that was a mystery to him. She'd lived in Portland and hung out with a lot of cool inked people around the city. He was still amazed that she'd spoken to him in the Harbor Park, and now he was having sex with her and they were hanging out all the time.

"This is Ethan and Sophie," said Jared at the door. "They want to see your designs."

"You can have a look, but I can't tattoo you."

"You can't?" Ethan seemed surprised.

"No. You're underage." She looked at Jared. "You know that."

"Oh, yeah," he said, as if he'd forgotten.

Ethan and the cop's kid were disappointed.

Kids were always coming in for tattoos. They had no idea.

"I can give you an ink transfer that stays on for about two weeks."

"You can?" said Ethan.

"Sure." Ashley opened the door wider.

Inside, Jared, who knew his way around the studio now, showed them books of designs.

"Did you have an idea of something?" Ashley asked.

"A name," said Ethan.

Ashley opened a book of fonts. She slowly turned pages: words, names, letters. All the blocky, curlicue, calligraphic variations of each style represented in its own font.

"So, it's going to be Ethan, right? And . . . ?" She looked at the girl.

"Not our names," said the girl.

12

It was a freaky afternoon at Hannaford. A lot of people in the store, their faces clouded, fearful, glancing around furtively, looking away, avoiding eye contact. They were buying food quickly, in bulk, as if stocking up for a hurricane.

Isabel filled her cart with cereal, eggs, milk, tofu, vegetables, pasta, spaghetti sauce, Annie's Organic mac 'n' cheese. Food for him, food for her.

Before Ethan was born, she sailed with his father, Joshua, from Maine to the Caribbean and back again. At the beginning of the voyage, as the Maine coast disappeared astern and the ocean floor beneath them dropped away to thousands of feet, Isabel was terrified by the thought that only three-quarters of an inch of wood, the boat's planking, separated them from the depths. But Joshua's confidence and joy, and the rhythm of the waves passing day and night beneath the hull, lulled her fear, and she discovered in the enormity and solitude of the ocean, and Joshua's calm and skill, a peace she had never experienced.

They set off with everything they imagined they might need stored inside the boat's lockers: cans of food, yeast for making bread, seeds from which Isabel grew sprouts, a dental repair kit, spare gear for the boat, the books they wanted to read. And each other. The sense of completeness gave Isabel a security she had never known before.

Or since.

When they returned to Maine, Ethan was born, and she and Joshua and their baby were wrapped in another kind of completeness. But after Joshua sailed off to England and disappeared, eleven years ago now, Isabel was left with an emptiness as large and unfillable as an ocean. There was no membrane now between her and terror, no Joshua to soothe her. The only thing that made her feel better was having ample food and supplies—paper towels, underwear, socks, flashlight batteries, and lightbulbs—stored in the house.

"Isabel."

She was at the end of the aisle—she could have kept going, pretended not to hear, she wasn't in the mood to talk with anybody—but she turned, reluctantly.

"Oh, Roger"—she was relieved—"it's you."

"How are you doing?" he asked. He was still in his Settlement apothecary clothes. He evidently liked the outfit; she'd seen him wearing those same clothes, the long vest, around town on days when he wasn't working. He was holding a red shopping basket partially filled with vegetables. The compassion in his face intensified. "How's Ethan?"

"Oh, God. You know him. He won't talk about it. He's bottling it all up inside. It's terrible. I don't know what to do for him, Roger."

"You know I'd be happy to talk to him. Let him know that. Or maybe I'll just try to catch him somewhere. You know I care about him. All those kids."

"Thank you, Roger. I know you do."

Home again, she cracked the door to the basement, heard Ethan tinkering below, was instantly reassured by the knowledge he was safe, and closed the door again. She made a cup of detox tea, placed her space heater so that its noisy stream of warm air was aimed at the sofa in the living room, sat down to sip her tea, and tried to read her book. *A Lady's Life in the Rocky Mountains*, by Isabella Bird, an Englishwoman who had traveled alone by horseback through Colorado in 1873. She'd picked it up for a dollar at Body and Soul, thinking it might take her far away, absorb her.

But Shane floated up before her. His exuberant laugh, his generosity of spirit. How would any of them bear it? She'd lost touch with Doreen since she'd married Dennis Wisner. They'd had Skye, but she couldn't imagine how Doreen would take it. She was heartbroken for Ethan. Those boys had loved

each other all their lives. They were closer than brothers. She saw them together, Shane, Ethan, and Jared. Here in her house, in the backyard, swimming off the docks in the summers, beautiful wet slippery bodies like seals.

This would be as devastating for Ethan as the loss of his father.

She tried concentrating on the book again. But now Alex's face and voice
were also getting between the pages. Until today, she hadn't seen him up
close for five years. He looked older, grayer. White bristles. Haggard. But
the voice was still the same. The accent, the slight rasping quality she'd loved.

She'd first seen him onstage, reading, at the Granite Harbor Opera House.
The witty writer. Afterward she'd bought his novel about two families living
on the same street in Northern England. Stood in line for him to sign it.
The characters were English, they spoke in their Manchester slang, the place
was surrounded by old industrial brick buildings. But she saw it, that world,
the people there. Afterward she felt she knew the author. That by reading his
book she'd looked into his brain and heart.

It was the first time since Joshua had disappeared that she felt she might
want to know another man.

Flynn came into the living room, sat upright close to the sofa, and looked
at her. Now she saw the light was falling outside.

"All right." She sat up. "Let's go."

Flynn whirled around and rushed into the mudroom.

Isabel opened the door to the basement and called down, "I'm taking
Flynn for his walk. Back soon. Okay?"

No answer.

"Ethan—"

"I heard you."

"Then let me know, okay? We'll be back soon."

Back home forty minutes later, she fed Flynn and made two more meals:
baked cauliflower, eggplant, onion and garlic for her. And—because Ethan
wouldn't eat much of what she wanted to eat—tofu, penne, arrabiata sauce,
broccoli, and a glass of milk for him.

She opened the basement door. "Ethan!"

They'd talked about her not having to shout for him while he was wearing
headphones.

"Ethan!"

Isabel flipped the light switch off-on-off-on inside the door. The basement light sent its message.

"Ethan?"

She went down the stairs. He wasn't there.

He wasn't in his room upstairs either.

13

In the van, its headlights carving out the road ahead, Jared took a hit from the pen and passed it to Ethan.

Ethan examined it. Short, elegant, the molded mouthpiece neatly screwed onto the transparent cartridge full of oily brown wax. "Did Ashley get this for you?"

"No way, man. She won't even buy me a beer. She's very strict about the law. She told me she wouldn't have had sex with me if I wasn't sixteen. Otherwise it would be statutory rape."

"Wow. So where'd you get the pen?"

"Donnie. His parents got him a card because he's got epileptic brain waves and they want to get him off his other medication."

"What did you pay?"

"I don't know. Like twenty-five?"

"Cool," said Ethan. He took a hit and passed the pen to Sophie, who was squeezed beside him in the passenger seat. She wiped the mouthpiece with her finger, sucked and coughed.

The GRANITE HARBOR LIVING HISTORY SETTLEMENT sign came up in the lights and Jared turned.

"Dude, use the service road in case anyone's still here." Ethan pointed at a gap in the trees. "It's another way in."

"How do you know?"

"I came up here with my mom a few weeks ago when she was thinking about working here. We drove around."

They came to a clearing, stopped, and climbed out of the van. It was almost pitch-dark. A wind off the sea made the treetops wave and groan overhead.

"Man, this is creepy," said Ethan.

"I know, right?" said Jared. "We came here in third grade and I thought it was real. I thought the people were all real and lived here."

They stumbled in the unseen ruts of the road. Jared pulled out his phone and turned on its light.

"Turn it off, bro," said Ethan quietly. "If anyone's here they'll see it. It doesn't help anyway."

They walked on slowly, shoulders bumping, Sophie in the middle, until they were out of the trees on the open ground of the Settlement. There were no stars, but they could make out the hulking forms of the cabins, the small outbuildings, other shapes around them.

"Dude," said Jared. "I feel like I'm in third grade again."

They stood still.

"This is definitely creepy," said Sophie. Her hand tightened around Ethan's arm. "Why would you leave England to come here?"

"So do we know where they found him?"

"Near some vegetable patch, my mom said."

"Fuck. Where's the vegetable patch?"

Ethan started laughing. "Somewhere, man."

Then they giggled together, a sudden stoned release, until their laughter subsided, the last of it blown away by the buffeting salty air.

"Shane!" Jared shouted into the wind. "Where are you, man?"

They heard only the sound of the surf breaking beyond the rocks above the beach.

"That looks like something," said Sophie. She raised an arm. "It's got a fence around it."

They walked slowly toward the faint rectangle of darker space that did appear to be outlined with a low fence.

"Let's do it here," said Sophie.

They sat on the ground, close together.

Jared held up his phone, and a dim green light illuminated the ground in front of them. "There's no one here, man. We need to see. It's like lighting a candle." He pulled a pack of American Spirit cigarettes and a Bic lighter from his pocket and placed them within the light. "He loved American Spirit. He said the packaging was cool. This'll get you to Valhalla, dude."

Ethan placed beside it a key ring holding a bright trinket on a patch of leather.

"What's that?" asked Jared.

"It's the EGA. The eagle, globe, anchor. The insignia of the US Marines. He was going to join after high school. He wanted to get out of here." Ethan's voice cracked as he rubbed the insignia with his thumb.

"He mentioned it," said Jared, "but I didn't think he was serious."

"Well, now he can."

Sophie reached out to lay something dark next to the cigarettes and the key chain.

"What's that?" asked Ethan.

Sophie's shoulders shook. She was crying. "It's a brownie. I didn't know what else to give him. But he liked my brownies."

Ethan put his arm around her. "You made them?"

"Yes."

"Sophie, it's beautiful. He would have loved that." He held on to Sophie as she shook against him.

Jared turned his phone off. Another light briefly glowed in front of his face, and he passed the vape pen to Ethan. Ethan pulled at it. "Here," he said to Sophie. She took it, and its light glowed again.

"Shane, man." Jared released a choked breath. He lay backward on the ground, his arm covering his face. "What the *fuck*, dude."

"We're here for you, always, man." Ethan lay back beside Jared and pulled Sophie down into the crook of his arm. "We miss you. Like . . ." He couldn't speak any more.

"He was the best," said Sophie.

They looked up at the clouds scudding low overhead.

"And he had the worst shit to put up with," said Ethan. "It's not fair."

"Who's got the—"

Sophie saw it and screamed before it even happened.

A portion of the sky detached itself, swirled overhead, and dropped on them, heavy, damp, coarse. Ethan tried to sit up, but a great blunt weight hit him and forced him down and knocked the air out of him.

"What the f—" Jared started to say.

As they struggled, moving against each other and trying to push upward, the black overwhelming pressure spread and settled over them, forcing them down and flat. Dull blows hit them repeatedly on their faces, heads, bodies. Sophie screamed again, muffled, and the boys made angry fear-filled noises. They heard grunts above them, men's snarling tones. More heavy blows, partly absorbed by the heavy suffocating cloth between them and what was pushing them down. Soon they were unable to move and lay pinned and breathless.

A man's voice barked overhead. "Stop moving!"

"Get off!" shouted Ethan, terror giving strength to his voice.

Another voice came from above. "What are you doing here?"

Both voices seemed familiar to Ethan. His fear that they were about to be killed subsided. "We're friends of Shane's."

"Who is that?"

"Ethan Dorr. My mother works here."

The weight on them shifted. The heavy canvas that had been flung over them was pulled aside.

Ethan saw the dark shapes of two men. One of them, holding an axe handle, threw it aside.

"Ethan, what are you doing here?"

"Roger?"

"Yes."

"And who's that?" Ethan asked.

"Your archnemesis," said the other man, larger, stockier.

"Chester?"

"None other."

"Fuck, man!" said Jared. "Why'd you jump on us like that?"

"What do you think, Ethan?" said Roger. "You know what happened here. We didn't know who you were, or what you were doing. You shouldn't be here."

"Chester, get off me, man." Jared pushed aside the heavy canvas. "What is this?"

"It's a tarp," said Chester, getting to his feet and pulling the canvas off them.

"Who's that with you?" asked Roger.

"Sophie Brangwen," said Sophie.

"Well, you need to go home, all of you. Are you all right?"

A flashlight beam stabbed through the air.

"My God," said Roger Priestly. He swung the flashlight across their faces. His own face partly lit up, filled with shock. "What the hell have you done to yourselves?"

14

He picked up the van on Elm Street. Easy to spot, an old Econoline, once white, rust beneath the fenders and quarter panels. And now he noticed the right rear brake light wasn't working. *Better get that fixed, boys, you might get pulled over for that.*

He was two cars behind. Then the car in front of him turned right on Belmont Avenue and he was behind the van. It was dark, and even if they were looking, they would only see his headlights, but he hung back, and then slowed to allow a car leaving the post office to enter traffic in front of him.

They weren't paying attention anyway. The van was moving erratically. Three of them in the front seat. The two boys weren't old enough for a full license; they could only have learner's permits, and obviously needed the driving practice.

The van turned up Chestnut Street. *Good. Drop the girl off first.*

That's exactly what they did. He stopped a block down the hill and turned his lights off before the van turned into the big house, the mother's place. He didn't see the girl get out, but the van reappeared quickly, continuing on up Chestnut.

Where now, boys? Go hang somewhere, play with your phones, smoke some weed? Drop your guard?

A wave of feeling swept over him. It made him think of other feelings. *Is it like hunger? Or arousal?* No, this was stronger, almost violent. His body shuddered. He had to grip the wheel as it surged through him. It left him with an ache. *Was it the coyote's appetite, the directive now lodged in his blood?*

Maybe it would happen now. He was ready. *Keep going, boys . . . keep going . . .*

The van turned onto Jacobs Avenue. *So you're dropping Ethan off.* He slowed again before the turn.

Okay then. I am ready for you, Jared.

But Jared didn't drive home. He drove to the public parking behind the Calder Mill. He jumped out of the van, and before the driver could park or even stop his truck, Jared had skipped across the narrow wooden footbridge over the Meguntic River and disappeared onto Main Street.

He drove the long three blocks up Washington, along Cross, down Mountain—observing the stop signs, he was only two blocks from the police station—and back onto Main Street.

But there was no sign of Jared.

Never mind. It would happen. At the right time.

15

Isabel heard the van pull up on the street. She looked out the mudroom
window and saw Ethan get out.

It was all she could do not to shout with fury as he came through the
door. "Ethan!" She quivered. "Where have you been?"

"I don't want to talk about it."

"Well, I do—"

"*Well, I don't!*"

He pushed past her into the kitchen.

"Are you all right?"

"Yes."

"Are you sure?"

"Yes! I'm sure!"

A rush of relief, love, gratitude flooded through her. Her anger was gone.
He was here. He was home.

"Then we'll have supper. It's ready. Sit down, please."

He sat at the kitchen table.

She scooped his penne into a big white bowl. She brought it to the table
and placed it in front of him.

"Remove your hat, please."

"Mom, it's freezing in here. You're wearing a hat."

"You don't need a hat, you've got hair. Lots of it."

She brought her own plate to the table and sat down facing him.

"Ethan, take off your hat, please."

He was already hunched over his bowl. "I want it on."

She reached her hand across the table and held his. "Ethan. Sweetheart. I'm happy you're home. I love you. Please don't argue with me. It's us. Remove your hat, please."

With slow deliberation, releasing long strands of curly hair that took flight with static, he pulled it off.

She screamed.

16

She wasn't physically hurt or Morgana would have told him right away on the phone. She simply said, "You need to come over here—*now*—and see your daughter."

Their mother-daughter power struggle had intensified with Sophie's adolescence. Increasingly, Morgana called Alex saying, "I can't handle her. I need you to come over here. *Now.*"

"Morgana," he'd say, "you both have to work it out. This is your week together."

But with the onset of Sophie's teen years, the court-certified custody schedule had broken down. More than once, Morgana's giant truck had pulled abruptly into his driveway—he heard its powerful snorting from anywhere inside his house—and Sophie, stone-faced, climbed down out of the passenger seat dragging a bulging duffel bag, exiled to stay with her father for an indefinite period. Dad as punishment. Dad as purgatory.

"Morgana," he said now on the phone, "this is—"

"*Someone has done something illegal to our daughter!*" An unusual edge of hysteria to her voice.

"What?"

"You need to come and see."

"Can't you just tell me?"

"Do you want me to call *another* policeman?"

He drove past the formal parking area, the front door, circled the fountain, and parked steps from the kitchen door, where he knew she would be. It was after dark. Sure enough, he saw her inside, sitting on a stool at the granite island.

But when Morgana saw him at the kitchen door—her face immediately annoyed—she waved him away, throwing her arm repeatedly toward the front entrance he'd driven past, halfway back through the vast house beyond the kitchen. He turned and walked back along the front of the house.

"I don't like you coming to my kitchen door," she said, as he came into the large front foyer. "You're not a friend. Use the front entrance."

At the time he met Morgana Claymore in London, Alex had moved south from Manchester to work at the *London Review of Books*. He'd published two books, was no longer a celebrated British novelist under thirty, but well into his fourth decade and struggling with his third novel. A friend of Morgana's, an editor at the *Smithsonian Magazine*, who had commissioned an article from Alex about the industrial waterways of Northern England, gave Morgana, who had come to London to take the Collector's Art Course at Christie's auction house, Alex's phone number. She called. Following a brief phone conversation, they agreed to meet for dinner.

He was living in a small flat in Putney, with a large Conran sofa he'd bought with his first royalty payment, when he'd anticipated literary success and a move to larger digs across the river, but that had never happened. He traveled by 14 bus to South Kensington, where Morgana was renting an entire detached house on Cranley Place. A furiously yapping dachshund launched itself at Alex's leg as the door opened. Not actually biting him but giving the impression of wanting to.

"Diego, get back in here!" commanded the tall, lustrously dark-haired woman in her . . . early thirties, he guessed . . . who must have been out riding somewhere. She was dressed for an equestrian event in breeches and a black velvet hacking jacket. A knee-high black riding boot corralled the dog and maneuvered it back inside. "My guard dog," she said, opening the door wider. Strong dark eyebrows lifting with amusement over large disarming blue eyes.

He took her to La Bouchée, nearby on Old Brompton Road. "Decent French," he'd been told by a friend when casting about for where he should take someone to dinner in upmarket South Kensington. When Morgana walked ahead of him for a few paces on a narrow stretch of pavement, he noticed the play of pronounced but firm buttocks beneath the flapping vent of her jacket. At dinner she held her thick dark hair aside to keep it out of the *soupe de poisson*. At moments when he appeared to be looking thoughtfully away from her compelling eyes, Alex watched a blue vein pulse in her ivory throat.

His dour, mordant Mancunian wit, a staple of the English sensibility that was met by British women with glum acknowledgment, made Morgana hoot loudly, double over in her chair, and slap her thighs. An unrestrained American laugh, as spacious and uninflected as a stretch of prairie. Alex was amazed that he could produce such a reaction. It felt like the sudden acquisition of an undreamed-of talent, as if he were able to let loose a Chopin polonaise. The more she laughed, the funnier he grew. She was strikingly un-English. Her boundless positivity and optimism contrasted with the pinched, self-deprecating qualities of his country's national character. Two evenings later, he decided that her sexual proficiency must be American too: an acrobatic repertoire wholly alien to the uniformly cerebral English girls he'd known.

By the time the Christie's course ended six weeks later, Morgana had become "your biggest fan in the world." They'd been to Paris by Eurostar, first class—she wanted to show Alex the flea markets at St. Ouen—and they'd decided to marry and have children. Morgana had always known, she said, that she would be a mother. There was no reason to delay. She'd sailed in the Mediterranean, spent more than enough time in New York, Santa Fe, Paris, and Rome. She'd always felt herself to be European in culture and sensibility, she said. She *loved* London, "the best of all worlds," and was ready to settle down there.

They imagined their life together. Morgana knew Alex would write increasingly successful books that would gain him awards and money. Through Morgana's eyes, he acquired a new view of himself: a natural wit on the cusp of literary renown. He began to understand how support and belief from the right quarter could be self-fulfilling conditions. She would deal in fine paintings and antiques. Her eye, of which she was no less certain than his literary talent, would leverage her to the status of an important collector. By then it was clear to Alex that Morgana had money, which, with typical British delicacy, he chose not to inquire about. But when they discussed, over dinners, in first-class railway carriages, in bed after lovemaking, what they would be able to give their child—the finest education, trips throughout Europe and the United States, unmatched cultural advantages—he appreciated what Morgana would bring to the table.

They married at Chelsea Old Town Hall. Her mother, Philomene, a Texas gentlewoman, came for a week. She stayed at the Dorchester with Dandie, her small white Coton de Tuléar dog. She was a large woman who moved with the stately grace of an ocean liner, inspecting and touching the furniture alongside her everywhere, in the hotel, in the offices of Chelsea Old Town Hall. Philomene had stayed at the Dorchester on her trip around the world with Morgana's father, the second of her four husbands, before Morgana was born.

"The world was so nice then, Alex," she said wistfully. "Before the Arabs bought Harrods." It sounded like a Noël Coward song.

He was dismayed when, a week before the wedding, in Philomene's hotel suite, he observed Morgana and her mother screaming at each other like teenage girls over the wedding dress. Morgana had chosen it with great deliberation, had it altered to her satisfaction, but Philomene was dismissive of the dress and its designer.

Alex took Morgana downstairs to tea. He tried to soothe her. "Don't let her upset you, sweetheart. It's your dress, your day."

"She's part of the reason I want to live in Europe," Morgana said, her breast heaving with emotion as her Lapsang souchong grew cold.

None of the rest of Morgana's Texan family was able to make it over for the wedding, though they sent large checks, including several for Alex. Alex's parents and his sister, Liz, came down from Manchester. His best man, David Burdett, a novelist, from nearby Richmond.

"You've got a tiger by the tail, wi' that one, lad," his father said cheerfully, quaffing the Ruinart Blanc de Blancs champagne at the wedding lunch in the Dorchester Grill. After lunch his parents caught a train back to Manchester.

"Just get a child, Alex," Burdett said emphatically. "For your old age."

To that end, Morgana directed their efforts. They made love every afternoon in the large bedroom overlooking Onslow Gardens. Morgana consulted an ob-gyn, a briskly efficient woman at the Harley Street Clinic, who told her they could increase their chances by less frequent lovemaking to conserve Alex's sperm. They monitored the growth and production of her eggs with ultrasound. Three months after their wedding the ob-gyn said, after a scan, "Try Thursday." That Thursday they made love by candlelight through the darkening afternoon and ate dinner again at La Bouchée.

Like making a battery out of two potatoes, it was a home chemistry experiment that worked startlingly well. Morgana was pregnant next time she checked. But her ob-gyn was knocked off her bicycle in Regent's Park and Morgana did not like her replacement, a man who called her "Dear Girl" and said "prepare for the puncture" before plunging the long amniocentesis hypodermic needle into her belly while looking sideways at the ultrasound monitor, "to avoid stabbing the fetus." Afterward, at Cranley Place, Alex made her a cup of tea while she cried in bed and said it was the most painful thing that had ever happened to her.

"I want to have my baby at home," Morgana said.

"Don't you think a hospital might be safer?" Alex asked, couching the question as tentatively as possible. He'd heard that American women were keen on having babies in bathtubs attended by doulas.

"I mean in America."

This was so unexpected that Alex was unable to formulate an answer before Morgana went on:

"I don't like the doctors here."

"Really? Well, actually, our National Health system—"

"Alex. Your pregnant wife needs to feel comfortable while she's having her baby."

"Of course you do, sweetheart. But, I mean . . . well, we live here—this is home. We work here. We've talked all about—"

"You can stay here. I'm going back to America to have my baby."

Shocked by the matter-of-factness of tone, short-circuited by an overabundance of possible responses, he said simply: "What, to Texas?"

"No. *Definitely* not there. I need to stay away from my toxic family. We can go to Maine. It's beautiful. You'll love it there. It's full of writers. We can come back later, I'm not talking about any great change in plan. I just want to have my baby in the States."

My baby, she kept saying.

She emailed him links that showed pictures of fall foliage and harbors full of sailboats. She'd gone to college in Boston and had rented houses in Maine. He'd missed that part. There was so much he didn't know about her.

She was commandingly resourceful. She arranged a shipping container for the antiques and paintings she'd bought in London, and there was room for a few boxes of Alex's books, and his sofa. From a website, she rented a house on Bayview Street in Granite Harbor, on the Maine coast, and somehow had it stocked with groceries when they arrived.

Morgana beamed with relief after their first consultation with Dr. Bob, her new ob-gyn at Midcoast Obstetrics, who sported an armful of tattoos and wore Birkenstock clogs. He grimaced sympathetically when she recounted the episode with the amniocentesis hypodermic.

"We don't go in for pain here," Bob said.

Morgana looked at Alex and teared up with joy.

Dr. Bob explained the rotation of the doctors in the practice, but not in a way they understood, so they were surprised when Morgana went into labor and Bob was unavailable for the next five days.

"It's my first baby!" the attending ob-gyn, Sarah, a partner in Bob's practice, told them excitedly—on her watch, she added. She'd delivered hundreds of babies, of course. This was her first as presiding physician. But after a long day of the worst pain she had ever felt, Morgana told the doctor she wanted a C-section.

"I know it's hard," said Sarah, not unsympathetically, "that's why they call it"— she flicked her fingers to make air quotes—"labor—"

"IT'S NOT COMING OUT AND IT HURTS TOO MUCH!" Morgana screamed at her. "I WANT A C-SECTION—NOW!"

Sophie was delivered by Caesarian half an hour later.

With what seemed like divine providence, a film option on Alex's Booker short list novel came shortly after Sophie's birth. He was offered a couple of semesters teaching writing at Bowdoin and Colby Colleges. But the film option expired, and the teaching gigs paid little more than gas money and were soon over. The strands of his long-labored-over third novel unraveled like overcooked noodles. He ran out of money. He borrowed a little from his sister, a computer programmer in the burgeoning Northern tech industry.

Morgana knew how things were with him. He'd always been honest about how little he'd made. It was all going to change with the next book—the bestseller Morgana was expecting—but waiting for it to appear had turned her brittle and short-tempered.

"I'll be better off when we go back to London," he said. He'd be back in his world, he explained, where he knew magazine editors and publishers, where he had friends and contacts, and people understood who he was and what he wrote about. "Out of sight is out of mind. When I see the people at the *LRB* again—"

"I'm not going back to London!" Morgana said, as if he were a moron. "Sophie will be completely disoriented. My milk will stop if we move. People don't make any money in England anyway. You need to get a real job."

When Sophie was ten months old, Alex laid her on the living room sofa to get her into her down-filled snowsuit to go outside and see the wonder of falling snow. When she was all zipped up, he laid her on the floor so she wouldn't wriggle and fall off the sofa while he went to fetch her boots. As he bent down in the mudroom and put his hands on her little red boots, Morgana screamed from the living room:

"YOU FUCKING IDIOT! SHE FELL OFF THE SOFA ONTO THE FLOOR!"

She wasn't mollified when he told her he'd put Sophie on the floor because he'd anticipated that possibility.

From that moment on, Alex was an impediment between mother and child. A clear and present danger to Sophie. Except at night, when Morgana was too exhausted to breastfeed and Alex got up to give her warmed bottles of expressed milk and walk her around the quiet house.

Naively, he'd accepted the picture Morgana had presented of herself: a collector of antiques, fine art, with a good eye that she'd parlayed into a career that would no doubt improve after her Christie's course, just as he had accepted her statement that she wanted to live in London, "the best of all worlds."

Once the divorce commenced, the real Morgana, what lay behind her lifestyle that was, he found, independent of any cultural aspiration or commercial effort, came out. The Texas and Oklahoma mineral rights and gusher monthly income that fluctuated with the price of West Texas Intermediate crude that had generated the family trusts, the phalanx of lawyers, and her father's Chinese factotum, a frequently invoked savant named Ming Huang who had overseen the prenup. Alex had seen the prenuptial agreement as a peculiarly American tic and cheerfully signed it to reassure her that he wasn't after her furniture, her paintings, her well-earned livelihood of which she was so proud. But now he was hog-tied, gulley washed down-ditch, and horse-whipped with legal costs.

At Morgana's urging, he'd applied for U.S. citizenship, available through their marriage, as soon as they'd arrived in Maine. There would be tax benefits, she said, for the money he was going to make as a bestselling author. By the time Sophie turned three he was a divorced American. He hoped his new status would get him better teaching positions, or any legal job. But jobs in Maine were hard to find. The state was full of Pulitzer Prize–winning authors, and MFA-degreed academics in their twenties and thirties who filled positions at all the colleges Alex applied to. Cold necessity finally forced him to inquire about jobs, with benefits, then being offered by the town.

At the time, there were just two. High school custodian and police officer.

Police officer applicants in Maine had to be over twenty-one—there was no upper age limit. He passed written and physical tests, a polygraph (Have you ever taken drugs? Well, a bit of pot at university, actually. Oh, heck, we expect that.), and the Police Board interview. He was accepted into the eighteen-week police training course at the Maine Criminal Justice Academy in Vassalboro, a castellated brick building that appeared modeled on the Tower of London, sitting with its back to the forest, facing the Kennebec River, an hour's commute each way.

His patrol officer's starting salary was $42,500, with health benefits that included Sophie's pediatric care. For years he'd lived hand to mouth as a writer, occasionally buoyed by an illusory sense of success and prospects. More often, and most recently, he was anxious and frightened about money. Now he was stunned at the regularity of the biweekly checks.

He began to wonder if he would ever write again.

Sophie would have no memory of her father in his dark blue uniform, shiny badge, black duty belt, and the holstered gun he wore for two years. Alex made detective and was back in his own clothes before her fourth birthday.

His salary as detective rose to $49,500. He traded in his old Jeep wagon for a late-model Subaru Outback, and bought a bed, desk, and bookshelves for Sophie's bedroom in his rented house on Mountain Street. He was no longer anxious about becoming homeless, but he didn't know who he was anymore. He felt *deracinated*—the word that kept coming to him. Torn up by the roots, cut off from the world that had produced him, set down in an alien landscape. He liked Maine—it was beautiful and unspoiled—but he was no longer who he had been or might have been going to be. He'd lost his identity.

He was a divorced policeman in America.

"Where is she?" he asked.

"Upstairs in her room."

"What's happened?"

Morgana let rip one of her intentionally fake theatrical cackles. "Go up and see for yourself."

Upstairs, at the end of the long, wide landing, Alex knocked on Sophie's door.

"Sophie, it's me."

"Come in," he heard her say quietly.

He opened the door. Sophie was sitting on her bed, beneath the Matisse, girls in airy frocks floating against a blue background, her back against the wine-colored toile headboard, knees drawn up, reading an actual book. She looked up at him. Her expression was open, even affectionate.

"Oh, Sophie." A convulsion squeezed his chest and he thought he was going to burst into tears.

"Dad"—a *calm down* tone to her voice—"it's not real."

He crossed the room and sat down on the bed beside her, looked into her face for a moment, then reached out and touched the dark, blue-black letters, an inch and a half high, that spelled SHANE across her forehead. He moved his thumb with a soft kneading pressure across her brow, as he had when she was a baby in the way that used to make her eyes close and send her to sleep—remembering this even now, the long early nights cradling his beautiful new little girl—across the letters that seemed embedded in her smooth pale skin.

"It's not a real tattoo?"

It certainly looked it. The thin and thick strokes consistent, the letters evenly situated across the whole frontal plane of her forehead for maximum effect.

"No, Dad." She gently pulled his hand away.

"It washes off?"

"No. It fades."

"How long?"

"Ten days maybe, two weeks. It depends."

"Not a needle?"

"*No*, Dad. It's drawn on, with a pen. It's ink that goes just beneath the surface so it doesn't wash off. But it fades completely. It's not illegal. It's just a drawing. With my permission. It's no different than someone writing on my arm with a Sharpie."

He looked at the rest of her face now. Her big eyes were looking down at her hands. "You knew him?"

The eyes flew up at him, hurt. "Dad! *You* knew him! He came to our house—Shane! You don't remember?"

She'd brought many friends, boys and girls, home to his house. They mostly stayed in her room, playing music, laughing, on their phones. He'd tried his best to give them space.

"I guess," he said. "You've had a lot of people over. Was he a boyfriend?"

"No." She made an annoyed face. "What, just because he was a boy? *Dad*—I have friends who are boys, just like girls. And nonbinary and trans friends."

"Right. I understand."

"Shane was friends with everybody."

"That's what I'm hearing. And why did you want to get this tattoo?"

"Because we're not going to forget him. Ethan and Jared got one with me."

"They did?" Alex had just seen Ethan that morning—since then? Did Isabel know? "Same thing, on the forehead?"

"Yes."

"When?"

"This afternoon. We did it together."

"But why on your face, Sophie? Why not on your—"

"Because then everybody will forget! People are always forgetting kids who get killed! We're not going to forget Shane!" She began to cry.

"Sophie." He held her tight and stroked her hair. "I'm so sorry. Sweetheart, I'm so sorry." His mind was filled with pictures—Sophie in all the stages of being a little girl: Easter egg hunts, parties with his friends, a carousel whip-pan of images—and her friend Shane strung up with a frog coming out of his stomach.

Sophie released him and pulled back enough to look up into his face.

"Who killed him? Are you going to find who did it?"

"Yes." Alex leaned forward and kissed her forehead.

"Can you get Mom off my back about this, please?"

He kissed the top of her head.

Morgana was on her feet when he came downstairs, standing near the kitchen door. She was dressed, as always, in an equestrian outfit, as if she were on her way to a dressage performance, or a fox hunt. Shirt and tie, tweed or velvet hacking jackets, leotard slim cream or khaki breeches with suede fabric seats and inner thighs and knees, riding boots. When he first asked her about this unvarying costume, she replied, "I dress for work." This had been the habit of her grandfather, a Texas rancher, whom she referred to in tones of respect and awe. "Dress for work and people will respect you," he had inculcated in her, and she'd adopted the practice.

Now her jacket was draped over a stool at the vast granite island. She was in waistcoat and shirtsleeves, black kerchief still knotted at her neck.

"You need to make an arrest," she said.

"It's not a real tattoo. It's temporary and it fades. I can't arrest anybody for that."

"This is the *disfigurement* of a child! A minor!"

"It's not illegal."

"Are you kidding me? Someone who did that to a minor, who doesn't know any better? Corrupting a minor?"

"She's not corrupted. She's expressing grief."

"Oh, for God's sake! I can take care of her grief—I'm her mother. I know how to help her. But *this*? She's supposed to go to school like this? For *weeks*? With that thing on her forehead? She has band practice! And she just got home, God knows where she's been."

"This is not a police matter, Morgana. Sophie did it, I believe, as an act of solidarity. I think it's more positive than some other ways she might be expressing herself—"

"You're pathetic. I might have known—"

"Right, cheerio," said Alex, heading for the kitchen door.

"*Use the front door!*"

He was already out, Morgana's squawked command spilling out behind him. He turned toward his car—

A rustle in the bushes on his left, movement in his peripheral vision, made his head spin to the side, and he saw a man in a baseball hat. Crouching.

Alex began to turn and orient his body in a defensive stance against the child killer here for his little girl. Until a quick, anxious voice stayed his hand already grasping the gun in his armpit.

"Oh, hey, Alex! How're you doing?" said Glenn Bell, in a greasy tone of casual surprise. "Oh, hey, Morgana." He looked different, hiding in the shrubbery, wearing a hat, than he did behind his desk at the Historical Society. "I was just taking a walk down to the shore, cutting through your yard, I hope you don't mind—"

"Shut *up*!" Morgana snapped at Glenn, who drew back. She reached Alex, and before he saw it coming, *pushed* him hard toward his car, shouting, "*Get out! Get off my property!*"

Inside his car, pulling away, he looked back in the mirror and saw Glenn standing beside Morgana, both looking in his direction as he sped out of the driveway. Then Alex saw Morgana turn toward Glenn in an unmistakable manner. He was about to hear from Texas.

Naturally, there were men who were attracted to Morgana. Local wealthy types, who spoke of their helicopters and houses in Aspen. Nothing ever came of it. Morgana was an autocrat. Normal intimacy didn't work with her. It would be like having a relationship with Mussolini. It could only be an affair of mutually advantageous power brokerage, and he saw no contenders in Granite Harbor.

Morgana and *Glenn?*

His stomach muscles contracted reflexively. He took a breath and it was expelled before he could pull in enough air. He couldn't stop laughing. It was the first funny thing that had entered his mind for ages.

17

O h, Chester, I've been calling you and texting you," said Nancy as he came in the door. She rushed to him and hugged him. "Why didn't you answer?"

"I'm sorry." He made a confused face. "My phone was in the cupholder."

"I was worried about you." Then she hated hearing herself say that. She didn't normally call or text him, most of their interaction was face-to-face. She didn't want to crowd him. "It's just that after everything that's happened..."

"Roger and I were cleaning up. The police and everybody were there all day and they made a lot of mess. They dug things up and moved things around and we had to put it all back. I'm sorry. But I'm okay."

He looked so apologetic that Nancy hugged him again, tightly. She stood on her toes, still unable to reach his cheek and kissed him where she could find his warm flesh, low on his neck beneath the beard. "That's all right, darling. Don't worry about it. I've made us dinner."

"I'll go wash up," said Chester. He bent down to unlace his boots and took them off. When he stood up he smiled at Nancy and she would have hugged him again but he turned and walked toward the bathroom down the hall.

Oh, what is this? Nancy thought, as she had so often in the last month and a half. *This crazy thing called Chester.* This bulky, rough-looking man, who beneath the beard and the construction clothes and boots and calloused hands and the reserve she had come to understand was a mask for an immense shyness, who now seemed to her sometimes like a boy. A sweet, shy boy, who was slowly, slowly opening up to her and making her feel . . . what? Love? It wasn't like any love she remembered. But she was no longer the woman who had fallen in love with her husband Graham and lived with him for thirty-four years. What was that expression: *never the same river twice*? She was sixty-seven and Chester was thirty-nine, and it was absurd—except for the tender lovely feeling that had grown inside her for Chester, and that he seemed, in his way, to return for her. It was the last thing she had expected to happen to her after Graham died. Thirty-four years and she was then sixty-five, and she'd assumed that was it.

Nancy certainly wasn't looking for another husband. Or a lover—unimaginable. Or a *partner*, that tepid description of a comfortable companion that many people seemed to find, or put up with out of fear and loneliness in their later years. She was quite happy on her own. She hadn't even been that lonely since Graham died—that had been a relief after eighteen months of aggressive, metastasizing prostate cancer. Nancy had been busy, first with the sale of Belvedere, the enormous old captain's house she and Graham had run for years as a bed-and-breakfast, and getting rid of *so much stuff*, and her move to her new house, a small Cape overlooking the harbor. And her new job at the Settlement. Exciting, all of it, and she'd felt at peace. Happy.

Chester was simply her new coworker. He made a convincing seventeenth-century settler in his beard, old felt hat with the feather poking through it, and his big leather jerkin. He was familiar. She'd seen him around town for years, she realized, when, in his own everyday clothes, he looked like a builder, or the construction workers or landscapers one saw everywhere in Granite Harbor. But she hadn't known or noticed him. He was *nice*—that was the word she'd decided upon at first. Nice and quiet, and reserved.

She heard he was selling some cordwood. She needed some—she had a nice, efficient woodstove now—and decided to buy it from him, someone she knew. He brought it over to the house and stacked it on her deck. It was late in the afternoon, that hot spell at the end of September, and afterward she invited him inside to give him a glass of water. He saw a photograph of her sitting on a camel, from the trip she and Graham made down the Nile.

He was fascinated that she had seen the Pyramids. They're still there? he asked. Oh, yes, she said, and told him about them. He sat down, sipped his water, looked at her as she spoke, and asked questions.

After that, at work, when they found time, eating lunch or at the beginning or end of the day, they talked about the Settlement, the settlers, what life must have been like for them on this cold, forbidding shore. And in these heavy woolen clothes—Nancy wondered how they'd lived without fleece and Gore-Tex. Chester said he liked to imagine them going about the same things they were doing, on this same ground they stood on, 381 years earlier.

He had books about early American history—Nancy was surprised. Chester hadn't seemed bookish, but apparently he read a lot. He brought books to work, and offered to lend them to her. She took them, partly because she was interested too, but mainly because she was touched that Chester wanted to share them with her.

What is this? she began to ask herself, when she realized she was looking forward to seeing Chester. Or when they parted at the end of the day, after talking about history. Or at home, when it occurred to her that she would like to ask him over for dinner. When she realized she wanted to see more of him.

But what would that look like? Quite apart from the age difference. Chester looked like the sort of man, the construction crews, the lobstermen, who went to Captain Smithy's pub after work. For all she knew, he probably had a lady friend somewhere—one of the tattooed women at Captain Smithy's. Nancy had never been in there, but she saw the people going in and out. She couldn't ask him over for dinner. It would make him uncomfortable. Then they'd both be embarrassed. It would be the end of their sweet friendship

Then Chester asked her if she would like to come out for dinner with him. There was a special on Wednesdays at the Wharf. "Oh, how nice," Nancy said, with an air of pleasant surprise. "I'd love to."

Chester picked her up at her house. They went to the Wharf and ate seafood. Chester was shy and quiet, as if, Nancy thought, wondering what he'd done in asking her out. So they talked, at first, about the food eaten by the early settlers, what they'd gathered in the woods and from the sea; how much that seventeenth-century menu might have resembled the Wharf's: they might certainly have gathered scallops, mussels, oysters, mushrooms, grown squashes. It was a way of continuing their ongoing conversation about the Settlement. Then Nancy asked Chester how he'd discovered the Settlement, why he was working there. Roger had told him about it, he'd been there now five years, but he was more interested in hearing about Nancy. He wanted to know where else she'd traveled to. She told him how she and Graham had tried to escape the Maine winters, sometimes going to Europe, Greece, Egypt, as he'd seen, to Mexico—Chester wanted to hear all about those places.

He paid for dinner and he drove her home. Nancy asked him if he'd like to come in for a coffee or tea, but Chester said he'd better be getting home. They agreed it was a nice evening.

A week later, Nancy asked him if he'd like to come to dinner at her house. Sure, Chester had said, with a shy pleasure.

She didn't often eat red meat, but she thought Chester might, and that night she made filet mignon. Before dinner was over, Nancy realized that it was now more than just a sweet friendship. She was almost sure that Chester liked her in that way, and she had begun to imagine them in bed—but she was equally sure that he would not initiate anything. She felt as if he were a horse that might bolt if she startled him.

After dinner, Chester offered to help her with the dishes.

"Oh, no, thank you, Chester. I'm just going to rinse them and put them in the dishwasher."

But he stood beside her at the sink, without speaking, apparently intent on watching her hands and the running water. Nancy heard him breathing, she was aware of his physical bulk inches away, and she was flooded with a wild desire. *I don't care*, she said to herself. When she closed the dishwasher she turned to Chester, stood on her tiptoes and put her arms around his neck, and kissed him gently on the mouth.

He didn't bolt. He remained still for a moment, his lips unmoving. Then she felt his arms encircle her, and he returned her kiss.

That night was beautiful to Nancy. He came willingly when she led him into the bedroom, but he seemed unsure of how to move, whether to sit or stand, or when and where to start removing his clothes. She helped him. In bed she nearly swooned to feel the size and shape and strength of him, a burly, very hirsute young man, so utterly different from Graham's long and delicate thinness, and the near total absence of hair on his body in his later years. But Chester had difficulty. He was uncertain how to touch her, though she helped him with that too, gently and encouragingly.

"I hope it was all right," he said to her afterward as they lay side by side.

"Chester, dear, it was lovely. It always takes time for two people to learn each other. But this is so lovely. Just being here with you. You're a very beautiful strong man, Chester. You have quite thrilled me."

"You're very beautiful too," Chester said.

"Oh, I'm an old maid!"

"No," he said, gazing at her as they lay on the pillows, "you're beautiful."

That was what was so sweet about him, she decided. He was genuine: she believed he meant it. To him, she *was* beautiful.

Their lovemaking improved. Chester remained tentative, but they began to grow used to each other. They made love at Nancy's. He didn't invite her to his house. She imagined he might be self-conscious about it. It was some distance out of town, in the farming country toward Hope. Perhaps it was a manufactured home, or a trailer. She didn't care. She liked having him come to her. Soon he was there almost every night after work. Unlike Graham, with his four or more trips to the bathroom through the nights, Chester slept soundly, deeply. Like a child. Nancy would wake in the night and listen to him breathing. This beautiful, gentle mass of man beside her.

What was this?

18

"What sort of frog?" asked FBI Special Agent Brad Harris, as if the classification of species might help the investigation. He'd driven up from Boston the night before to be present at the 7:30 A.M. autopsy in Augusta.

He looks like Tintin, Alex thought. Blond hair very short all over except for the small gelled quiff sticking up like a feather at the front. Small button eyes. Impossibly young. Taut, smooth-skinned, not like a cut gym rat, but like a boy. Yet his every remark implied long years of fieldwork. As if he'd become an agent at six years old.

"Not a frog," said John Barney, herpetologist and professor of biology at U Maine, Orono, who had driven down to the medical examiner's office in Augusta. "*Anaxyrus americanus.* Eastern American toad. Female, judging by the size of the tympanum."

"It was inside the body, is that right?" Phil Gressens, the medical examiner's senior forensic technician, looked at Alex. With a long braided gray ponytail, Gressens was tall, his height accentuated by Dr. Scholl's slip-resistant work clogs.

"Yes," Alex answered.

All four men wore white Tyvek overalls.

The toad was still alive, smeared with blood, coagulated in places and glistening wetly in others. It had accompanied Shane's body in a plastic evidence Ziploc bag in which Patrolman Mark Beltz had poked breathing holes. Gressens had kept it overnight in the Ziploc, in an unsealed Tupperware container. Now the toad, still inside the Ziploc, sat on a bright stainless steel autopsy table, where it appeared to be in a state of Zen repose.

Shane's body was out of sight in a cold drawer. The windowless room was brightly lit with overhead fluorescent lights. Glass-fronted, kitchen-looking cabinets showed an array of small electric saws and other tools.

"What's the difference?" asked Harris. "Frog, toad?"

Professor Barney had already pulled on a pair of surgical gloves. With practiced movements, he removed the toad from the bag. "Taxonomically, they're both amphibia. Frogs belong to the Ranidae family, toads are Bufonidae."

"Perhaps without the Latin, please, Professor?" said Alex. "For me anyway. What's the basic difference?"

Professor Barney turned on a tap and gently washed the blood off the toad. His tone was affable, yet still pedagogical. "Frogs have longer, meatier legs, as any Frenchman will tell you. They jump, they move around more, explore farther afield. They exude a mucous film on their skin, which acts kind of like a wet suit, because they spend more time in ponds and water habitat. Toads—this creature here—have shorter legs, dry skin. More woodlands habitat, though they need freshwater ponds for reproduction. And here"—he pointed with his pen to two raised mounds on the toad's head behind each eye—"these are the paratoid glands. In here the toad produces and retains a reservoir of bufotenin."

"What's that?" asked Agent Harris.

"It's a toxin," said the professor.

"Enough to kill a person?"

"Oh, no. Well, certainly not *Anaxyrus americanus.* Toxic for small animals, predators. Grab a toad—like a dog will, say, in its teeth—and it will eject bufotoxins. A Florida cane toad could certainly harm, possibly kill a human if the toxin entered the eye. This toad would not cause death to a human, but its toxin might cause palpitations, disorientation."

Professor Barney shut the water off and placed the toad in the palm of one hand.

"Why would a toad crawl into a dead body?" asked Harris. "And how would it get up there, if the body was hanging, suspended off the ground?"

"It wouldn't. That would not present as a hospitable habitat. And they don't fly."

"So it must have been put there," Harris observed, shooting a penetrating glance at Alex.

Alex nodded back, arranging his face obligingly, as if to say, *Good call.*

"I would say so," said Professor Barney.

"Has it been harmed, mutilated, in any way?" Alex asked.

Professor Barney picked the toad up with his other hand, turned it over, inspected it again. "She looks unharmed to me. What are you going to do with her?"

"From my point of view, it would appear to have nothing to do with cause of death," said Phil Gressens. "But I'm going to autopsy it. See what's in the stomach. How should I humanely kill it? Preferably without injury."

"Rub her all over in benzocaine," said Professor Barney. "Use a whole tube of Orajel. Give her a few minutes and she'll be on her way." He handed the toad to Phil Gressens, who was also wearing gloves.

Gressens looked at Alex and Agent Harris. "There's a Walgreens up on the corner. Two minutes. Maybe one of you could run up there? I'll have the boy's body ready for you when you get back."

"I'll go," said Alex.

He saw Professor Barney out of the medical examiner's office, thanked him, agreed upon the details of the delivery of his report. He walked on to the Walgreens. When he returned to the autopsy room, Shane's body was laid out on a stainless steel table. Alex's nostrils tingled anew with chemical odors. Harris was walking slowly around the table, studying the corpse.

Alex handed Gressens the tube from a Walgreens bag. "Generic benzo-caine. I presume that's okay."

"Works for me," said Gressens. He squeezed most of the contents of the tube into a stainless steel dish and began to gently smear it over the toad. When it was covered with gel, Gressens placed the creature in the dish.

All three men looked at the toad, which appeared unperturbed in its coat of death gel.

"If toads could talk," said Harris.

Earlier in the morning, before they had arrived, Gressens had prepared the body, he told them. He'd weighed and measured it, made a close external examination. He had placed a rubber block beneath Shane's back making it arch, projecting the chest upward, causing the long incision to gape open.

Shane's head tilted backward. His eyes were still partly open, the lids half closed.

Agent Harris pulled a small bottle of Vicks VapoRub out of his pocket, opened it, and dabbed a finger beneath each nostril, and offered the bottle to Alex.

"No, thanks."

"That stuff's not good for your lungs," said Gressens.

"Works for me," said Harris.

Alex had previously attended only two autopsies—both in this very room—during his training at the Maine Criminal Justice Academy. They had been performed on donations to the Academy: elderly bodies, shriveled, diminished carcasses that had appeared more like archaeological finds, the life long ago sucked out of them. The deaths he'd covered as detective had required little initial investigation before being ruled accidental or suicidal; the cause of death evident, there was no need for him to be present at the autopsy.

On the clean stainless steel, Shane—his upturned face anyway, despite the cold blueish color—still looked like any boy in Granite Harbor. Alex tried to recognize him, place him.

In his house, apparently.

He shook his head as an image of Sophie herself on the table in front of them flashed through his mind.

Gressens's gloved finger pointed to the left side of Shane's neck where it met the shoulder. It was vividly bruised, blotchy purple and brown.

"He received a blow to the right side of the neck some hours before death. Enough time for considerable bruising to collect in the area."

"Looks like a brachial stun," said Agent Harris. "Inflicted by a southpaw—left-hander."

Alex looked at Harris and then to Gressens.

"Certainly a blunt force injury to the brachial plexus," said Gressens.

"Brachial stun," Harris said again.

"What is that?" asked Alex.

"A blow inflicted with the forearm to the brachial plexus. Not a punch or a karate chop, but a blow carrying the entire weight of the attacker's torso. Like this."

Harris stepped toward Alex. Slowly, he swiveled his entire upper body.

Although it came at him slowly, Alex tensed at the sight of Harris's entire arm swinging horizontally through the air, moving not like an arm at all but a separate attachment strapped onto his shoulder and having its own momentum. Harris stopped it as his forearm reached the side of Alex's neck, low down, but he allowed some weight to land with the impact.

Alex felt it. He understood then the power it might have contained. The recipient poleaxed by something like a small tree limb hitting the neck where it joined the shoulder.

"The force behind that, if I were doing it for real, would exceed my body weight by many times. Like a bag of wet cement. If it lands on the brachial plexus, it shocks the carotid artery and jugular vein, and causes immediate unconsciousness. It'll land right side or left, according to the swinger's right- or left-handed preference. The attacker here was a left-hander."

"It would certainly explain the bruising," agreed Gressens.

"Cause of death the wound down the stomach?" Alex asked.

Gressens shook his head. "No. The cut's not deep, just through the abdominal wall. It would have bled, but not a lot. Not a gusher source. On its own, not nicking arteries or vital organs, it wouldn't result in death." He raised first one and then the other of Shane's half-closed eyelids and pointed out the bloodshot hemorrhages in the whites. "Petechiae, generally present in asphyxia deaths. And"—he pulled Shane's lips open—"slight bruising inside the lips showing pressure on the mouth holding it closed. Trace bruising against the nostrils to block air intake. Not hard pressure. No signs of struggle except for the light bruising around the wrists and ankles. Probably tied down but not so much that he struggled against the restraints. Which suggests he might have been sedated. Blood work will show what sedative, if any. I would say he died of suffocation. Nostrils pinched, hand over the mouth. Probably post incision, because the edges show bleeding."

"Cut open while he was alive?"

"Yes," said Gressens. "Subsequently suffocated. Almost an act of mercy by then. He would have been in great pain."

Alex sensed Harris observing him. He didn't want to show his face, so he looked away. In the stainless steel dish, the toad, glistening in its thick wet suit of benzocaine, had slumped forward onto its chin, its hind legs splayed out beneath it. Its eyes were closed.

Part Two

19

The first time the boy saw a frog—or toad, he couldn't tell the difference until long afterward—was beneath the white hammering light of the Florida sky, when his dog Boon dropped the creature from his mouth and started to shake his head so violently that the boy thought the dog's brains would begin to fly from its ears. A flow of drool gushed from some impossible reservoir out of its mouth, and the high voltage convulsions continued long after Boon had fallen to the dirt, emitting the piteous howl that subsided into a wheezing organ note from deep inside his chest as he lay dying at the edge of the muddy, reeking canal.

Thereafter, a phalanx of frogs and toads leaped through the boy's life. As if they'd chosen him.

His father, Frank, found the dog, a large mutt, at the animal shelter a week after his son was born. He was determined that his little boy would have a dog, learn to look after it, feed it, take care of it, and be responsible for it, something Frank had learned and loved from his own boyhood.

Frank and Eileen, the boy's mother, and the boy and the dog, lived in a small white house on Mallard Lane, on the swampy outskirts of Fort Lauderdale, Florida, in a development of shallow brown canals that allowed the builders to claim that each of the ninety-three houses was "waterfront property." Frank hadn't gone to college, he'd never held a job for longer than a

week or two at home in Connecticut, and the house on Mallard Lane had
been bought for him by his family. It had a dock, and Frank bought a small
Sea Ray sixteen-footer with a Bimini top. He liked to speed down the South
Fork of the New River, up and down the Intracoastal between West Palm
and the Keys. He was handy—he replaced the windlass on his boat and put
in a new hatch, and rigged new outboard-to-cockpit controls. Sometimes he
worked on other people's boats. He could have established himself as a small
independent contractor, a boat handyman, zooming around with his tools,
and he would have liked that, but he had no gift for enterprise, and, more
crucially, no motivation to make money.

When he met her, Eileen was waiting tables at a crab house on Pelican
Landing. She had a dazzling smile. Right off, she picked Frank out with it.
She seemed to see something in him that no other woman had. At thirty-
seven, Frank already had a good beer belly and had lost some teeth through
an aversion to dentistry, but Eileen found him—no doubt about it, he had
to conclude after a very short time, marveling at his luck—she found him
handsome and attractive. She was Frank's age, or a little older. He took her
for rides in his boat.

She loved his house. He could tell, when he first brought her home, and
she sat down on the sofa and looked out at the dock. Then she looked up at
Frank, as if seeing him for the first time.

Neither of their families came to the wedding.

From the time he could walk to the end of the short driveway, the boy walked
away from the house because of the yelling inside. He and Boon explored the
canals of their waterfront development. Soon they went farther, along the
tributaries of the South Fork of the New River where these trickled out of
the Everglades.

That's where Boon picked up the toad in his mouth and died.

Eileen, who was given to fits of uncontrollable anger when she drank, told
Frank there would be no new dog. She couldn't deal with a dog anymore, she
said, *clearly, with bells on*, but he got one anyway. The new dog was not Boon.
It was just some dog. And the boy didn't want to take any more walks along
the canals.

One day, when he came home from school and refused to take the new dog for a walk, Eileen broke the boy's nose. Blood poured all over the kitchen. He ran away from the house alone. He missed Boon more than ever, sobbed, and wiped the slurry of blood and tears from his face.

It was after dark when Frank found him, walking along State Road 84, west of Bonaventure Golf Club. Frank's truck was packed with his toolboxes and some clothes for him and his son. Inside the cab was the new dog, whose name hadn't been fixed yet, and was called for the time being New Dog. At a rest stop in Georgia, New Dog ran into the woods. Frank wouldn't leave the rest stop for seven hours. He ran through the woods until long after dark calling for New Dog.

A day and a half later, after a long slog up I-95, they reached Frank's family compound in Guilford, Connecticut, where Frank was arrested for Eileen's murder, though he said it had been an accident. He was sent to the Union Correctional Institution in Raiford, Florida. The boy didn't see his father again before he was stabbed to death in prison.

He was taken in by Frank's sister, Mary, to live with his four cousins. Here was a real home, a big old house with four stories, and an attic room for the new cousin. There were bikes—the cousins had French Peugeots with drop handlebars, and the boy was given a battered Schwinn hand-me-down—and there was a dog, a golden retriever called Wally, but Wally wasn't like Boon. He was happy for the new child to pet him, but he seemed bored with everything and slept a lot, unless the children threw balls for him. The house was full of noise, screaming, fighting, arguing, calling upstairs and down, in which the cruel and mean behavior the children showed their cousin was absorbed and appeared almost normal. Even Aunt Mary and Uncle Bob soon ignored it. The cousins teased him, made him the butt of jokes, played tricks on him. But no one had ever paid attention to him before, and he loved them all.

The only thing against the boy becoming a natural, if grafted-on, member of the family, was the parents' odd habit of referring to him, when talking to their own children, as "your cousin."

In summer, the Buells—Uncle Bob's family name—vacationed at Prouts Neck, in Maine. They owned a house there, a maze of wood-paneled rooms with tilting floors and leaning stairways, a big grassy backyard between high hedges. The boy had been used to Florida water, and the sea in Maine took his breath away. They went swimming at Scarborough beach and ate saltwater taffy, and he forgot about the cold. They climbed the big rocks around Prouts Neck, they sailed in tiny boats. At night, fireflies glowed in the backyard, and they caught them and put them in bottles.

The summer he was eight, seven months after he'd moved in with the Buells, he and his elder cousin, Sally, who was fourteen, and Billy who was nine, camped outdoors in a tent in the backyard at Prouts Neck. Sally told ghost stories. When Uncle Bob called out to them "Night, night, campers!" Billy got out of his sleeping bag and ran into the house. When the screen door banged, Sally crawled into her cousin's sleeping bag.

Sally snuggled against him. She was small for her age. She hadn't grown since she was ten. Her parents had started her on development pills, she told him that night in the tent, and the pills were working, she said. She took his hand and pulled it under her T-shirt.

"I've got bosoms now. Squeeze the little buttons."

He squeezed the buttons very gently. Sally's breath filled his ear.

"Keep doing that. Harder."

She wore a bikini top when they swam and played on the beach and he'd thought of what was underneath there as private parts. But he was thrilled that he could do something that pleased Sally. And that she liked being with him in his sleeping bag. And that just the two of them were together in the tent. He'd never been alone with any of his cousins before.

Sally took his hand and pulled it down across her stomach and farther until it was between her legs. "Touch me here too," she said.

This was also a private area, but Sally made it seem like she was just asking him to scratch her back. It was wet where she pressed his fingers, slippery. She held on to his hand and kept it moving.

He felt her other hand pulling at the waist of his pajamas, and suddenly she was touching him there. He jackknifed away from her, although he didn't get far in the sleeping bag.

"It's okay," Sally said in his ear, soothingly. "We're doing sex. It's what grown-ups do."

He tried to lie still. Her fingers, cool and damp, were tugging at him. It was strange. Those were your *privates*. He wriggled, partly because it tickled and partly because he couldn't help it.

"See? It's getting bigger. That means it likes it."

Sally sat on top of him.

"Can we sleep in the tent again?" Sally asked her mother a few days later, when they were making sandwiches in the kitchen.

"Sure," said Aunt Mary. "I don't see why not." She looked around at the boy. "Would you like to sleep out in the tent again?"

"Yes," he said.

"You two are the champion campers!" said Aunt Mary.

A few minutes later, Aunt Mary said quietly to Sally, though he could hear, "You're being so nice to your cousin. Like a big sister. I'm proud of you."

They slept out in the tent all the rest of the time in Prouts Neck.

But back in Connecticut, Sally paid no attention to him. Sometimes he said hi to her, but she ignored him. Once, when she caught him looking at her, she hissed, "*Stop looking at me.*"

He tried to figure out what he'd done to make Sally not like him anymore. He went back over everything he could think of since they'd returned from Maine. That's when, looking at her, maybe across a room full of kids, she'd come by and hiss, "*Stop looking at me!*"

At night, in bed in his low-ceilinged room in the attic, he read the books he'd found on the shelf where the sloping ceiling met the floor. They were about a group of children called the Famous Five. He wanted to be one of the children in the Famous Five books, like Dick or Julian, and be friends with girls like Anne and Georgina, and have adventures at Smuggler's Top and on Mystery Moor. He read long after the rest of the house had gone quiet.

He was reading *Five Go Off in a Caravan* when the door opened and Sally came into his room.

She pulled the book away and got into his bed and turned out the bedside light.

"What are you doing?" he asked.

"This," she said. She snuggled against him like she used to. "Sex."

He couldn't believe she was there. She liked him again. He didn't understand why, but he was glad.

She pulled off her nightgown. Her legs moved up and down and she pushed herself against him. There was more room in his single bed than there had been in the sleeping bag. Sally pushed the covers off. She pulled down his pajama pants. He helped her, lifting his bottom, but Sally had a way of showing him what to do, even though he knew by now. When Sally was finished rubbing his hand and fingers on her and she was all slippery, she sat on him and they rocked back and forth the way she'd shown him.

He looked up at her. With the bedside light out, the room was blue from the lamp on the street and Sally's straight blond hair rocking back and forth above him was white in the blue light. He couldn't believe she was here, in his room in Guilford, where he'd spent almost a whole year alone. They'd be together again now—

The door opened, the light was switched on, and a strange noise came out of Uncle Bob as he pulled Sally off him. He heard more than felt the smack on his face. The room swirled around him and he was on the floor.

Uncle Bob went away with Sally, who was quiet. The boy lay on the floor, the room still whirling around him.

When Uncle Bob returned, it sounded as if a snorting animal had come into the small attic room. Uncle Bob shut the door. His face appeared overhead. Uncle Bob kneeled over him, gasping for air like someone who had run somewhere, a thread of snot hanging from his nose. Uncle Bob's hand rose and fell like an axe chopping at a tree, falling on each side of his face, and the room and the ceiling and Uncle Bob's head flew from side to side in time with his hoarse grunts.

"Animal . . . filthy . . . depraved . . . animal . . ."

It didn't hurt, like when you crushed your fingers in a door or window or fell on your knees. The boy hardly felt it. He just saw the room flying overhead, between the blue streetlight in the window and the sloping wall. He tasted blood in his mouth.

While Uncle Bob was hitting him, he saw Boon shivering and drooling on the ground. He saw the bright sky and the brown canal, as if it were happening all over again.

20

Alex's phone dinged at 7:25 A.M. Up at 5:30, he'd already hiked up Mount Meguntic, showered, eaten blueberries and granola, and was about to drive to the station.

My hotel ASAP, read the text from Special Agent Harris's cell number.

On my way, Alex texted back, putting away the mild annoyance at the peremptory command of the message. Harris was staying at the Lord Calder Inn. Brick-fronted, faux Colonial with pillars on Main Street, the inn was a four-story motel-like complex with views from most rooms of the police–fire station parking lot and the dirty brick facade of the disused Calder Mill.

"Pepsi, Fanta, in the fridge," said Harris as he closed the door, pointing to the kitchenette. He appeared to be newly showered, dressed in his suit pants and wearing a tie.

"A little early for me, thanks," said Alex.

Papers, manila envelopes, accordion files, neatly arranged, covered one of the two queen-size beds. Athletic shorts and a singlet were draped over the heater–air conditioner unit near the window. The room smelled of fresh sweat.

Harris sat at a table in front of a large Dell laptop, screen up and bright. "Take a seat." He pulled a chair around the table and turned the computer so that Alex could better see the screen. "Our office in Boston produced this

and emailed it to me this morning. It's a crunch of cold cases and method-
ology."

Alex sat and looked at the screen.

What he saw was so joltingly familiar that it took him a moment to
realize it wasn't what he thought he was looking at—Shane—but an older
photograph of the body of a naked young man hanging from a similar doorway frame, arms raised, both wrists bound together with rope. A slit down
the middle of the torso.

"My God. Where's this from?"

Harris didn't answer but touched the trackpad, bringing up another photograph, color, overlaying the first: a toad—Alex presumed—lying in a stainless steel dish. The animal was smeared with a thick coating of coagulated
blood. Both its eyes were open.

"Found alive inside the body," said Harris.

"*Where?*" Alex asked again. "And when? Who is this?"

Another file, a page from a police report with a photograph and printed
details, appeared on the screen.

"Byron Pugh. Twenty-six years old, resident of Brookline, Mass. Found
strung up in the backyard of a house at Prouts Neck, Maine, August four-
teenth, 2008. Last seen on vacation in Scarborough, four days earlier, August
tenth, 2008."

Harris turned to Alex. "A hundred miles away. Sixteen years ago. So we
have a serial killer. Who, unless we find another such killing, and we haven't
yet, has done a Rip Van Winkle and woken up and gone back to work."

"Unsolved?"

"Yes. Cold."

Alex was still trying to read the particulars of the file on-screen. "Cause
of death? Not the wound, I take it?"

"No. Nor this."

Harris moved his finger, tapped his trackpad, and another photograph
appeared on his computer screen. A closer shot of the corpse. Purple and
brown bruising on one side of the dead white neck and shoulder.

Harris read: "'Considerable antemortem bruising in the brachial area of
the *right* neck and shoulder.' Brachial stun, right side. Like Shane Carter. The
guy who did this, a southpaw, did the same thing to Shane Carter. Cause of

death . . ." He tapped and returned to the police death report. "Asphyxia-tion. With some bruising around the mouth and nostrils. His blood report showed trace amounts of DMT, suggesting he'd been doing drugs, probably shrooms, before death."

Again, Special Agent Harris turned to face Alex. "So what does all this tell us, Detective? Absent another body presenting in the same manner—that we know of—we've just got the two killings, same MO. Why Byron Pugh, Prouts Neck, Maine, 2008, and why Shane Carter here now? Why has this killer woken up after a long dormant period? And when will he kill again? Has he been in prison and now released? Gotten married, got a kid, had his hands full?"

The nerve of this kid, this weirdly adult boy. His Vicks VapoRub, and now the professorial tone Alex had heard from gruff, seasoned police instruc-tors during his courses at MCJA, coming from such a smooth youthful face.

"I don't know," said Alex, trying to keep a defensive tone out of his voice.

"Right. We don't know," said Harris disarmingly. "We can't know half of this now. But we know some stuff we didn't know before. We have a serial killer. A planned killing. Byron Pugh was someone the killer knew, or had observed—had chosen. The killer had his method, he had a place of operation—you don't do this sort of surgery beside the road or on a beach. Nor spur of the moment. He overpowered Pugh—who was a big guy, six two, young and strong—and brought him to his place, home, storage unit, whatever it was, where he could work on him. Then strung him up in some backyard at Prouts Neck."

Harris returned to his screen. "We're cross-checking all possible con-nections between Byron Pugh, his background, home, where he attended school, names of school classmates, friends, jobs, et cetera, with everyone Shane Carter knew, everyone at the Settlement."

"Good," said Alex. He was impressed. Tintin had come up with this cru-cial clue—a serial killer, an MO, a past—and now he and the full mainframe power and capability of the FBI were pursuing it. "Any idea why Prouts Neck?"

"Prouts Neck is an upscale summer resort. The Maine version of the Hamptons."

Alex knew this.

"Scarborough's the less fancy summer resort next door. The sort of place where a bunch of guys Pugh's age would share a house together for a few weeks. The police doing the initial investigations probably had the same questions, and I've already forwarded their report on to your email."

Special Agent Harris closed his laptop.

"I'm going down there to talk to the cops, a few people who are still in the area, look at the Prouts Neck address. Probably come up with nothing, the police did all that at the time, but you never know."

"When? Maybe I should come with you."

Harris blinked and looked even more like Tintin. "I'm going today. I don't think it's necessary for you to come. Obviously, I'll share everything I get with you. Doesn't need two of us."

Alex stood up. "So you don't see this as having much to do with the Settlement, where Shane's body was left? The people there?"

"We haven't found anything connecting Byron Pugh to Granite Harbor. Or this historical site here. The bodies were discovered here and at Prouts Neck. Might mean something, might mean nothing. A car crash can happen anywhere, and it's usually not the road conditions. It's more likely what's going on with the people in the car."

It sounded clever. Facile. Something Harris had picked up at the Bureau.

"Let me know when you get back from Prouts Neck," said Alex.

"Will do. Probably tonight. What are you going to be doing?"

"I'm going to research the history of the Settlement, the historical site. I'm still thinking there might be some connection."

"Good job!" said Tintin.

Alex disliked Special Agent Harris.

21

The Granite Harbor Living History Settlement was open for business again. The murder of a Maine high school student, the body discovered on the site of an early American settlement tourist attraction, though widely reported, seemed not to have affected the traffic of fall season tourists and leaf peepers whose cars now almost filled the small parking lot. In their teal, cranberry, royal blue fleece or quilted jackets, pink trainers, ripstop nylon daypacks, stretching their legs in their space-age SUVs, they looked like visitors from the future.

Alex did not resemble a tourist. His face didn't show their open, half-smiling fascination as they bent close to inspect the construction of the cabins or spoke with the "players." He kept to himself, wandering the periphery of the cabins and gardens, looking like a man who had lost his way. He peered into the trees that bordered the marshy wetland inshore of the narrow pebbled beach. Gazed across the marsh, stepping into it a few paces, gauging the soggy spring to the mossy earth. He walked through the knee-high brambles, goldenrod, and rose hip bushes, over the rocks onto the beach and looked up and down the shore. For what, he had no concrete idea. He wanted to see how the place made him feel. Where his thoughts went. What he might imagine. He had once lived by his imagination. Unspooling scenes of characters under pressure and distress.

Why *here*? Was it a reenactment of something that happened here at the

time of the Settlement, some nutcase with historical insight? Or a connection existing only within the mind of the murderer—who felt some bond,
association, attachment, to this place?

One of the players? The Agatha Christie dramatis personae? He watched
them as he sauntered around, not too closely, but observing. He'd read more
about them all, details about their lives from the statements they'd given
Mark Beltz. Nobody seemed a likely killer.

Chester Coffey, in leather jerkin and felt hat with a feather, making a great
show of pounding yellow hot metal on the anvil in the real working forge,
wheezing bellows, flurries of charcoal sparks, white-hot metal dipped with
tongs into buckets of water producing clouds of steam to the applause of
several visitors. He'd seen Chester around Granite Harbor for years, without
knowing him, as was common in a small town. No family, no apparent problems with money, a stable if static life.

Jeff Block—who had found Shane and called 911, an unlikely move by
a perpetrator, or a clever one?—had been a shipwright on high-end custom
yachts at the Lyman-Morse yard down in Thomaston, laid off by a downturn
in the economy, or luxury yachts. Here he played Isabel's husband, Goodman
Samuel Swaine, and got to fool around with the Settlement's fishing boat,
now hauled up on the riverbank. He was planing, fitting, and nailing new
planks onto its frames with square-cut nails.

Bill Conrad, retired builder, and Jan, married for forty-eight years—a
Goodman and Goodwife couple, he forgot the names of their Settlement
characters—were working the vegetable patch, explaining seventeenth-century
kitchen gardening to onlookers.

Nancy Keeler, looking like a Halloween witch without the hat—ludicrous
as the killer. Apart from anything else, she was tiny, and it seemed physically
beyond her to haul a dead body through the Settlement and string it up. He'd
known her for years. He'd recommended the Belvedere Inn to any friends
who came to town.

Monte Glover, Settlement magistrate, was talking solemnly to a group
on the green. He'd known Monte for years, but he knew better his partner,
Forest Albury, who owned the Dog Ear and Tatter bookstore and had hosted
Alex for readings of his books.

Roger Priestly he remembered as a teacher at the high school. He had retired early and was now hosting the apothecary shop at the Settlement.

He'd seen each of them in many places over the years: in the bank, the post office, the Granite Deli & Bagel, laughing with friends, nodding hello, shopping in Hannaford. Impossible to imagine any of them as killers.

As a writer, working at home, he'd been almost hermetically sealed off from the world around him. In his head all day, usually somewhere around Manchester, England, his fictional landscape. When he left home in the afternoons to pick up Sophie from school, it was as if he'd woken from a dream and found himself across the Atlantic, in small-town America. But since becoming a police officer all that had changed. Granite Harbor had a population of about five thousand people, and now it seemed that he somehow knew them all, if only by sight. His years of police work had brought him out of himself. He'd been involved with people all over town, seen them at their best and worst, heard about them through Mark Beltz and the other officers, through proceedings at court. This was his landscape now. He was familiar with everyone. And that made it even more fantastically improbable to imagine that anyone could have done such a thing—here.

And then there was Isabel. She stood across the central green talking to two women, one middle-aged, the other elderly, beside a small log cabin. They were asking questions, and Isabel, pointing out details of the cabin, answered earnestly.

In her black and drab seventeenth-century natural threads, she was a creature apart. She wore the period clothes well. He could imagine her in *The Crucible* as Goodwife Proctor. Or right here through the mists of four centuries. But it was more than the costume. He saw her face clearly even across a distance, devoid of any makeup, no hair to frame it, only the natural flax-colored linen coif she wore on her shaven head. Her large dark eyes, the asymmetrical dark brows. And her mouth, expressive in speech and repose.

He remembered her face inches above his own, her eyes fixed on his, mouth partly open, as they moved together.

Had it been love? Pretty close to it, or something just as good, once they'd decided to let go of their hesitancy, accommodate their baggage, and open up to each other. The deep pleasure he'd felt being in her home with her, entwined on the sofa watching TV or reading their books. The food they made together. A fire. Knowing the children were elsewhere. His house, when he could be sure Sophie was with her mother, was freer from the likelihood of interruption, but he'd loved Isabel's home. Away from the detritus and associations of his own life. The Sears, Roebuck house that had come on a train a hundred years ago. The cozy scale of the rooms. The bedroom's tongue-and-groove wainscoting. The bed. Isabel. Her acceptance, her appreciation of him. The way she'd let go. Her body, her long white thighs, what they did together and to each other. But most of all he loved her face. Up close, her breath, her eyes wide and boring into his.

They tried to do things with the kids, both the same age: musical events at the opera house, day trips to Mount Desert Island, kayaking on Lake Meguntic—but at eleven, their children wanted nothing to do with each other and rebuffed all efforts that might suggest a "family" appearance. *Ewww.*

Seven months. Long enough for them to think this might become the shape of the future.

It had all dissolved in a matter of minutes.

At the time, he was still in uniform. In a Granite Harbor Ford Explorer patrol vehicle with patrolman Frank Duggan, doing a speed stakeout on West Street. Out on the long stretch near the intersection with 17, just inside the town limit. A Wednesday night, around 9:45 P.M., clear and starry, no moon. Frank giving him the fine points on using the radar device, determining who you wanted to stop. Up to seven or eight mph over the limit—forty-five mph was posted there—you didn't bother. On a night like this, clear conditions, no traffic, it was reasonable for someone to speed a little. Unless you could see it was a kid, or someone just plain crazy speeding, doing sixty-five, seventy because the road was beautifully straight and no one was around.

The patrol vehicle was parked out of the light beside Granite Glass and Counter, about halfway between the lights at 17 and Meadow Street, the spot of maximum velocity going either way. A couple of cars went by, most doing between forty-five and fifty-two. They're fine, said Frank. He sipped from a thermos of coffee and imparted some insight into road surface. Major factor. A little light rain, even humid damp, was worse than real rain. That first drop on the windshield, you needed to slow down. That first sprinkle mixed with the oil on the surface, specially naturally greasy tarmac, made it slippery. People didn't even see it. A downpour was better, it washed the oil away, tires got a better grip.

A Subaru Forester shot by, fifty-nine on the radar.

"Let's go," said Frank.

The Subaru just made the light at Meadow Street, going through yellow at speed.

"This one's hammered," said Frank. "Not even slowing for yellow."

Frank turned on the roof strobes as they closed with the Subaru. It pulled over at Erickson Fields.

"License and reg. Get 'em out of the vehicle, heel-to-toe," Frank said. "Intoxilyzer. The works."

Before he reached the window, Alex knew it. He could see Ethan's wild hair in the passenger seat.

"Hi," he said, evenly, when she lowered the window. "Hi, Ethan."

"Hey."

"I have another patrolman in the car with me. So this has got to be by the book."

"I understand." Isabel was looking at his uniform, duty belt, the gun. He'd never worn them around her.

"You were speeding."

"Oh. I guess . . . Well, I'm sorry."

"Where are you coming from?" he asked.

"Jared's house. I had to pick Ethan up."

"I have to ask you this. Have you been drinking?"

"Yes."

"Alex, you can say you know us," said Ethan.

"Ethan, be quiet, please," she said.

"I have to go through this procedure," Alex said.

"Of course. Go ahead."

When he asked her to get out and walk nine steps heel-to-toe, Ethan got out, came around the car. "Why are you doing this?"

Frank Duggan got out of the patrol vehicle. "Back in the car, young man." His voice at bullhorn volume.

"Ethan!" said his mother. "Get back in the car! Now!"

"Mom—"

"Get back in the car!"

Ethan got back in the car. Frank Duggan remained standing ten feet behind Alex.

Isabel lost her balance and stepped sideways on her fourth heel-to-toe.
The Intoxylizer showed an alcohol reading over the limit.

For a first offense, with an aggravating factor—carrying a passenger under twenty-one years of age—Isabel's license was suspended for 150 days.
She was fined $500.

The next day, she was suspended from her job at Granite Harbor High.
Her contract with the school was terminated.

She stopped drinking. She went to AA meetings. By bicycle.

She forgave him, of course. You were doing your job, she said, it was my
fault. She said it simply, without any rancor.

But everything was changed. Alex couldn't forgive himself. She had lost
her job. Nor could he erase the picture of the scene, standing beside her window in a police uniform, making her walk the humiliating nine steps, blow
into the Intoxylizer. The smoldering fury of Ethan through the window, who
remained furious with him ever afterward. Something flattened inside Isabel.

They didn't break up right away, or on any given day, or moment, or in
a conversation. They tried. They were careful. But the wonder, the deeper
feelings they had begun to feel for each other, the unfolding view of what
might be, were gone.

Ethan wouldn't talk to him. He left the room or the house if he encoun-
tered Alex.

Even Sophie was angry. "Really, Dad? You *arrested* her? You couldn't do
something? She's a really popular teacher."

In town, at the supermarket, they said hi to each other, or nodded from
a distance, a bare polite acknowledgment, on the rare occasions they crossed
paths—less often than one would think. He didn't see her for a year or two.
Then her head was shaved.

She saw him now. She angled her head slightly. Like, *Can I help you?* He turned
away.

He'd already spoken with Sylvia Grinnell in the gift shop, and almost everyone else so far. The usual questions: if they'd seen anyone other than the tourists in the Settlement, or anyone striking them as odd. Or signs of anything unusual, footprints, anything missing. No, they'd answered. Nothing odd or unusual. He wrote their answers in his notepad.

His own schedule had prevented him from talking with Roger Priestly. He found him now inside one of the other small cabins. A plain sign painted above the door: BOWLES APOTHECARY.

"Mr. Priestly?"

"Yes?" He was grinding something in a large mortar and pestle.

The interior walls of this cabin were lined with shelves of jars containing colored powders and what looked like dried flowers and herbs. An old scale sat on a heavy, scarred, wood table.

"Could we talk for a few minutes?"

"All right," said Roger Priestly. "We'll have to stop if I get any visitors."

"Of course. So what have you got in here?" Alex nodded at the jars, the table.

"This is my rendering of the apothecary shop that undoubtedly was a part of the original settlement. Not as complete a range of items as would have been available but a representation."

"How do you know there was an apothecary?"

"He was listed as such in the few records we have. An important position: the local apothecary was the doctor back then. They used the medicines they found around them. What we're rediscovering now. Natural treatments. But he was more than that. Counselor, confidant. More vital to the health of a community than a preacher. They wouldn't have left England without an apothecary. It would have been like heading to the New World without an axe."

"I had no idea."

"Oh, yes." Roger continued grinding, looking down at his mortar and pestle, absorbed. "Most people don't."

Alex looked around. He read the paper labels on the jars—PURSLANE, LAMB'S-QUARTER, CREEPING CHARLIE. "Do you know of any—I'm not sure what to call it—practices or rituals, maybe witchcraft, involving animals, anything like that in the history of Granite Harbor? Back in that time?"

Now Roger Priestly looked up at him. "No more than what we know of the hysteria over the Salem witch trials. What you'd find in the library. American history, 970. Witchcraft would be Wicca, that's 299, I think."

There was a knock on the open door. "Oh, hey," said a smiling elderly man in an L.L. Bean jacket. "What've we got here?"

"If we're finished our business?" Roger asked Alex.

"Sure. I'll get back to you if I need to. Thank you."

Alex walked back to the parking lot, avoiding Isabel, where she was still talking to a small group beside one of the cabins.

He'd caught the note of . . . What was it? The former teacher's habitual manner? No, more than that.

Self-importance.

22

When he was thirty-nine, one of Roger Priestly's relatives, an aunt he'd never met, died. She had no children of her own and she left her house on Cape Cod and her Merrill Lynch account—all but the $75,000 bequest to People for Cats—to Roger. He promptly sold the modest gray-shingled Cape for $1.7 million, liquidated the Merrill Lynch account (he didn't want to follow those stocks and bonds going up and down), and put all the money into his Granite Harbor National Bank account. He retired from the high school, where he had been teaching social studies and history for seven years.

He bought himself a new house: a fifteen-year-old post-and-beam with an island kitchen open to a great room, fieldstone fireplace, a broad deck, views of Penobscot Bay from the great room and master bedroom, a full, *dry* basement, and a two-car garage, set on a mature pad of land on Meguntic Street.

All his adult life Roger had lived in schoolteachers' houses: small, poky rooms, sagging bookshelves, galley kitchens, cranky furnaces, drafty walls, damp basements, no garage, shoveled snow through the winters to get into his car to drive anywhere. Now he suddenly found himself living a version of the American Dream he had never imagined for himself.

He spent more time outdoors, hiking through the woods and along the shore. He became fitter than he'd ever been in his life. He let his salt-and-pepper whiskers grow and trimmed them short. Friends of long standing, of both sexes, and more recent acquaintances, alone or newly divorced, seemed to notice Roger anew in Brown & Cord, in the post office, chatting with him at an event at the library. They suggested a lunch, dinner, some engagement that was unprecedented in the existing configuration of the relationship. Roger would smile warmly, apparently charmed at the suggestion, but fail to follow up. He was then seen to be a determinedly solitary man. His sexual proclivity was speculated about but could not be backed up by evidential history or anecdote. Roger Priestly had never, as far as anyone in Granite Harbor knew, had an intimate relationship with anybody. He appeared to be what had once euphemistically been termed a "confirmed bachelor."

He already knew something of natural, wild edibles, but now, without a job and a professional schedule, he spent hours walking in the woods and along the tidal shores. He read *Stalking the Wild Asparagus* by Euell Gibbons. He stalked hen of the woods and other wild mushrooms, foraging far afield on long day trips into the boreal northern forest of Maine. He cooked himself "wild dinners," washed down with organic wines.

Life was better with money. It was true.

He searched online and bought older, rarer books: *Alchemy of Herbs*, by Rosalee de la Fôret, from which he produced new and strange herbal teas. A 2011 reprint edition of *Pharmacopoeia Londinensis*, by Nicholas Culpeper, originally published in Boston in 1720, which he read was the Betty Crocker cookbook for the settlers of colonial Massachusetts; and early editions of *An Account of Some of the Vegetable Productions Naturally Growing in This Part of America*, by Manasseh Cutler, Boston, 1785; and *American Medical Botany*, Jacob Bigelow, Boston, 1818. He pored through his books and photographed illustrations with his phone, gathered leaves and roots, brought home his finds, ground them in mortars and pestles, mixed, boiled, and brewed ingredients, rendering them palatable by adding maple syrup, honey, pine sap, ground fruits and nuts.

A chance conversation with Chester Coffey at the Granite Deli & Bagel reminded him of the old settlement on the Fairhaven Road north of town, where Chester worked. Roger had been there with several classes of history students, whose minimal homework reports left him with a sour association. Now, talking with Chester about the lives of the early settlers, he went back and looked around. He researched the period. He imagined the lives of those settlers on the rugged coast of Maine. Finally, he joined the players, taking over one of the log cabins as the place of business of Jonathan Bowles, the apothecary. Though not a doctor, Goodman Bowles would have ministered to the health and well-being of the settlers, preparing and dispensing the natural remedies, locally foraged, exactly as Roger had been doing for some time.

He decorated his apothecary shop with a rough table, clay and pewter bowls, mortars and pestles, scales, strips of linen for applying poultices, shelves holding jars of dried herbs and flowers. Pots of medicinal plants and flowers. There had been, he told visitors, a real apothecary Bowles in this very place, three and a half centuries earlier.

But all this was merely a diorama for tourists. The real manufactory of Goodman Bowles's apothecary business was the warm, dry, well-insulated basement of Roger's new house. He had brought folding worktables in through the wide cellar doors. Along the walls, he'd arranged laundry drying racks on which he hung the stalks, bunches, and string-bound bundles of foraged herbs, weeds, and flowers that formed the base ingredients of his apothecary's medicine chest: bee balm; birch twigs and leaves; purslane, a good source of omega 3; hyssop flowers; chickweed; lamb's-quarter; stinging nettles, that marvelous anti-inflammatory and peerless soup ingredient. Clover blossoms, he conveyed to the female visitors in his shop, provided a "female's most efficacious helpmeet in acute moments of periodic distress or the inevitable changes of advancing years." Because of the Settlement's non-profit designation, he couldn't sell what he produced, but he showed them to visitors in his apothecary shop, let them sniff, gave them printed recipes.

Roger became fascinated with the Settlement. Right here, hundreds of years earlier, a small group of Pilgrims had lived and struggled. After-hours, poking around the outlines of the dig started and abandoned by the U Maine archaeologists in the 1970s to 1980s, he unearthed a cache of small colored bottles and jars: pale and indigo blue, green, violet, square, wide and slim—apothecary vials dating from the sixteenth and seventeenth centuries, he discovered looking online. He displayed them on the shelves in his apothecary shop, stoppered with round nubs of cork, cloth, and string. He filled them with his homemade nostrums and electuaries.

• • •

The players brought sandwiches, salads, for lunch and ate whenever they got a break from the visitors. Roger joined Isabel when he saw her on the gray plank outside the small cabin, nominally the Swaine home. He'd made himself an avocado, grilled pepper, garlic aioli wrap.

"Wow, that looks good," she said.

"Would you like half? It's more than I can eat."

"Oh, no thanks, Roger. I can hardly eat this." She lay her fork inside the Tupperware container on top of a half-eaten salad, and closed the lid.

"How's Ethan? I saw the tattoo."

"Oh my God. It's not a real one, it fades—I hope."

"I guessed. But is he talking about it yet?"

"No, he's not—not to me anyway. But he's got his friends, which I'm so thankful for. They need each other." She looked at Roger. He was watching her in his concerned way. Always a dark study; she couldn't tell how he was taking it. "How are you doing, Roger? I know you and Shane were close."

"Yes . . . he was a wonderful boy. I'm just . . . devastated, like all of us."

Roger placed his wrap beside him on the plank. He reached into one of the pockets of his black seventeenth-century woolen waistcoat—it was like a French waiter's vest, long with many pockets for change—and pulled out a small, wide-necked blue jar, covered by a cloth held in place with string. He held it out to Isabel.

"I made this for you."

"For me? Thank you." She took it. "It's a beautiful jar. It looks old. What is it?"

"The jar is old. I found it here. I think it may come from the original Settlement. The contents though are fresh. Apothecary Bowles's Tonic Electuary. A natural remedy from back in the day."

"What's in it?"

"Mostly herbs, flowers, a little bit of willow bark, sassafras, this and that. A spoonful of honey to help the medicine go down. Try it. A pick-me-up, as the English say. If you're needing one. If you don't like it, wash it out and return the jar to me, please. If you like it, I'll give you some more."

23

Come up and get your specimen!" Mr. Williams called out to the class. He pulled a plastic package out of a cardboard box and held it up before him. Its contents were clear.

The classroom filled with cries. "Ewwww!"

Always the same response.

"It's not going to bite you—it's dead!" said Mr. Williams cheerfully. He loved giving his dissection class.

In ones, twos, and groups huddled together in revulsion, the students came up to the front of the class, picked up a small vacuum-wrapped packet, and returned to their desks.

"Gloves on," instructed Mr. Williams. "Then open your packet with your scissors, and lay your specimen on your tray."

"It smells."

"*It* does not smell, Julie. What you're smelling is an aqueous solution of formaldehyde that has preserved your specimen in its current clean, germ-free, useful condition. Put your gloves on. Open them up. Somebody tell me why we dissect frogs."

"'Cos they're disgusting?"

"No, Ralph. They're one of God's creatures—like you, in fact."

Comments arose comparing Ralph to frogs—

"*Quiet!*" barked Mr. Williams. "Or you can clear out and get zero credit." He pointed to the door and stared at the class. The room fell silent.

"We use frogs because the organ systems in a frog are laid out much as they are in the human body. They show us how our own bodies work. Also, we can see adaptations in frogs that illustrate how they evolved to suit their environment. For instance, the tongue of a frog has adapted to have great length, strength, and speed in order to effectively catch insects at a distance or in flight. Indeed, what a piece of work is a frog! Who hasn't got one?"

One packet still lay on his desk. Mr. Williams looked around the classroom. He spotted the lone holdout—normally one of his more avid students. He held up the plastic packet and looked at the student over his glasses. "Come and get it, young man."

Welldale Academy, near Gardiner, Maine, drew its student body largely from families who might have sent their children to some very fine schools: Choate, Phillips Exeter, the Groton School, Deerfield Academy. Welldale was just as expensive as those other establishments, though far less well-known. It came to light during the same unhappy search made by many desperate parents, its reputation broadcast mostly by word of mouth, and then it seemed a godsend: *You should look at Welldale.*

The brochure showed a photograph of a substantial early-nineteenth-century house that had once been the home of a whaleship captain. A handsome building that bespoke tradition and solidity. Parents coming to inspect the school met its founder and headmaster, Dr. Frederick Grayson, tall, sandy-haired, dressed like an English squire, in the main house, which contained fine furniture and paintings of the same era as the house's construction. The tone of the place reassured parents.

They were further reassured by the dormitory and classroom buildings not shown in the brochure: plain, efficient, rectangular structures of mid-twentieth-century construction that had the aspect of a minimum-security federal prison.

This was where some children belonged. Where, according to the brochure and website, they would at last flourish. "I was in a mental hospital before I came to Welldale," testified one student in the video on the Welldale website. "Now I have a sense of purpose and a future."

Dr. Grayson maintained Welldale's accreditation with the Maine educational authorities by providing a curriculum that embraced a wide range of developmental and educational challenges, a rigorous sports and outdoor program, and the HiSET or GED-equivalent diploma. The school's location suggested a wholesome environment. Here, at the edge of the Maine woods, the precincts of Thoreau and Maine summer camps, parents found a refuge for a child who had difficulties being placed, or remaining, elsewhere. Achievement and graduation, Dr. Grayson assured parents, were not in doubt. In due course, Welldale students reached the age of eighteen, graduated, and passed into the next phase of life, and parents and children could move on with the difficult high school years behind them.

The boy remained hunched in his seat.

"Everyone's got one. This is your guy. Come up here now."

The boy stood and slowly walked to the front of the class.

Mr. Williams pulled the last packet out of the box and held it up.

The boy stared at it with evident horror. "They kill," he said.

"Oh, yes, they do indeed with that flicking tongue. They kill bugs, small insects, slugs—"

"One killed my dog."

"Your dog? Where?"

"In Florida."

"You might be talking about a toad—perhaps a cane toad. Did your dog try to pick it up in its mouth?"

He nodded.

"That's possible—with a cane toad. But this fellow is a frog and he's quite dead. See? Preserved in formaldehyde in the bag. He's not going to hurt anything."

Mr. Williams saw that the boy was in an elevated state of fear. A funny kid, this one. He could see it in the way he interacted with others, observed them, stood back, a complicated wariness. But the boy's grades, in biology anyway, were excellent. He was quiet, he paid attention. *Give me a classroom full of this kid over the rest of them, frankly.*

"Come on, let's go get you started."

He walked the boy back to his desk. "Gloves on. Open the packet with your scissors."

The frog plopped into the steel tray with a splash and strong odor of formaldehyde. It lay on its back, stomach up, limp, legs spayed.

"Pick up your scalpel. You can do this."

The purple-gloved fingers of his left hand wrapped around the stainless instrument and raised it over the tray.

"That's fine. Now, you've seen the video. Hold him steady with your right hand, and start with a clean cut right down the front there. From the throat to the groin. Start at the top. That's it. Now open it with an incision at the top and bottom of that line, like you saw in the video—like you're crossing a *T* and underlining at the bottom."

The boy did as Mr. Williams instructed. The teacher saw that his fear was replaced by interest. His concentration was strong. He was cutting well.

"Well done. Now put down the scalpel and peel the skin back. That's it. And look what you've got. See that? All the organs beautifully laid out."

The boy looked up at him.

"You did it perfectly," said Mr. Williams. He clapped the boy's shoulder and walked back to the front of the class.

Every year, after spring break, Welldale geared up for its "Survival Games" program. Students ran along logs, crawled through large plastic pipes, raced to build stacks of cordwood, rode a zip line, and clambered up and over a net stretched between two rigid telephone poles driven into the ground. It was a cross between boot camp training and a dog show. The program culminated in the Survival Games Interscholastic Championship in late May. Two other alternative schools, Crandall Academy in Topsham, Vermont, and the Trantor School in North Conway, New Hampshire, competed against Welldale and one another. The games were held at all three schools on a rotating schedule. In the boy's first year at the school, it was Welldale's turn to host the games.

He enjoyed Survival Games training. He discovered that he was well-suited to strenuous nontraditional physical activities. He was particularly good at scrambling up and down the high net strung between the old telephone poles. In competition, he made a difference to Welldale's chances. Dr.

Grayson cheered him on during the events, shouting, "Good man! Good man!"

Byron Pugh was Trantor's champion. He'd helped his school win the games twice in the last three years. He was six foot two, with thick wavy blond hair, green eyes, and a heroic chin.

Byron Pugh was more than strong. "He's *sexy!*" the girls from all three schools said. The boy saw the way they looked at Byron Pugh and giggled and went all funny when he was around.

Sex. Sally had whispered it in his ear. That's what they'd done together. The boy imagined Byron Pugh doing sex with the girls who looked at him and giggled.

Teasing and roughhousing at Welldale was of a different order than at other schools, but it didn't bother the boy. Verbal chaff, however vicious, reminded him of his Buell cousins, and he enjoyed the attention. When he felt the presence of a physical threat, he displayed a subtle alteration of appearance, such as occurs in the animal kingdom: a flush of color in fish or reptiles, hackles raised, ears back. In the boy, this manifested as a noticeable stillness. His movements slowed. His senses of sound, vision, and space became acute. This had been apparent enough to dissuade most bullies.

The boy's antennae located the incoming threat—a purposeful stumble designed to knock him out of the lunch line—well before Pugh reached him. He deflected the contact by turning smartly aside, and his arm shot out, palm thrust forward like the end of a battering ram, into the side of Pugh's head. Byron Pugh crashed into a folding table and landed in a slick heap of potato salad.

There was a ripple of laughter along the line and at the picnic tables, and titters of surprise.

Byron Pugh got to his feet. He looked down at himself. His tight T-shirt, athletic shorts, fancy running shoes, were covered with food and mayonnaise. He tried flicking the mess off his clothes. Then he looked up. The laughter faded as everyone watched.

The boy remained standing casually in his place in the line.

Belatedly, Byron Pugh detected what he'd missed before: the boy's stillness, a sense of personal space. He walked around him—remaining beyond an arm's length of distance—looking him up and down. "Dude, hope you're okay. Didn't mean to barge in. But I got you an extra helping."

He flicked a handful of potato salad at the boy's face—but the boy snapped his head aside, and the potatoes flew wide.

After supper on each day of the games, the home and visiting teams were free to roam around the grounds, exercise, or practice for the next day's events, get together and socialize, or relax until bedtime.

On the evening before the last day of the games, the long Maine twilight, a month before the summer solstice, stretched out the light, softened the humid air and deepened the shadows imperceptibly as the students played and chattered and laughed until late.

The boy lay in the grass by himself, looking up at the white clouds moving slowly by overhead. Seeing the clouds made him feel peaceful. At home almost. He imagined himself up there looking down at the tiny people running around, playing, or stretched out in the grass far below. Way up there he would hardly hear the sounds they made, small cries and screams of delight blown away by the gentle but constant breath of the wind up in the sky. He had never been part of that tiny whirling group of human beings scattered across the surface of Earth. He was always far above them, floating like a balloon.

He didn't pay attention to the group of students who rushed by on either side of him until they dropped the Survival Games net on top of him. He sat up, saw what had happened, and tried to work his way out of the net. Without getting near him, the students, from Trantor and Crandall, well rehearsed, ran around him in a circle, holding the net down. He was snagged and wrapped in the net, and then they pulled him across the grass into the long grass near the trees, out of sight of School House and the other players.

Byron Pugh directed them. They pounded stakes into the net around him until he stopped struggling. He knew he was trapped. Tightly held down, lying on his back, arms pinned to his sides.

Byron Pugh's face loomed above him. "How's it hangin', dude?"

He drove four stakes into the ground alongside the boy's temples and jaw so that he was unable to turn his head aside but was forced to face the sky. He saw the clouds again, although now there was a net of rope across his face and he knew he was trapped back down on Earth.

Byron Pugh stood, pulled up the hem of his shorts, and urinated on him. One by one, seven students, three of them girls, did the same. The girls stood close to his head, legs spread, pelvises thrust forward, and hit him almost as accurately as the boys.

Then Byron Pugh took his shorts off, squatted over his head, and defecated onto his face.

Because of the stakes beside his head, he was unable to turn his face aside. He could only blow an airspace through the shit piling onto his face.

"Hey, check it out," said Byron Pugh. "Breakfast! Blueberry pancakes!"

Laughing, they ran back across the field leaving the boy pinned beneath the net.

Welldale's groundskeeper-handyman, Ivan Haney, a North Carolinian and Vietnam veteran, lived in what he called the Shack, a single-wide manufactured home parked out of sight behind a line of firs at the edge of the woods that bordered the Welldale grounds. The structure had been winterized by being completely encased, down to the cinder block surround, with four-inch sheets of foam insulation (holes cut around the windows), taped, Tyvek-wrapped, and sided with battens and tar paper. The home and materials for its improvement had been provided by the school. Haney had done all the work himself.

It was Ivan Haney's long ingrained habit to patrol the perimeter of the property before dark, walking with a ski pole that he poked into the brush here and there, and this evening he came upon the boy beneath the net.

Haney didn't think much of Welldale's students, or the Survival Gamers from the other schools. *Survival Games!* He would have liked to have seen them all shipped off to Nam.

But the sight of this netted boy caught inside him. It took him back to things he had seen. He freed the boy, brought him to the Shack, hosed him off, and gave him some spare clothes that were much too big.

For the rest of his time at Welldale, four years, the boy spent a few hours a day working around the grounds with Ivan Haney. Dr. Grayson approved and awarded him athletics credits.

He liked working with Ivan. He admired Haney's mastery of Welldale's natural surroundings, and his knowledge of the world. ·

Haney taught him many things. Tricks of woodcraft, how to use, sharpen, and maintain tools. The secrets of the wild vegetation. Natural foods and medicines, he said, available for the picking all around them. Haney would snatch up nuts, berries, flowers, and herbs growing in the woods and fields, chew them with relish and share them with the boy. He made wine from wild berries and teas sweetened with maple sap and wild honey collected without a sting as bees flew around him. The boy watched and drank.

In light of his capture and treatment by the enemy schools, Haney taught the boy how to defend himself and, if he felt threatened, how to attack. How to swing his arm with all his weight behind it like a club to fell a boy or man like a puppet with the strings cut.

Occasionally, Haney asked him about his studies. He was contemptuous of his dissected frog.

"Frogs are trash. Nothing but wet skin and throwaway parts. Toads are what you want. They got some powerful juju. We'll get to that."

24

In the library, Alex started, as Roger Priestly had suggested, with American history, 970. He took a small stack of books to a table and settled into an armchair.

The upstairs reading room was wonderfully quiet. It was a good afternoon to be indoors with books: the air outside smeary with fine rain, the top of Mount Meguntic shrouded with low cloud.

Alex had a gnawing sense that he was hiding out here in the library, while FBI agent Tintin Harris was on the case, chasing down the only real lead they had. But he'd spoken with Chief Raintree about the investigation, and run down a bullet list of what he'd done, what he was waiting on:

- He'd taken statements from Dennis and Doreen Wisner.
- He'd spoken with Shane's best friends, Ethan, Jared McKinnon, their mothers, and Shane's other friends, and their parents. Jared confirmed Ethan's account of the boys' skateboarding evening and their last sighting of Shane—the last anyone had seen him—on Limerock Street.
- He'd read through the sixteen-year-old police report of the murder of Byron Pugh in Prouts Neck. Both he and Agent Harris and the department's IT man, Kevin Regis, had looked for any connection between Byron Pugh and the smallest mention of Granite

Harbor, and Granite Harbor Settlement and its players and their backgrounds and histories, with no result.

- He'd examined, in the basement of the William P. Merrill Station, the simple, unbolted two-by-fours of the structure from which Shane had hung, and read the report on same—standard Douglas fir framing timber, approx. two yrs old, probably grown in the Pacific Northwest, used for housebuilding all over the United States, available at Home Depot and Lowe's stores and local lumberyards everywhere in the country, including Maine. Cut to size without any lot numbers or identifying marks. Lumber anyone could have bought anywhere. Put together with neat but simple carpentry skill. Examined for prints, any trace of DNA, without results.
- He was waiting for the autopsy report, due today or tomorrow.

Meanwhile . . . It felt self-indulgent, sinking into a chair with a book. This was what he loved to do, almost more than anything else: read, tune everything out, leave the confused and messy world around him for the contained and organized world of a book. But right now, this seemed, intuitively, the way forward.

"Writing is like driving at night in the fog," E. L. Doctorow had famously said. "You can only see as far as your headlights, but you can make the whole trip that way."

Solving this murder felt like writing a novel. He couldn't see it yet, but it was all there—in the night fog—ahead or in his peripheral vision. The only way to figure it out was to grope his way forward into the dark.

He opened several of the books, read a few pages of the early chapters. Paleoindians were hunting caribou in what was now Maine thirteen thousand years ago. . . .

Alex flipped pages. . . . "Upon landing," wrote a French chronicler who navigated up the Penobscot in 1606, "we saw a great multitude of native people coming down upon us in such numbers that you might have supposed them to be a flight of uncountable starlings. They all greeted us in the most affectionate manner, declaring that they were our friends. Having remained in this place for five days, we weighed anchor, and, parting from them with a marvelous contentment on both sides, went out upon the open sea."

Yet soon the natives, that "flight of uncountable starlings," "suffered a great depopulation of the country by the plague imported from the Europeans."

He opened another book, *A History of Maine*, by William Smith Cabot, Benjamin Russell Publisher, Boston, 1825. He thumbed pages, skimmed . . . then the book's loosened binding fell open at this: "In the year 1643, a small company sailed from Weymouth, England, to Maine, aboard the ship *Hope*, under the direction of Sylvanus Clews. The Brethren purchased from the local natives one thousand acres of land, one half on each side of a river they named after the same in Dorset, the Frome. . . ."

This had to be it. The Frome River ran alongside the Settlement.

The early news was encouraging. Cabot quoted an unnamed source: "'The creek mouth abounds with fin and shell fish and a strong tide goeth in there. The river runneth up into the main, through verdure crowned banks and headlands, presenting green meadows stocked with beaver, otter, musquash. Wood abundant for winter fires and a great amount of game in the forest, raccoons, foxes, rabbits, and fowls of many kinds. Upon the hills grow notable high timber trees, masts for ships of 400 tons burthen.'"

So what had happened?

The books contained accounts of other early settlements in Maine—Popham, Castine—but no more mention of Granite Harbor or the Frome River.

He changed tack, went downstairs, and settled in at a computer carrel and typed *frogs, toads, rituals, witchcraft* into Google. Up came the same vague information he'd found through his own laptop at home: the Frog and Toad book series by Arnold Lobel; witchcraft sites, Wicca blogs; the Frog & Toad bookstore in Providence, Rhode Island, purveyor of candles, celestial animal print dresses, "soap for Cat People."

A link he hadn't seen before produced a pdf translation of the *Malleus Maleficarum*, written by Catholic clergyman Henricus Institor, in Latin, published in Speyer, Germany, 1486. A testimony, by man or woman was unclear: "Then she came up and touched my belly with her hands, and it seemed to me that she did take out my entrails, and put in something which I could not see." But no mention of frogs or toads. . . .

Inside the head-high barrier of his carrel, he'd become aware of the increasing buzz of people coming into the library, the mechanism of the outside door opening and shutting repeatedly. At first it was the noise of younger kids, mothers, middle schoolers. Then the noise increased by many factors. He looked at his watch: 3:44 P.M.—high school was out. He put his notepad and pen back into his coat pockets, got up, and left the comparative peace of the rows of carrels and turned into the main room, heading for the door.

They appeared ahead, rising above the smaller kids, shuffling in movement, like a phalanx of zombies from a TV show: four abreast, three of them girls, with the same stark, black brand across their foreheads: SHANE.

One of them belonged to Isabel's son, Ethan. The boy turned to face Alex, and their eyes—Ethan's boring out beneath his billboard brow—met.

Then, his eyes drawn swiftly by instinct, he saw Sophie standing beside Ethan.

They were all staring at him, accusingly. For a long moment, he thought the slight change of one letter was real:

SHAME slammed into him like a wave. He *heard* it, a chorus of accusation shouted inside his head.

Alex automatically walked toward Sophie, but she veered away. Ethan stopped moving, refusing to let go of Alex's eyes.

Another SHANE-branded high schooler called out to him: "What are you doing about it, Detective Brangwen?"

Alex's phone began to vibrate in his pocket.

"I'm investigating. Is there anything you can tell me about Shane? Anything might help."

They looked at him as if he were the murderer. Then they turned and slouched off toward the carrels.

Outside, the green lawn of Library Hill fell away to the windjammer schooners and the moored yachts and floating pontoons, the beautiful harbor opening out to Covert Island lighthouse and Penobscot Bay. Alex couldn't see any of it.

All he saw was SHAME, the Britannic Bold letters filled his mind with the power of klieg lights still burning behind closed eyelids.

It's not an M, he had to force himself to remember. It was still an *N*.

In his car, he pulled out his phone. The missed call was from a 207 Maine number he didn't recognize. He tapped it.

"Detective. This is Phil Gressens, medical examiner." It took Alex a moment to come back to the present, and then came the picture of the tall, ponytailed medical examiner. "I've emailed you the full autopsy report. But I thought I'd call and let you know a few highlights. Your victim was not sexually molested. No sign of ante- or post-mortem activity on or in penis or anus. No semen or other collectibles."

"Thank you."

"But I have a trace blood result. Organic DMT—dimethyltryptamine."

"DMT?" An echo, something recent . . .

"It's a psychedelic. There are various DMTs, but for a recreational high it's usually something like psilocybin, or magic mushroom."

"Shane was on mushrooms?"

"I can't tell you the source. Except that it's organic, not lab manufacture. So that would indicate something like mushrooms."

"So he was high before he died?"

"Possibly, but not very. As I said, there wasn't much, but enough for a trace. Doesn't stay in the blood for more than a few hours, so that would indicate ingestion of the drug, followed by the toad business. Then death by asphyxiation. All within two to four hours."

"So he was probably hanging with someone he knew and getting high."

"I'll leave the deductions to you, Detective."

He had to drive back to the office and open the file on his computer to make sure: Byron Pugh, the Prouts Neck victim from sixteen years earlier, had DMT in his system.

25

The lights dimmed in the conference room of the William P. Merrill Station, the pull-down screen on the wall was illuminated, the slide projector whirred, and Special Agent Harris, sitting before his laptop, began his PowerPoint presentation.

In the glow from the screen, he looked ludicrously young. A kid playing a video game. But Alex had read through Harris's CV: graduate of FBI Academy, Quantico, obviously a far more sophisticated program than the instruction on note-taking and basic deductive skills Alex had received at the MCJA. He had already spent six years in the field, attached to notable investigations. He came with the vast resources of the Bureau, its scientific and technological databases. All its deductive machinery and history.

Faces now appeared on the screen. "Local sex offenders," said Harris.

But there had been no apparent sexual interference. Alex had shared this finding from the autopsy with Harris. So what was this?

One by one, each on a separate PowerPoint slide, the booking photos for the town's four registered sex offenders, three men and one woman, appeared on the screen. Alex knew them all by face and file. He'd seen them, too, around town, the way you saw and were familiar with everybody in such a small town after so many years. But in these cases, he'd read their files as a matter of due diligence, he knew where they worked, knew their friends and family, and he didn't see any of them as Shane's killer.

But it was correct of Harris to present them. To round up the usual suspects, if only to dismiss them.

More photos. Harris continued: "The eleven convicted adult and juvenile drug dealers who have had any connection, past or present, to Granite Harbor and the midcoast region, whether still living here or not."

One by one, faces you would steer clear of on the sidewalk. All marked by something clear but indefinable: a feral quality. People who had never learned to run with the herd, staring into the headlights of an ill-begotten fate, as if they hadn't seen it coming.

More due diligence. Alex was suddenly disappointed. This is what the Bureau serves up?

He was startled by what came next: slides showing five of Shane's high school friends, including Ethan Dorr, Jared McKinnon, and others in grades above and below him, each shown with an official high school yearbook photograph, and the student's current address in town. Alex knew them all. It was jarring to see their faces, names, and addresses on the screen with the sex and drug offenders. It felt obscene.

He looked covertly along the table, suddenly aware of the waves of brooding displeasure pouring off Chief Raintree as she sat still as a Buddha in the darkened room.

But he had to be impressed by Harris's industry—he'd only told him about the finding of DMT in Shane's system the afternoon before.

"Why these kids?" Alex asked. "What are you suggesting?"

"I'm suggesting this is where we look."

"Seriously? Our local high schoolers? These are my daughter's friends. Yes, there's weed and drugs and alcohol out there, but DMT seems like another order of recreational drug-taking. College students maybe. And I presume you're not presenting these kids as murder suspects."

"The children no, not for the murder. And, full disclosure, Detective, I don't have children. But I'm familiar with your response. We hear this everywhere. 'How can this happen here, to us? Our children?' Of course, it *does* happen here. *Everything* happens here, every day. I put the children up here because they suggest a clear avenue of investigation."

Harris clicked, and another slide showing Ethan Dorr appeared on the screen. Not a high school yearbook photo but a shot of the boy in front of one of the town's brick buildings, standing with other kids. Harris clicked again: Ethan coming out of the Shed, the teen after-school hangout—Alex was jolted to see Sophie beside him. He felt an instant surge of anger toward Harris. In both photographs the depth of field was flattened, taken with a telephoto lens from some distance away, from inside a car maybe.

"Who took these pictures?" Alex asked.

"I did," said Harris. "So here is Ethan Dorr. One of Shane's friends. Maybe a friend of your daughter's, Detective, I don't know. This kid has dropped out of school. What's he doing? His mother, Isabel Dorr, is broke, she's in debt—"

"How do you know she's in debt?"

"Credit report," Harris said. "She makes hardly anything working in the Settlement. So you have to ask, what's the kid doing wearing expensive fashionwear—"

"Expensive fashionwear?" Alex almost laughed. "I know this kid. He wears the same clothes as everyone else—"

"I don't think so, Detective."

New slides appeared. Screenshots of clothing from websites: a wool watch cap, with the label SUPREME on it; price: $104. A sweatshirt: the logo *BAPE*—

"Bape—Bathing Ape fashionwear. Here we see a Bape camo shark hoodie, $440."

Harris clicked back to the street shots of Ethan. He was wearing the same sweatshirt, the same hat. Harris had organized his slideshow well.

"They're fake," said Alex. "Cheap knockoffs. Anyone can buy that stuff online." Sophie had acquired shoes, handbags, jackets, Versace, and other gaudy high-end designer brands, that Alex presumed had been bought for her by her mother but learned that they were cheap imitations Sophie had bought online. *Mom would never get me this shit*, she'd told him.

Harris, one half of his face lit by the screen, looked across the conference table at Alex. "I mean no disrespect, Detective, but I don't think you know what you're talking about. That's true for many items, but not these. These items are real. And you know where we see this?"

More slides: they looked like stills from the television show *The Wire*: drug dealers on a city street, looking around, a deal going down, hands exchanging small packets.

"What does any of this have to do with Shane's murder?"

Another slide appeared. Alex recognized the file photo he'd seen on Harris's computer. The slit-open torso of the body found at Prouts Neck sixteen years earlier.

"We know Shane Carter was doing drugs from the DMT in his blood. So was Byron Pugh in Prouts Neck. I'm sure you've read the report."

The photo of Ethan and Sophie coming out of the Shed reappeared on-screen.

"What I see here, is that this boy, Ethan Dorr, is a drug dealer. Hardworking single mother has no idea what he's into. Maybe Ethan is Shane's dealer, though Shane didn't have any money, but Ethan's got money to burn if he's buying Bathing Ape hoodies; he can afford to give his friend a ride. Shane comes from neglect at home. He was cutting school too. Both of these boys are vulnerable. I don't see either of them spending hours bushwhacking in the woods up around Baxter State Park looking for *Psilocybe quebecensis*, the shrooms that can give this sort of buzz, so they're getting it on the street—here, or Rockland, or Fairhaven. This is a classic drug-taking situation here. Shane had it in his blood."

"How does this fit in with a murder in Prouts Neck, which happened around the time Shane was born?"

"Same presumption of Byron Pugh doing drugs. He went to a therapeutic boarding school for difficult kids, he was a troubled child like these others. What I'm saying is, these boys are exposed and vulnerable to the criminal element. They're getting drugs from someone they know, somewhere close. This is how serial killers and sex offenders—they go together, of course, Jeffrey Dahmer, John Wayne Gacy—find their victims: among vulnerable, neglected youths. They prey on them with drugs. Detective, you ask why these kids, *kids you know*, are up there"—Harris nodded at the screen—"with those criminals, sex offenders, drug dealers? Because they go together like peanut butter and jelly. There's no mystery here. This is the paradigm. This is textbook."

"You're presuming," Chief Raintree said, "that Shane took the drug voluntarily. What if someone gave him the drug, spiked a drink or something, and then killed him?"

"Yes, ma'am, I'm assuming he took drugs voluntarily. That's what I see here. I'm looking at this with a broader view than simply an autopsy finding. I look for patterns. What I see here is kids doing drugs, and behind that a killer. The drugs make them vulnerable prey to a serial killer."

"And the toad?" asked Chief Raintree. "Where does that figure in?"

"It figures in with madness. That's obviously what we're dealing with here. A fetish, a fixation, an association. A childhood hangover thing, a gruesome show-off device. Who knows. You catch the lunatic and then you figure out his crazy. I'm not too hung up on the frogs—toads. That's a detail. The crazy thing a killer does is almost incidental. A serial killer will kill to a pattern."

Chief Raintree asked another question. "Who owned the property in Prouts Neck where the other victim was found?"

"Family named Buell. No known connection, place, or the family, to either victim, Byron Pugh or Shane Carter. The only common elements here are the murder details, the toads, and the drug, DMT."

Harris closed his laptop.

Chief Raintree stood and turned on the overhead lights, and turned off the switch that powered the projector. She sat back down at the table. "Thank you, Agent Harris. And why do you think Byron Pugh's killer has not killed, or such a killing has not come to light, and now woken up and begun killing again in this pattern after sixteen years?"

"We may not learn that, ma'am, until we've apprehended him." He looked respectfully at Billie Raintree. "Or her. But, as you know, most serial killers are male."

Harris stood. He placed his computer in a rigid molded attaché case that looked as if it had been designed to carry a small nuclear weapon. "I'll be in my hotel if you need me."

When Harris had left the conference room, Chief Raintree said, "What do you think?"

Alex looked at the white screen. "It was well put together. Impressive." Alex shook his head slowly. "I just...don't see it. I don't like the logical neatness of it." He looked at Chief Raintree. "Do you?"

"My only like is for the truth. And for information that leads us to that. Our job is to not turn away from where that takes us. The drug finding is significant. We have very little else. Apart from frogs. Which clearly mean something to the killer."

"Toads."

"What's the difference?"

He tried to recall what Professor Barney had said. "Habitat. Warts—the toad makes a toxin."

"Enough to kill?"

"No. But . . . you don't think it suggests spells and witchcraft? Shakespeare mentions them—"

Chief Raintree exhaled noisily. "I don't. Perhaps you'd have to be a woman to understand. Witches—women. It's a tired trope, but go ahead and prove me wrong." She stood up. "What are you planning to do?"

"I'm going to talk to Ethan Dorr about his fashionwear."

26

At dinner, Isabel said, "Alex wants to talk to you again."

"Fuck. What for?"

"Ethan, please stop saying that."

"Do I have to?"

"If he needs to talk to you about—"

"Okay. Fuck."

"Ethan! Stop saying that!"

"*Okay!* When?"

"I don't know. I think tomorrow, he said."

Ethan hunched over his plate.

"The school is doing grief counseling. I think it would be—"

"I'm not doing that. I'm not going there."

"Lots of kids are. I want you to."

"Well, I'm not going to."

"Would you like to talk to somebody else? Roger said he'd be happy to talk with you."

"No."

"Ethan—"

"Mom, *stop!* I don't *want* to talk about it." He pushed his plate aside. "It's freezing in here. It's like fifty degrees."

"No, it's not."

"*It was this morning!*" he shouted at her across the table.

"Ethan, please don't shout at me."

"But this is ridiculous! Who lives like this? What are we going to do about the furnace?"

"We're going to get a new one."

"When?"

"When I make some more money."

"I'll get one. How much do they cost?"

"About four thousand dollars."

"Really? Can't we get one secondhand?"

"No. People keep them until they break down and then they get a new one. Like us. That's what we have to do. If it was fixable, we'd fix it."

"Well, I'm going to sell something. It'll make me a lot of money."

She pretended it was a possibility. "That would be nice."

"I'm serious. You don't believe me. You'll see."

"That would be great. It would be wonderful, Ethan. Do you want any dessert?"

He stood up. "No thanks. I'm going upstairs. I going to get into bed—where it's warm."

He took his plate and glass to the sink, washed them, placed them in the dish rack. "Thanks for dinner," he said, and disappeared upstairs.

She pushed away her own plate—she'd barely eaten anything—and sat at the table.

A great sadness enveloped her. Ethan seemed unreachable. This wasn't just Shane. He'd changed completely since he was fourteen. Where was her little boy? This taller, lankier dude was morose, unhappy, with a constant, simmering anger.

He's a teenager, people told her. *Welcome to the club, this is what happens.*

Then she thought, *Why wouldn't he be angry?* His father disappeared. His mother's a freak who pulls out her hair, shaves her head, lost her job, and now dresses like a witch. And they live in a freezing house.

He didn't know the half of it, thank God. How she felt in the mornings before she forced herself out of bed to take Flynn out to Calderwood Point. To put one foot in front of the other to avoid the total collapse she felt she had in her.

She'd been angry too, at herself, worried about money, how to pay for
college—if he went—at the terrible abyss that seemed to yawn before them
both. The shame she felt, the sense of failure as a parent. The almost overwhelming fear of everything collapsing, losing the house if she couldn't make
any money. She was getting close to telling Ethan to get a job—a real job, not
his model-making—if he wasn't going to school. They needed the money—
anything would help.

She'd changed too. He must have seen that. She'd been happier when she
drank.

She cleared away her plate and washed the dishes. She was disgusted with
her self-pity. She made a cup of Herbal Wellness tea. Her attempts at healthy
eating didn't seem to help much—where was the *wellness*?

When she set the cup down on the counter she saw the little blue jar
Roger had given her. He'd pasted on a paper label, written on it in black ink,
in a flowing cursive script: *Bowles's Electuary. A Beneficent Tonic for Spirit and Physik
Humors.*

Isabel untied the string, removed the cloth, and sniffed. Pungent, earthy.
Mostly herbs, flowers, a little bit of willow bark, sassafras, this and that, a spoonful of honey.
Dark, like tapenade. She dipped a finger and brought it to her mouth and
sucked. Rooty, like root beer, not too sweet. She spread some on a pita chip. It
went well with the tea. Something in her that hadn't wanted supper wanted this.

Again, the thought of Shane broke over her like a cold wave. Isabel shuddered. *Why?* She had her own grief over Shane. He'd been over a lot, eaten
with them, remained a loyal friend to Ethan at an age when kids dropped
friends and made new alliances. A beautiful, sensitive boy.

Her mug was empty. She'd polished off a third of the jar of thick jam-like
stuff, and now it was filmy on the roof of her mouth. She put the cloth back
over the jar, tied the string, and put it in the refrigerator. She drank a mugful
of water, washed the mug, and went upstairs.

27

Something woke him. A noise?

Alex's house, a small converted barn, made noise in strong winds. When spring and fall equinoctial gales came, and during the winter northeasters, it moved. It swayed and groaned. He'd mentioned it once to his landlord, Ed, who'd smiled and said, "Oh, sure." Ed pointed out the barn's structural members, the rough-planed eight-inch-square beams joined to the massive ten-inch vertical posts, the hand-chiseled mortise-and-tenon joints. "She's stout. But maybe think of it as an old wooden schooner. She won't sink, but she'll heave, and she'll let you know about it."

Alex knew the noises by now, and he believed in the soundness of the building, and when the wind blew and he lay in bed at night and heard the groaning timbers, he felt secure. The old barn would carry on till morning.

Now he sat up and listened. This was not a known and cataloged creaking post or beam. It was new. Not wood on wood. It was oddly soft.

Sophie, he reminded himself, was at her mother's. But just to be sure— she might have come over and crept in—he got out of bed, went to her room, and opened the door. Bed empty, room dark.

Then he heard it again . . . from the kitchen.

Back in his bedroom, he pulled the small gun safe from under his bed, punched in his father's birthday, and pulled out the Glock.

Inside the kitchen, he paused, then stepped soundlessly to the back door that opened onto the deck. There was some wind, but it wasn't blowing hard. . . .

The inner kitchen door was closed; locked, he was sure. But the storm door beyond it was moving . . . slightly. An animal trying to get in?

Or someone had tried to?

The sky was overcast, but there was enough moon above the cloud ceiling to give him a clear view of the backyard through the den windows. Nobody visible.

The noise again . . . there was something between the two doors. Not a person.

Alex stepped forward, unlocked the inner door, and opened it gently—

Something leaped at him—he jumped back, his foot twisted on the braided carpet and he stumbled—hissing *Jesus!*—as his hip hit the floor—

It was coming at him across the floor. He rolled away, hissing again, channeling fear into what sounded like anger—*What the fuck!*—checking the impulse to point the gun—it was small. . . . It stopped moving. Then it trembled. Brown, crinkled, the size of a clenched fist.

A leaf, for fuck's sake? A *leaf* made that noise?

Or the storm door? It moved again, its weather stripping rubbing on the raised threshold. The leaf whirled across the floor, and something heavy tumbled into the doorway. Alex reflexively aimed his gun—

Then he slid it away from him across the carpet. It was what he hated about guns: if you have one, you're waiting to use it.

He was shaking. He stood up and pulled the storm door shut until he heard the latch engage. He closed the inner door, locked it, and opened the plastic bag that lay on the floor. Butternut and acorn squashes. Gifts from Ed and Joan, his landlords. They often set bags of fruit, tomatoes, or, now, fall squashes from the garden inside his back door. These were large, and the storm door had not latched.

Alex picked up the leaf, crushed it in his fist, and threw it into the garbage beneath the sink. He put the squashes on the kitchen table. Thanks a lot. He returned the gun to its safe and crawled into bed.

He tried to relax. *What is the matter with you? Pull yourself together.*

He'd been sure—just for a moment—that a toad was leaping toward him.

28

She woke gasping for breath. She was out of bed, stumbling across the hall, pushing open the door to Ethan's bedroom before she even realized it. Then she was tearing off the duvet, pulling at the sweatshirt he wore. A wild woman.

"Mom . . . what the . . ."

"*Where is it?*" she cried, searching frantically, trying to roll him over, running her hands over Ethan's body, his skin beneath the sweatshirt.

"*Mom!*" Ethan sat up and backed away from her. Wide awake, terrified. He tried to pull the duvet over himself. "What are you *doing?* What's happening?"

"Where is it?"

"Where's what, Mom? What the fuck?"

"There's something on you. Let me see—"

Again she tried to pull at his sweatshirt. Clawing at him.

"*Mom, stop!* There's nothing on me! What are you doing?"

She stared at him. He was fine.

"You didn't feel anything? Crawling over you? In your bed?"

"No! *Like what?* Like how would you know, Mom? Did you see something?"

Yes. But not in here.

"You're okay?"

"Yes! I'm fine. There's nothing in my bed." He threw the duvet aside to show her and then whipped it back over him. The letters SHANE still starkly visible on his forehead beneath the mop of curly hair. Below that, his eyes were bugging open at her. He was still moving away from her.

"I'm sorry, Ethan. I guess it was a nightmare."

"Mom, I'm fine. Nothing was in here. You were like . . . berserk."

"Okay." She saw it was still dark out his bedroom window. She was sweating, but it was clammy cold around her torso beneath her T-shirt. "I'm sorry, Ethan. Go back to sleep." She stood and went to the door.

"Yeah, right."

29

Sophie ordered a chai, Ethan a latte with an extra shot. They took their drinks to a corner table whose legs tottered on the thick, uneven floorboards of the Shed, the café in a former boatshed hanging over the water at the inner end of the harbor. Long and narrow, tilted out of all level planes, the Shed's largely unimproved, old-world ambience made it a favorite of local artists, writers, lobstermen, construction workers, and high school students who wanted to avoid greater numbers of their peers in the library or the Granite Deli & Bagel.

After years of staying away from each other, repelled by the association of their parents, Sophie and Ethan had felt mysteriously drawn together since Shane's death. The inking had been Sophie's idea, and after that they'd found it natural to hang out.

Ethan pulled off his beanie, flicked his head, ran his fingers through his dark curly hair, pulling it away from his forehead in a self-consciously casual movement. The letters of his SHANE tattoo were slightly faded, like day-old Sharpie pen marks. He looked over at Sophie and found she was looking back at him over the rim of her large mug.

"Can I see your ship models?" she asked.

"How do you know about those?"

"Everyone knows. You sell them. That's cool. Can I see them?"

"Sure. They're at my house. When?"

"Like now? Will your mom be home?"

"I don't know. It's after work, but she might be shopping or walking the dog. My stuff's in the basement anyway."

A thick hairy hand dropped onto Ethan's shoulder. He had to turn his head up and around. "Oh, hey, Chester."

"You're lucky I didn't bop you on the head with an axe handle." The face, largely hidden by beard, was amused. "That's what I was going to do. I was ready to pound the hell out of whoever it was. The tarp was Roger's idea."

Roger appeared beside him. He looked at them both, shaking his head. "What were you thinking? We're still on pretty high alert there."

"We were just . . . We were there to say goodbye to Shane."

Roger nodded. "I understand. But after what happened, sneaking around there at night?" His expression softened, he fixed his gaze on Ethan. "Look, Ethan, why don't you come and talk to me? I hope you know I'm always there for you. You know that?"

Ethan nodded. "I do, Roger. Thank you."

Chester now dropped his face close to Ethan's. His eyes became small beads, his expression a mask of annoyance. "I'm still looking for a pair of needle-nose pliers. And a C-clamp." He looked Ethan up and down, into his lap, as though he might be hiding them in his clothes. "You don't happen to know where they are?"

Ethan smiled gamely. "I wouldn't know."

Chester glared at both of them. "One of these days I'll get you back."

"Yeah, right."

Chester lumbered away.

"Call me, text me," said Roger.

"I will, Roger."

Roger put his hand on Ethan's arm and squeezed. "Take care," he said to both of them." He headed toward the door.

"Who was that guy with Roger?" asked Sophie. "Why was he talking about tools?"

"That's Chester. He's just joking. We took some of his tools years ago when he was building stuff at the Y for the summer camp. We hid them all over the place, so it was like an Easter egg hunt, he had to find them all. He's always joking about it."

"So, can we go see your ships?"

Sophie looked through the wavy glass of the bottle as Ethan explained what was happening to the ship: it was stuck in the ice, probably sinking. Those were Eskimos looking at it.

Sophie shivered. It was almost as cold as the Arctic in the basement. "Why's your house so cold?"

"The furnace is broken. I can make a fire upstairs."

His mom was out. Ethan made tea and a fire in the woodstove in the living room. They ate crackers covered with some jam he found in a little blue jar in the refrigerator.

Sophie's phone vibrated in the pocket of her jeans.

"Do you want to get that?"

"No," she said. "It's my mother."

For some reason they both found this funny. They began giggling. Ethan pulled a throw over themselves on the sofa. Ethan heard his own laughter, which sounded young and babyish, but he couldn't stop it. And Sophie was making the same sort of noise, higher-pitched and sweet. When there was a pause, Ethan reached for the little blue jar he'd found in the refrigerator. He stuck his finger into the sweet-but-earthy-tasting jam. It had produced a slight, pleasant bubble effect on his tongue.

"Want some more?" He offered it to Sophie.

She shook her head and sat up. "I better go soon."

They both heard knocking on the door. They dropped down onto the sofa cushions and stared at each other.

Ethan whispered, "At least we know it's not my mother."

They tried not to laugh. Sophie put a hand over his mouth, and Ethan put his hand over her mouth, and they were reduced to stifled snorts. He pulled her hand away and gasped for air. Sophie rolled on top of him and clamped her hand over his mouth again, her face inches above his.

From outside the door. "Hello?"

Sophie's eyes widened with alarm. "*It's my dad!*" she whispered.

148

PETER NICHOLS

"Hello? Isabel?"

They stared at each other, aware of their bodies sandwiched together, and the new thing that was happening between them.

"Hello? Ethan?" Sophie's father—*the detective's voice!*—

Sophie's phone vibrated again. It was in the front pocket of her jeans, vibrating between them. Ethan felt it throbbing into his crotch.

"Oh wow—"

"*Shh!*" Sophie dropped her face until her lips covered Ethan's. He felt their swelling size and soft shape. He opened his mouth slightly, and her lips parted too and their tongues met, warm, wet, tentative. His eyes closed, and for a moment he existed entirely inside their two mouths.

They both heard the car start and drive away. Sophie raised her face, her mouth still open.

Ethan said, "My mom'll probably be home soon."

"I better go home." She rolled off him and pulled out her phone to look at it. "Yeah. My mom. Once she starts she never stops."

They stood up, swayed and held on to each other. Sophie looked at his full lips and kissed him again.

30

"Why aren't you eating your dinner?" Morgana asked. "That's a beautiful and perfectly cooked piece of wild salmon. From Alaska. Eat up."

Sophie saw that poor wild salmon with a big hook in its mouth, twisting violently as it was pulled out of the water, then its rotting flesh as it was shipped thousands of miles on a bed of slushy ice. "I'm not hungry," she said.

"What is the matter with you?" Morgana peered into her face. "You're white as a sheet."

Sophie thought she was going to throw up. "I don't feel well."

"Then you'd better go up to your room." Morgana removed the plate and put it on the granite counter near the sink. "You can eat it for breakfast."

Sophie almost barfed right then. She got off her stool, scooped up Bella, her dachshund, and left the kitchen.

Her bedroom on the second floor of Belleport was not like the warm, mussed, comfortable, personalized bedrooms of her teenage friends, full of untidily tossed fleece throws and posters of boy bands, Taylor Swift, makeup, clothes stuffed into corners—or her room at her father's house, with the books he'd bought her that she didn't read, but with her own stuff she'd put on the shelves, photographs and pictures on the walls that she'd chosen. A room she'd made her own and liked to spend time in with her friends.

Her bedroom at Belleport was like a museum space. A young lady's bedroom designed, curated, a showplace for the treasures Morgana had bought for Sophie over the years: the Matisse with the floating girls, the original Broadway poster of *The King and I* starring Gertrude Lawrence and Yul Brynner. The French cabinet with beveled glass holding netsuke pieces from the Edo period. The four Noh masks, faces of highly individual character, yet scarily devoid of the spark of life, hanging on a wall. All were as familiar to Sophie as her own hand, but they meant nothing to her. She was allowed to sleep in the hand-painted bed, use the en suite bathroom and walk-in closet, the leather-topped French Empire desk with a protective plastic sheet on which to do her homework, but she wasn't allowed to touch the treasures or be messy and make more work for Roxanna, her mother's cleaning lady.

Twenty minutes later, she was lying on her bed, rolled over on her right side facing away from the door, wrapped around Bella, Snapchatting with her friend Christina, when her mother abruptly opened the door.

"Get up," said Morgana.

"What?"

Bella leaped off the bed and shot out the door.

Her mother took Sophie's hand and pulled her onto her feet. "Come with me."

"What? What's going on?"

Morgana opened the door to the bathroom, pushed Sophie in, and handed her a tall water glass. "Pee in that."

"What?"

"Pee."

"*Mo-om?* What's going on?"

"That's what I want to know." Morgana stood implacably before her, her closed fists pushed into her hips. "You're not leaving this bathroom until you pee into that glass."

Sophie sat down on the toilet seat. "Why are you doing this?"

"Because you're high as a kite. What is it?"

"I'm not."

"Don't lie to me. I know you've taken drugs, Sophie. I *know*, okay? Do you think I, your mother, who knows you better than you know yourself or anyone ever will, can't see it?"

"But I haven't! I haven't, Mom."

Abruptly, Morgana's face crumpled and she began to cry. "Sophie, you have no idea what I do for you. What I've tried to give you. I love you more than you'll ever understand. And I can't imagine you would ever do this to me if you loved me." Morgana leaned back against the sink and wailed with a long keening sound.

Sophie began to cry. "Mom, please don't cry. You know I love you too." She stood up and hugged her mother, and they cried together. "Mom, I know what you do for me, and you know I love you."

They hugged and wept, and each said *I love you* to the other several times.

"But I haven't done anything, Mom."

"Well, we'll see, right?" Morgana gripped Sophie's arm with one hand, pushed her down onto the toilet, and held out the glass with the other hand. "Weed? Bong? Ecstasy? Something *mellow* for sure, because, darlin', you are out of your gourd. And you think I can't even see it."

"I didn't take anything!"

"I've got all night," said Morgana, blinking her tears away furiously.

Still crying, Sophie unbelted her jeans, pulled them down, sat on the toilet. After a while, it came. Sophie's shoulders were shaking as she handed the glass to her mother.

Morgana placed it beside the sink and drew out of her pocket the Walgreens twelve-panel drug test she'd just raced out to buy, and placed the panel in the glass. "We'll just see."

Sophie pulled up her jeans and returned to her bed. Morgana came into the room and sat down on the bed. She stroked Sophie's hair.

"Darlin', you think I don't know anything about drugs? My dear, I took *everything*. But later, when I was at college, not at your age. I know what happens. Who was it? That big cave boy Jordan? Richie Podolsky?"

Sophie didn't answer. Her mother stroked her hair for another minute, before she got up and went into the bathroom. Then she came back.

"Take a look."

Sophie didn't move for a moment. But she was curious. Her mother was right: she wasn't herself. Things had been intense with Ethan. They hadn't been able to stop laughing. But the salmon. And the way her bedroom sort of . . . *barked* at her when she came into it this evening.

She rolled over and took a look at the closely spaced thin panels her mother was holding between her thumb and forefinger.

The panels were clear.

"These tests are useless on hallucinogens. So what was it? Acid? Mushrooms? You need to tell me, Sophie. Or I will ground you for a month."

"I've told you, Mom. Nothing."

"I know you're on something. It's not alcohol, so what *is it*, Sophie? Tell me!"

"Nothing!" Sophie sat up. The clear panels fueled her outrage. "I told you, I didn't take anything! Stop bullying me!"

"Bullying you? I am your mother. I'm *in charge of you. And your well-being.*"

"So? Does that give you the right to bully me? Leave me alone!" A force welled up inside her like a sneeze, filling her with a molten fury. She shrieked. "*Go away! Go AWAY!*"

Morgana was startled. Sophie had never spoken to her like this. Her face was contorted and strange, white with striations of color on her neck and cheeks. The big SHANE letters on her forehead still dark and horrifying. "Sophie, what is happening to you? I don't recognize you."

"I recognize *you!*" Sophie rose on her knees on the bed and at the same time backed away from her mother, holding a pillow to her chest. "You're a bully. You bully me and you bully Dad." A fury, validated by the clean results of her drug test, filled her. "Now *leave me alone!*"

Sophie's face transmogrified, quite suddenly, from a familiar cast of small, hurt, unhappiness, into a mask of eye-blazing hatred.

Morgana's own eyes hardened into a calm, stone-cold regard. Her daughter was clearly in the grip of whatever had violently distorted her personality. Ayahuasca? Who knew what was available to schoolchildren now. And her father—the *policeman!*—unable to stop her. More likely unaware. A fool.

She spoke now in a voice Sophie had learned to dislike. The acquired moderation of her accent slipped away and the words came in the broader twang of Morgana's natural West Texas Hill Country: "You better mind your p's and q's, my girl, or you're going to *thrive.*"

Sophie was suddenly afraid. "What do you mean, thrive?"

Her mother laughed, softly. "Oh, that's just a lil'ol place down in Texas."

Morgana left the room. She closed the door with an expensive click that was satisfying to them both.

Sophie rolled off the bed and went to her desk. She opened her computer and typed into Google: *Thrive Texas.* It came up immediately.

Thrive Girls Ranch & Home

A year-round Christian boarding school in Central Texas for girls ages twelve to seventeen who are misbehaving and struggling with self-destructive or dangerous behaviors. We help girls transform into responsible, respectful, and gracious young women.

31

Isabel was sitting on the granite steps outside his kitchen door when Alex pulled up in his Subaru. She stood as he got out of his car and came toward her.

"I need to talk with you," she said.

Inside, Alex made tea. She sat as she used to on the big sofa in the breakfast room off the kitchen. The wall of double-glazed windows looked out at the garden, now almost tucked in for its dormant winter.

Five years in a blink.

He'd found the house, a small converted barn, in the classifieds of the *Granite Harbor Herald*, when it was still printed on paper, the first place he looked at and took immediately as Morgana moved swiftly to divorce him, thinking it would do for a while. He'd now lived here twelve years, longer than he'd lived anywhere since leaving his childhood home in Manchester.

He brought in two mugs of tea, placed them on the coffee table, and sat in the threadbare armchair facing her across the coffee table.

"I was hoping to talk with Ethan. I went by the house, but no one was home."

"I'm sorry. I didn't get it together today. He's home, he texted me. What do you want to talk to him about?"

"His clothes. Apparently, he wears some expensive hoodies."

"It's all secondhand. He buys and sells used clothing and sneakers online.

He makes a little money from that and from his ship models, but none of the stuff he buys and wears is expensive."

"Maybe it's more than you know."

"I know how much it costs, and what it costs new. He shows me. It's not expensive. Why?"

"Do you know if he's doing any drugs?"

She looked at him sharply. "I don't know. Maybe some weed. Why?"

"Anything harder? Any mushrooms?"

"I don't think so. Why? Was Shane?"

"We're looking into everything." Alex tried to make it sound vague. "Why are you here?"

Isabel took off her hat, a slouchy snood, throwing it on the sofa beside her coat. He'd made a point of not looking at her closely in front of Ethan in their kitchen. She'd worn her hair—which he'd loved, dark and wavy—below her shoulders when they'd been together. Now he looked at her buzz cut. It was still dark, and thick, with new hints of white. She was all face now. As though she had stripped naked, with nothing to conceal her.

"I never told you some stuff. About me."

"Okay." He sat back in the chair and sipped his tea.

"I knew Joshua wasn't coming back. I knew it before he left. I didn't tell him, I didn't want to sound hysterical or irrational. As you know, I sailed to the Caribbean with him before Ethan was born. He knew what he was doing. Lots of people sail across the Atlantic all the time, alone, and they're usually fine. There was no reason for me to think that anything would happen. He was very capable. So I didn't say, 'I'm sure you're going to die, please don't go.'"

"It was probably natural."

"No, it wasn't like that," she said quickly. "That's what I'm trying to tell you. I saw his boat being destroyed. It was very specific. I saw it being crushed and splintered, going down fast in the water. I *saw* it. Vividly."

"What, like—"

"Like I was there. *Not* like a dream. I saw it, felt it, heard it."

He nodded, trying to make his face open, nonjudgmental.

"I'm getting to my point—why I'm here. I have to tell you this first."

"Okay."

"As you know, Joshua never arrived in England. There was no weather system around him when we last heard from him. I'm sure he was run down by a ship. Maybe I told you that."

"I remember you saying something like that."

"The point is, I knew Joshua wasn't coming back because *I'd seen it.*"

"Okay."

"Since then, I've seen other things. A girl, Amy Leroy, went missing in the winter, four years ago. I saw where she was, though I didn't know the place. I'd never been there. I told the state police—"

"The girl in the toboggan chute."

"Yes."

"The official story was that someone provided information, but in the department we heard that it was a clairvoyant. Or something like that. That was you?"

"Psychic, clairvoyant, second sight—all those labels carry associations. I knew people would start asking me all sorts of things, so I told the police I didn't want anyone to know it was me. And it doesn't happen often."

"So, you've seen something?"

"Alex, stop interrupting me," she said impatiently. "You're always doing that."

"I'm sorry," he said. He knew he had a tendency to finish other people's sentences, move a conversation along.

Isabel's eyes bored into him "There's a trigger. And an association. With Joshua, I was helping him get ready for his race, stowing things aboard his boat. One of them was a flare kit. It's like a little toolbox with a flare gun and flares to shoot off if you're in trouble. You can shoot off a flare that might be seen by ships in the area or maybe an aircraft, especially at night. I was putting the kit in a locker in the boat and I was suddenly aware that there wouldn't be time to get it out and shoot off a flare. I had the kit in my hand and those words came into my head: 'there won't be time.' And then I saw the boat being crushed and going down fast. Like I was there. I saw it. I heard it."

Alex remained still. He waited a moment, almost asked a question, and then she spoke.

"The trigger for the toboggan chute was Ethan. He'd met Amy three weeks earlier on a school ski trip to Sunday River, and he was upset when she went missing. She'd given him a friendship bracelet she'd made. When he showed me the bracelet I touched it, and I saw her in the toboggan chute. I knew she was there and very cold. I felt the ice and the tightness of the toboggan chute that was holding her in. Like I was there too."

After a long moment, he said, "Can I ask a question?"

"Yes."

"So it's touch? The flare kit and then the bracelet?"

"That, and maybe other things. All I know is it's connected to someone close to me: Joshua, and then Ethan—it had nothing to do with the girl, but he had feelings for her. It's something that affects someone I love."

"Got it."

She took a deep breath, sipped her tea, and held her mug in both hands.

"Last night I saw something again."

"Okay."

"It was on Ethan. It was trying to get into him."

"What was?"

"An animal. I was asleep but I saw it . . . it wasn't a dream, it was very real to me. And then I went into his room and stripped his bed while he was in it and looked for it. But of course it wasn't there. But it was as real as Joshua's sinking and the girl stuck in the toboggan."

"All right. And how do you mean, it was trying to get into him?"

"It was burrowing into his stomach. There was a hole in Ethan's stomach and it was trying to get in."

Alex couldn't wait any longer. "What was it? The animal?"

Her eyes found his and focused. "A frog."

32

The toad, the location of Shane's wound, had not been released to the public. No one knew these things except the police, Agent Harris and the FBI, the forensics team from Bangor, the medical examiner, and the murderer.

Yet Isabel knew.

What would a real detective do with this? Alex asked himself. Because he didn't feel like a real detective, particularly at this moment, when he wanted to believe Isabel, wanted to believe that she had conjured up this information from her dream or whatever it was, and had not killed Shane herself.

Because a *real* detective—*you understand, Alex,* he heard himself saying to himself—a real detective would now realize that Isabel was mad. A psychopath who was having visions and was now, right in front of him, making a subconscious confession, or giving a cry for help. The real detective, an organized, methodical professional, would have had his wits about him and recorded this conversation. Because it would now be clear to that detective that Isabel was the murderer—how else would she know these details? She'd broken into the William P. Merrill Station and opened his computer?—and he would arrest her, take her off to the station, and put all the other stuff, Byron Pugh, etc., together with Special Agent Harris, who would help him see how it all *must* fit together.

Because otherwise, he was an unprofessional credulous fool, who didn't want to believe that this shaven-headed, obviously distressed woman, was a mad killer. Alex, the sham detective, wanted to deny every shred of the real evidence that had just been presented to him, suspend common sense, believe in supernatural visions, and put his arm around this woman, whose warm scalp he kept wanting to put his hand on.

"What was the trigger?" he asked.

She looked at him, trying to think.

"The flare kit with your husband, the friendship bracelet with Ethan. What was it this time?"

"I think it was something I touched—or ate. A blue jar. The electuary."

"Electuary?"

"It's like a jam—a tonic, Roger called it. What the early settlers used to take, like a medicine, when they weren't feeling well. I ate some last night."

"Roger Priestly—the apothecary at the Settlement . . . He gave it to you?"

"Yes. He makes it. He makes stuff, natural things, potions, whatever. He gave me a jar yesterday and I ate some last night. It made me feel strange. Almost like I was on something. And then . . . I had this experience."

"And the connection to someone you love is obviously Ethan."

"Yes."

"Did the frog get into him? Or it was just trying?"

"It was trying. There was a hole, or a wound, and it was trying to get in."

"But Ethan's okay. Or do you believe now that something will happen to him?"

"I believe something will happen to him. Now please tell me how Shane died. Did something like that happen to him?"

"Well, there were a number of—"

"*Alex!*" She almost screamed across the coffee table at him. Her face carried what she had seen—or was still seeing. "Do you hear what I'm telling you! I'm terrified for Ethan. Can't you be open with me? For God's sake, Alex. Tell me what's going on. What happened to Shane?"

"He had a stomach wound. It didn't kill him."

"Was there an animal—a frog? Inside him?"

How could she know this?

But if he wasn't going to arrest her and bring in a criminal psychiatrist, then he was committing himself to another path.

Because, if he persisted in believing her, ignoring fact and common sense, it was a lead.

"Something like that. Yes. A wound. There was a toad inside him. The wound didn't kill him. He was asphyxiated."

Isabel dropped her head in her hands and sobbed. He resisted the impulse to cross the room and put his arms around her. He got up and came back with a glass of water and a tissue, which he put on the table in front of her.

She took a sip of water. Dried her eyes with the tissue.

"Isabel."

"Yes?"

"Have you still got it?"

"What?"

"The stuff Roger gave you. That you ate. And the jar?"

"Yes."

"Can you give it to me? I can have a lab look at it. See what's in it. Is there any left?"

"Yes, I didn't finish it."

"Do you think—I understand what you saw, it's horrible—but if you ate some more of that stuff, do you think you might . . . see more? Like—I don't know—who's doing it? Or does it not work like that?"

33

Today, Isabel tapped gently on Ethan's door—she had learned in every unwelcome way the mother of a teenage son might, not to enter his room unannounced, except in panic. Hearing nothing, she gripped and turned the vintage brass doorknob—obtained along with all the others in the house at a restoration supply barn in Hallowell, a relic of the happy time when she and Joshua had renovated the house in the months before Ethan's birth.

She pushed the door open.

The skinny lower legs, now showing dark hair, and long—lengthening weekly—feet stuck out of the comforter. She knelt beside the bed where his head was mostly hidden except for a mass of curly brown hair.

"Ethan."

For a moment nothing. Then his face appeared beneath an edge of the comforter. "Oh, Jesus, not again." He snatched at the comforter and rolled away from her.

"It's okay, don't worry. I'm just . . . Did you eat the electuary? The stuff in the blue jar. Like a jam? It says 'Bowles's Electuary' on it. I can't find it."

Silence from under the covers. "Oh . . . yeah."

"You did? You ate it?"

"Not all of it."

"Where is it? I can't find it."

"I don't know." He sounded annoyed. "That's what you woke me up for? Mom, you're kind of losing it, you know."

"Don't worry about me. Did you finish it?"

"No. I don't know, Mom. Let me sleep. Jesus." He moved even closer to the wall.

"How did it make you feel?"

He didn't answer and for a moment she thought he'd fallen back asleep. Then he rolled over and lowered the comforter from his eyes, still holding it over his nose and mouth. "It was kind of weird."

"How was it weird?"

"I don't know." He pulled the comforter over his head again.

In the kitchen, she looked in the garbage beneath the sink. There was the jar, pale blue against the white plastic garbage bag, like a watercolor wash.

Not quite empty. Round smears left by a swiping finger near the top. A teaspoonful maybe at the bottom.

Alex was waiting outside his kitchen door as she turned into his driveway on Mountain Street. Hunched shoulders inside his morning running clothes, sipping coffee. She knew his routine: he'd already run up and down Mount Meguntic. She pulled forward. He came up as she lowered her window. She handed him a Ziploc bag with the little blue jar inside it.

"Ethan got into it. Is there enough in there for a lab?"

He held up the bag. "Probably. They don't need much. Is there enough for you to take some more? Is it eating the stuff or touching the jar? The trigger?"

"I don't know. I've touched the jar plenty this morning. I can ask Roger for some more."

"Don't do that. Please."

"Why not?"

"Just better if we keep this between us. When do you want to try again?"

"I'll let you know," she said.

"I want to be with you when you do. Is that all right? Could you maybe do it here?"

"We'll see."

As she backed out and drove down Mountain Street, she saw him in the mirror watching her, until the house blocked her view of his driveway.

She had an errand in town at the end of the day. It was dark when she got home. She called downstairs. "Ethan, are you home?"

"Yes," came the reply.

"I'm going to take Flynn out and then make dinner."

"Okay."

"Don't go anywhere, please."

Annoyed shout. "Okay!"

After the walk, she took a brief freezing shower—she'd gotten used to it. She rubbed coconut oil over her buzz cut, into her face, and dressed in sweats. She brought the space heater downstairs to the kitchen, made her nonalcoholic cocktail—tonic, bitters, slice of lemon. The soothing placebo effect was immediate.

She set the table. She lit candles. She used linen napkins instead of paper towels.

"Ethan," she called downstairs.

Just before she was about to call again, he came up and sat at the table. He was looking at his phone, thumbing the screen.

"Put the phone away, please," she said as she brought their plates to the table.

She sat down across the table from him.

"Ethan."

"Okay," he said, eyes glued to the screen, thumb still tapping as his hand moved to lay the phone down.

"Away, please. Not on the table."

"Okay!" He put the phone in his pocket. He reached for his glass of milk. He picked it up, sipped, and looked across the table at his mother.

"*Whoa!*"

The milk spilled as he set the glass down with a bang.

"*Ohhh* . . . Oh . . . my . . . God. Mom . . ." His eyes ranged across her forehead.

"You approve?" she asked.

He lowered his gaze and looked into her eyes. Then back up at her forehead again. The inked SHANE was fresh, dark. A big smile spread across his face. "Yes, I approve. Wow, Mom. I can't believe it. I love you."

"I love you too, Ethan."

34

In the afternoons, the boy worked with Ivan Haney to clear the tree limbs downed by winter storms around the Welldale grounds. They chainsawed them into short logs ready for splitting into cordwood, spattering new blond sawdust and wood chips over the clean snow.

Beneath the snow, where it was thin along the edges of the woods, mice, voles, and small creatures scurried. Woodcocks and whip-poor-wills laid scrape nests on the forest floor, which drew the foxes and coyotes he'd seen loping in the distance across the fields against the white snow as the trees grew bare in the winter.

Here, along the rodent runs, Ivan Haney had set the rusty spring trap, its arcing sawtooth jaws black with old blood, except for the bright steel where Haney had filed the teeth sharp. Its chain was secured by an eighteen-inch spiral anchor screwed deep into the ground, and they found the trapped creature when they tramped across the meadow after lunch with their axes and chain saw. Its right foreleg was clamped tight in the black and steel-shiny teeth. He saw the white bone glinting above the jaws where the animal had tried to gnaw its leg free.

"He'd a chawed that leg clean off in another hour," observed Haney.

He was surprised by the animal's size: it was as big as a large dog. But he could see it was no dog. Its fur was thick and rippled in waves along its spine as it trembled. In its eyes, fixed on them as they approached, he saw a wildness, a hatred of the two men he had never seen in another animal.

"Is it a wolf?"

"Nope. No wolves in Maine. This here's your eastern coyote. He's smarter'n any wolf. Canny as a fox. More adaptable."

"He looks big," said the boy, standing a little behind Haney.

"Yup." Haney looked the animal over with satisfaction. "He's a big ole warrior male. He's got a fierceness and a cunning in him you won't see in another animal. Except some kinds of human beings."

Haney pulled a coiled length of cord from the oil-stained canvas bag they carried with them. He tied a bow at one end and ran the other end of the cord through it, making a sliding noose.

The coyote's eyes fixed on Haney, the alpha of the two humans, the one who spoke and directed the other. It tried frantically to leap away as Haney stepped toward it, its leg hauling the trap along the ground as the chain rattled until it straightened, quivering along its full length to the anchor. Haney stepped on the trap, causing the coyote to roll on its side, and then put his other boot onto the coyote's neck. His enormous hands worked deftly as he slipped the noose over its waving nose, over the head and ears and pulled it tight around the neck. He smartly wound the rest of the rope around the writhing coyote, binding it tight. Then he opened the trap jaws and freed the coyote's leg.

"Find me a toad, Mister," said Ivan.

The boy knew where to look. In a short time, he found one hibernating beneath a log beside the small pond at the edge of the field. He ran back and presented the toad.

"Put him in your coat pocket."

Haney hauled the trussed coyote by the cord through the fields as it emitted a long guttural whine, half terror, half threat. The boy followed, carrying the opened trap and chain and the canvas bag. His eyes were fastened on the squirming animal. Even bound with rope, he was afraid of it. It was like a creature in a story, not from real life. But here it was. He felt its eyes on him. He didn't get too close.

In the small aluminum Quonset hut adjoining the Shack, where Haney kept his own supply of cordwood and larger tools, he laid the coyote on the ground. It twisted violently, arched its back, and tried to snap its jaws at Haney as he tied more rope to its legs and the ends of the rope to fixed points at the four corners of the hut, until the coyote was splayed open, outstretched. Its mouth snapped the air, but its waving head had a short reach.

He didn't see the buck knife until Ivan put it in his hand.

"Open it."

He pulled with his fingertips. The blade emerged from the bone handle like a long limb from clothing. The carbon steel stained dark as a winter sky, except for its quicksilver whetstoned edge.

Then Ivan gripped the boy's hand inside his own. Almost a creature itself with its thick carapace and arthritis-bulbed joints and long, blood-dried appendages. Before he understood what was happening, he and Ivan were pushing the blade into the fur just below the center of the rib cage.

"Not deep. Just through the wall. Like a pie crust."

Or the skin of a frog embalmed with formaldehyde. This was thicker and Ivan's hand determined the pressure, but he felt the puncture of the wall, how just the tip of the blade floated beneath it.

Ivan released his hand. "Now draw it downward through his belly. Same depth, just like you got it. Straight down, like you're undoing a zipper."

A long squeal came from the coyote's throat. The animal twisted frantically, but Haney again placed one boot on its neck and the other on its tail, and this curtailed its struggle. The fur was short beneath the ribs and gave way to pink skin on the belly and the blade left a clean opening with barely any blood in its wake.

He unzipped the coyote.

"Good," said Ivan. "Keep going down. That's good. Gimme the knife."

Ivan wiped the blade with a cloth, and closed it.

"Now get your toad."

The boy had forgotten. It was still in his pocket. He fished it out. Ivan pulled open the slit he'd cut in the coyote. The boy recognized what he saw from Mr. Williams's class, though now the living organs heaved and pulsed beneath the fur.

"Slip Mr. Toad in there. Just push him in."

He did as instructed. He felt the heat of the organs. It was easy. Ivan removed his bloodied hands and the incision closed over Mr. Toad while the coyote continued to struggle against the ropes and its stomach rose and fell.

"Will the toad die in there?"

"Nossir. He'll be fine. He'll probably have himself a warm nap. We done this with our captured Cong. The kind of toads we found in the jungle in Nam was called Uncles of Heaven. Because they're brave, or lucky, or some such thing they say there. They were big fellas. Their bitter pus was some powerful juju."

"You put them in people?"

"If you want to call 'em that."

As always, the boy took in the competence of Ivan's skill, his knowledge of the coyote, its behavior and anatomy, the woods, the arrangement of the trap and where to lay it, the efficiency of his rope and knife work, the fluent deployment of his large hands, still nimble enough to thread a needle. He had never admired another person, except his father in dimly remembered moments when his father steered his boat and maneuvered it alongside a dock. Ivan was master of the world around him. His knowledge of everything he touched was a lodestar to the boy. The stirrings of thoughts about what he himself might someday be capable of.

"We'll leave Mr. Toad to marinate for a while."

In the kitchen, Haney washed and dried his hands. He went to a bookshelf and pulled out an old brown, leatherbound book. "Now you sit."

They both settled into their customary chairs at the table.

Haney put on a pair of goggle-size readers, opened the book and laid it on the table.

"'*Principia Magister,*'" he read slowly from the title page, separating and enunciating the syllables. He looked across the table, his eyes huge through the lenses. "That's Latin for 'Principles of the Master.' Now . . ." He turned pages slowly, his eyes wavering over the text. "'If a live pigeon be cut through the heart . . .'" He looked over at the boy again with a poker face.

He understood that Ivan was being funny and emitted a small laugh.

"We don't need to know the properties of the pigeon right now."

He turned pages. Then flattened the book and read again. "'*Bufonus Medicamen.* Both Paraclesus and Helmont agree that the Toad hath a natural abhorrence to the sight of Man that congeals into a hatred he carries in his head, lodged behind his very eyes, so that a poison ariseth in the Toad and is released in the foulness of his pus. *Ex turpi serpentis nova essentia creata est.'* That means, 'Out of the foulness of the toad is created a new essence.'"

Haney looked over at the boy. He closed the book. "I'll spare you the Latin lesson. Point is, you place a toad inside the viscera of a host—in its guts—and it absorbs the properties of that host. Then you pull it out and take into yourself the bitter pus of Mr. Toad, and thereby acquire the properties—the character, the essence—of that host. You got me?"

The boy blinked.

"Never mind. Come with me."

Out in the Quonset hut, the coyote was still wriggling at the apex of the ropes binding it to the four corners. Haney again placed his foot on its neck.

"Take that toad out."

He put his hand into the coyote. It was blood warm. Everything in there was heaving, as if pulled by a tide. Except for one thing. His hand closed over the toad, and he pulled it out.

In the kitchen again, Haney turned on the tap over the sink.

"Wash that blood off him. Now put him down there." Indicating the kitchen table.

Haney lit the kerosene lamp that swung over the table. The toad's shadow moved around it on the tabletop, making the animal appear to waver and lurch from side to side. It seemed none the worse for its immersion inside the coyote. Its eyes were half closed.

Now Haney picked up the toad. He arranged it in his left hand, closing his fingers over most of the body, leaving only the large head exposed. With his right thumb he began to press on the raised lump on the toad's head, behind one eye. Drops of white fluid popped out of the pores of the skin beneath his thumb.

"That's where Mr. Toad keeps his bitter pus—his juju juice."

The toad seemed unperturbed, staring unblinking into space as Haney continued to press until the drops merged into a larger blob, like water forming a small puddle from a series of drops.

"Now scoop that up with your finger and rub it around inside your mouth. Over the gums, under the tongue. Like you're rubbing salt into meat. Then suck your finger clean and swaller it all down."

The boy hesitated.

"Go on now."

He wiped his finger across the bulge where the white secretion had pooled. He spread it around inside his mouth as instructed. It sure tasted bitter.

Haney swabbed at the gland with his own finger and sucked on it. Then he moved his thumb and pressed down behind the other eye until it exuded more white secretion. "Take another swab."

The boy rubbed the goo again around his mouth.

"Swaller it down."

The boy gulped and swallowed.

Haney held the toad beneath the kerosene lamp, and looked at it. "Mr. Toad absorbs into his own self the qualities of the host's nature. When you take his bitter pus into your own self—like you just done—the particular nature of that host, Mr. Coyote, becomes a part of your nature. *'Ex turpi serpentis nova essentia creata est.'* Out of the foulness of the toad is created a new essence. You will now have the essence of this coyote—his fierceness and his cunning—in your own nature. You got me, Mister?"

"Yes, Ivan." His tongue was moving around inside his mouth, which was feeling numb.

In the hut, the coyote's mouth gaped wetly as it panted.

"Now return the toad to the host."

He pushed the toad back into the blood-smeared wound.

"That binds you and the host together. You got me?"

"Yes, Ivan."

Haney gathered some lengths of lumber. He tossed a hammer and nails into the oil-stained canvas bag.

"Here, you carry this. And some of these sticks. We're going to build us a proscenium. You know what that is?"

The boy shook his head.

"The host shall afterward be displayed in a public place, within a proscenium. That's the space inside of a theater between the curtains. Or like a picture frame. The proscenium frames your new powers for the world. You don't have to show everybody, but it has to be out there, in some place where you are. They don't need to know you done it, but they'll feel your new power."

He untied the coyote's legs. They twitched but its body no longer twisted, its strength gone. He dragged it by the noose around its neck back into the woods. He knelt in the snow and quickly, efficiently, nailed together the pieces of lumber into a crude rectangular frame, about the size and width of a door. He leaned it against a tree. He threw the line over the top section of the frame and pulled until the coyote's body was hoisted within the structure, and he tied off the cord. Still the animal shuddered as it dangled.

"This is what we done to our Cong prey in the jungle. They were some will-o'-the-wisp jungle creatures, them skinny fucks. They moved through that vegetation like snakes and bats. After that, we acquired their essence, their jungle cunning, and we became like snakes and bats. Now you say it. '*Ex turpi serpentis nova essentia creata est.*' Out of the foulness of the toad is created a new essence."

"Out of the—"

"You got to say it in Latin." Ivan repeated it again, slowly. "*Ex turpi serpentis . . .*"

"*Ex turpi serpentis . . .*" the boy repeated.

"*Nova essentia creata est.*"

"*Nova essentia creata est.*"

"There you go," said Ivan. He clapped the boy on the back. "You have acquired the essence of Mr. Coyote. What runs through his veins will now run through yours."

The boy stared at the coyote hanging inside the frame. One of its eyes fixed on him.

Then the coyote addressed him by name.

"Yes?" the boy answered.

"My essence is running inside your veins now. You have my fierce strength and cunning. You will have my power over all the creatures of the woods and fields. Do you feel your new strength that came from me out of the bitter pus of the toad?"

He did. He had swallowed the bitter pus of the toad that had been pulled from the bowels of the coyote. He'd felt it tingling in the roof of his mouth, in the back of his throat. And now he became aware of the sleek, wild power he had seen in the live, quivering animal. It was coursing through his body. He trembled with it. His muscles rippled beneath his skin. He had become the master predator of his domain.

"Yes, I feel it," said the boy.

"Okay, then," said the coyote.

35

Isabel didn't want to do it alone.

"Absolutely," said Alex over the phone. "I want to be there with you. Maybe you'll talk out loud, or remember things you'll forget later. Your place or mine?"

His, they decided. She imagined Ethan coming in unexpectedly and finding Alex leaning over her unconscious body. And it was warm at his house.

They waited two days, until Ethan was spending the night at Jared's, and Sophie was at her mother's. Isabel arrived at 6:00 P.M. She'd brought crackers and detox tea.

"Can you boil some water, please?"

She sat on the sofa and took off her coat and beanie.

"Oh——" His stare landing just above her eyes. "You got one too."

Her hand went automatically to her forehead. "Yes."

"I imagine Ethan was pleased."

"Yes, it meant a lot to him. You should get one." Alex looked tired, she thought. The circles under his eyes were almost as dark as her tattoo.

"Perhaps another time."

When the tea was ready, he set it on the coffee table in front of her. She opened the blue jar and spread the dark goo on a cracker. "There's not much left. It probably won't work anyway."

"I understand. I appreciate your trying, though."

She looked at the cracker with its smear, and took a bite.

"What does it taste like?" he asked.

"Rooty . . . earthy. Sweetened with something."

The cracker and its topping became liquid in her mouth. A dark, earthen soup. She swallowed and almost retched.

Alex was staring at her. "Are you all right?"

Why had she agreed? To help him find the killer, of course, if this would help. To protect Ethan. But now that it came to it, she didn't want to. She didn't want to see that thing trying to burrow into Ethan again.

"I think I'm afraid. I don't want to see it again. I don't think I'll see anything else."

"I understand. But here you are. And you've started, you've eaten some of it. How are you feeling?"

She was still holding a small piece of the first cracker, with the stuff on it. She put it down. "Sort of . . ."

The musky taste, a filmy slickness, like oil, coated the roof of her mouth. Her mouth was empty but she swallowed spasmodically. Her throat contracted.

"You look kind of—"

She jumped up and ran through the kitchen to the bathroom. It was in her mouth before she knelt over the toilet. It surged into her nose and splattered, a thin dark gruel, into the bowl. She'd eaten hardly anything all day, there was nothing inside her to come out, yet she retched convulsively. She flushed the toilet, continued to retch and flush again, producing nothing further than a long string of viscous drool that hung and would not fall from her mouth.

As the racking heaves subsided, she realized Alex was kneeling behind her, his hands on her shoulders. When she could, she sat back on her heels.

"Here," he said. He handed her a small towel. "Are you okay?"

"Yes."

He helped her stand. They returned to the breakfast room and she sat down on the sofa. He brought her a glass of water. She was shaking.

He left the room and returned with a small red fleece throw. He sat down on the sofa beside her and draped it over her.

"Were you sick, or did you feel sick, last time?"

"No."

He put his arm around her. "Is this okay?"

She didn't want to answer.

He moved closer.

After a little while, she stopped shaking. She felt warm again.

She remembered the time they'd spent on this sofa together. Hours. For months.

She was aware of his arm around her. His breathing. The rise and fall of his chest against her.

A tremendous warmth arose between them.

She stood up.

"Are you feeling sick again?"

"No. It's not happening—it's not going to work." She started pulling on her coat.

He stood too now. "Wait—are you sure? You're reacting to something, I can tell. People throw up on ayahuasca when their bodies begin to register the effect. It's a sign of something happening." He put his palm across the SHANE on her forehead. "You're hot. Flushed, I can feel it."

"I'm all right. I'm going to go."

She pulled on her beanie.

"Isabel, wait. What if it comes over you when you leave?"

"It won't. I'm sorry I threw up. Your phone's been vibrating in the kitchen."

He followed her outside. As she opened her car door, his hand gripped her upper arm, pulling her toward him, to face him. For a moment the movement filled her with sense memory. She pulled her arm away and got into the car.

"Isabel." He looked alarmed. "It's dark. Let me drive you."

"I'm okay." She slammed the door and started the engine.

"Call me when you get home, please?" His voice was distant, muffled.

She nodded, turned her head, and backed out of the driveway. She drove off down Mountain Street.

She'd wanted him to kiss her.

36

He watched her car until it turned onto Cross Street and disappeared. *Fuck.* He should have insisted on driving her home. He'd call her in a minute to make sure she got home.

He picked his phone up off the kitchen table. Two numbers had been trying to reach him. Both had left voicemails. One was Mark Beltz. The other he didn't know, a 207 number.

He called Mark without listening to the message.

"Detective, it's your daughter—"

It hit him in the middle of his stomach. "Oh Jesus—"

"She's *all right*, Alex"—a rare use now of his first name from Mark— "don't you worry. She's fine."

Mark's voice carried the whole weight of his large, solid frame, and Alex believed him and felt weak with relief.

"But you need to come over here," Mark added.

"Where?"

He tried not to speed through town, across Harbor Park, down the long stretch of Sea Street behind Seafarer Marine. It was dark.

Hadn't Morgana missed her? Had Sophie told her she was going to his place?

What was she doing way over here across the harbor, about as far as she could get in town from both her mother's and father's houses?

That was the point, he supposed.

He spotted Mark's cruiser parked beside an old, scuffed, and rusty Toyota Camry. It was parked conspicuously all by itself near the end of the fuel dock, below the Ocean View condos. Mark was standing at the rear of the car, writing in his pad. In the dock lights, Alex could make out four figures slumped in the seats looking down at their phones.

Alex parked and got out of his car. "Hi, Mark. What's going on?"

Mark jutted his chin in the direction of the condos. "Got a call from someone up there. A car parked at the end of the dock with four kids. Smoke coming out the windows like a bonfire. I'd'a let it go but they called it in twice."

Mark opened a large fat hand to reveal a vape pen with a dark oil-filled cartridge.

"Cannabis?" Alex asked.

Mark nodded and angled his head at the car.

Alex walked to the driver's door. He knocked on the window. As it was cranked open, the smell came out, thick and sweet, like a miasma in a cartoon. The driver was Dickie Emmett, a senior, whom he'd recently questioned about Shane. He recognized the girl in the passenger seat—magenta streaks in her thin blond hair and a small gold stud in the middle of an inflamed spot in her upper lip—one of Sophie's newer high school friends, but he didn't know her by name. Ethan Dorr sat in the backseat, beside—only now did he look straight at her—Sophie. She was looking away out the window.

He opened his mouth, but he knew the wrong things were going to come out.

Mark saved him. "Detective?"

Alex turned away and joined Mark, who was now standing beside his cruiser.

"As you know," Mark said, "we don't usually pull them in for this. Not these days. Unless, you know, they've got more than two-point-five ounces. We could check the car, but this is probably it."

"Sophie can't have any special treatment, Mark."

"I'm not booking them. I had to turn up because it was reported." Mark inclined his head again toward the condos. "The courts don't want to see these kids. What I usually do is release them to the parents. I just called you first."

"So . . . that's it?"

"That's it. Just take her home."

37

Alex didn't trust himself to speak in the car. He was afraid the conversation would get away from him.

He could feel her seething, icy cool in the passenger seat beside him.

He'd tried for years to understand and correct his increasing inability to exercise calm, self-assured parental authority over his daughter. After the divorce, seeing her at first only every other weekend, he'd feared losing her. He'd tried too hard to please her. He hadn't anticipated failure as a father, two toxic parents, Sophie torn between them like a rag doll coming apart. No wonder she was self-medicating, smoking dope in a car, with an angry tattoo stamped across her forehead.

"When one's young, everything is a rehearsal. To be repeated ad lib, to be put right when the curtain goes up in earnest. One day you know that the curtain was up all the time. That was the performance."

Something he'd read by the novelist Sybille Bedford. Now it haunted him. He was always going to be a better father the next time. Next incident. Summon sounder parental judgment, find the wise words and actions to help Sophie—and himself—achieve more constructive outcomes. Work at fashioning a healthier relationship with Morgana. Be closer with Sophie—like they'd been when she was younger. But there was no going back and redoing any of it.

The curtain was up all the time. That was the performance.

"Dad, where are you going? I'm not going to Mom's house."

"It's your week with her."

"I was going to spend the night at Kendra's."

"Did you tell your mother?"

"Yes!"

This teenage autonomy—Sophie going where she wanted, whenever she wanted, maybe Morgana had agreed to it, or maybe Sophie had told her she was spending the night at her father's place—was driving him crazy. She was only sixteen. And now there was a killer on the loose.

"Well, you're not going to Kendra's place now."

"So I'll stay with you. Can we go get pizza?"

"Don't you have homework?"

"I've done it."

"Already?"

"Yes! I did it at school."

"Okay." He didn't want to be that kind of policeman.

At Granite Pizza, they ordered a large Margherita. One half with anchovies for him.

"Are you and Ethan seeing each other?"

"*Dad.* We're friends." A finality of tone that stopped further inquiry. "You can't tell Mom about tonight."

"Sophie, I can't not tell her. It'll come out—"

"*You can't tell her, Dad!*"

"Sophie, lower your voice, please."

"You just can't tell her. She's been talking about sending me away to some Christian boarding school in Texas."

"Well, that's not going to happen. She would need my permission to send you anywhere. Particularly out of state."

"Really? She can't send me away?"

"Really. No way. But, Sophie, you can't be doing this. Cannabis, weed, whatever you want to call it, is a regulated substance in Maine—like alcohol—and you're underage, and I'm a policeman—"

"This isn't about you, Dad. I'm just hanging out with my friends, doing the normal things everyone else does."

"Really? Where'd you get it?"

"Oh, right, like I'm going to tell you. The police."

She was looking at her phone.

"Would you please put that away."

She sighed loudly and threw the phone into her bag. "We didn't think anyone would see us there."

"Four kids in a car at night in a boatyard right beside Ocean View condos, which is full of retirees looking out their windows? You'd've been better off parking in front of the post office, or Brown and Cord—or anywhere."

"Okay, thanks. Next time we'll go to the post office."

Their pizza arrived. Alex placed slices onto their plates.

"So will I have to go to court?"

"No."

"Did you get me off?"

"I certainly did not. You're underage, you could have been arrested, but it was Officer Beltz's call. He's not charging you—"

"So it was all bullshit. You were just fucking with us!" She was quivering with rage.

"*Sophie!*" He glanced around the restaurant. The policeman and his out-of-control daughter. "Please don't talk to me like that. We're not playing with you. What you did was illegal."

"Dad, you've got better things to do—like catching Shane's killer."

"Yes, quite. I've got better things to do than dealing with kids in cars smoking weed."

He picked up a slice and pushed it into his mouth. Sophie picked up her knife and fork and cut into her slice.

"You're going to catch him, right?"

"I'm doing my best."

The fork stopped at her mouth. "So it's not certain you'll catch him?"

"We're investigating. The FBI is involved. There's a process. You mount an investigation, you look at evidence—I can't talk about it."

"So you've got evidence?" She put the fork into her mouth, chewed. Threw back a gulp of Coke. "Like what?"

"Sophie—I can't talk with you about it. And you can't talk about it with your friends. You and I don't talk about my work. You have to understand that."

"I won't say a thing," said Sophie. "Your secret is safe with me."

"Dad," she said in the car driving home, "are there a lot of people like you who don't have a dog?"

"Of course there are. Lots of people don't have dogs."

"I don't know anybody who doesn't have a dog."

"You already have Bella. You don't need another dog at my house."

"It wouldn't be for me, it would be for you. You'd have someone to come home to."

"I have you."

"It's not the same. It's a forever companion."

"You'll be my forever companion."

"No, I won't. I'm growing up. I won't always be here."

Pantomime shock. "You won't?"

"I'm serious, Dad."

"Well, dogs don't last forever."

"Then you get another one. It's statistically healthier than being alone. You can look it up. You need a dog, Dad. I'm worried about you."

He'd never heard her speak this way. This concern for him.

"Don't worry about me, sweetie. I'm fine."

"No, you're not, Dad. You're getting old. And you're kind of out of touch with reality."

I won't always be here. He knew that. But it was something else to hear her say it.

She was barely here now. When they got home she vanished into her room.

Alex poured himself a finger of Johnnie Walker Black and sat on his sofa. The big tea-stained floral Burnham from Conran. He didn't want dog hair all over the place.

He spread his hand over the depression in the cushion where he and Isabel sat beside each other an hour earlier.

Isabel had a dog, and she certainly wasn't happy. Dogs were a nuisance, always barking, wanting to go out. His sister, Lizzie, was always grumbling about what she and Tony couldn't do because of the dogs.

You're kind of out of touch with reality—

His phone vibrated in his pocket.

"Detective Brangwen? It's Rob Reilly. I'm a technician at the police lab in Bangor. I hope it's not too late to call, but I'm working late this week and I have some results from a substance you sent us. Some kind of jam?"

"Oh, yes. Thank you. Go ahead, please."

Reilly read from a list. Cellulose, chlorohydro-something, carbon compounds.

Alex interrupted him. "I'm sorry, those chemicals—they're from plants, right?"

"Mostly, yes. Roots, flowers, herbs. Some kind of holistic-type organic mix—except for a tryptamine."

"A what?"

"DMT. Dimethyltryptamine. A psychoactive chemical found in several recreational drugs."

"The stuff I sent in to the lab had a psychedelic drug in it?"

"Yes, sir."

DMT in both Byron Pugh's and Shane's blood. *Something like mushrooms,* Phil Gressens had said.

"Mushrooms?"

"Could have been. It's hard to nail down the chemical signature of origin. It can be produced inorganically in a lab. But your stuff was organic."

"Was there a lot of it? If someone ate a couple of spoonfuls of that jam, could it be like an acid trip? Hallucinations?"

"I couldn't say. People have different susceptibilities to chemicals and drugs. A couple of tablespoons you'd feel a buzz."

As he hung up, Alex saw the small blue jar beside the plate of crackers on the coffee table.

38

They drew stares as they strode through the village, heading without pause or glance aside down the gravel path toward the small log cabin. Alex felt theatrically conspicuous, flanked by Special Agent Harris and Patrolman Mark Beltz. They resembled, he thought, characters in a western. As much as the Settlement players evoked the early settlers.

He felt rather than saw Isabel watching him. He hadn't called her since she'd left his house. And she hadn't called him.

Alex knocked beside the open door, beneath the sign painted with two words: BOWLES APOTHECARY.

Roger Priestly was standing at a heavy table, like a rough butcher's block on legs, pulverizing something in his mortar and pestle. He looked up.

Alex stepped in and handed him an envelope.

"Roger Priestly, this is a warrant for search and seizure. For your premises here, and at your home."

Roger's eyes took in the three men standing in the doorway, and lingered at Agent Harris. He looked back at Alex. "Am I under arrest for something?"

"No, but we want to know what you're making here."

"You mean my herbs and flowers?" He waved a hand at the bunches of dried stalks tied with wool yarn hanging from the low roof beams. "Go ahead."

Agent Harris and Mark Beltz entered the shop. They'd already put on latex gloves. Mark Beltz began picking up the small jars and placing them in a large Ziploc bag.

"That's my property. What do you want it for?"

Alex pointed at the table. "What is that?"

"Detective, as I've already told you, I'm the village apothecary. Like it says on the sign"—he pointed outside the door—"'Bowles Apothecary.' You know what that means in the context of the seventeenth century? I'm the pharmacist. I make what we now might quaintly call folk remedies out of herbs and flowers, tree bark, roots, Saint-John's-wort, that sort of thing. Other natural ingredients. What do you want with it?"

"What's this?" Alex picked up a small, old-fashioned-looking green bottle—a vial—dark with substance inside it.

"That's my electuary. See the label? 'Bowles's Electuary.' It's an old-fashioned tonic."

Alex handed it to Mark Beltz, who put it in a Ziploc. "Can you give me a list of its ingredients?"

"It's just natural stuff. Weeds and flowers and herbs, and tree bark, pine sap, things like that. You mean each ingredient?"

"Yes. And their source."

"I forage for everything. In the woods and along the coast mostly—like the original Apothecary Bowles. You want me to write it down now?"

"After we're finished here and at your home will be fine."

"Why my home? Can you tell me what you're looking for? Do I need a lawyer?"

"Not unless you think you do," said Alex. Everyone was better off with a lawyer, and entitled to one if requested. *Not unless you think you do* was a response Alex had learned at the Academy.

"But why? You can't think I had anything to do with Shane Carter's death?"

"Did you?"

"Of course not. This is absurd. You both know me—Officer Beltz, I've had both your boys, Brian and David, in my history classes. Not that they paid much attention."

"I guess not," said Mark Beltz, who was making a methodical, practiced examination of every square inch inside the small building, feeling along the roof beams, testing the floorboards for any loose or not nailed down. "My boys aren't big on homework. I wasn't either."

"We'll go to your house now, Mr. Priestly," said Alex, when they were finished.

All the other players, Isabel, Nancy, Chester, Jeff Block, Monte, the Conrads, and the few early visitors, stood aside as the four men walked up the gravel path across the Village green. Alex and Roger in front, Mark behind them carrying a large canvas tote bag, Agent Harris in the rear.

"Isn't this what you call the 'perp walk'?" said Roger. "Aren't you supposed to handcuff me for maximum humiliation?"

"I haven't assumed you're a flight risk," Alex said. "You're just helping us with our inquiries."

He saw Isabel standing near the other cabin. Her eyes were locked on him.

"What about my car?" asked Roger when they neared the parking lot. "Are you going to bring me back? If you release me, that is?"

"You can drive your own car. Just drive to your home. We'll follow you."

"You know where I live?"

"It's a small town, Roger."

39

Roger led them directly from the gravel driveway through a door beneath the deck, into the basement. Inside, he turned on lights.

"Oh my," said Mark. "This is quite a space you got here."

"Yes," Roger agreed. "It runs the whole sixty feet of the footprint."

It looked to Alex like an indoor organic farmstand. Folding tables were arranged in two neat rows down the length of the basement, beneath regularly spaced warm LED lights hanging from the overhead joists. The tabletops displayed dried herbs and flowers, loose and string-tied bundles, wooden baskets of twigs, sticks, roots, tree nuts. Rows of shelves against the walls held Tupperware containers, bottles, and screw-topped jars containing substances that ranged in appearance from sauerkraut to thick dark soup. Drying racks supported long stems and flowers.

"Quite an operation," said Alex. "Are you supplying other people?"

"No. It was just a hobby before I joined the Settlement." He looked at Alex. "What exactly do you want to see?"

"Got any mushrooms?" Agent Harris asked.

Roger's expression didn't change. It was something behind his eyes, Alex thought. A penny dropped. "I don't use mushrooms."

Alex cut through the tension crackling between the two men. "Please show us what you've got here."

Roger turned and spread an open palm across a table covered with dried flora. "These are woodland herbs." He moved to another table. "These are barks. Dried berries. This is sassafras. Elderberry. You've heard of elderberry wine, I'm sure. It has excellent medicinal properties. Very high antioxidant."

"I had no idea," said Mark Beltz, sounding quietly astonished.

Agent Harris walked away from Mark and Roger. He bent forward at the waist, inspecting, sniffing, looking at tools, peering into containers.

He reached the bottom of a staircase and disappeared.

Alex followed a few minutes later, leaving Mark Beltz absorbed in Roger's enthusiastic presentation and its properties.

He found Harris in the study off the great room: a desk, armchairs with reading lights beside a fireplace; walls hung with botanical prints, old maps, a series of hand-tinted photographs of rural Maine and the coast, shelves of old and rare books.

"Take a look," Harris said. He was peering closely at a grouping of framed photographs on the wall.

Alex walked toward him, but before he could see anything of the photographs, a voice spoke behind him.

"By all means make yourselves at home," said Roger, with a tight note in his voice as he came into the room.

"Nice home for a retired high school teacher," Harris said.

"Isn't it," Roger agreed. "I'm fortunate. A small inheritance. You might ask me if you want to look around, what you're looking for. I might be able to help you."

"Who are these kids?" Harris pointed to the photographs.

Alex was close enough to make them out now. The sort of thing you might see in a house belonging to grandparents: photos of children. Though these were not very young or old children; most were between the ages of about ten and sixteen. Some were shots of kids staring pokerfaced at their opponents across chessboards at long tournament tables; others showed Roger with these same kids holding trophies, medals, grinning broadly into the camera.

"They're my chess kids," Roger said. "At tournaments. I coached the school chess team."

Alex caught the note of pride. "Are you still coaching chess?"

"Not at school. A few privately."

"Privately?" said Harris. "What exactly does that mean?"

"You've heard of after-school tutoring, I presume, Officer, or Agent, or whatever you call yourself?" Roger said, patiently. "After-school math? Piano lessons?"

Harris tapped a finger on a photo. His eyes swung first to Alex, then to Roger. "Shane Carter was on the school chess team?"

"Yes, he was. For four years."

Alex had seen numerous pictures of Shane, at different ages. The photograph in the eight-by-ten black frame was recent. He was grinning and holding a trophy.

Alex heard a low roaring in his ears. His heart. "When was this taken?"

"At the state tournament, last spring."

"You're still coaching the school chess team, even though you've retired from teaching?"

"I was last spring. There's not much of a team this semester."

"You coached them and took them there?"

"Yes."

"Shane's parents paid for chess lessons?"

"No. They weren't interested."

"So you taught him chess for free?"

"Yes. He was a good player. I wasn't going to turn him away. I informed his mother about the tournaments whenever we went out of town. She didn't ask anything about it, or how he was doing, though I told her he was good. She didn't seem to care."

Alex's eyes were drawn to another player.

"Ethan Dorr was on the chess team?"

"Yes, he was."

"And you coached him too?"

"Yes."

How had Alex missed that?

"Detective?"

Alex, Roger, and Agent Harris turned away from the photographs. They hadn't heard Mark Beltz, now breathing heavily, or his creaking belt, approaching through the great room.

"Yes, Officer Beltz?"

Mark's eyes were fixed on Alex. "Something I'd like you to take a look at, please."

They followed Mark downstairs. Harris in the rear. Mark walked carefully the length of the basement, making sure his bulky duty belt avoided contact with the tables, shelves, furniture, all so carefully lined up. He led them to the back door, opposite where they'd entered from the driveway.

Because of the house's situation on the hill, the basement was half underground, half above it, the back door opened straight out onto the sloping backyard. Mark stopped in the shadow beneath the overhead deck. He looked again at Alex, and then pointed to the small area beside the concrete foundation wall, about five feet square, that held what appeared to be a homemade cage of fine mesh wire.

Inside the cage was a jumbled arrangement of small bushes, ferns, tall weeds drooping over mossy grass, a mound of pebbles, a dash of rocks, and a large pan of muddy-looking water. A small, landscaped habitat. Like an outdoor terrarium.

Alex looked at Roger. "What is it?"

"See for yourself."

Alex kneeled, leaned closer, and looked through the wire, into the ferns and weeds. An earth-colored patch of ground moved—

Hopped, in fact.

"Frogs . . ." said Mark Beltz, in a voice from the crypt.

"Toads, actually," said Roger. He pushed his hands into the pockets of his baggy, Goodman apothecary trousers and gazed down into the wild place he'd made for them inside the wire. "Eastern American toads. *Anaxyrus americanus.*"

40

Alex turned on the tape recorder.

"Roger Priestly interview. Attended by Detective Alex Brangwen, Granite Harbor Police, at William P. Merrill Station, Granite Harbor."

He read the rest from a card. He knew it by heart. He'd read it aloud enough during police training, and several times for real afterward, but this was procedure, to ensure that the wording was correct: "You have the right to remain silent. Anything you say can and will be used against you in a court of law. You have the right to an attorney. If you cannot afford an attorney, one will be appointed for you."

"Thank you," said Roger Priestly.

"Do you want your attorney present?"

Roger looked directly at Alex. "I'm happy to help you, Detective. I have nothing to hide."

There was one interview room at the William P. Merrill Station. Downstairs in the basement rooms, no window. Two small CCTV cameras in different walls recorded the interviewee and a wider-angle picture that took in the entire room.

In the room next door, Agent Harris and Chief Raintree sat watching the interview on monitors.

"Thank you, Mr. Priestly." Alex got through the perfunctory questions:

Roger's full name, age, address, how long he had lived at that address, before
asking him, "How long have you been working at Granite Harbor Settlement?"

"Three years. Three and a quarter, actually."

"How long have you known Isabel Dorr?"

"About seven years."

"How do you know her?"

"We were both teachers at Granite Harbor High School."

"So you're friends?"

"Yes."

"Close friends?"

"Good friends."

Alex pushed a sheet of paper across the table. "This is the chemical
breakdown of the contents of a jar you gave to Isabel Dorr. Which she ate
with some crackers."

Roger looked down at the paper. He read, then pushed it back.

"The dimethyltryptamine. Where does that come from?"

"From my toads."

Before the interview, Alex had reached Professor Barney, U Maine at Orono
herpetologist, on the phone.

"Professor. That toxin you mentioned that toads secrete—"

"Yes. Bufotenin."

"What are its chemical properties?"

"It's a tryptamine derivative. Specifically, a DMT. Dimethyltryptamine."

"Is that the same DMT found in magic mushrooms, psilocybin, peyote?"

"It's very similar. Dimethyltryptamine presents as various tryptamine compounds: 4-PO-DMT, 4-HO-DMT, 5-MeO-DMT, and so on. Bufotenin is
5-HO-DMT. All are structural analogs of tryptamine. It's found in many
plants, fungi, and some animals. They can all produce a psychotropic experience, depending on the amount ingested and the susceptibility of the individual taking the drug. To answer your question, yes, it's virtually the same
psychoactive component found in psilocybin, ayahuasca, magic mushrooms."

"You thought Isabel needed a psychedelic experience?" Alex said now to
Roger.

"Not at all. She needed a tonic. A pick-me-up. A very small dose of bufo-tenin can biosynthesize in the brain and set off neurotransmitters that have an effect on the production of serotonin. It acts as an antidepressant."

"Did you tell her that your tonic contained a psychotropic drug, a con-trolled substance, extracted from toad glands?"

"Of course not."

"Why not?"

"People don't need to know such things. Medicine practiced on hu-mans"—a flat pedagogical tone took over—"has always been full of ani-mal products. Heparin, insulin, and pituitary hormones are animal derived, from dogs and pigs and cows. Premarin vaginal hormone cream comes from the urine of pregnant mares. The traditional vaccine industry was based on chicken eggs. Had any organic vitamins recently? Porcine and bovine gelatin capsules."

"Are you a doctor, licensed to prescribe medicine?"

"I'm the *apothecary*."

He's mad, Alex thought. "Tell me what that means to you."

"The apothecary in colonial times was like the pharmacist or doctor in today's society. He foraged for ingredients. He knew where to look and when to gather. He was a chemist who knew what affected the constitution of his patients and customers. He was the front-line consultant in a community's mental health. Women didn't talk to their husbands about their personal and physical concerns—they might talk with other women, but the whole reli-gious overlay of the times made honest inquiry and admissions dangerous. They *hanged* people for strange behavior. But in the apothecary, people ex-pected the confidentiality one now expects of a doctor or lawyer—or a priest."

"A special trust, then."

"Absolutely."

"And you took that position of trust on yourself."

"Absolutely."

"You don't find it strange that you put a controlled drug into a folk rem-edy and gave it to an unsuspecting person?"

"I was helping a friend. I told her I made it. She didn't have to take it. She hasn't mentioned any problems to me. I produce an authentic remedy for distress. You saw my library in my house—there's probably not another one like it in private hands anywhere. I've been studying the pharmacology of natural plants and medicines for years. Toads were a mainstay of apothecary ingredients in colonial and precolonial times. The secretion of the parotid glands was used extensively in ancient cultures and in religious ceremonies. It was a popular remedy in Mesoamerican, pre-Columbian—"

"So you were aware you were breaking the law?"

"I didn't think about it, to be frank."

"Did you ever give Shane Carter, or any of your students or chess players, your electuary?"

"Of course not," Roger said sharply. "An electuary is for people who are ailing, who are unwell, tired, dispirited, falling into despair. Shane was young and healthy."

"How would you characterize your relationship with Shane Carter?"

"Shane was my chess student," said Roger.

"That's all?"

"I saw him several times a week for years for chess club, and we developed, as I did with a number of students, a warm friendship."

"What do you mean by a warm friendship?"

"Nothing inappropriate, I can assure you, if that's what you're insinuating—"

"I'm not insinuating anything. I'm talking to everyone who knew Shane. Everyone who could tell me something about him."

"I can tell you that Shane was a smart, exuberant boy, with a neglected homelife. His friends and his activities, both in school and out, were very important to him, in the absence of any kind of love and attention at home. I saw Shane grow up, from the age of eleven onward. From a troubled boy into a strong young man. I saw him master the game of chess to a high level. If he had a passion for something, if he loved it, it had his whole attention, and he did well at it. He was a wonderful boy. He was well-liked, indeed loved, by everyone who knew him. If you've talked to his friends, you already know that."

"Did you love him?"

In the observation room, Agent Harris exhaled audibly and said, "Finally."

He was standing, hands making fists in his trouser pockets, staring at the two monitors. One showed Roger's head and shoulders. The other gave a higher, wider view of the interview room, showing Alex and Roger Priestly in profile facing each other across the table.

Chief Billie Raintree sat at a desk behind him. She stared impassively at the monitors.

"I was close to Shane. I've been close to many of my students, the boys and girls in my chess club. If you're a teacher, some children stand out. You watch them grow and evolve into the people you hope and imagine they might become. It's a natural human connection. Or you're an inhuman teacher. And a few . . . you invest yourself in them, and you take into your heart."

"Did you ever know a young man named Byron Pugh?"

Roger tilted his head and gave it some thought. "Byron Pugh . . ."

"Before you moved to Granite Harbor, you were living in Westbrook and teaching at U Maine Orono, correct?"

"Yes."

"Byron Pugh took your course"—Alex looked down at the small yellow pad on the table, the results of research by Agent Harris and the Bureau— "BIO 205—Field Study in the Natural History of Maine, U Maine, Orono, fall semester, 2002."

Roger raised his eyebrows. "That was a long time ago. But you seem to know. I don't remember him. What, apart from that possible connection, does he have to do with me?"

"Did you have a relationship with him?"

Roger's expression changed abruptly. "I've told you I don't remember him, as a student or in any other way. Is this about my electuary—which I've been happy to help you with—or what?"

"Did you have a relationship, romantic, sexual, or otherwise, outside of your role as teacher, chess tutor, with Shane Carter?"

For the first time, Roger looked up at the camera on the wall facing him, behind Alex's back, then he looked back at Alex.

"This has now become offensive. I want my lawyer."

41

"Means, motive, and opportunity," said Special Agent Harris.

"What's the motive?" asked Francis Doyle.

"Love," answered Harris. "One of the most common of all motives for murder."

"So, he's a serial romantic, then, my client?" Doyle looked blandly across the table at Alex and Chief Raintree in the conference room of the William P. Merrill Station. "Twice he's killed for love?"

His client was in a holding cell downstairs.

"People date serially, fall in love serially," said Harris. "He knew both boys, Byron Pugh and Shane Carter, more than a decade apart. Taught them both. Both dead, same MO."

"Are you serious?" Doyle gave a good impression of trying not to laugh. "Roger Priestly's been a teacher here in the state, in Orono, Portland, and here in Granite Harbor, for years. He's met and taught a great number of students. Knowing those two is not even coincidence, it's a statistical probability."

"It's also supportive history, counselor," said Harris. "And the specific mutilation of both boys is no coincidence."

"I've known Roger for many years. Making a natural remedy according to his own recipe, without a full acknowledgment, perhaps even to himself, of its chemical contents, I can see that—I mean, with Roger. He's an avid and dedicated amateur biologist. He's an unusual man. But murderer—*serial murderer*? Impossible."

"Why do you say that?"

"Because I've known Roger for many years."

"Then you're in the company of all those people who lived next door to serial killers for years, decades even. And their wives, families, children, friends, who also claimed they knew them. Who said, 'Seemed a perfectly nice man, normal, like anyone else, you'd never think he could do such a thing.' My time investigating and studying violent crime with the Bureau has taught me one fact more than any other: *nobody really knows anybody*."

"Agent Harris, I respect your professional experience. I'm just telling you that, quite apart from what I know of Roger, I believe your conclusions in this case are circumstantial coincidence, and that suggests to me that you must be grasping at straws."

Small-town lawyer was the label that came to Alex. It was a cliché, and what, beyond Granite Harbor, did he know about American small towns? In fact, Francis Doyle seemed more a Jarndyce or a Pumblechook. Midforties, not shabby but self-neglectfully groomed in a fashion that stretched all the way back to Dickensian. His pinstripe suit, shiny with wear, broad-lapeled, might once have been baggy but was now too small for the straining belly and well-established love handles. The hair was too long, a neglected Beatle cut that didn't work then or now, the beard, thin, overlong. But Doyle's small eyes were sharp, his mouth set in a small, persistent wry smile.

Doyle—Chief Raintree had filled him in—had handled Roger's inheritance from his aunt's estate, the subsequent purchase of his big post-and-beam house. Doyle had also defended a murderer at trial—a local man, a lobsterman, who had killed his mother, an Alzheimer's sufferer, when he no longer felt himself capable of caring for her. He'd smothered her with a pillow. The visiting nurse reported her suspicions. Doyle had represented him pro bono, and obtained a reduced sentence of community service.

"And there's the toads," said Harris. "And the presence of DMT in both bodies, conforming to the same animal source of DMT found in Roger Priestly's electuary."

"We'll supply our own laboratory report," said Doyle. "You're talking about a chemical coincidentally found in the bodies, that is common to any number of recreational sources."

"I'm talking," said Agent Harris, "about a preponderance of multiple source association that would dispense with any notion of coincidence."

Doyle looked at Alex. "Then why aren't you arresting him for murder?"

"For the moment we're dealing with the manufacture and distribution of a Schedule One controlled substance."

"Agreed. A trace, given to a friend." Doyle stood up. "The rest is circumstantial phooey." He glanced at Chief Raintree. "Chief," he said.

"Mr. Doyle."

When the lawyer left, Chief Raintree turned to Agent Harris. "You believe Roger Priestly killed Shane Carter?"

"I do."

"Detective?"

"We've got him for manufacture and possession of a trace amount of a controlled substance, and giving it to a friend." Alex turned to Harris. "You see him carving up his unrequited love objects and putting toads inside them. There's no evidence. Seems a bit of a stretch to me."

Agent Harris made a polite face. "Sexual need, dominance, obsessive fixation, can present in the mind of a killer as romantic love. Roger Priestly fits the bill. He's a loner—no spouse or partner. He's got money, privacy, time. He's got that big house and basement. He's got toads. He knows both boys. I'm telling you what I see here."

"It's not evidence. It's all circumstantial. There's nothing there to convict."

"We'll see. The forensic crew went through his house. The lab will look for a DNA link between his toads, and that stuff you got from Isabel Dorr, and the trace found in Shane. Siblings, same batch, type, something like that. We'll get there."

Harris stood up. "Detective. Chief Raintree, I'll be in my hotel. Writing up a report."

When Harris had left the conference room, Alex looked at Raintree. "What do you think, Chief?"

Billie Raintree's face was inscrutable. "As you say, it's not evidence. But it doesn't look good for Priestly. You don't agree?"

Alex shook his head. "I see him as a loner, obsessive maybe—that apoth-ecary business. I just don't think it's him. I think it has something to do with the Settlement. But not Roger."

"The intuition of a novelist?"

"Not a very successful one."

"Maybe a better policeman," said Billie Raintree.

42

The arraignment had been short but frighteningly real. Francis Doyle had driven Roger to the Calder County Courthouse in Fairhaven.

Francis counseled him to plead not guilty to the charge of possession and distribution of a controlled substance. "We'll admit the toads but argue against knowing possession of a substance and the intention to distribute. You gave it to her, you didn't sell it. They have very little to present. We'll plea a deal. Your record is unblemished, your character is exemplary, you're a member in good standing with the community. You have character witnesses. I've known you for years. Everybody at the Settlement will speak for you."

"How do you know?"

"Because they told me. Isabel Dorr, Monte Glover, Chester Coffey, Nancy Keeler, Jeff Block, the Conrads. They all said they'd speak for you."

Roger began to cry in the car.

"It won't be bad, Roger. You'll get off with a fine and possibly some community time."

In the brief court hearing, Detective Brangwen presented what evidence they had: the lab report showing the presence of bufotenin containing dimethyltryptamine found in the blue apothecary jar, and the discovery of the toads at Roger's house.

Doyle drove him home and briefly came in, but Roger told him not to stay, he'd be okay.

"Call me anytime, Roger, day or night. This will all pass."

The lawyer squeezed his arm and left.

Roger went downstairs to the basement. The police had been in the house all day. His entire collection of foraged and dried and prepared materials, many of his tools, dishes, jars, had been taken away. Some of it he'd get back, Francis had told him.

His toads were gone. He'd caught them over a period of several years, housed and treated them humanely, doted on them and their needs, used their secretions sparingly, gratefully. Their individual features and the personalities—they had them—had aroused his affections. What would become of them? he'd asked, but no one had been able to tell him. He was sure they'd be destroyed—or killed and kept as evidence.

He could find new plants, although it was now November. He could order some of it online. He could put it all together again, catch toads even, but for what? When people learned what he'd put into his electuary, they'd be disgusted. He'd be linked with the deaths of Shane and the other boy, Byron Pugh. He'd be tainted. There would be whispers. People—parents and children—would avoid him. He'd become the boogeyman.

He turned off the lights and went upstairs.

The house grew dark, and he didn't turn on any more lights. Night came early now. He sat in the great room and watched the daylight fade over the sea, the molten texture of the waves grow faint, until it was a depthless slate medium below the pewter ceiling of clouds.

A feeling came over him, almost physical. He'd been aware of it before, the thin maggot edge of it nibbling away inside him, at his peace of mind, but he'd been able to push it away with industriousness, his immersion in his pursuits, talk and plans with the other Settlement players. What passed, for him, as social activity.

He'd heard all about it from the mothers—the parents he'd dealt with most—when he ran into them at Hannaford or Brown & Cord, and they told him that Alice or Jack or Britney or Everett was doing well at U Maine, or BU, or, if they'd been exceptionally bright and lucky, at Colby, Bates, or Bowdoin Colleges.

"Yes! Alice is *gone!* Flown the coop. Can you believe it? *Eighteen!* It's like everyone says: it goes by fast! The days are long—*oh my God!* Sometimes I couldn't wait for a day to be over—the sun over the yardarm—but the *years* . . . whoosh!"

The mothers were most affected. The fathers all worked. Roger generally only saw them, if at all, at school events, concerts, sometimes at chess tournaments. Some of them even lived in other states. Some were absent from their children's lives altogether. Most of the mothers worked too, sold real estate, taught yoga, started a web design business, a local baking company, been a doula or a life coach. But they'd all been mothers and homemakers first.

"It happens to everybody"—Sara or Gretchen would roll her eyes at the cliché she was suddenly experiencing—"your kids leave you. Like, all of a sudden, it's over. It's what you want, of course"—a forced laugh of relief— "they're launched!"

But also a tone of dismay. "I'm an empty nester—I can't believe it! She has her own life now, it's great"—Sara or Gretchen put her hand on Roger's arm, the laughter pierced with a sudden note of hysteria—"I just have to figure out what mine is now! Ha-ha-ha! Like . . . who am I now?"

Roger said: "Well, now you can go to Paris, Sara," remembering how they'd talked about her dream of spending a few months there, doing a cooking or a wine course, or taking a cruise on a canal barge. Or Spain, where Gretchen had talked of walking the pilgrim route to Santiago de Compostela.

"Right! I can do that now—maybe I will. But you've been spared all that, Roger—you don't know what you've missed."

But he did know, and at one time he'd been glad. For years Roger had felt a complacent satisfaction that his life wasn't measured by the passage of children. The grind he'd witnessed of parents seeing kids through school. The unremitting, largely unrewarded, effort. The small triumphs, sports, chess tournaments, the dates, the proms, the GPAs, the gradual, then increasingly fraught garnering of academic achievement, the looming approach of college. The growing, deepening anxiety that overwhelmed the parents and their children. The disappointments were large, often crushing. The diagnoses, the Ritalin and the therapists, Zoloft for everyone in the household, the weed, the car crashes—sometimes worse.

Roger had frequently shuddered with relief.

"His" kids had stopped in his classroom for a year or two and moved on. Pushed through like peristaltic action. His chess players had stayed longer, like children who stuck with music lessons through elementary and middle school and beyond. With some of them he'd formed real attachments, completely unlike the temporary association with his academic students. A real bond. Especially during the chess club years. Week after week, semester after semester, for years. A connection far beyond the stratagems of chess, the fun of tournaments. He had felt about some of them—Shane—what he imagined he might have felt, just a little, about sons or daughters. He'd been involved with their lives. He'd discussed them with their mothers. He'd rooted for them, driven them to tournaments, fed them, supported them, talked with them, watched them grow up.

Roger knew he'd been granted a high privilege: he'd been witness to—he'd experienced—the beautiful natural flowering of a personality, a sensibility, of a young child evolving into the embodiment of so many hopes. To feel such an investment—such an attachment. That exquisite human connection.

Yes, love.

Then gone.

They never called. They moved on. They dropped him.

So easily.

Roger too had finally become an empty nester.

And then Shane—murdered. He'd been shocked, of course. Immensely saddened. Perhaps because of Shane's neglected homelife, he'd felt a greater pull of compassion for the boy. But many other things. A beautiful, funny, charming boy, so full of life.

Yes, Roger had loved him. And he could grieve with nobody.

Gradually, as the shock of his death wore off—no it didn't wear off, but he made some daily accommodation for the fact of it—he'd been overcome with grief. How did you get over something like that, the murder of someone like Shane?

He'd kept busy. Concentrated on his remedies and nostrums.

Now it would get out. In the *Granite Harbor Herald*, on the radio, on the television news.

They would have to let him go. No more Settlement, no more Apothecary Bowles.

He saw the way they would see him now—all the kids he'd known for years, their mothers, everybody: a weirdo who'd put toad stuff into his remedies. It would work retroactively. They would see—they would believe—he'd always been like that. Twisted. A creep.

He could hear it: "Roger . . . *Eeeewwww . . .*"

43

Isabel turned on the WCSH Portland News Center evening news at six. A young woman's gratingly strident voice was screeching from the TV. "—Granite Harbor man, Roger Priestly, was arrested this afternoon on a charge of possession and distribution of a Schedule One controlled substance."

Roger, still in his Apothecary Bowles outfit, was caught in the TV lights penetrating the early dusk. A man with a scraggly beard and a bad suit led him by the arm as they came out of the Calder County Courthouse. Roger looked small and old. And angry. The Pilgrim clothes made him look like a crazy homeless man. After a moment Isabel recognized the other man: Francis Doyle. Her friend Lisa had done paralegal work for his law office. He took the difficult cases that made the news.

She opened the basement door. It was dark downstairs. Still she called. "Ethan?"

No answer.

Back on TV, Roger and Francis Doyle moved through a small group of police and reporters and got into a Jeep, Doyle's she supposed. The Jeep drove away.

The scene cut to a head-and-shoulders shot of WCSH reporter Ella Blake, a young blond-haired woman with carefully curled beach waves. As she spoke, her eyes repeatedly popped wide for emphasis. She was standing some distance away from the front of the courthouse.

"The retired former local high school teacher also works at the Granite Harbor Settlement Living History Museum north of Granite Harbor, where, just two weeks ago, the body of murdered Granite Harbor High Schooler Shane Carter was discovered. It's not clear, Pat and Frank, whether the current arrest is connected in any way with Shane Carter, although Priestly is known to have been a mentor to the deceased teen. Priestly was released on his own recognizance. From the Calder County Courthouse in Fairhaven, this is Ella Blake. Back to you in the studio, Pat, Frank."

They were linking it to Shane. Making Roger sound unsavory. Isabel, and everyone else, Chester, Jeff, Monte, had watched Roger being escorted away from the Settlement by Alex Brangwen and the FBI agent. They'd seen his apothecary jars carried away from his building by Mark Beltz. It was all they talked about for the rest of the day.

"Not for Shane, surely?" Nancy Keeler had said.

"Impossible," said Jeff Block. "Absolutely not possible."

It couldn't be anything to do with Shane, they all agreed, so what else was going on with Roger?

Only Isabel had any idea. Alex had called her that morning and asked her if she had any more of Roger's electuary.

"No. I left the jar at your house. Why?"

"There was something in it."

"What?"

"I can't go into it," Alex said. "But it's spiked with something. That might have been why you had a reaction."

"What do you mean, a reaction?"

"I don't know. But maybe it caused what happened to you."

"It was the *trigger*, Alex." Now she was pissed. He didn't get it. "It wasn't what was in it. I wasn't *tripping.*"

"Isabel, I'm just saying there was something in it, so if there's any left, don't take it. I'll talk to you later."

He hung up.

A Schedule I controlled substance, the woman had said on TV—a drug? That's why they took him away?

She went upstairs. "Ethan?" She knocked, paused, opened the door. He wasn't home.

She thought about changing—she actually started, removing cape and bodice—then she was rushing down the stairs, grabbing a down jacket from the mudroom, and driving up Meguntic Street.

44

She saw no lights on in the house. Roger's car was there. Maybe he was still on his way home or with the lawyer. She climbed up to the deck and looked in the kitchen window. No lights anywhere inside the house. The door was locked.

She went down the stairs. The basement door was unlocked. She turned on a light. She'd been down here before, seen Roger's collection of herbs and supplies. The place was stripped, the shelves empty.

"Roger?" she called, loud enough to carry up to the first floor.

She climbed the stairs to the wide-open post-and-beam great room. "Roger?"

A movement caught her eye. Up on the second-floor landing. A line out of alignment against the vertical wooden posts—moving back and forth. She followed it down and screamed—

"No!"

He was still swinging, swaying slowly a few inches either way, on the end of a white rope. His feet were only eighteen inches or so off the floor. A dining chair lay on its side.

"Roger!"

Isabel rushed forward and wrapped her arms around his legs and lifted.

"Roger! No, you can't!"

She tried to lift him—maybe it wasn't too late and she could hold him up—he was surprisingly heavy. Deadweight.

"*Roger!*"

45

Special Agent Harris stood in the open doorway to Alex's office and knocked.

"Hey," he said. Then stepped in. He looked neat, close-shaven, brushed, gelled. He placed a manila envelope on Alex's desk. "Here's a copy of my report. I've already filed it with the Bureau. I'll be in touch. It's been great working with you, Detective." He stuck out his hand.

Alex looked at the hand and up at Harris's face. "You're leaving?"

"Yup. Heading out." The hand remained steady.

Alex rose and shook it. "Why are you leaving now?"

"I think my work is done here. Roger Priestly's suicide is as good as an admission. I'll be down in Boston but I'll continue to work with you to find the pieces and put it all together. You need me to come up, I'll come up."

"So you're convinced that Roger Priestly was a serial killer, who killed Byron Pugh years ago, and then killed Shane Carter?"

"It fits, Detective."

"It's all circumstantial."

"Occam's razor. The simplest explanation is the best."

Alex hated sounding pedantic, he knew it wouldn't help. "Actually, Occam's razor is the principle that fewer entities are preferable to explanations that posit more. That's different."

Special Agent Harris smiled. His teeth a white not found in nature.

"Detective, I know you write novels. You invent characters. You try to give them credible motivation—what's credible to you. You're projecting your own normal associations. You try to wrap up a story in a way that makes sense. That doesn't work for serial killers in real life. You don't need to look under the bed for this one. It fits. Take a load off, Detective. You should go home."

"Have you read my books?"

"I read reports. I don't have time for novels."

Harris left his office.

Alex sat down. He looked out the window. One of those clear, cool, amazing Maine fall days. Red and orange leaves from the trees were scattering on the breeze up Mechanic Street. People would be hiking up Mount Meguntic. Buying pumpkins and squashes out at Cobb Hill Farm. Alongside a monster. Someone everybody knew and smiled at. A neighbor, a coworker, a friend. Out there now.

And Alex had nothing. Except the weekend wait to see if the bufotenin from Roger's toads matched the DMT found in Shane's blood—and Isabel's jar of electuary. The RapidHIT ID DNA processing only took ninety minutes, but Maine.gov officials didn't work weekends, and the lack of agency resources and queue of samples in the state lab meant he would hear nothing till Tuesday. Alex wasn't holding his breath.

Meanwhile, there were no leads. No credible tips from the tip line.

Harris was mistaken. A common mistake. Alex didn't invent characters. He didn't try to give them credible motivation, project his own parameters of behavior onto them. Writing wasn't like that. Characters appeared, whole, strange, sui generis, with their own flaws and quirks. They weren't like you at all. You followed them, watched what they did, groped to discover and unveil the world they inhabited. You learned them. You were often astonished by their behavior.

Harris's "Occam's razor" was a contradiction. The logic he applied to Roger's supposed means, motive, and opportunity was too convenient, too forced.

Alex didn't believe it.

46

Kathy McKinnon hadn't wanted to impose a curfew on Jared. She wanted to instill in him independence, personal responsibility. She didn't want to nag or worry about him. She didn't like reducing him to a child.

Her own schedule was varied and uncertain. She taught yoga during the day and several evenings a week, sometimes private classes. She didn't always know when she'd be home. She often missed dinner, ate what she needed before or later. Then Jared had to fend for himself. Make his own dinner, do his homework, be home in time to get a good night's sleep. She had to trust him to do this.

His life as he'd grown older had become complicated, but it was also acquiring structure, habit, solidity. He had friends, school, activities. If Kathy didn't know where he was, she could make a good guess. She tried to have faith in Jared and the world he lived in.

But Shane's death had changed everything. Every moment her son was out of sight now left her terrified.

And since he'd started seeing Ashley Green, he'd been coming home late at night, or early in the morning before school.

Her fear made her strident, overbearing, not at all the way she wanted to address the situation. "Jared, you can't be doing this! Out late on a school night, wandering around in the dark! Do you hear me? I want you home by nine o'clock! At the latest!"

Jared's response when she spoke to him like this was the opposite. He hated arguing with his mother. He dialed it all down to what she wanted to hear, and what he would try his best to deliver. "Okay, Mom."

"I'm serious, Jared. Promise me."

"I promise, Mom."

And for a moment, they both believed him.

But Jared was also a teenager. Their brains were undeveloped, lagging far behind their physical appearance. They were tall, their bodies bursting with hormones, growth spurts, developing muscles. They were all about their culture and its language. They thought they were grown up. But they didn't know what they didn't know. They were capable of doing idiotic things, forgetting everything, being totally unaware of the repercussions of their actions or what was going to happen in the next minute.

It was almost eleven, and Jared wasn't home.

He was jogging up Chestnut Street. It was after ten—like ten twenty or something. He didn't wear a watch and his phone was dead, but he knew it was late and his mother was probably calling him, her calls going straight to voicemail, and she would be upset with him when he got home. His van was where he usually parked it, in the public parking behind the Calder Mill, because there was no room in the driveway at home, and he'd gone straight from school, by school bus, to Aerie Ink.

He felt bad. He wanted to be better. But Ashley, man. It was like some spell or witchcraft or something. She was cool about him going home—"okay, bye," she'd say, her breathy voice sounding like she was falling asleep, though she was on her phone—but he couldn't seem to get out of bed. He'd make the effort, sit up, put his feet on the floor, but first he had to rub his face one more time across her stomach and he'd nuzzle in down there, snaking his arms around her again. And then it would be half an hour later, and Ashley would be listening to some podcast while he was dozing on her stomach.

So he ran. And now it was raining and foggy and he could hardly see anything. It would be at least ten minutes running through this shit until he got home. Most of it uphill. *Fuck.*

A vehicle slowed beside him, the passenger window lowering.

"Hey, Jared. You need a ride? I'm going up past Cedar."

"Oh, hey, man—Yes! Thank you! It sucks out here!"

The truck stopped. Jared tried the door but it wouldn't open.

"It gets stuck," the driver said. "I got to do it."

He got out and came around the truck.

47

The place gave her the creeps now. Every morning as Isabel walked into the Settlement from the parking lot, she could see plainly the spot beyond the vegetable patch where Shane's body had hung on that first morning—her first day here. She hadn't seen the body, but she knew where it had been found, and her whole impression of the Settlement dated from that moment. Every dark morning—it was now less than two months before the winter solstice—when she came to work, she saw it as she imagined it might have looked 381 years earlier. Dark, gloomy, no sign of light, except sometimes a flickering fire as Chester pumped the bellows in his forge. In the cabins, they lit flickering oil lamps and made smoky fires in the fireplaces. God, what an awful place. The settlers must have gone out of their minds.

The woods looked impenetrable where they bordered the marsh. She could imagine Hannah looking at them from the cabins, fearful of whatever might be lurking in there, looking back at her. Natives, wolves, other creatures. What had lurked closer, in plain sight, right here in their midst? What had happened to them? And why had they left?

It was cold and damp every morning in Goody Swaine's claustrophobic log cabin—as cold as her own house. Every morning she made a fire with the kindling and logs stacked beside the crude stone fireplace, and the small interior warmed up quickly. But it remained an unwelcome place.

She shivered inside the raw wooden structure, bare except for a rough chair, a stool, a table, and a pot that might hang over the fire if she wanted to demonstrate meal-making to a visitor. All those layers of her historical outfit were insufficient. The wool grew wet with sweat or rain through the day.

Today, the Settlement glistened in a mist of fine rain. When Isabel lit the fire, wet smoke billowed from the fireplace and filled the room instead of going up the chimney. She opened the windows and the small door, but that just seemed to pull more smoke into the cabin. She couldn't remain inside. She couldn't even get close enough to the fireplace to put it out.

People came running. Jeff Block, Monte Glover, Bill and Jan Conrad. They fanned the fire, swung the door open and shut to try to improve the draft. Nothing worked. They began to cough. Monte fetched a bucket of water and poured it over the fire, which smoked worse.

They stood around outdoors in the rain.

"It's okay, folks," Monte bellowed at the few early visitors who had gathered to watch. "Just a blocked chimney."

"That's what I'm checking on," said Chester Coffey. He was walking with a ladder—a neat handmade contraption fashioned from long saplings that appeared to be of genuine colonial design and ancestry. His felt hat with the feather was clamped down over the thin wet strands of his hair. His leather jerkin was shiny wet. In one hand, he carried a long, nearly straight branch, its smaller limbs hacked off.

"Chester, please don't go up there in this rain," said Nancy, walking quickly behind him. She carried a basket holding a few small squashes and carrots. "The roof will be slippery."

"It'll be fine, you'll see," said Chester. Then he addressed Isabel. "Goody Swaine, has your fire been smoking before today?"

"A little but not like today."

"We'll take a look." Chester laid the ladder against the eaves of the roof and began climbing.

"Chester, please," Nancy said again. "The house isn't on fire. You don't have to go up there now. Monte, do tell him to come down."

"She's right, Goodman Denham. It'll keep for another day. I put the fire out. No need to head aloft at the moment."

But Chester was already on the roof. He pulled a small hatchet from his belt and swung it without force into the thick shingles, where the edge of its blade lodged. "See. Got a good handhold. I'm not going anywhere."

He moved easily across the slope of the roof, releasing and sinking the hatchet blade for a secure handhold, until he reached the stone chimney. There he straddled the ridge, where he appeared quite safe and comfortable, a foot planted on either side.

"Oh, do take care, Chester," said Nancy.

The small group of people, most of them the players in their old clothes, standing in the rain around the small cabin watching Chester on the roof, made Isabel think of a scene in an old painting.

Chester maneuvered the long pole until he was able to thrust it down the chimney. He lifted and plunged the pole several times. What had been thin wisps of smoke now thickened and rose out of the chimney, swirling around his head.

Chester started to say, "Got a nest or someth—"

The shriek of the visitor right beside her startled Isabel more than the animal shooting out of the chimney straight at Chester's head. Dark brown with long pink hands, clawed fingers stretching forward. Because of the scale of the cabin, it appeared huge, the size and shape of a football. It landed on Chester's head, scrabbled for footing on his hat, the hat came off, and the creature leaped into the air. Gasps, more shrieks, people jumped as the writhing bundle sailed over their heads. It landed ten feet from the house, a rolling ball of fur, then scurried away.

Someone shouted again—Isabel looked up to see Chester slip. He slid down the wet shingles. Then he was airborne, twisting, midflight.

Nancy cried out, "Oh, no!"

He landed heavily and they all heard the breath expelled from him by force.

"Chester!" Nancy dropped her basket and rushed to his side.

"Oh my God," said several visitors.

Everyone drew close.

"Stand back now," said Monte, in his deep voice, and they did.

Except Nancy, who dropped to her knees beside Chester's head.

"Chester, darling," she said softly, bending over him.

Isabel saw the way Nancy smoothed the thin hair away from his face, her palm lingering as it passed across his furry cheek.

"Is he okay?" said one of the visitors. "That was some fall!"

Chester rolled onto his back and tried to sit up. "I'm all right," he said. He put his hand on his leg, staring at it, and fell back.

"Chester, *please* lie down," urged Nancy.

Monte squatted beside Chester. "Chester, I want you to lie still. I'm going to call an ambulance. You need to be looked at properly. No fooling around here."

"No, no ambulance," said Chester. He was trying to sit up again. "I'm all right. I just need to go home."

Monte pulled a phone from inside his jerkin and punched the numbers. "I don't think so," he said with a tone of great good humor to the assembled group. "Don't try this at home, folks."

"Where's my hat?" said Chester.

"Chester, do sit still," said Nancy. "Look, I've got your hat." She showed Chester his hat and put it in her basket.

By the time the ambulance came, Chester was visibly upset, attempting to stand and resisting Monte and Nancy who were trying to keep him down. "I want to go home!" he kept saying.

The EMT team, a man and a woman, with pleasant, imperturbable assurance, took control, told Chester to lie still, bound him to a gurney, and took him away. Nancy followed in her car.

She left her basket behind.

48

The ringing phone jolted Alex awake. He raised his head abruptly and realized he was staring at the Granite Harbor Police Department screen saver, which showed the Chamber of Commerce town photograph: a sunny, summer view of the harbor filled with boats. And the time, floating slowly across the screen: 7:26 A.M.

It was his own cell phone ringing on the desk in front of him. Not his department phone. He reached for it, looking to see who was calling.

Thirty-two hours earlier, 11:30 P.M. night before last, Kathy McKinnon had called the station to report her son, Jared, missing. On-duty officer Becky Watrous had taken the call. She phoned the emergency room at the Penobscot Medical Center. A quiet night so far, no teenagers. Becky knew Jared McKinnon was Shane Carter's friend, so she'd called Detective Brangwen.

He was at Kathy's house fifteen minutes later, at midnight.

Jared had been coming home late since he'd started seeing Ashley Green, she told Alex. She'd talked to him about not being out late, especially now, but she couldn't *keep* him at home.

"I can't stop him," she said helplessly. "He says yes, like he hears me and understands, and then he just . . ."

"Believe me, I understand," said Alex. "At least he's saying yes."

He asked her the routine necessary questions. Any reason he might have run away? Gone to see his father, who lived in California? Could his father have turned up and persuaded him to go away with him? No way, said Kathy.

Outside, he called Mark Beltz, told him Jared was missing. "Jared and Ethan have a van. Registered to one of them. They keep it parked in the lot behind the mill. See if it's there, anything in it."

At 1:00 A.M., he called Ashley and drove to her grandmother's house. They talked in the living room. Jared had been there earlier, but left—she wasn't sure—like around ten thirty?

In his car at 1:25 A.M., he called Isabel.

"Oh my God," she said. "No, he's not here."

"Can you wake Ethan and ask him when he last saw him?"

She brought the phone with her—he heard rustling, movement—he imagined her in the upstairs hall. He heard her knocking on the door, Ethan's croaking voice, resentful at being woken. She put the phone on speakerphone and asked him when he'd last seen Jared. Alex heard the spatial echo of the room.

"Why?" Ethan said.

"He's not home," Isabel said. "Kathy's worried. When and where did you last see him?"

"Umm . . . At the Shed. Yesterday—no, the day before yesterday. After school."

"Do you hear that?" she said.

"Yes," said Alex. "Ethan, do you have any idea where he might be—now, at almost two in the morning? Anything at all you can think of?"

"Maybe with Ashley? The ink artist."

"He was with her earlier in the evening, but not now. I've just seen her. Anything else?"

"No. Mom, what's going on?"

"Alex, do you need anything else right now?"

"No, thanks. Thank you, Ethan. Obviously if you think of anything, call me, please."

"Alex, please let me know when you hear anything."

"I will."

His phone had been buzzing, two calls from Kathy. He called her back. No Jared. Could she talk more now if he came over? Yes, please come, she said, no way could she sleep.

She was in sweats. She was going out of her mind. Was he thinking it had anything to do with what happened to Shane?

"Let's hope not. He's a missing teen. It's not that unusual."

"It is for us."

"What did they share, do together, Shane and Jared?"

"Everything," said Kathy. "The three of them, Jared and Shane and Ethan. They did everything together. They shared everything, their whole lives. Summer camp at the Y, chess—"

"Chess with Roger?"

"Yes. He was wonderful with them. All three of them had chess lessons with him, went to tournaments. I don't believe Roger had anything to do with what happened to Shane. And obviously not Jared."

3:00 A.M. She made chamomile tea. She talked about her breakup with Jared's father, who'd gone to California. Jared went out there for a few weeks every summer. What a mistake that had been. She hadn't known him at all. She'd fooled herself. Her fault as much as his father's—different temperaments, different values—different realities! She was a perfectionist and he was—never mind. *Ha!* So have a child together! She spoke with lacerating guilt, self-blame. But she had Jared . . . Oh my God . . . She began to cry.

He made more tea. Then said, "I've got to go. I'll come back in the morning. Call me of course if he comes home. If you think of anything."

At dawn, with a sudden wild sense of dread, exaggerated by a lurid yellow sky, he tore north doing eighty on the Fairhaven Road to Granite Harbor Settlement. He walked all over the place. Into the woods, the marsh, onto the beach, looking in the waves along the shore. He checked the dumpster behind the gift shop. Nothing.

At six thirty he stopped at the Granite Deli & Bagel and bought six bagels and six donuts. Back at the station he made coffee. 8:00 A.M. department meeting with Chief Raintree and all officers. Procedure cranking up. Missing Persons bulletin issued to agencies statewide. Media outlets alerted. He sent Mark Beltz to check out Roger Priestly's house—no logic to it if Mark asked him why, but he didn't ask. Just go through the place again, everywhere, every closet, Alex told him.

Nothing here, Mark reported back by phone an hour later.

Alex called Doreen Wisner, Shane's mother. Asked her if she could think
of anywhere Jared night be. She couldn't.

Midmorning, Alex and Mark went to the high school. Through his own
boys, Mark knew most of Jared's and Shane's friends and peers in the junior
and senior classes. They were taken out of class and brought to Alex and
Mark in the principal's office. They'd already spoken about Shane but now
the questions were about Jared. Where did they think he might be? Could
possibly be? The kids shrugged. Several mentioned Ashley. They talked with
Sophie—it was certainly easier for Alex with Mark in the room.

Nothing.

In his car, he called Agent Harris in Boston.

"So I grant you it's not Roger," said Harris. "But all you've got is a missing
teen. Not something I would come up for. Kids go missing all the time, usually
for no more than a few hours. I'm not downplaying anything, Detective, but
any association with the other boy, Shane Carter, is right now just coincidence. They're friends at school. Let's hope the boy is found. You get anything, give me a call."

The television trucks and generators descended on the William P. Merrill
Station for the press conference outside the station at noon. Chief Raintree
made an appeal to anyone who might know of anything. Then the TV reporters shouted questions, the inevitable linking and revisiting of stories—
was Roger Priestly responsible for the murder of Shane Carter? Did Jared
McKinnon know Roger Priestly? Was Roger Priestly's suicide an admission
of guilt? Had Jared and Roger Priestly been close?

In the afternoon, Alex and available officers drove around town, looked
inside the dumpsters behind Hannaford, Brown & Cord, and Seafarer Marine, not because of any connection but because they were large enough to
hold a body. They walked in a rough grid formation every possible route between Ashley's grandmother's house on Atlantic Avenue and Kathy's on Cedar Street. Looked at every possible detour through backyards, walked empty
lots. This was police work. That and just driving around, trying to think,
hoping unreasonably that Jared would somehow pop out of the shroud of
absolute disappearance that had dropped over him.

Harbormaster Dave Pixley drove Alex around the harbor in his Whaler.

They peered under docks, floats, cruised around the few boats still not hauled out for the winter. Then along the shores of Watson Cove. The tide was low. They skirted and nosed among rocks covered with seaweed. Bell buoys clanged out in the marked channel. The afternoon was growing dark. An icy damp floated above the water like a blanket.

Nothing.

Nothing from nothing leaves nothing.

A total absence of any kind of clue, sighting, basis for conjecture. Alex felt unprepared for this. An amateur. Ashamed at his powerlessness.

Who do you call if you're the police?

He called Kathy—her voice clutched, choked, seeing who was calling. No news, he told her immediately. But could he come over?

Her face had collapsed. Eyes sunken in their sockets, the pigment around them dark. Deep hollows in her cheeks, around her mouth. As if the essence beneath the surface of her had ebbed away.

"Kathy, are you eating and drinking? Is there someone who can come over—"

"Oh . . ." She waved a hand. "People are calling. I can't . . . What's going on?"

"Could I borrow something of Jared's?"

"What?"

"His skateboard."

"What for?"

The lie came easily. "Just to see if anybody recognizes it."

Isabel answered immediately. "Any news about Jared?"

"No," said Alex. "Where are you?"

She was at home. She'd been at work at the Settlement, she told Alex, but Chester Coffey had fallen off a roof, and Nancy had left, and Isabel couldn't stay any longer, she was too worried about Jared, so she'd come home.

"Could I come over?"

"What for?"

"I need your help."

When he knocked, Flynn barked. He watched through the mudroom as she opened the door to the back deck and the dog rushed out. When she opened the door to him, she didn't look much better than Kathy. She was in jeans and a sweatshirt. No hat.

Pointing down at his hand. "What's that?"

"It's Jared's skateboard. I wondered if . . . perhaps you could—"

"It doesn't work like that, Alex." She sounded annoyed.

"I know—or, I don't know. I just thought . . ."

She looked down at the board again, stood aside, and opened the door wider. "Okay—of course."

In the kitchen, he said, "Where's Ethan?"

"Downstairs. In his workshop."

He followed her into the living room. She sat on the sofa he knew so well.

"I don't suppose you've got any more of Roger's stuff?"

She glared at him. "No." She held out her hands.

He handed her the skateboard. Then backed away and sat in a chair facing her.

She laid the board across her legs, top up, knees together between the wheels. She placed her hands flat on the black sandpapery griptape where Jared's feet would have stood. She looked up at Alex. They locked eyes.

Maybe thirty seconds later, she moved her hands to the sides of the board, holding it where he might have held it. She returned her gaze to Alex. Her face was haggard, drawn, crushed, pale, and five years later. They would grow old, not together but in glimpses, across town from each other, yet he knew he would always love her face.

Her eyes were ranging in quick shifts across his face too. What was she seeing?

"I'm sorry, Alex." She lifted the skateboard and placed it on the floor.

He brought the skateboard back. Nothing, I'm afraid, he told Kathy. He spent an hour with her, drinking tea, both of them looking often toward the door.

"Alex, there's nothing you can do here. I appreciate it. But you haven't had any sleep. Go home."

He couldn't go home. He went to the station. He sat helplessly in front of his computer and tapped to open the screen saver. He pulled up Weather .com. He'd talked with the chief about mounting outdoor search parties in the woods around both Mount Meguntic and the Settlement. That would be a depressing exercise, an admission of an abject lack of evidence, and Jared had not been known to wander lonely through the woods. Yet it would be something to do—and they'd be seen to be doing something. The forecast for the next week was cool, partly sunny.

He heated a ramen in the microwave and slurped it in front of his computer. He pulled up other cases of Missing Persons on the Maine State Police site:

> **Case date:** 11/14/2004. Aspin, Jonathan (4/08/86). Jonathan was last seen running down a rural road in Warren, Maine, in a delusional state. Jonathan has not been seen or heard from since . . .
>
> **Case date:** 10/04/1973, Lewis, William (11/04/1958) was reported missing by his father on 10/03/1973. He was last seen on 10/03/1973 in Porter, Maine, supposedly going to spend the day at Fryeburg Fair . . .
>
> **Case date:** 6/14/1993. Wilkinson, Gretchen (3/19/78) was last seen playing with friends in Belfast Park on 6/13/1993. She said she was going home . . .

The photographs were old high school yearbook photos. Thirty-four outstanding cases. About half of them kids, teens. Last seen . . . decades . . . gone forever.

He had the feeling—not a good one—that this would not be forever, a blank silent curtain drawn over Jared.

The ramen was congealed and disgusting. He pushed it aside.

He scrolled through the files of the local registered sex offenders—again, an admission of total cluelessness. Each mug shot was a picture of Dorian Gray, marked not so much by moral transgression as pathological neglect, unhappiness, anger, physical dissipation. Could any of them have overpowered an athletic six-foot teenager—and for what? To stuff him with a toad?

He was wondering what else he might constructively do on the computer when his phone rang. On the desk in front of him.

He'd been asleep—it was 7:26 A.M.

"Yes, Mark."

"We've got a body."

49

It was found by two hikers with a dog. In front of a camp on Moody Pond. They've just phoned it in. They're staying there till we get there. At 27 Thorndyke Road. I'll text it to you. Off Molyneaux Road, southwest shore of the pond. I'm heading there now. Judy's calling the crews."

"Male? Female?" Alex was already outside the station, climbing into his car. "Any description of the body?"

"It's naked. They haven't looked closely. They're keeping the dog away. They think it's male."

"On my way."

Mainers called any residential structure on a lake, from a fishing shack to a Hamptons-style mansion, a "camp."

The house at 27 Thorndyke Road was a sizeable cedar-and-glass house with vaulted ceilings. It was shut up for the season. Had not been broken into or entered. Mark had already contacted the owners, who lived in New York City and had not been in the house since Labor Day weekend.

Mark's cruiser was in the driveway, no other vehicles had arrived yet. Alex walked around the house.

Mark was standing with a middle-aged couple holding a Lab on a leash. They were halfway between the rocky shore and the deck running along the shore-facing wall of the house. Brown leaves littered the lawn.

He saw the body. Lying on its side, knees pulled up in a fetal position, its back to him. Naked, white. A long back, muscular in the shoulders, narrow in the waist.

The dog whined and pulled at the leash, straining toward Alex as he approached the group. Mark started talking. David and Mary Chapman, South Fairhaven, morning walk.

"Logan ran almost up to it and started whining, so then we saw it, and we called 911. . . ."

"Did Logan touch it at all?"

"No. He just started whining and came running back. . . ."

Alex walked slowly toward the body. He looked down carefully around his feet as he walked. He couldn't make out any sign of footprints, dragging, flattening of grass, any disturbance in the leaves that had blown off the surrounding trees and scattered over the lawn. But it was a windy morning, leaves were blowing through the air around them, settling on the lawn. He got within eight feet and began circling the body.

Yes, male—a boy. A teenager. Long hairy legs, folded over each other. The muscled arms tucked into the chest, as if trying to keep warm, hands together below the chin, as if sleeping on his side. Alex saw beneath the elbows, where these were tucked protectively over the stomach, the long line of the incision parting the dark belly hair. The edges lifted, puckered, showing the epidermal and subcutaneous layers, the abdomen distended where, in such a perfect, young, toned body, he would have expected to see a six-pack.

As he continued circling the body, the front came into view. A few steps more and he saw the inked SHANE, faded but clearly legible across the forehead.

Oh, Kathy. Alone in her house. No nearby sister. No other children.

This would not be like his interview with Doreen Wisner. *How do I tell Kathy that her beautiful boy, her only child, who did not live in a corner of the basement but for whom she had made a home and life and done everything, has been so horribly*—he wouldn't tell her about that . . . yet—*and I have no clue who has done it or why.*

Now Alex noticed the wrists and ankles. Dark, purple and blue rings; deep abrasions of the skin, which would have appeared chafed raw and bloodied in a living body.

Jared had been bound tightly at the wrists and ankles and then somehow freed. Escaped or released?

Again, Alex scanned the ground around the body, the lawn. No apparent (others would look more closely) flattening of the grass, trail of disturbed leaves that might indicate someone carrying or dragging a weight.

He looked at the neighboring houses: all appeared to be summer rentals also closed for the season.

Now he turned toward the water. A light breeze stippled the pond's flat surface with small cat's-paws. No dock, no boat. Jared was cold, but his dry hair was lifting on the breeze.

He would need a photograph for Kathy. He aimed his phone. Just the face. Jared's mouth was slightly open. He could have been asleep, untroubled by dreams.

50

A week after the boy's eighteenth birthday, a registered letter arrived at the school, the first piece of mail the boy had ever received. It was sent by a law firm, and informed him that a trust set up by his father's grandmother, having bypassed his deceased father and been held in trusteeship by executors, had now passed on to him, on reaching legal age. A lump sum and a small annuity. The letter requested that he contact the law firm at the earliest opportunity.

He showed the letter to Ivan Haney and asked him what it meant. He watched Ivan's face as he read the letter.

Haney smiled, moving his head side to side in a wondering way, as if listening to music. "You have not been forgotten in the grand scheme of things, Mister." He explained the terms in the letter, and the route by which the windfall had reached him. "You got an inheritance."

Then Haney sat him down at the table in the Shack and stared at him more forcefully than he ever remembered. "You need to get out of here, Mister. You need to go off into the world now and make a life for yourself. Now you are fixed up good for the world out there. But you must shepherd and conserve your assets with foresight and planning. So you listen to me now. I'm going to tell you how to do that."

"I can't stay here?" The boy felt an end coming again. For a moment, the memory of his dog Boon lying beside the canal passed across his mind.

"Nossir," Ivan said emphatically. "This place is trash, though it's done well enough by you and me, but it's time for you to go. This is a fortuitous occurrence, and you have to make the best of it."

In short order, Haney helped the boy craft a response to the law firm. Helped him open an account at the Bangor Savings Bank in Gardiner, into which his inheritance of $763,431 was soon deposited. He'd already taught the boy to drive, now they bought a truck, a 2007 Ford F-150 with 37,600 miles on the clock.

"You go out into the world now and buy yourself a small house. A man needs his own place, if he's fortunate enough to be able to procure it. A property that will provide for you all you need but no more. Comfortable enough for a man alone, but not a burden to him. A place with a sticker price that will not make too big a dent in your inheritance. Low property tax. Then you get yourself some work. A man needs to work. Find something that suits your temperament. Then you will have two incomes: your savings from your inheritance, and your wages. You must spend less than incoming every month, and put aside the surplus amount of the leftover in your bank each month, where it will *accrue*. In this way, you will continue to profit all your days, so you will hereafter be a free man on this Godforsaken earth, free to choose your work and go about your business and be beholden to no man. Or woman—by far the trickier of the two types of humans you will encounter. Don't let one of them get her hooks into your money. You got me, Mister?"

A great opaque space yawned in front of the boy. How did you go out into the world? But Haney had planned for that. He presented him with a large road atlas of Maine. "This'll get you where you're going. You just stop and orient yourself when you need to. Head east, north, south, doesn't matter—though I would counsel you to go north—mark your direction, speed, and time, like we done in the woods—dead reckoning, like I showed you—and you'll know where you are. You drop me a line when you're fetched up."

As he drove through Maine, in a northerly direction, and looked for a home, the boy carried with him the memory of his father and the way he loved traveling up and down the New River and the waterways in his runabout, and brought his son to share his joy. Coastal properties, he found, were far outside his budget, and the expanse of Atlantic Ocean water stretching away to the horizon too lonely. But he found many small houses— "camps," the Realtors called them—along lakes and rivers. One of these, five miles inland from a coastal town, beside a pond that was part of a network of waterways that led to the sea, already furnished, with a small barn in the back, seemed to fit.

Looking through the atlas, he had seen, with a shock at reading the words, the name Prouts Neck on one of the pages. The configuration of the page, white where the land was, curving diagonally beside the blue representing the sea, made him remember the long curving beach, and the round outcropping peninsula—the *neck*—where the jumble of big houses sat on the granite rocks above the coastal path. Where, in the backyard of one of those houses, he and Sally slept in the tent. Long ago. Ten or twelve years, he wasn't sure. He wondered if she still remembered him.

In August of the year following his departure from Welldale and the purchase of his home, he drove south.

But when he got close to Prouts Neck, small movable wooden fences stopped him in the middle of the road. Young men and women in white polo shirts and khaki shorts smiled as they said, "Do you have a sticker? I'm sorry, sir. This road is open only for residents."

He turned around and drove up one street after another, trying to reach Prouts Neck, but the whole area was full of private roads with little wooden fences and signs announcing that parking was for residents only, policed by the young people in white shirts and khaki shorts.

His simple plan foiled, he retreated. The narrow tree-shrouded lanes and hedges and the little fences gave way to wider streets with no fences or young people guarding them, and the houses were smaller and closer together. He passed a pharmacy, a hardware store, a sandwich shop. He turned in behind them and parked in the public parking area beside the low coastal sand dunes.

He walked through the dunes to the beach. He took off his shoes and walked into the water. He remembered that the seawater in Maine was cold.

Far down the beach, the granite outcrop of Prouts Neck rose above the sea.

There were no fences on the long beach. Just people lying in the sand, running, kicking balls, swimming in the waves, just like he remembered. No one stopped him or looked at him as he walked down the beach. They were all having a good time. They looked like they belonged there.

Above the soft rhythmic roll of the waves breaking gently on the shallows and the approach and retreat of the water washing around his ankles, he heard a voice he remembered.

It had been three years since he'd seen Byron Pugh at his last Survival Games. He was bigger, even stronger-looking. His hair was longer. A girl in a bikini was sitting on his shoulders, her thighs wrapped around his neck. She was pretending to ride him like a horse while he chased another girl around their towels in the sand. The girls were shrieking with laughter. Then they changed places, and the other girl rode him and he chased the girl who had been on his shoulders. He noticed how tightly the girls clamped their brown thighs around Byron Pugh's neck and the firm, comfortable way he held on to their legs, as if he owned them.

Sexy, he remembered the girls saying at the Survival Games.

The boy continued plodding along the sand. He turned his head often to see Byron Pugh and the girls until he lost sight of them behind the other people on the beach.

He found the Buells' house right away. The shingles painted yellow at the top. He found the hole in the hedge. He stood to the side and listened. Laughing. Children calling to each other, parents calling to children—the sounds of the life he had been close to and listened to for less than a year living with the Buells—*his cousins*, after all. *His family*—

"Sir!" The voice rang out clear and sharp.

Two men with short buzz cut heads, dressed in uniforms, were walking toward him. An SUV, the words BLAZE SECURITY on its doors and panels, was parked at the corner of the road behind them.

"Are you a resident, sir?"

"No."

"Are you staying with friends here?"

"No."

"Step away from the hedge, please, sir."

"What are you doing here?"

"I'm just walking around."

They'd reached him now. They were tall, strong-looking men, with tight perma-creased khaki uniforms that stressed their physiques. They wore duty belts with pistols and small boxes of equipment. At first he thought they were policemen, but now he saw they didn't have badges.

"This is all private property, sir. What are you doing trying to get through that hedge?"

"I'm not. I was just looking."

"I'll ask you again, sir, what are you doing here?"

"Nothing. I just walked up here from the beach."

"Where's your vehicle?"

"It's not here."

"Where is it?"

"I parked it. At the other end of the beach."

"What's your name?"

"Ivan Haney."

"Can you show me some ID, please?"

"I don't have it with me."

"You don't have your wallet, driver's license on you?"

"No." It was true. He'd never owned or carried a wallet until Ivan had bought him one when he'd acquired some money and a driver's license, and he'd taken to keeping it in the center console compartment of his truck when he left his house. It felt more secure there.

"Come with us, please, sir."

They put him in the backseat of their SUV. They drove him through the narrow gated streets until they reached the wider streets with smaller houses closer together, where the stores began, not far from where he'd parked. They stopped. The security man in the passenger seat got out and opened the rear door.

"You can get out here, sir. Stay away from Prouts Neck. That's all private property. You understand?"

"Yes."

The security man got back into the SUV. The vehicle made a U-turn in the street and drove back toward Prouts Neck.

As he walked through the parking lot behind the stores, he heard that voice again.

"Whoa! Look who *it is!*"

He turned and saw Byron Pugh coming out of the back door of the pharmacy. He was alone. He was carrying a small plastic bag of his purchases. He was wearing clothes now: baggy shorts to his knees, sport sandals, a billowing pink T-shirt.

"*Dude!*" Byron Pugh sounded as if he'd found an old friend. He stopped, closer than he ever had at school, and looked him up and down. "How's it hangin', man?"

As if everything around him had become liquid and he could detect the least ripple in the air, the boy took in the stillness of the parking lot, the configuration of the parked cars.

He stepped back on his left foot, turned partly away from Byron Pugh, leaning backward as if to reach for something, then rotated his torso forward again in a whipping motion, his long left arm fully extended and swinging through the air with a momentum gathered from his whole body weight rising through his back and shoulder and transferred down his arm until the thickest part of his forearm slammed into Byron Pugh's neck. Byron dropped as if he'd been held up by a string that had suddenly been cut.

Always keep a roll—better, two—of duct tape with you, Ivan had counseled him.

Three days later, he found it was surprisingly easy to get into Prouts Neck in the middle of the night. All the wooden fences and their young guardians were gone. The streets were deserted. He was able to drive right up to the hole in the hedge surrounding the Buells' house. There were no lights on— except for the blue streetlight he remembered.

Time collapsed. It all looked so familiar. It seemed just an hour since he had come out the back door onto the deck. The flat spot beneath the tall oak tree was where they'd pitched the tent.

He looked up at the house. Maybe Sally was still in there. Was she with her husband?—Did she have a husband? Was she all grown up, big like a woman? He pictured her still small like she was when she was taking her development pills.

She would be impressed by him now. He'd acquired Byron Pugh's essence.
He would be *sexy* now. But he didn't need her.

He set up his two-by-fours to make a proscenium.

She would see it in the morning.

51

O h my *God...*"

Alex heard her voice fall away as she dropped her arm—he could see it, the hand holding the phone falling to her side. He heard other voices, conversations some distance away. She was at the Settlement. He could see the scene, the visitors walking around the log cabins. She raised the phone to her mouth again. "This can't be happening."

"Isabel, can you please help me? I've got to go tell Kathy. Can you come with me, please? She'll need somebody—you."

They met at Isabel's house. He was there first, parked on the street. She shot into the driveway, just behind him, got out of her car and into his Subaru, her costume piling around her.

"Tell me."

"What?"

"Is it the same thing?"

"I can't tell—"

"For *God's sake*, Alex! *Is it the same?* Just tell me that."

"It appears to be. Sort of."

She stared at him. Her face went white in seconds. "Ethan's next."

"No—why do you say that?"

"Can't you *see?* The three of them were always together, and now they're being targeted. You need to, to *stop this!*"

He tried not to let his voice betray him. "We're doing everything we can." *We* indicating the larger crime-solving machine he wished he was or had access to.

"This is crazy, Alex. You have to catch this person. You've got to do *more*."

"It's police work—"

"*It's obviously not enough!*" She threw open the door. "I can't go over there like this. Two minutes."

Kathy knew the moment she opened the door, the moment she saw both of them. Her eyes flying between them trying not to see or know. Her face coming apart in small places not even identifiable as components. Isabel held on to her for a long time. Kathy barely made any noise. Except a gasping.

Alex put on the kettle—*because I'm English?* he wondered. Tea, the British national panacea for every calamity. Cliché of the culture. But it had gotten them through two world wars and everything since, and it was the only thing he could think of doing. He poured water over the bags in mugs and put them on the table.

Finally, Kathy said, "How?"

He felt Isabel's eyes on him.

He told Kathy where he'd been found. "He was naked. Hypothermia, we think."

"My God . . . Was he . . . harmed?"

"There was a wound. On his stomach. We're not sure what made it. But that wasn't the cause of death."

One last awful appeal, her voice, low and quiet but filling the air as if out of a ceramic vessel: "Are you sure it's him? . . . Jared?"

Alex pulled out his phone and handed it to her.

Kathy dissolved in Isabel's arms.

"I'm sorry," he said. And to Isabel, "I have to go."

"A toad, yes," Phil Gressens told him over the phone. He'd arrived at the house on Thorndyke Road after Alex had left. He'd be doing the autopsy early in the week, but he had some preliminary information. "It was still alive. We'll look for a DNA match with your other toads. But no water in the body cavity. He got there dry."

"So he was brought and dumped there?"

"I wouldn't say dumped. The arrangement of the body, the limbs, was consistent with a natural self-determined position. Looks more like he lay himself down, curled up, and went to sleep. Right there on the lawn where he was found."

"Cause of death?"

"As with the other boy, not the incision. A clean cut through the rectus abdominis—the abdominal wall—but not deep. No fatal loss of blood. No internal organs cut or nicked. But no sign of asphyxiation this time. Cause of death most likely hypothermia—exposure. Looks like he'd been there all night. The low last night was around forty-two. He'd have probably made it if he'd gotten to a hospital."

Alex wished Phil hadn't said that.

"Then there's the abrasions on the wrists and ankles. Looks like severe rope burns. Much more pronounced than the other boy. A real struggle. Like he was restrained by a synthetic fiber rope—polypropylene, common stuff, often yellow. A coarse plastic, not smooth and pliable like nylon. Cheap, strong, but prone to chafing. Also, it's slippery, knots don't hold well in it. Not my place to make a reach this far, but I would say it's possible he was tied down with poly, then left long enough to struggle until he either chafed through the restraints or the knots unraveled, or he freed one and untied the rest, something like that."

"While his stomach was cut open?"

"He's young and strong. That chafing around the wrists and ankles, he did that to himself, struggling. For a long time. Then—maybe—he got away. Crawled there somehow. No other marks on him. Got there, lay down, and died."

"But he hadn't swum ashore?"

"I can only tell you he had not been immersed."

52

Alex strapped his kayak to the top of his Subaru, drove to the "camp" on Thorndyke Road, carried it across the lawn, and pushed it into the water.

Moody Pond was part of the Loon River waterway, which had its source somewhere deep in Maine, far inland from Calder County. From there, the water flowed in a series of runnels, streams, rivers, ponds, occasionally widening out into lakes. How much of it was navigable, Alex didn't know.

But it all flowed one way: from the higher inland elevations toward the sea.

He clambered in, settled quickly into his seat, and pushed off from the small rocks at the edge of the lawn. He paddled only a short distance from the shore, then raised the paddle and let the wind and current carry him where it would. He resisted dipping the paddle to keep his bow oriented to the direction of travel. He let go and watched to see what the kayak would do.

The closed houses next door and their garages and outbuildings had been entered and searched and revealed no signs that could be associated with what had happened to Jared. Other houses in the neighborhood had also been visited.

Alex felt sure Jared came ashore from the pond behind the house. But he hadn't been in the water—"not been immersed"—no water in his body cavity. His hair had been dry.

So he'd come by boat. Alex saw it clearly in his head. Somehow he'd freed
himself, found a boat tied to a dock, crawled in, untied the line, pushed off
or drifted away. Not strong enough to row or paddle, he lay down and went
where the boat took him—*downstream*—until it bumped into the pondside
backyard of 27 Thorndyke Road. There, Jared crawled out, across the grass
toward the house . . . but had not made it. Cold, horribly injured, he curled
up and went to sleep.

But the boat kept going. Lightened of its load, not tied to the shore,
turned by current, buffeted by wind, it would have drifted on. Alex wouldn't
find it where it had come from, one of hundreds of properties with boats
tied to docks on the waterway *upstream*. Jared's boat, hopefully identifiable by
name or registration number, lay somewhere *downstream*.

The kayak soon reached the eastern end of Moody Pond. As the shore
drew closer together on each side, the speed picked up as water funneled
into the narrow entrance back into Loon River. Alex had looked on a map,
but this had told him nothing of the depth and navigability of the rocky
bottom ahead. He knew only that Loon River led into Fellows Brook, which
in turn debouched into Coleman Pond, and from there the flow ran in
twisty stretches to Fairhaven and the sea . . . but he didn't think he'd have to
go that far.

Rocks hove up without quite barring his way into Loon River. He dipped
the paddle a few times to avoid the rocks but he tried to let the kayak find
its own way. That was the whole plan. Float, drift, spin, run aground in the
wake of Jared's boat after it left the Thorndyke Road lawn.

Then—what he hadn't noticed or taken in on the small-scale map—
the river divided ahead into two forks on either side of a small "island," a
midstream mound no larger than a tractor trailer, but solid enough to be
overgrown with small trees. The water flowed into each narrow fork with the
same force.

Which one? The kayak had to decide. He let himself be sluiced sideways,
to the right, into the faster fork.

As the island slid past, he saw where the two forks merged ahead in a
jumble of rocky shallows, and there it was. Lodged in a thicket of fallen tree
trunks on the right bank. He stepped out of the kayak. The water was no
deeper than the ankles of his hiking boots.

It was the sort of boat you saw everywhere in Maine. A johnboat, they were called. People hunted from them, or just tooled around ponds and lakes. Wide, flat hulled, easily driven by a small outboard. Nothing to tell one from another. This one was plain aluminum. The small outboard engine was still clamped to its stern, but tilted up and sideways, its propeller lodged into a rock as it trembled and bobbed on the water coursing beneath it. The hull was dented, maybe from before, maybe from its passage down Loon River and over the rocks.

He reached it and looked inside. A plastic red gas tank in the stern with a line to the outboard. Water lay in the bottom.

On one of the wide aluminum seats stretched across the middle was a broad thin smear of brown, not quite dried, blood. Alex pulled his collection pack out of his jacket: a Ziploc bag and his own business card. He scooped up a teaspoon of blood with his card and popped it into the Ziploc.

He walked to the bow. There were the little black adhesive letters and numbers, peeling, but all there: NC 3704 JH.

He shot a photo of the numbers, another of the boat, and sent them to Kevin Regis, with the message: *Find me this boat's owner, address, phone.*

53

The response to the press and media release that a second Granite Harbor High School student had been found murdered was unsurprising. Trucks, generators, cameras, reporters, and a small but growing crowd watching them, appeared outside the William P. Merrill Station almost immediately. The further announcement from inside the station that there were no details, no location, time, or cause of death, that the Granite Harbor Police Department would provide information "soon," only added to the noise outside.

Inside the station foyer, Morgana and her group of "concerned"—they called themselves—parents staged something like a protest, until Chief Raintree invited them into the conference room.

Then it felt like a private harangue aimed directly at Detective Brangwen by his ex-wife.

"Our children are not safe," Morgana barked at him, at commanding volume. She stood in the conference room in her Texas horsewoman outfit, raising a fist with a forefinger sticking out of it, like a Colt 45 aimed straight at Alex. "And we need to know, *now*, what you're doing about it."

The other parents—Morgana's posse of Realtors, Rotary Club members, business owners, and Tinker Bell—stared, first at her, and then at Alex. Another scene straight out of a western: the fearful citizenry mobbing together, in the church or saloon or outside the jail, clamoring for protection by the clearly overwhelmed, outgunned, harried law officer.

Chief Billie Raintree, front and center in the conference room, waited until Morgana had finished speaking, then raised a hand. Raintree's bearing, commanding physical presence, implacable demeanor, and not least her unassailable straddle of social dichotomies brought the clamor to a sudden silence.

"Ladies and gentlemen. I appreciate that 'doing everything we can' may sound to you right now as effective a measure as 'thoughts and prayers.' But it's no less applicable, and I promise you it will be a lot more effective. We are engaged in multiple crime and scientific detection procedures, with the cooperation of many people and agencies. It may seem slow or vague to you, but it has to be, as you can imagine, deliberate and painstaking, and it will produce results. This is police work. And I ask you to please let us get on with it. That is all we can tell you now. You can help by maintaining contact with us and with each other. By staying close to your kids and families and friends. Our officers all have children too, right here in Granite Harbor. We share your concern. But a gathering like this keeps us from our work. It doesn't help us right now. Or you. Thank you."

As in a western, the citizenry disbanded. Muttering, some placated, some disgruntled. Morgana mounted her Ford and drove away.

Back in his office, Alex looked at his phone, which had been vibrating inside the pocket of his jeans. A message from Kevin Regis, the department's IT guy: "Boat reg info sent to your dept email." Alex sat at his desk and opened his email:

North Carolina registered watercraft. NC 3704 JH; Year: 1993; Length: 11'; Material: Aluminum; Mftr SEARS. Model: Swampfire Jon Boat. Engine: Johnson 12 hp, 2005.

Registered to: Frederick Maroni. #14, Neuse St, Oriental, NC, 28571.

Maroni is a tax resident of Oriental, NC, receives his credit card bills, etc., at that address; but owns lakeside property at 31 Beaucaire Ave.,

Granite Harbor, ME 04842. Only phone number found so far: NC area
code: (910) 357-1608. Working on it. Kevin.

Nothing fit. Apart from the wild-card North Carolina stuff, the Beaucaire Ave. address was on Lake Meguntic, miles east and downstream from
Moody Lake and not part of the Loon River waterway. No way could that
boat have reached Thorndyke Road by water from Lake Meguntic.

Alex called the phone number. *"The number you have called is not available. Please
leave your message after the tone."*

"Hello. This message is for Frederick Maroni. I'm Detective Alex Brangwen from the Granite Harbor, Maine, Police Department. I'm calling about
your boat, North Carolina registration NC 3704 JH, which is here in Maine.
It is urgent that you give me a call back as soon as you can. Thank you." He
gave his cell and department numbers.

54

Sophie's voice on the phone had been small, shaky, and at the same time shrill. "Come and get me, *please!* I'm scared! I don't want to be alone!"

She was waiting for him outside her father's house on Mountain Street when Ethan pulled up in the van. School was out again. Kids were home.

"Go," she said, climbing in.

"Where? My place?"

"No, your place is freezing. I don't want to go there. Go!"

Ethan floored it and the van rumbled up Mountain Street.

"Okay, where?"

"I don't want to go anywhere. Let's just drive around. Anyway, it's warm in here."

"You want to get some weed? We could go—"

"No, I don't! I'm freaked out already, I don't want anything. Ethan, what is *going on?* Jared's *dead?* What's happening? I'm so scared." Sophie sat hunched into herself in the passenger seat, where she'd been crammed against Ethan only a week ago when Jared had driven them to the Settlement. "I don't understand. Why Shane and now Jared? Someone's killing *kids?* Who's next?"

"Me," said Ethan.

"What do you mean? Why you?"

"I don't know. But, you know, Shane. And now Jared. So I must be next."

"What did you do?"

"We didn't do anything! Jesus! What do you think?"

"I don't know! But why you?"

"I don't know either! But, like, it was the three of us, and now"—Ethan started to cry, but forced himself to look ahead through the windshield—"it's just me."

Sophie leaned sideways and took his nearest arm in both hands. "Ethan, I'm sorry! Do you want to stop?"

"No! I don't know what to do."

She stroked his arm. "But . . . did the three of you do something together—"

"Yeah! We fucking went skateboarding!" He tried blinking away his tears. "We went skateboarding, and we went to the lake, and the beach, and we went to camp and school and parties, and we played video games and did crazy-ass stuff together—all our fucking lives! And now they're *both gone!*" He shouted through the windshield: *"What am I going to do?"* He began to cry again, his body racked as he tried to hold on to the wheel.

"Ethan, pull over. Right here. Stop. Stop driving now."

He pulled violently toward the curb and the van stopped abruptly. He dropped his face into his hands and sobbed. Sophie unclipped her seat belt and put her arms around him.

"Ethan . . . I'm sorry."

"Oh, God, what is happening?" he cried through his hands. "Shane and Jared gone. Dead. What the fuck is happening?"

"I don't know. But I'm here. I know it's not the same—"

Ethan turned sideways and hugged Sophie with all his strength.

She held on to him while he shook, and they said nothing for a while.

Then Ethan rubbed his eyes and looked up, again through the windshield. "I can't take it in. I don't know what to do." He looked at Sophie. "I'm so glad you're here."

"Me too."

Ethan looked into the rearview mirror, put the van in gear, and drove on up Mountain Street.

"Where are you going?"

"I don't know. Let's just drive around. Unless you want me to take you somewhere?"

"No. I don't want to go anywhere, but I want to be with you."

Ethan turned down Gould Street, drove to the bottom, and pulled into the Meguntic Market.

"What are you doing?" asked Sophie.

"I need something to drink. Like a Coke or whatever. Do you want something?"

"I'm coming in with you. You're not leaving me in here alone."

Sophie held tightly on to Ethan's arm as they went through the market. They bought Cokes, iced tea, a bag of pretzels, and a bag of potato chips.

As they drove away from the market, out of town on Route 52, and were among the woods again, Sophie said, "Let's go far away somewhere."

"Like where?"

"Like Canada."

"Canada?"

"Yeah. Just for a while. I'm scared here. I don't want to stay at my mother's or father's house. Do you want to stay at your house?"

"No fucking way. So some insane killer can come and get me?"

"Then let's go. I've got some money on me. I know my mother's American Express Platinum number. We can just stay away for a while."

"Where'll we sleep? We can't get into a motel, we're minors."

"We'll buy sleeping bags at Walmart or something. And we can buy food anywhere."

"Really?"

"Yes! I want to get away from here! You want to stay?"

"No. But my mom'll worry herself sick over me."

"So call her later when we get somewhere. Or text her and just say you're okay."

"Fuck. Let's go." He looked into the rearview mirror and saw a truck with a snowplow blade on its front closing behind them so he pulled to the right to give it room to pass. "So where?"

"Canada. I'll look on maps." Sophie pulled her phone from her jacket, held it in front of her, but it flew out of her hands when they were rammed from behind. She screamed.

"What the fuck!" yelled Ethan as he struggled with the wheel, trying to keep the van from slewing sideways. He got it straightened out and was braking when they were rammed again.

55

During a winter storm that passed through Gardiner, Maine, a tall oak tree blew down on the Welldale grounds. Its trunk was caught in the embrace of an old American elm. Two hundred years earlier, perhaps from being nibbled by wildlife, the elm's young bole had sprouted into four separate stems. The oak lay like a spear lodged twelve feet above the ground clutched in the fist of the elm.

In April, Ivan Haney filed his chain sharp, oiled and fired up his Husqvarna chain saw, and went to work. He began cutting the outer web of the oak's pale roots, releasing whatever force still held the tree to the ground. He stepped smartly back after each cut to inspect his work and the force still contained in the oak's desire to complete its fall. Then he stepped forward to cut again.

He didn't remember afterward hearing a crack or tear, or seeing the elm's fist explode.

He was lying on the ground beneath a thicket of trunks and branches, the chain saw pinned over his leg, still running. Haney knew pain and injury—you only felt the pain afterward—and this was not pain so much as an awareness of his finger still pulling on the saw's trigger and the chain reaching bone.

. . .

The VA medical clinic in Augusta fitted him with a prosthetic leg, but Haney couldn't abide it—here was the pain now, compared with which chainsawing halfway through a leg was like a paper cut. Hurting where there wasn't even part of him to feel it. The whole thirty-six inseam from his phantom toes up to the thigh that had been whittled to a nub for the prosthesis socket, now ablaze. But strapping on that plastic-and-titanium pogo stick gave him a new leg from hell. Haney told them where they could shove it.

Dr. Grayson, Welldale's principal, came to see him. He was happy and relieved, he said, to see Ivan sitting up in bed sounding much like himself. He shook his head in a marveling sort of way. Dr. Grayson had visited the scene of the accident and taken a look for himself.

"I crawled out of worse," Haney told him.

Dr. Grayson laughed and said, "I'll bet you have, Ivan, I bet you have."

He outlined the leg half-there side of the situation: the accident fell incontestably under the heading of on-the-job injury. So the Academy's insurance was picking up all Ivan's medical costs not covered by the VA, and was even able to provide him with a small disability pension to augment his VA disability. But after giving it *much thought*, Ivan, said Dr. Grayson, as if he were still deeply puzzling over the situation, he had reluctantly come to the conclusion that it might be some time before Ivan would be able to resume his duties, if even then. So the Academy had hired another groundskeeper.

"I figgered," said Ivan, pulling deep on a Camel.

Dr. Grayson asked if Ivan had any family who could now help him. No next of kin was listed in his file with the school. Was there no one, Dr. Grayson wondered, whom he could contact? A friend, anybody, who might help Ivan in the next difficult stage of recovery?

The boy—now a well-bulked-out young man—liked having Ivan living with him full-time. He'd always missed him when Ivan went back to Welldale after his two weeks' summer vacation. They were a real household now, something the boy had not known since he'd lived briefly with the Buells as a child. It made him happy to shop for Ivan, cook for him, look after him, and smoke with him, to leave work for the day and find Ivan at home when he returned.

But once away from Welldale, Ivan's former robustness quickly faded. His immobility, only able to hop painfully around the house, outside to the porch—he didn't care to go to town—soon reduced him to a wheezing old man sitting beside a humming tank with an oxygen tube around his face.

As he watched Ivan's health fail—as Ivan became wheelchair- and finally bed-bound, unable even to sit in the living room with his tank, gaunt and wasted on the few mugs of chicken noodle soup he could get down—the young man began to anticipate his death. It had never occurred to him, and now he saw that it was going to happen soon.

Two realizations came to him. First, that when Ivan went, everything he was, everything that he carried inside him, would go with him. This shocked the young man. Gone, taken out of the world, would be the great store of Ivan's particular knowledge, his life experience, and his skills.

Second, he began to understand the absence that would descend on his life.

There had been no one in his life like Ivan. Ivan had taught him everything he knew. He'd shown him how the world worked, how its parts fitted together, and his own place in it. Ivan had molded him, witnessed his growth and accomplishments, been proud of him.

Even after he'd left Welldale, Ivan had continued to be the largest presence in his life. They wrote letters to each other—Ivan's were detailed accounts of the animals he had seen or killed, the work he did on the grounds, and the fat, lazy, pissant students who now attended the school—and Ivan came to stay at his house at Christmas and during his summer vacations. They were like a family.

"I feel like you're my son," Ivan had said to him several times after he came to live with him.

This meant, he knew, that Ivan loved him.

How would he live in the world without Ivan? When you were part of a family, you were real to someone. It seemed to him that with Ivan gone, part of him would also be gone. He would no longer be seen by anybody. If no one saw him, would he even exist?

One night, during the time this weighed on his thoughts, the young man dreamed of the coyote. It was hanging in the proscenium Ivan had made, dangling on the rope tied to its paws. Its vivid eyes fixed on him. The coyote spoke to him.

"Do you feel my strength and cunning inside you?"

"Yes," he said.

"Okay, then," said the coyote.

The following weekend, he wheeled Ivan in his chair across the grassy driveway to his barn workshop. He lifted him from his chair, laid him flat, and tied him spread-eagled onto the plywood workbench. Ivan didn't protest. He hadn't brought the oxygen bottle, and Ivan was in respiratory distress.

But once laid onto the plywood bench, Ivan relaxed. Long breaths wheezed out of him. He seemed at peace.

"Mister Toad," Ivan said, with what sounded like fond recognition as the young man held one of the animals above his face.

He squeezed behind the toad's eyes until the bitter pus popped out of its skin and he swiped it up and rubbed his finger over Ivan's discolored gums, freed of his full-mouth dentures. He could feel Ivan's gums clamping over his fingers.

Ivan hardly moved as the honed blade went in and was drawn down through his navel. His eyes popped open more than usual, his head straining to look down, as the young man pushed the toad into him. Though his stomach muscles were no longer knit together, his breath came in short exhalations as he fixed his eyes on the young man. His mouth pursed to a small round hole.

"I've got you, Ivan," said the young man.

Ivan's whole body became still. His feet splayed wide. His open mouth widened slowly, exposing his discolored gums.

"Okay, then, Chester," Ivan whispered.

Part Four

56

Morgana called from her truck. Heading down Chestnut Street at the height and speed of a low-flying aircraft.

She just knew. She *knew* because she was a *mother*. Mothers were from planet Mother, a place of inescapable gravity, a consequence of masses that fathers, tumbling endlessly through space, could never understand. Alex groped around parenthood like a blind dog looking for crumbs on a floor. Morgana was connected to Sophie on another level. She knew *everything*. In real time.

"Morgana, I'm in the middle of—"

"IT'S. ABOUT. OUR. DAUGHTER." She had him on speakerphone.

"What's up?"

They both pitched their voices to be heard above the roar of the Ford's engine.

"She's offline. And she's moving around town in an erratic manner."

"I thought she was at your place."

Morgana briefly chortled her mirthless stage snigger, loudly enough to carry through the phone, over the Ford engine noise. "She told me she'd be staying with you."

"Well, maybe she's there now. I'm at the station—"

"Alex—" Morgana pitched his name with the warning tone of a dog owner about to press hard on the button of a shock collar. "I've told you: *she's moving around town in an erratic manner.*"

"What do you mean? How do you know that?"

"I follow her phone."

"What—"

"Shut *up*, Alex, and *listen to me.* She has an iPhone—I can track it. She's not at your place, she's not at my place. She's driving around town in someone's car. Fast. And she's offline."

"What do you mean she's offline? How do you know?"

"Seriously? You're a *policeman*? I monitor her phone. I know when she's on it, and where she is. She is *NEVER* offline—don't you know that, Alex? There is *no activity*, on her social media or anything. And she's moving around town fast."

"Then how do you know where she is?"

"GPS? Hello? Right now she's on Elm Street, just passing Hannaford, coming back into town from Rockland—"

"From Rockland?"

"I'll be outside in two minutes."

57

Alex came out of the William P. Merrill Station, phone to his ear. The press vans and onlookers had disappeared. It was getting dark. "That North Carolina boat registration number has expired," said Kevin Regis. "And since the boat is here, it was obviously towed up at some point. Either the owner, Maroni, hasn't reregistered it, or he might have sold it to someone local who hasn't registered it. It's an old boat, maybe not used much, whoever owns it hasn't got around to it. I'm still looking for more phone numbers for Maroni."

Morgana's truck shot past him like a train. She was impossible to put off. She *did* seem to know, at times, with a parental clairvoyance he evidently lacked, what was going on with Sophie. He was trying to hold on to the threads of Jared's murder, the boat's passage down Moody Pond, but now Sophie was missing—yet moving around nearby—and Morgana was scrambling his brain.

"Okay, thanks, Kevin. Keep me posted."

She parked in the lot beside the station and jumped out of the cab, literally airborne as she flew to the ground, her hacking jacket fluttering behind her like a cape. Her boots ground grit underfoot as she strode toward him like a soldier. Her face was white and fierce in the station's harsh exterior lights, which flooded the early evening dark.

"We'll go in your car," she said, climbing into his passenger seat. "It's perfect. Every other car on the road is a Subaru Outback."

"Right," said Alex. He didn't disagree, and he ignored her contemptuous tone.

Morgana stared at her phone and flung out an arm passing close to his face. "Go up Quarry Hill Road."

"How long have you been tracking this car?"

Morgana exhaled a sharp burst of breath, a sound lasting no more than a second, resembling a brief cough, but somehow conveying the message that she'd been surveilling Sophie for years.

"Left here!" She jabbed a finger at the windshield. "You know what they're doing, don't you?"

He didn't waste breath telling her he knew where the turn was. "Who's they? What are they doing?"

"Drugs. Looking for it. Or selling it."

"What makes you think that?"

"Because she's been high, Alex. Just days ago. I drug-tested her."

"Really?" He was surprised. He hadn't yet found a good moment to tell Morgana about Sophie's drug bust in front of the Ocean View condos. She hadn't been arrested, but he was unsure what Morgana's response would be. Probably angry that he or Mark hadn't enforced an arrest, as they could have done, and hauled Sophie down to juvie in Rockland to give her a scare. Make her accountable for her behavior—the whole Texan ride-tall-in-the-saddle thing that Morgana trotted out in teachable moments of child-rearing and withering criticism of Alex, who had failed all tests of Texas-style manliness. Evidently, she didn't know, or he'd have heard. "What was it?"

"It was psychedelics. I know because the drug test was unable to show that, yet she was definitely on something."

"But it didn't show—"

"I could tell! She was high. I'm her mother, I know. So this fits. She's in a car driving all over town in directions that make no sense. They went halfway to Rockland, then back as far as Cobb Road, stopped, turned, and headed back into town the long way. They stopped again on Mechanic Street and then they moved on. She's out scoring or selling drugs."

"Did you see the car, whatever they're driving?"

"I didn't want to get that close. She'd spot my truck. We can only hope to God it's not fentanyl."

"I'm sure she's not doing fentanyl—"

Another sharp cough from Morgana, while she looked down at her phone.

"Go back down Union Street . . . toward Elm . . . slow down . . . *slower* . . . They're pulling into the Stop-and-Go . . . *Stop*."

Alex pulled over. He could see the lights of the Stop-and-Go ahead. He looked at Morgana's phone. "They're stopped there?"

"Yes."

Alex punched a number into his phone.

"Who are you calling?"

The number answered. "Mark, are you busy? Meet me at the Stop-and-Go. Kids in a car, maybe some drugs . . . I may need you there." He put the phone down.

"You need reinforcements?"

"If we're stopping Sophie in a car with drugs, I'll need Mark—"

"Someone else to play father—"

"No, Morgana. Conflict of interest. It wouldn't help anybody. He's a minute away."

"Okay. Go, get going. They might leave."

Alex breathed in, exhaled, put the car in gear, and moved forward. Round the curve, he pulled into a parking space at the edge of the small convenience store–cum–gas station. There was only one car at the Stop-and-Go. It was parked not at the pump but taking up two customer spaces.

"Sophie's in that car."

"I don't think so," said Alex.

"Yes—" She waved her phone's screen, the proof, at him. "She's *in that car*."

They both stared at the long, low-slung, dark green Cadillac sedan DeVille, circa 1979, with a TAXI sign on its roof. A tall, shambling man with long stringy gray hair got out of the driver's door and walked into the store. The interior of the car appeared empty.

"Who's *that*?" Morgana asked.

"That's Gene Hurlbut. He's a local taxi driver. That's his taxi. I can't see anyone in it. Unless they're crouching."

Morgana looked down at her phone's screen, then up, around, back at the

Cadillac, then at Alex. "Her phone is *in that car*. If she's not in the back, then she's *in the trunk!*"

Alex opened his door—Morgana opened hers—

"Morgana, *stay in the car*. This is police business now. Don't get in my way."

"She's in that car!"

"We'll see. There's a procedure. Shut your door, please."

He waited.

She pulled her door shut.

Alex walked to the Cadillac. He bent close and looked through the front and back windows. He walked around the rear and tapped on the trunk. "Sophie? Anyone in there?" He looked over at Morgana, shook his head, then walked into the store. Inside, he watched Gene Hurlbut buy a packet of cigarettes and a Maine Mega Millions lottery ticket. He saw Mark's patrol car pull up outside. Then he heard Morgana and looked through the window.

She was pounding on the Cadillac's trunk, shouting, "Sophie, are you in there?"

Alex followed Gene Hurlbut out of the Stop-and-Go.

"Hey!" said Hurlbut. "What the hell are you doing? Stop that!"

"Open this trunk!" Morgana shouted.

"What the hell?"

"Gene, I'd like you to open your trunk, please," Alex said.

"Why? What are you looking for?"

"Where is my daughter?" Morgana shouted at him.

Hurlbut's face was a mass of twitches. "I don't know. . . . Who are you?"

"Open the trunk, Gene," said Mark Beltz.

Hurlbut opened the trunk. It was wide and deep, and showed a folded blue tarp, small red jerry can, a few pieces of cordwood. He looked at Morgana, Alex, and Mark Beltz. "What's this all about?" he asked. He was frightened.

"You've got my daughter's phone!"

"No, I don't."

"Mark, look in the car please."

Mark opened the Cadillac's doors and bent in. Hurlbut watched him carefully.

"Have you had any kids in your car recently?" Alex asked him.

"No, sir. No kids at all. I don't take kids."

"You're lying," said Morgana. "You've got her phone! *Where is she?*"

"Look, I don't know what's going on here—"

"Detective?" Mark Beltz called. He was standing at the open rear door, holding up a phone. Alex recognized the kiwi green case.

Morgana said, "That's Sophie's phone!"

58

E than?" Isabel shouted into the house from the kitchen.
Flynn leaped and pranced around her.
"*Down*, Flynn."

She let him out the back door. She could tell he'd been inside for hours. Ethan was usually good about letting him out and back in.

She opened the door to the basement. It was dark but she called down anyway. "Ethan?"

He'd called earlier. His voice in pieces. "Is it true, Mom? Is Jared really dead?"

"Sweetheart. How did you find out—"

"Mom! It's on the fucking news! When did you know? Why didn't you tell me? Are you at work, at that fucking place?"

"No, Ethan, I'm at Kathy's. I'll be home soon. I wanted to tell you myself when I got home—"

"Mom! This is fucking crazy!"

"Ethan, I'll be home soon. Stay home—"

Ethan hung up.

She ran up the stairs. He might be in his room, ears plugged with head-phones, but unlikely to be far from his phone, not noticing her repeated calling.

She rapped her knuckles hard, reflexively, then barged into his bedroom. Not here.

She turned in his room, facing the door, and screamed. *"Ethan!"*

Downstairs, she stood in the kitchen, ready to go, drive like a maniac to get Ethan—but where? With who—if not Jared?

Sophie? Alex's house?

Flynn was pawing at the door. She let him in and fed him while she phoned Ethan again, and again got voicemail.

"Ethan, I don't know where you are. You're making me sick with worry. You can't do this—*what are you thinking? Please call me and come home!"*

She couldn't stay here in the house going crazy with worry.

As soon as she opened the car door she saw Nancy's basket that she'd picked up after Chester had fallen from the roof. She'd forgotten about it. It smelled of something rank. She grabbed it and brought it inside, into the kitchen. Flynn leaped and barked again, sensing some kind of freaky excitement. She opened the back door, and he ran out, barking into the backyard.

What *was* that God-awful smell? She looked at Nancy's basket. Chester's hat. The feather sticking out. Shiny with wear, almost black with what looked like years of sweat soaking into it. Disgusting. She certainly didn't want to touch it.

But she saw her hand—as if in a dream, already dreaming—reach out and pick it up.

59

He'd found the phone in a van on the side of the road out on 105, Gene Hurlbut said. Mark was following Gene's taxi there now. Alex was following Mark's patrol car. He'd called Judy Waite at the station to send a team out to the van to dust it for prints. He'd tried calling Ethan too. Voicemail. "Ethan, this is Alex Brangwen. Is Sophie with you? Please give me a call as soon as you get this message. Let me know how you are anyway. Thanks."

"Don't lie to me," said Morgana, sitting beside him, "you know that man." She gave him the evil eye, Texas style. "Who is he?"

"Gene Hurlbut. That's his taxi. He's a registered sex offender."

"Jesus Christ, Alex!"

"That's why he doesn't give rides to kids. Did you hear him? He can't take kids. He's known. He'd go straight to jail. He hasn't seen her, or any kids, and I believe him. But he still has the reflexes of a petty criminal, and he's probably not very bright, so he found the phone and took it, thinking he could sell it."

"*Jesus Christ*," said Morgana. "I want it. Give it to me."

"It's police evidence now," said Alex, firmly, "so it stays with me."

The van sat at an angle on the grassy verge, leaning toward the roadside ditch. The passenger door hung open. The rear end on the driver's side was crumpled inward with collision damage.

"Mark, let's take a look."

Mark pulled on a pair of surgical gloves and pulled open the sliding rear passenger door.

Gene Hurlbut opened his driver's door and put a foot on the ground.

"I'd like you to stay in your car please, Gene," Alex said. "Where was the phone?"

"Yessir." Hurlbut withdrew his leg and shut his door. He was quivering like a dog that had been repeatedly kicked. "It was on the back floor."

"What were you doing here?"

"I was going by with a ride and I saw the van."

"You stopped then?"

"No, sir, I came back."

"Why?"

"Because it looked like this." He nodded at the van. "Like something was wrong."

"You didn't call the police?"

"I was going to, but I wanted to check it first before I sent you all out here for nothing."

"So you looked inside and found the phone. What time was that?"

"Must've been a little before five."

"What were you planning to do with the phone?"

"I swear to God I was going to take it into the station. I haven't had time, I've had one ride after another all afternoon."

"Detective." Mark Beltz made a motion with his head. Alex walked to the van. Mark was standing near the open rear passenger door. He held up a hat. "I found this on the backseat."

Alex had seen it before—or a picture of it. In Agent Harris's PowerPoint presentation. A white wool watch cap. SUPREME woven into the front.

Alex stepped away. He called Isabel's number. It rang and went to voice-mail.

"Whose hat is that?" Morgana demanded.

"It's Ethan's."

"Who are you calling? Her? Of course."

Morgana started walking toward the van.

Alex stepped ahead of her, placing himself between her and the van, and spoke quietly. "Morgana, get back in the car, please. I'm going to take you back to your truck but I need to deal with this. Give me some room here."

She straightened herself to her full height, her head tilting into his. "*I am a mother—*"

It rose up in him, into his head, like some blood rush, like a volcano—

"Daddy, I *need* you," Sophie said a number of times when she was two, maybe less, when she was learning words, putting together expressions, finding out how to express what she wanted to say. She'd say it with a conversational tone, but he knew she was saying, *Daddy, I love you.* Already his marriage with Morgana was foundering and he was feeling the bewildering rupture of his new family, a force separating him from his new daughter. "I need you too, sweetheart," he'd say, playing the word game. But he was beginning to know how much.

From the moment of her birth—hours before, even, as Morgana began demanding a C-section—Alex had feared for his daughter. He supposed it was every parent's existential fear, but he hadn't imagined being invaded by such a constant anxiety for her safety. Then Morgana divorced him and ever afterward he was afraid something would happen to Sophie. For a long time he saw her only on weekends, and in between those times he felt powerless to help her, protect her.

Once she began saying *Daddy, I love you*, she stopped saying, *Daddy, I need you.* He didn't remember her ever saying it again. But as the years went by, he needed her more and more. And his need made him more fearful. What if something happened to her? What if there were a school shooting? He told a therapist about his fear and she told him that this was normal, every parent felt such a fear. He dreamed of people coming after Sophie in his house, he told the therapist. Was that normal? We express normal fear in different ways to ourselves, his therapist said. When Alex became a policeman and started carrying a gun and keeping it at home, those dreams—someone coming after her in his house—stopped.

Now all his fears were real. And they needed each other more than ever.

"For *fuck's sake*, Morgana—" He stood close to her, his back to the others. Then he controlled himself. "I'm working on it. I'm going to find her. I'll let you know as soon as I know anything. But I need you to leave me alone now. Let me do my job."

Morgana spun around and strode away.

He tried Isabel again. No answer.

He walked to the van. "Mark, stay with the van. Send someone to my house. It's unlocked. They have my permission to go inside, look for Sophie and Ethan, and wait there for the time being."

"Yes, sir. Where will you be?"

"I'm going to the Dorr home."

60

When Ethan opened his eyes, hands hovered above his face. Cupped is if in prayer, or cradling something. The hands parted, revealing two bulging eyes, a wide mouth, mottled skin—

What the . . .

A frog?

The hands turned the animal slowly in the air, giving Ethan and the frog a close, rounded view of each other.

Then a thumb belonging to one of the hands pressed down on the frog's head. White drops appeared above its eye. The frog and hands were withdrawn.

Ethan tried to shout but could only grunt, his mouth taped shut. He was lying flat, hands and legs outstretched, wrists and ankles held down. He tried to look around—*OH GOD MY NECK*, shooting pains through his neck and shoulder and head . . . He remembered the vehicle hitting them from behind, fighting the wheel . . . *Where was Sophie?*

Ethan began to hyperventilate when a wet hand clapped over his face, and his nostrils were squeezed shut. For a moment, with his mouth taped closed, he couldn't breathe at all. He squirmed, made noises in his throat. Then the tape was torn off his mouth. As he opened it, gasping, sucking for air, a fat coarse finger poked into his open mouth. A thick goo, like runny glue, was swabbed onto his tongue, under it, around his mouth. A bitter taste.

The thick finger and nail moved around, scraped the roof of his mouth, his gums, rubbed the goo over his teeth, gums, into the salivary glands under his tongue. He tried to jerk his head away—*fuck, his neck*—but it was clamped or taped down—

As he thought about biting down on it hard, the finger was gone and a strip of tape plastered across his mouth again. The finger and thumb let go their grip on his nostrils. His chest heaved as he sucked in air, simultaneously gagging at the bitter, horrible stuff in his mouth. There was no way to get rid of it. His cheeks bulged, air and snot blew out of his nostrils, and his lungs sucked it all back in. He tried not to swallow, but reflex took over. It came up again, his stomach and throat convulsed, it rose into his nose, his air passage plugged, he aspirated the bitter flow. He thought he was going to die.

Then Ethan felt a hand on his stomach. The pressure on his stomach increased.

At first, a small sensation below his breastbone. Contained in one spot, like a sudden deep itch . . . The itch intensified rapidly, deepened, no longer an itch but—he could feel it, saw the feeling with his brain—a cut deep into the skin, a sharp searing line, spreading downward over—*into*—his stomach—

O-my-God-O-my-God-my-God-my—

His body was writhing with a will of its own. Heaving at the sharp restraints that held his wrists and ankles as he tried to pull his stomach away—a scream erupted out of him, blowing out his cheeks, mouth clamped shut by tape, pouring from his nose, filling his head, a muted roaring in his throat and ears:

OH-MY-GOD-MY-GOD-MY-GOD-STOP-IT-PLEASE MAKE-IT-STOP—

61

The swirly-patterned Damascus steel drew the skin apart like opening a Ziploc bag. He had sharpened the blade first on the Arkansas
stone and then on the soft suede strop and he had used the knife for
nothing but this. So smooth and quick the first seconds of the cut that for a
moment there was no blood, just the white V that widened as the tension in
the young skin pulled it open before the neat runnel filled with red. A perfect
incision, the thin line beginning to shine red down the smooth pale surface
only lightly ruffled with small hairs—

The only difficulty, beginning a few seconds into the cut, was the violent
contractions of the stomach muscle that made the surface rise and fall with
sudden heaves and drops that the other hand, his right hand, even pushing
down hard, could not stop. He tried to keep it as neat as the beginning but
soon there was enough blood pooling into the concavity he made pushing
down with his right hand that he had to stop to wipe away the blood to see
his work—

He cut through the belly button, the knife and his hand hardly registering
the change in thickness, and stopped a few inches below.

Ivan was with him now. Through his eyes, Ivan saw and guided him, held
the knife with him, steadied his hand. Good cut there, Mister. Make it clean
and true.

He was not distracted by the noise and movements made by the boy under his two strong hands. The moans and motion weakened with the cut through his abdominal muscles—he could no longer make his instinctive crunches, flex his torso. The blood flow lessened. He mopped it away. He'd cut no organs. Finally, the opening was complete, top to bottom.

He could see things inside. He always remembered the frog in Mr. Williams's class. He'd learned more than he'd imagined.

Now he picked up the toad, which he'd placed in a small bucket on the table as he'd worked. It was not large. He spread the cut open by slipping his fingers in and turning his hand sideways, and pushed the toad in. It couldn't escape until he was ready to take it out, the tension in the tissue would close over it. The toad would be happy in there. It was warm, but not too warm. Not as warm as lying on a rock in the sun.

He tuned out the noise made by the boy. So he heard the new voice clearly. Right outside.

"Chester . . . ?"

62

Nancy was relieved. Chester was home, his truck in the driveway, parked between the house and the garage. But then she was alarmed again—the house was dark.

She hadn't spoken to him since leaving him at Penobscot Medical Center the day before. His leg had been x-rayed and showed a possible fracture between the tibia and fibula, but he'd also hit his head on his fall from the roof of Goody Swaine's cabin, and they wanted to keep him in overnight for observation. She'd kissed him goodbye and left relieved that he was in the Med Center.

Since then, she'd called repeatedly, but he hadn't called her back. He was often slow to respond. She knew he didn't look at his phone for hours.

She'd finally called the Med Center. The receptionist, a very young-sounding woman, asked who was calling.

"Nancy Keeler. I came in with him last night. I'm his friend. . . . I'm his partner, actually."

"Oh, okay. Let me see . . . Coffey . . ." She was breathing heavily into her mouthpiece. . . . "He's no longer here."

"You mean he was released?"

"No . . ." It sounded as if she was reading, scrolling through her screen. "He wasn't released. . . . It looks like he checked himself out, though I don't have confirmation—"

"When was that?"

"It doesn't say. Because we didn't release him. So he must have just left?"

Now she was worried. She pictured Chester lying dazed or even unconscious in his funny little house.

She'd been to Chester's home only once, weeks earlier, in September, when they were just getting to know each other. She'd asked him if he wanted to come with her to the Common Ground Fair in Unity. He didn't seem to know about it. "You've never been? Oh you'll love it, Chester," she'd told him. A celebration of old-timey crafts and organic farming, farm animals, old tractors, artisan toolmakers, pie contests, hay wagon transport from the parking area—a *Whole Earth Catalog* come to life every fall. If he liked the Granite Harbor Living History Settlement, she said, she was sure he'd get a kick out of the Common Ground Fair.

His house, out on Moody Pond Road, was on the way.

"I'll pick you up," she'd told him.

"What if I meet you there? Or at your house?" He sounded evasive.

Maybe he was shy about her seeing his house. Which made her more curious. "Chester, dear, it's on the way. It just makes sense for me to pick you up."

She was surprised when she saw the place. A pin-neat, plain little 1950s Maine farmhouse, small garage, a barn of weathered gray boards beside the garage. The land sloped to a dock on Moody Pond and a view of the hills of Mount Meguntic State Park in the distance.

"Chester, your house is *darling!* You furnished it yourself?"

"It was like this when I bought it." He'd purchased the place complete, he told her, with all the furnishings inside. It looked like the estate sale of a deceased elderly woman or couple: green wallpaper, pleated curtains, rag carpets, old lamps, prints of snow-covered fields. An authentically unimproved blue Formica kitchen and Sears Kenmore appliances. And it was full of books: decades of Book-of-the-Month Club editions in the bookshelves, and others, older books, on shelves; a number of them lying open on the coffee table.

"Chester, you're a reader!"

"Well, I like the history books. Old ones. I buy them too."

"You do? Where?"

"Oh, garage and library sales, things like that."

"Chester, you're an intellectual!"

"Oh, no." He smiled, almost embarrassed. "I didn't read much at school. Only later. I just like history."

At the fair, Chester was like a child at a circus, seeing things he'd never imagined before. At moments he came to a standstill, unable to decide in which direction to move. He was fascinated by the animals, the tools—everything. Nancy was happy and gratified watching him take it all in.

As the Settlement's blacksmith, he was naturally interested in the metal forging. At the Zoltan Blades tent, he watched the video of how the blade-smith made his knives by folding and pounding together alloys of Damascus steel. After a circuit of the fairgrounds, they returned to the Zoltan Blades tent and Chester bought a short "Peregrine" knife with a burl maple handle and squiggly lines and whorls like wood grain along the gray blade. It came with a deep leather sheath worn on a belt, and a fine grit Arkansas sharpening stone and leather strop in a small wooden box. The whole rig cost six hundred dollars, which Chester handed over in cash.

"Good lord," said Nancy. "That must be a good knife, Chester."

"This is an heirloom-quality item, ma'am," said the bladesmith, a rugged-looking man in denim overalls, with a long, dense, gray-flecked beard. "I believe Chester here understands that."

She left her car running, the headlights on. She got out her phone as she walked to the front door and turned on its flashlight. No motion sensor light came on; the electrical system was probably as old and unimproved as the house. She pressed the doorbell button, heard a ring inside the house. She opened the storm door—Chester had replaced the screens with winter-season glass panels—and raised the green brass eagle knocker and rapped it down twice, hard.

"Chester?" she called through the door. "Chester?"

The front door was locked.

As she walked around the side of the house, she aimed her phone's light into the truck's window. The front seat was empty.

But the truck, she realized, was warm. She felt the heat coming off the hood in the night air.

Nancy was relieved again. She'd imagined Chester, concussed by his fall, lying for hours inside in the dark house . . . but he'd obviously just been out in his truck.

She walked to the kitchen door at the side of the house, farther out of the loom of her headlights. The kitchen was dark too.

"Chester . . . ?" she called again, louder. Several times. Was he in the cellar? She tried the kitchen door, but it too was locked. She started walking back toward her car.

"Nancy."

She turned. He was coming out of the little barn in the back. She'd only glimpsed it briefly when she came to take Chester to the fair, but her impression then was that it was abandoned, leaning off-kilter, unused. Now she saw light from inside the building, framing Chester for a moment in a small doorway before he closed the door behind him. He was moving toward her.

"Oh, Chester! I'm so glad to see you! I was calling you. Didn't you hear your phone? You left the Med Center. I was worried about you."

"Oh. No, I didn't hear it."

"Why did you leave? You were supposed to be under observation for a concussion."

"I felt okay."

"But, darling, you can feel okay and still have a concussion and then get worse." She noticed his hands were wet, dripping water, and the large roll of tape he carried in one hand. He was in his socks, no shoes on his feet.

"Chester, you're not wearing any shoes."

He looked down at his feet. His face was partly lit by the headlights behind them. He seemed confused.

"What am I to do with you, Chester?" she said. And she heard what sounded like love in her voice.

"I don't know," he said, as if thinking hard about it. He was standing close in front of her now. There was an unusual vertical line between his eyebrows.

"You don't seem yourself, dear."

"I'm just busy right now. Nancy, you go home and I'll see you later."

"But, Chester, I'm worried about you. Come home with me in my car and I'll drive you back tomorrow."

"No, I'll come over tomorrow. I'll see you at the Settlement."

"Then I'll stay here. I don't want to leave you now. You may not be entirely well. I'll make us dinner here, how's that?"

"I want you to go home now. I'll see you tomorrow."

"No," she said firmly. "I'm not leaving you, Chester. I love you and I'm
worried about you. You've become very dear to me, and I'm not going away."

Chester looked at her for a long moment. *Yes,* thought Nancy, *that was a
mouthful,* but she wanted him to know her feelings now. She wasn't going to
walk away and let him neglect himself. They were past that. She was sure too,
that in his way, Chester reciprocated her feelings.

He put a hand on her arm and turned her toward the back door of the
house. "Let's go into the house."

"Okay, let's. That's good. Let me turn my car off."

"I'll get it," he said, steering her toward the house. Chester pulled out a
ring of keys and opened the back door, and they went into the kitchen. He
turned on the low-wattage ceiling light. Not the most flattering light for the
old kitchen.

"You could do with some under-the-cabinet lights in here, Chester.
Nothing fancy, just a touch."

"Okay." He was propelling her through the kitchen, down the hall toward
the bedroom, his grip now tight on her arm.

"Don't you want me to make dinner?"

"Not now."

"Chester, you're definitely not yourself. You're not well, and you're dripping with sweat. You have to trust me, dear. I want to take you back to the
hospital."

In the hall, he turned on another light, identical to the old ceiling fixture
in the kitchen, the same dim light. His hand on her arm kept them both
moving into the bedroom. He didn't turn on a light.

Now he released her arm. "Lie down on the bed."

"Chester . . . this isn't how we are together." Though now that she thought
about it, Chester's lovemaking had changed markedly in the last ten days or
so. He'd become unusually urgent, more confident, thrusting into her long
and powerfully. She'd become sore and had needed a few days off. "I'm not
actually ready for this now."

"We're staying here."

His face was peculiarly set.

"Chester, listen to me—"

Holding her arms with his hands, he forced her firmly down onto the bed. "You have to lie down now."

She tried to rise. "Chester, I don't want this—"

"Lie flat." He pushed her back down.

Chester dropped to the bed. He swung one knee over her, put his hands on her shoulders, and firmly pushed her flat onto the mattress. He straddled her, a knee pinning each shoulder flat. He was not rough with her, but firm, powerful, heavy.

Nancy felt a rising panic. She knew he was a gentle soul—something had happened with the fall from the roof. She felt the incredible strength of him—not as he'd shown it in their lovemaking, in his new stamina. This was the man who moved rocks and trees around the Settlement Village, pounded metal at the forge. She'd watched and marveled at what he did. But this was too much now, and Chester didn't seem to know it.

"Chester, you have to stop this now. I'm serious. Listen to me. I don't like this. Please let me up."

With deliberate power, Chester straightened her arm. She heard the sound of tape being pulled from the roll in his hand. He started wrapping tape around her wrist. Thick gray duct tape, she saw now, around and around her hand and wrist and then ran the tape to the corner of the wooden headboard, and around her hand again, several loops, until her arm was stiff, all but im-movable. He did the same to her other arm. Then he pulled her legs apart.

"Chester *stop!* Darling, listen to me . . . I don't want this! Stop, Chester. *Chester . . . please!*"

Chester didn't seem to be listening to her at all. His eyes were on his hands as they worked with the tape, absorbed with this task. Nancy was sud-denly breathless, she began panting. He moved to her feet—she tried pulling her legs away but he pulled them straight, spreading them open. Wrapping tape around her ankles.

Her clothes were still on. Was he going to rip them off?

"Chester, no! *Please, stop this!* I don't want this!"

Nancy was spread-eagled, her arms and legs held fast in a web of tape to each corner of the bed.

Chester stood up and looked down. He walked around the bed and moved her arms and legs slightly, gauging the tension of her bindings.

"Does it hurt?" he asked her.

She couldn't catch her breath. "Chester . . . are you going to hurt me?"

"No. I don't want to hurt you."

"Oh-h-h . . . Chester . . ." She heard her voice: it was small and weak—not like herself at all.

He kneeled beside her and raised her head off the pillow with his hand. She heard the sound of tape being pulled off the roll. The roll went around her head—"*Ches*—" until it sealed her mouth. Around and around three more times, he took care not to cover her nostrils before he ripped the tape free.

"*Mm-n-m-m-m—!*"

Chester stood and drew the curtains across the two bedroom windows.

"Don't worry, I'll be back," he said. "I won't leave you here long. I just have to do some stuff. You'll be okay."

He left the room. Nancy heard him walking down the hall. The hall light went out. The faint kitchen light was turned off. She heard the kitchen door open and shut.

She heard his footsteps through the window on the driveway. Then her car, still running, was turned off.

63

The driver's door on Isabel's car was open. From the driveway Alex could hear Flynn barking like crazy in the backyard. He knocked on the kitchen door. No response inside. He tried the door. It was open.

"Isabel?" he called.

Alex went through the mudroom into the kitchen. The house was freezing.

The dog was going berserk through the glass door on the deck, which could have been a trampoline with the height he was achieving. The dog saw him and his barking intensified, insanely. But Alex saw that Flynn was focused on something inside the kitchen, out of his line of sight, the other side of the small central island.

She was lying curled on her side on the floor, between the island and the stairs, in full sight of Flynn. Tremors shook her like a dog in the grip of a mad running dream.

"Isabel . . ." He knelt down and touched her arm. She was rigid—was she having a seizure? He thought of trying to get something into her mouth— he'd done EMT/CPR courses at the Academy. Call 911? But he saw her mouth was open, not clamped shut, not biting her tongue; no froth or blood. She was talking, babbling something he couldn't make it out.

Her head was cut, bloody above the temple. Had she fallen over?

The knuckles of one hand were white. She was clutching something tightly. A hat—surely not hers, brown felt, shapeless, filthy, pierced by a feather.

"Isabel!"

He placed one hand beneath her neck, just taking the weight of her head. He pressed the heel of his other palm against her forehead, between her full eyebrows. The skin was warm but not hot. He held his palm against her with pressure, the way he used to with Sophie when she was going to sleep.

But her arm leading to the hand clutching the hat was stiff, inflexible. Her whole body was rigid, as if she were being electrocuted. He reached for the hat and tried to pull it from her hand. He had to use both hands and considerable strength, to pull it from her tight fist.

Her body went limp.

"Isabel . . ."

The dog was still barking insanely.

"*Isabel*—"

Her eyes opened.

Flynn stopped barking.

"Are you all right?"

She sat up abruptly. She looked at the hat lying on the floor, then at the hand that had been clutching it, and she pulled the hand to her heart.

"Chester . . ." she said hoarsely.

"It's his hat? That's the trigger—it's him?"

She nodded.

"Ethan!"

"Someone you love."

She turned to stare at Alex again.

"And Sophie."

64

I love you, she'd said. *I'm not leaving you, Chester.*

He played the scene with Nancy over in his head as he drove the truck. Carefully, not over the speed limit. He didn't want to get stopped. And people might be inbound.

You've become very dear to me, and I'm not going away. He could still see and hear her saying that. And he could see she meant it.

In his whole life, no one had ever said that to him. Not Sally. She didn't love him. He understood, deep down, that Ivan loved him too, in the same way he loved Ivan. They wouldn't have said it like that, because they were men. They wouldn't have used the word *love*. But they were a family.

With Nancy it was different. This was men and women love. With sex. Which was better since Shane.

Nancy would probably think what he'd done, tying her up with the tape, was weird. But he didn't hurt her, and he didn't mean it to be weird. It was for her sake. *I love you and I'm not going away.* She was telling the truth. So it would just be a one-time thing, like a mistake. He'd apologize, and they could keep going like they were. He imagined what it would be like if he and Nancy weren't together anymore. He didn't want to go back to that, being alone at home and thinking all the time and not *making love*—that's what she called sex—with Nancy. The thought of it made him feel scared and lonely again.

He would explain it to her, without telling her the real reason, and tell her he was sorry. He was in the middle of something and it could have been dangerous for her so he had to protect her. Something like that.

She just showed up. He wasn't able to think about what to do with her. She never came to his house, except once on the way to the fair, so he couldn't have done anything else. He couldn't have figured it out that fast. It wasn't his fault.

And after he tied her up and came back into the barn, Ivan started talking to him.

"The jig is up here, Mister. If that one knows you're here, someone else might too. They could be inbound any minute. You best get your party out of here now, Chester. Take them Uncles of Heaven with you, and finish up in-country. You hear me? Go on, now."

Chester wouldn't have said it like that, used those words—*inbound, your party, in-country*—that was the way Ivan always talked, army language, though Chester always knew what he meant. And nobody else ever called him *Mister*. So he knew it was really Ivan talking to him.

"Okay, then," Chester had replied.

So he got Ethan and Sophie in the truck and the Uncles of Heaven and all the rest of the stuff and got out of there. Nancy would be okay. She wasn't hurt and the tape wasn't too tight and she could breathe. He'd come back and untie her and figure something to tell her about why he'd done it. He couldn't think of anything now but he would later, when it was all finished and he had time to think. And then they'd be like they were, only better now.

Because . . . now that he thought about it since Nancy said it . . . he loved Nancy too. He'd loved Sally, but she didn't love him and made it all a secret. Nancy was the way she was with him in front of other people, calling him *dear* and being nice to him. It made him proud. They were having a real man-and-woman relationship like he'd never had before. And the sex part had just got better. Now it would get a lot better.

It hadn't worked so well after Byron Pugh. He'd gone to a few bars up in Bangor, far from Granite Harbor so nobody would know him, and met some girls. They wanted money and he paid a few times, but he could tell they were probably just doing it for the money. He didn't do it well then either. Maybe because they didn't love him and he didn't love them.

Now it was different. Nancy laughed when they did sex and made noises out loud, small cries and moans. More than Sally ever did. He could tell she was really liking it. So much that it even hurt her, she said.

He'd seen the boys, Shane and Jared and Ethan, with those girls. They were *sexy*. They had it. There were always lots of girls around Shane, and Jared had hooked up with that weirdo Ashley, who could probably get a much older man, and he could see the way Ethan's girl liked him. They had the essence. It worked for them. And fuck them for hiding his tools and making him look for them and laughing at him in front of the other kids.

The first time, with Nancy, he could see she was just being nice to him. He wasn't able to control himself, worse than with Sally, worse than with the girls in Bangor, and it got all over the outside of her. They wanted it inside. He was embarrassed. He'd wanted to get out of bed right then and never come back. But Nancy made him feel it was okay. She held on to him and told him it was wonderful even when it wasn't.

It got better after he got the essence out of Shane. It would have been even better if Jared hadn't gotten away while he was in the hospital. He got his essence but he didn't display him in a proscenium.

Ex turpi serpentis nova essentia creata est. Now, with Ethan's essence, the sex would be a lot better. Nancy would love him more. They'd be a family.

He didn't want anything out of the girl. He didn't know what he was going to do with her. Ivan would call her collateral damage. Something that got in the way. But she'd seen him, so he'd have to do something with her. Maybe just hit her on the head and bury her somewhere.

I was doing an experiment in the barn and it was dangerous and you wouldn't leave so I had to tie you up to protect you and I had to get back to it right away . . . with gasoline, so it could have exploded . . . or something like that. He'd have to figure out what and make it sound realistic. . . .

Chester reached the Fairhaven Road and turned.

65

They were back in the truck. Ethan remembered it from earlier, before the thing with his stomach. Now what? Sophie was beside him again, rolling against him as the truck bounced and swerved. Had Chester done the same thing to her stomach too? She was making noise, like crying or whimpering, but her mouth was taped shut too.

He was cold. He felt the cold truck bed beneath him. On his skin. Was he naked? Was Sophie? He couldn't see. His head rolled around as the truck moved, but he had no strength to lift it.

It felt like a dream, because the pain was in his body and Ethan had left his body. He was stoned . . . or something, he knew it . . . because he was floating inside the truck's hardtop, hovering over his body and Sophie's. But he could see shapes of moonlight in the clouds through the rear window.

One cloud looked familiar. As he looked, it acquired shape and definition. It was his father. Right through the truck window. Not a cloud now, nor a dream, but his father looking back at him. He was laughing, bending over Ethan, tickling him like he used to without mercy, on the pink sofa in the living room. Only his father always had the power to tickle him senseless, until he was writhing and screaming, about to wet his pants. No one else. Right up until Ethan last saw him, before he sailed, and his father tickled him on the sofa. He saw him now, in vivid detail. Every whisker of his droopy mustache, his teeth and tongue as he laughed, hovering over Ethan, tickle-attacking him on the sofa.

"Dad—stop!" he said, trying to talk through his giggles. "I want to tell you about this ship in a bottle. You'd like it. It's made me think about you a lot."

"Tell me."

"Dad, it's the *Concordia*. One of the Arctic 1871 ships. The scene inside has icebergs. The glass is wavy and uneven and makes the ship look almost like you're seeing it through a storm. I think whoever made it must've been there."

"I'm sure you're right, Ethan."

"I'm trying to fix it the way it was made, not too good but with some rough parts, like matchsticks or chopsticks for the spars, and keep the scene there the way the builder saw it. It makes me feel closer to you, Dad."

Ethan had always wanted to have this conversation with his father. He was the only person who would get it, really understand what he saw in old ship models, ships in bottles. "I'm learning how to use your tools, Dad. I'm doing what you used to do."

"I can't tell you how happy that makes me, Ethan. What are you going to do with the *Concordia* when you've finished?"

"I want to try to sell it. But someplace important, where they'll recognize what it is, and pay me well for it. Like maybe a museum—it's like a museum piece, you'd know it right away if you saw it. I want to sell it for enough money to buy Mom a new furnace for the house."

"It's so good to hear that you're looking after your mother. How is she?"

"Oh, Dad . . ." Now Ethan felt the years since his father had gone. All the things he'd missed. "You don't know how things have been. Mom pulls her hair out. . . . We really miss you, Dad. Where are you?"

"I miss you too, Ethan."

"Where are you, Dad?"

"I'm at sea."

"I wish I could hug you, Dad."

"I'm hugging you now, Ethan."

The truck bumped beneath him, pulling him back down into his body, where he felt the fire that was burning through his stomach.

"Daddy?"

The hardtop window showed only hazy moonlight.

• • •

The truck lurched to a stop and he felt himself rolling into Sophie. She was crying.

He heard noise through the roof of the hardtop. Now it was sliding over the roof. Then the noise of wood and metal outside. Something being put together. . . . He remembered Chester making the obstacle course for camp at the Y, bolting long pieces of wood together . . . when they hid his tools all over, and it was hysterically funny watching Chester looking for them. . . . Was he still pissed off because of that? Is that what this was about? What had happened to Shane and Jared? Really? So why Sophie?

The hardtop window was pulled open, the tailgate dropped down. Ethan felt himself sliding feet forward, his bare butt dragged across the truck bed. Turned upside down. Bumping, lurching, floating like flotsam on a jerky sea. Beams of light and shadow played around the head rocking above him, the hair diffusing into wisps and halos. A great buffalo head snorting plumes of vapor.

He was on the ground. Buffalo Head stepped away and came back in the white lights. Huffing and puffing, steaming. Ethan's hands were lifted and pulled together above his head. The fire inside him had turned to ice. His arms jerked up above him, pulled upward. His shoulders lifted after them. His arms stretched to new pain from his shoulder sockets and he was dangling, spinning like a fish on a hook.

His head fell down onto his chest, and he saw he was naked, bloody—and *what the fuck?* The front of him, all down his stomach, open like an unzipped jacket.

Buffalo Head came into view. Chester pushed his hand through the zipper in Ethan's stomach.

Just. Too . . .

Chester drew out his hand—Ethan's head still fallen over his chest, nowhere else to look. The frog again. He lifted it close to Ethan's face.

"Ex turpi serpentis nova essentia creata est."

What?

Chester was squeezing the frog's head again. The white stuff oozing out through the skin. Chester raised the frog to his mouth and sucked at its head.

66

In the car, Alex jabbed his thumb at his phone. "Mark! Get out to Chester Coffey's house—fast. Something may be going on there. If Chester's there, bring him in. Take backup. Let me know what you find. I'm on my way to the Settlement, with Isabel Dorr. There may be something happening there too. I'll call you. Call me when you get there. Get there fast."

Five minutes later, Isabel grabbed his arm. "Here!"

"I know." He braked hard at the GRANITE HARBOR LIVING HISTORY SETTLEMENT sign, drifting through the turn.

It was all she'd said on the frantic drive. Did you see Sophie? he'd asked. She nodded her head. Where? Is she okay? She would only jab her finger at the windshield. The blue lights in his Subaru grille strobing the road as he tore on.

She pointed through the windshield. They were descending alongside the blueberry barren, almost at the parking lot. "Take the service road. Not the parking lot."

"Why?"

"I can't—" She shook her head briefly with frustration. "Take the service road!"

Alex slowed and turned into the unmarked gap between the trees. It curved in a rough semicircle through the woods—

"There . . ." Isabel's voice came with a sudden inhalation of breath. She pointed out her passenger window, where the arc of the service road was

revealed by the high beams of a stationary vehicle through the trees. "...
There!"

Alex saw the lights. Whoever it was had no route of escape without re-
turning along the road and meeting them. He sped up, a volley of gravel
striking the underside of the car as they skidded around the long bend
through the trees until his headlights crossed the beams ahead, and the scene
in the clearing came into view.

A stark chiaroscuro: Chester's truck, angled with its row of high beams
above the snowplow blade boring a cone through the fog swirling off the
marsh, illuminating Ethan's body, white except for the dark wet slash and
rivulets down the front, hanging suspended by his bound wrists. A night-
marish reproduction of what had been devised for Shane. Identical to the
photograph he'd seen of Byron Pugh dangling at Prouts Neck. But Ethan
was moving. Revolving slowly on the rope, as if just hoisted.

Where was Sophie? The truck? The hardtop's rear window was open, tailgate
down—

"Isabel—*wait!*—" She was opening her door. The car was still moving.
He braked, grabbed a sleeve, but she wrenched it free and was out the door,
running.

Alex fumbled maddeningly for a moment with his seat belt, then was
running around the car after her, slipping on the gravel.

"*Wait!*" he hissed. *She was running straight into it.* He thought of calling Mark
again, but there was no time. He ran after her.

No sign of Chester, but he had to come lumbering out of the dark any
moment, out of his truck maybe—still running, powering the high beam
with the big engine idle. The sound filled the small clearing like a waiting
school bus.

Alex's hand went to the Glock under his arm, but he withdrew it. He
needed both hands to get Ethan down—

She was shrieking. A mother's primal howl. She reached Ethan and
wrapped her arms around his legs, trying to hold him up. "*Ethan! Hold on!
Help me! Help me get him down!*"

"*I am...*" Alex followed the rope up from Ethan's wrists to the overhead
strut, down to where it looped around the galvanized cleat bolted to the

vertical frame—at the same time trying to look around. He raised the first loop, lifting the line over the top prong of the cleat—

An electric shock coursed through his upper body. Concentrated in his head, neck, right shoulder. He lay on his back looking up at the swirling vapor in the air. He didn't pay attention to the screaming until it stopped. It ceased abruptly and then he heard its absence, like the sudden cessation of the drone of cicadas. He tried to turn his head, triggering another stabbing electric jolt in his neck. He felt paralyzed.

At the edge of his vision, against the light-filled swirling air, a figure bobbed, working in small deliberate movements. That noise. *Eeeoow*—the noise of tape peeling off a roll.

He tried again to move his head, a few millimeters for a better view. He made out the dark bulk of Chester bent over Isabel—her shorn head—a few feet away. He was wrapping tape around her head and hands.

He understood what had happened to his head and neck. The brachial stun. He was literally stunned, as if Tasered. If he tried to move, do something, he would have no strength—

Where was Sophie?

Ethan still revolving above, in the headlights. Streaks of blood down his legs.

Alex lay on his right side. He'd collapsed on top of his right arm, which was stretched out almost straight behind him. He twitched his right hand, to see that it worked, would work. He would have to roll off his arm, pull his hand free, bring it across his chest and beneath his coat—*was his coat open?*—to reach the Glock. Chester was four feet away, bending over Isabel. There would be no time for a fumble or a misplaced movement. Roll, reach, draw, swing, aim for the center of the bulk, and fire. And keep firing.

He'd never fired his gun outside a practice range.

Go. He rolled, got his hand out from beneath him, reached, dug into his armpit—the Glock was gone.

Chester turned his head almost lazily to watch. He rose to a crouch, crossed the few feet, and bent over him. The woolly head, the flyaway hair and furry beard, backlit against the vaporous lit-up air—holding a roll of duct tape. Alex could smell rank sweat. Chester flipped him over onto his stomach, pushed a knee into his back, pulled his arms roughly together.

Eeeooww . . . Tape bound tightly around his wrists.

"Chester . . ." His voice was strangled, his throat felt numb. But he pushed out words. "Chester . . . stop. This can't work. . . . It's over. We know it's you. People are on their way here. Your plan won't work—"

"You don't know what my plan is." Chester had no tone to his voice— rather, a monotone entirely without pitch. Alex had spoken with him before, but he only noticed it now. Chester was engaged in some strenuous effort, the unfolding of his big plan, much of it physical, yet he spoke as if reading aloud letters on an eye chart exam.

"Tell me about your plan," said Alex.

Pretty lame, but it didn't matter. Had to keep him talking. That was what you did with loony killers—inasmuch as he knew anything about it. You kept them talking to stretch out the seconds until something happened, the reinforcements arrived—Mark and Becky at some point. Would they go to the main entrance? Would they hear the truck, see the lights through the trees on the service road?

"You can't get away with it, Chester. We're onto you—we found you. Others are coming. What do you think you're going to achieve by this?"

You talked to the killer. Tapped into his insane ego because he was dying to tell you, somebody, his clever plan, while time elongated and something might stop him. The killer needed to tell the world how smart he was. You kept them talking until you could make your move—you talked because it was all you could do. Your last card.

"Chester, tell me about the toads. I don't understand—"

Eeeoow—tape sealed his mouth. Chester's hand pressing it hard, then he wound the roll around Alex's head.

Talk wasn't going to work.

Alex was left with only his eyes. So now he watched, all that was left to him.

How much would he see? *Oh God, Sophie dragged out of the truck and strung up?*

He watched as Chester's left hand, holding the short fat knife, lowered close to his face and then dropped out of view below his nose. Alex's entire nervous system gathered to feel the first prick of the blade. His eyes fixed on

Chester's head and upper body, bending close, his stench prickling the inside of his nose—

Too fast for comprehension, everything transformed.

Chester's left side was slammed backward by the kick from an invisible horse's hoof—

At the same time the enormous *boom*, like a cannon—

The dark leather at Chester's left shoulder exploded outward in red and white tissue—

Hot, wet, sharp on Alex's cheeks and forehead, in his eyes—

A second kick hit Chester's chest. Another eruption spattering the rest of Alex's face . . .

Chester lay almost still across his legs. Alex wriggled free like a trapped fish. His movement was violent and uncontrolled and he rolled away until he lay on his back, winded, looking up—

Above him, not two feet away, against the dark sky and the filmy, light-saturated air, he saw Morgana from the knees of her riding breeches up, legs apart in the shooter's stance she'd learned as a child from her granddaddy. The short, bulky stainless steel revolver—not a lady's gun but the up-close-and-personal snub-nosed killer she favored—in her two-handed extended grip.

She remained rigid, unmoving. Nothing was ever finished quickly with her. Nothing she enjoyed was cut short. So she deliberated now—he saw it, knew her and understood as he watched—then she fired two more shots, spaced a long, gratifying second apart.

67

Morgana didn't stop to free Alex. He rolled on his side and watched as she ran to Chester's truck. He saw her pulling Sophie out—he didn't see any blood—saw her hands pulling the tape off, sharply, efficiently, and then he heard Sophie's whimpers.

Somehow, Isabel was up, pulling tape off her arms and legs and scrabbling with the rope holding Ethan up.

Alex sat up. He made noises through the tape over his mouth. He wanted to say "Let me help . . ." But the two mothers didn't need his help.

Then he saw the flashing lights . . . Mark running into the scene. Behind him Becky Watrous and Chief Raintree. They went to Ethan and Sophie. . . .

An ambulance, big and red, came into the clearing. The trees were full of the strobes of flashing light.

It was Sophie who finally came and freed him. Pulling the tape off him. "Dad"—she was crying—"are you okay?"

"Yes, sweetheart. Are you?"

He hugged her until she said, "Ow, Dad."

"What? Are you hurt?"

"You're hurting me."

Mark had released Nancy from the cobweb taping her to Chester's bed. He'd helped her out to his cruiser, and then they'd driven through the night faster than she'd ever traveled in a car in her life while Mark spoke to people on the radio, and then they arrived at the Settlement. . . . She'd held Isabel while the EMT people worked on Ethan.

Finally she was alone. One of the EMTs had given her a Mylar blanket, and she hugged herself.

The EMT team was strapping Chester onto a gurney. Nancy walked toward them.

Chester's mouth was open and gulping for air.

"Oh, Chester," she said.

Chester's eyes, roaming overhead through the lights in the trees, dropped and found her.

Nancy stared at him. "I thought you were . . . so sweet."

Chester opened his mouth. A bubble of blood rose out of it and grew almost translucent as it enlarged, and then more blood filled it and spilled over his lips into his thick beard. He tried to make his lips work.

"I . . . am . . . sweet."

"I have to ask you to stand back, please," said the female paramedic, working with three male EMTs.

Nancy stepped back. They lifted the gurney until its collapsible legs extended beneath it, and maneuvered it toward the ambulance.

Part Five

68

Often in the night now Isabel woke as the furnace came on. A small rumble barely at the threshold of sound from the basement two floors below. January in Maine, and the house was warm. It seemed like a miracle.

The ticking of the radiators brought an additional, immeasurable warmth. In some way Ethan had brought his father home. Joshua's passion picked up spontaneously by his son, self-taught, resulting, across the decade and more since his disappearance, in a boy with a passion, a new furnace, a warm house. She had no words.

"You'll see, Mom," he'd said, "this'll bring in the bucks. I'm going to buy you a new furnace."

"That'll be great," she'd said, pretending to shiver, or really shivering, wrapped in a fleece throw as she left a tray on his table. She was simply relieved he had something to take an interest in. That he was coming back to life.

"You don't believe me. But you'll see."

She was happy that he believed it. They were both happy he was able to work bundled in bed with blankets and comforters against a bank of pillows, while the house remained frigid.

She bought a hospital tray table that moved on casters and allowed him to position the bottle, with clamps from his workshop, at eye level, over his chest, and concentrate on it through weeks of pain.

When he was finished, Ethan sent an email, with photos, to Llewellyn Cruikshank, director of collections at the New Bedford Whaling Museum. He wrote that he believed the ship in the bottle ("please see attached photos"), the *Concordia*, might be the same *Concordia* owned by the Howland Whaling Company that had been one of the fleet of thirty-two New Bedford whaling vessels trapped and sunk by ice off the coast of Alaska during the unseasonably early onset of winter in 1871. He believed that the ship in the bottle might have been made by a member of the *Concordia*'s crew. And it was the rare ship in a bottle that offered a perspective scene, rather than simply a ship viewed from either side of the bottle.

Three days later, Llewellyn Cruikshank himself drove up to Granite Harbor to see it. He took many photographs with a Canon SLR camera and several lenses.

"Fascinating," he said, peering through the wavy glass. "An estate sale? Well, of course, there was a strong connection between Granite Harbor and New Bedford. The ships built here brought a lot of granite and lumber down to us, and your shipyards built some of our whaling vessels. And you did the restoration yourself, Ethan?"

"Yes, sir." Ethan showed him the before and after pictures.

Two days later, Mr. Cruikshank phoned him. Michael Dyer, the museum's Curator of Maritime History, believed Ethan's ship in the bottle was the work of African American boatsteerer Archaelus Bowen, whose work was characterized by views of historical incidents rather than simply ship reproductions, and was highly esteemed. The museum had several other works by Bowen in its collection. Bowen had indeed sailed to the Arctic aboard the *Concordia*, his name recorded in the ship's log. Both Cruikshank and Mike Dyer were highly impressed at Ethan's deduction that the creator of his bottle had been aboard.

"Cool," said Ethan.

"You may certainly look elsewhere"—Cruikshank named several institutions and collectors, Ethan was familiar with some of them—"but I don't think you'll do better than what we're prepared to offer you. We feel strongly that New Bedford is the proper home for such a representation of a famous local vessel, and one of the 1871 fleet. This, and Bowen's almost certain authorship, informs our evaluation. The museum will be happy to make you an offer of twenty-five thousand dollars."

Ethan's phone was on speakerphone. Isabel was standing beside him. He'd told her he hoped they might offer $5,000—enough for a furnace and its installation.

Isabel put her hands to her face and stared at Ethan through her fingers.

He'd practiced his response—for $5,000, but it seemed to work for this price too. "That will be acceptable, thank you . . . sir."

Two men drove up from the museum to collect it, assembling their own crate in Ethan's workshop to transport it. A week later the money was deposited in his bank account. Ed Jackson of Maritime Energy came to the house with catalogs, and together Isabel and Ethan chose the new furnace. It was in and humming, sending out hot water, radiators ticking, by Christmas Eve.

Mr. Cruikshank called again in late December. They would like to do an event, he said, an official unveiling of the Bowen *Concordia* in the museum's Harbor View Gallery. They greatly hoped that Ethan would give a presentation, with photos, of his restoration.

"Yes, of course," said Ethan, not really understanding what this meant, but grateful and wanting to be agreeable. As the date approached and he emailed and Zoomed in preparation with the museum staff, he got scared shitless.

It was scheduled for late January, when Ethan's recovery would permit him to attend.

Isabel called Alex, told him about the sale, the event at the museum, and invited him to come with them.

She'd seen him only three times since the night at the Settlement. Once when he interviewed Ethan at the Maine Medical Center in Portland. He'd waited a week after Ethan's surgery, until Isabel told him he was well enough to talk. She was present when he told Alex what he could remember about that night. How Chester had taken them from the van, cut him open in the barn, pushed the toad into his stomach. How Chester rubbed the frog's white stuff around in his mouth and how it made him feel. He hadn't mentioned any of this to his mother.

She became so upset that Alex stopped the interview.

She'd had no idea Ethan had known Chester for years.

Alex visited twice after Ethan came home. Once to ask him more questions about Chester, and once just to see how he was doing, he said.

Isabel asked him to stop by again, anytime, and stay longer. She invited him to dinner, but he stayed away. She sensed he was avoiding her. She felt like they'd been in a storm or a shipwreck together. She wanted to talk with him, see him again in what was beginning to resemble normal life.

She missed him.

"Ethan would really like you to come with us," she said on the phone. "I would too. We could drive down to New Bedford together. I think Sophie's coming—not with us, but I'm pretty sure she's coming. Most of the Settlement people are also coming. I'm sure everyone would like you to be there."

"I'd be honored to come, thank you."

Sophie had thought of going with Ethan and Isabel—Isabel had invited her too—but she wanted her mother to come and see what Ethan had done, and what a big deal it was. It was difficult to get Morgana to go anywhere. She detested flying and preferred to drive everywhere, unless she had to cross an ocean, but Morgana hated to be driven. She never went anywhere with anyone else driving. She agreed to drive down to New Bedford in her truck if Sophie went with her and they made a mother-and-daughter stop in Boston on the way back. They would spend two days at the Beacon Hotel and shop. Sophie accepted her conditions.

They were in a new phase of their relationship. Sophie had been totally creeped out to learn that her mother had been tracking her phone. She asked her to promise not to track her anymore. She talked about her right to privacy, and Morgana emitted her theatrical cackle. There had been some tension between them, even though everybody thought it was awesome that Morgana had shot and killed Chester Coffey and saved Ethan and her father and herself, by tracking her phone.

Morgana had long held a concealed-carry permit issued by the state of Maine, and no charge had been brought against her after the shooting, although the Calder County DA had, pro forma, asked for an explanation of the circumstances and her presence at the Settlement on the night in question.

Her lawyer drew up a response that represented her actions as entirely reasonable, especially given the presence of her daughter bound in duct tape in the back of Chester Coffey's truck, and the DA's office and the Calder County Court agreed and troubled her no further.

For about a week, a group of people, headed by Glenn and Tinker Bell, including Ralph Lansing, who every day of the year hung a large American flag and the sign GOD BLESS OUR TROOPS outside Lansing Liquor on Main Street in Granite Harbor, had lobbied for Morgana to run for Calder County sheriff, or legislator, or any public office.

Sophie was intrigued by the idea of her father being the Granite Harbor police detective and her mother the Calder County sheriff. How would that work? Alex hadn't heard anything about it, and he reminded her that he didn't like being pranked and this one was particularly unfunny.

"No, it's serious," she said. "Glen and Tinker Bell want Mom to be sheriff."

Her father pretended to laugh, poured himself a Scotch, turned on BBC Radio 4 to a show he liked to listen to called *The Week in Westminster*, which featured grown men in Parliament braying like sheep. He sat down on his English sofa and started drinking.

She asked him who would have more authority, a police detective or a sheriff, and he told her they would have different responsibilities and there would be no conflict between jurisdictions. Sophie said that was ironic, because it would be the only area where her parents wouldn't have conflict.

Since leaving Maine Medical Center, Ethan had traveled no farther from home than to friends' houses a few streets away. For the ride down to New Bedford, Alex and Isabel made him comfortable lying across the backseat of Alex's Outback, propped up with pillows. Isabel sat in the front passenger seat and fed them grilled cheese and vegetable sandwiches on sourdough focaccia that she'd made for lunch.

In the car, Alex was aware of a strange doppelgänger dislocation. It was like being part of a normal family—mother, father, child on an outing—something he'd never experienced as long as he'd been a parent. He'd seen them on the roads, parked in state and national parks, families talking and eating in cars and enjoying one another's company. The sandwiches were delicious. Isabel reached over and tucked a cloth napkin into his shirt collar while he drove and gave him paper towels to wipe his hands on. They drank Perrier. Ethan told Alex more about the Bowen bottle, and what had happened in the Arctic in 1871.

Alex couldn't believe how nice they were to him. What sweet, decent people they were. The way they all talked together. This other life some fathers had known.

South of Hampton Toll, Ethan fell asleep. Isabel wore a long creamy cashmere sweater dress that draped around her like a fleecy throw. She sat angled comfortably in her seat with her back against the door, her down jacket a cushion, half facing Alex, one black stockinged knee crossed over the other, close to the gearshift so that he kept seeing it.

The Harbor View Gallery was packed. Half of Granite Harbor seemed to be there. The Granite Harbor Settlement players: Monte and his partner Forest, Nancy Keeler, Bill and Jan Conrad, Jeff Block.

Chief Raintree and her wife, Barbara.

Morgana and Sophie.

Sophie was suddenly with them, hugging Ethan, carefully. Then she hugged Alex, which somehow made the entire trip to New Bedford worthwhile, and she and Ethan moved away to find their own private museum space beside a wall of bent harpoons. Both had been receiving counseling through a school-appointed therapist, and they'd become inseparable in the weeks after their abduction. Sophie had spent hours in Ethan's bedroom as he worked on his bottle.

More than half the assembled audience were people he'd never seen before. Museum members, donors, supporters, trustees, staff members, and board members. Cashmere coats, bright winter sweaters, wool pants. A heaving sea of white hair like whitecapped waves, interspersed with a surprising number of younger people, in fleece and nylon.

An intimidating audience for Ethan. Easily over two hundred people in the large room. Alex had never faced such a crowd at his best attended book reading.

Llewellyn Cruikshank thanked everyone for coming, expressed pleasure at the turnout, declared the evening an exciting start to the museum's fundraising year. He thanked Senior Curator Mike Dyer and the museum staff. Finally he introduced the evening's guest.

Ethan rose stiffly and stood before the room. Sophie's tattoo had at last faded completely. Isabel's too. Ethan's curly dark hair fell loosely, parted in the middle, and from the second row in the gallery, Alex could still see, curtained between strands at the side of his forehead, a faint SHANE on the smooth skin. As if that name still pulsed inside Ethan and would not be dimmed or forgotten.

He wore a small microphone on his shirt collar. He held a remote device in his hand and raised it toward the projector.

The screen lit up with one of his earliest "before" photographs. The bottle, and the wreck inside.

"I saw this bottle at an estate sale. . . ." Ethan cleared his throat. "It didn't look like anything at first. It wasn't like an ordinary ship in a bottle, where it's usually just a model of the ship and you see it from both sides. This wasn't like that at all."

A series of photographs moved around the bottle—revolving it in effect—showing different views through the wavy glass.

"This one was only meant to be seen from one side. It tells a story. . . ."

Lots of people wanted to talk with Ethan after his presentation. He sat at a table beside Llewellyn Cruikshank. Isabel stood nearby, leaving him alone but watching people lining up to talk with her son.

Alex sipped a glass of wine and walked along the gallery walls, looking at the glossy oil portraits of whaleships and their owners and masters.

"Good evening, Detective."

Alex turned to see Chief Raintree and Barbara approaching him. He was startled to see lipstick on Chief Raintree's lips, rouge on her swarthy cheeks. She was dressed like a golfer at a country club dinner: white turtleneck, bright green blazer, cream slacks, and large deck shoes.

"Ethan has you to thank for this," said the chief.

"I was too late—"

"Alex." Chief Raintree gripped his arm. "You did a great job."

"I don't think I've yet figured it out. Not all of it."

He'd finally got a call from Frank Maroni, the North Carolina registered owner of the johnboat. He'd sold it to a Chester Coffey, he said. He
guessed Chester hadn't reregistered it. Was there a problem? This only confirmed what Alex now knew, that Chester's property lay on the Loon River
waterway, that Jared had somehow escaped in the unregistered johnboat
that had been tied to Chester's dock. Alex had explored and laid out his
conclusions in his lengthy report, but he knew a lot of it was guesswork.
And the toads . . .

That would take a novel to figure out. Getting inside a serial killer's head,
letting imagination take over . . . but that wasn't the sort of character or fiction Alex knew anything about.

"Are you working on the Granite Harbor history for the Historical Society?" Barbara, Chief Raintree's wife, asked him. Her eyes crinkled with
something like kind concern, as if asking him how he was doing with che-
motherapy.

"I've decided not to. I don't know how to write that sort of book."

"Then I hope you'll write another novel," said Barbara. "I would love that."

"I would too," said Chief Raintree. "As long as you don't leave us. Whatever's going on in there"—she tapped her own head—"is working for you as
a detective. The department needs you, Alex."

He'd thought about it. The horror of what had happened—had almost
happened to Sophie, and to Ethan. He wanted to hold on to his gun.

"I'm not going anywhere," said Alex.

"Good," said Chief Raintree.

And he accepted that he was a detective now. It was not unlike being a
writer. Nobody told you what to do. You had to figure stories out for yourself. Like driving in the dark.

Agent Harris had called him. He'd been generous. "You picked up on
things I didn't, Detective. It's good for me to see that."

He felt an arm slide through his, an unfamiliar sensation. Isabel was beside him.

"We'll let you go," said Barbara, pulling the chief away.

"You've been weird," said Isabel. "I've asked you over, for dinner, for whatever, doesn't matter. Both of us just wanted to see you, and say thank you.
Why have you stayed away?"

He hadn't been able to tell her how haunted he'd felt. He'd been seeing a counselor too. Now he tried.

"Well . . . I think there was more I could have done. I'm not sure what, I'm still trying to figure it all out. But if I'd known . . . more . . . what to do . . . maybe Jared wouldn't have been killed. Maybe I could have prevented what happened to Ethan."

"That's ridiculous, Alex. You *saved* Ethan. *And* Sophie. You found Ethan's hat in the van, you came and got me. You *listened* to me, you *believed* me. You could have thought I was crazy. All sorts of things could have happened. It's ridiculous to feel that way."

"I almost got us killed. I was unprepared. We were lucky she"—his eyes darted toward Morgana—"turned up."

"Are you upset that she was the one with the gun? That she shot the bad guy? She got there because she tracked Sophie's phone in your car—she followed *you*."

"No. I'm glad she did what she did."

Isabel found his hands with hers, gripped them fiercely, and pulled him closer. Her eyes blazed at him. Making a small private tunnel between them in the museum crowded with people.

"Please stop thinking this way. I don't know about police work and how things are supposed to be done, but everything you did worked out *perfectly*, Alex. Everything. All of it."

Her hair was about three inches long all over, dark, shot through with gray, but thick, tousled, a windblown effect. Like the hair curling and flapping around the heads of the whaleship captains in the portraits around the room. A style, maybe a fashion then, that made them all look storm-tossed. He'd only seen her recently in her cold house with a hat. Until today.

"You're growing your hair out."

"You noticed."

"Yes. I always loved your hair. Is it hard?"

"So far it's working. Ethan shouts at me if he sees me tugging at it. And I'm going back to school."

"You are? Where?"

"Stonecoast."

"The MFA writing course?"

"Yes."

"You want to write?"

"I've always wanted to. I want to write a novel."

"Really—?"

"Mom!" Ethan was grabbing her arm. One arm was wrapped around his stomach, but he was almost bouncing on his toes.

"Yes! What?"

"Llewellyn wants me to do more restorations for the museum! I might be able to work here someday! Can you please come and talk with Llewellyn? They're going to train me! Can you come now?"

"I'll be right there."

Ethan moved away.

"Go," Alex said to her.

"Alex. Will you stop this, please, whatever it is, and come to dinner? Unless you don't want to."

"No, I want to," he said.

"Really?"

"Yes."

"Soon?"

"Yes."

She squeezed his hand and left him amid the whaleships, the God-fearing captains, the storms, the harpoons.

Yes, I said yes, filled his head, *I will, Yes.*

fin

Acknowledgments

My literary agent, Patrick Walsh, does what I have not heard of many other agents doing: he line-edits my drafts, on paper, by hand, before and after the sale of a manuscript. As I write this, with *Granite Harbor* in production, he's still scribbling on and sending me pages. We talk and Zoom for hours about story, characters, writing. This is sorted and attended to before we ever talk about where and how to market the finished product. Dream agent. Thank you, Patrick, and all who work with you: Margaret Halton, Rebecca Sandell, Emily Hayward-Whitlock, Cora MacGregor, and John Ash.

My editor at Celadon Books, Ryan Doherty, saw what this book could/should be when I hadn't, quite. He and associate editor Cecily van Buren-Freedman tirelessly read and edited many drafts, helping me reduce a vast, baggy story—I don't want to belabor the metaphor, but it went from sprawling forest to neatly trimmed bonsai. The most compressed and indelible writing instruction I've ever received, and I'm more grateful than I can say.

The quality at Celadon Books is evident to me at every point in production. I'd like to thank publisher Deb Futter, associate publisher Rachel Chou, Jennifer Jackson, Jaime Noven, Randi Kramer, Sandra Moore, Rebecca Ritchey, Anna Belle Hindenlang, Julia Sikora, Anne Twomey, Erin Cahill, Jeremy Pink, Vincent Stanley, Emily Walters, and Faith Tomlin.

I've published six previous books, enough to know what a privilege it is to be copyedited by Shelly Perron. Will Staehle designed the beautiful cover.

A number of people read drafts and gave me hope and insight: Peter Selgin, Gillian Stern, Lara Santoro, Kate Christensen, Debra Spark, Katherine Howe, Tony Cohan, David Nichols, and my sister, Liz Sharp, who was always insightful and involved with the changes and path of the book from the very beginning.

Thanks to Roger Salloch, Yvonne Baby, Olivier Fourcade for the opera at your dinner table on Sunday nights in Paris, and Adrian Leeds, Jennie and Oskar and Katya von Kretschmann, Tina Sportolaro, Jane Gay, Julia Gay, Clemence Demaison, and Camille Michel Gay for friendship in Paris, where much of *Granite Harbor* was written. Caitlin Shetterly for giving me an outlet to write about Paris. David Nichols in Rome, Liz and Tony Sharp in Faversham, England. Tony Cohan, Lois LaRock, Tara Keairnes, Bob Block, and Sherwin and Peg Harris in Mexico.

The love and friendship of the dedicatees at the front of this book sustained me through the writing of it. I can't thank you enough.

And Gus, I celebrate you and all you've done during the time I worked on this book. Amazing.

About the Author

PETER NICHOLS grew up in the United States, England, and Europe and has lived for long periods in France and Spain. He is the author of the bestselling novel *The Rocks*; the nonfiction bestsellers *A Voyage for Madmen* and *Evolution's Captain*; and three other books of fiction, nonfiction, and memoir. His novel *Voyage to the North Star* was nominated for the Dublin IMPAC Literary Award, and his journalism has been nominated for a Pushcart Prize. He has an MFA from Antioch University Los Angeles and has taught creative writing there and at Georgetown University, Bowdoin College, and New York University in Paris. Before turning to writing full-time, he held a 100-ton U.S. Coast Guard Ocean Operator's license and was a professional yacht delivery captain for ten years. He has also worked in advertising in London, as a screenwriter in Los Angeles, a shepherd in Wales, and has sailed alone in a small boat across the Atlantic. He is a member of the Explorers Club of New York. He presently lives in Maine.

Founded in 2017, Celadon Books, a division of
Macmillan Publishers, publishes a highly curated list
of twenty to twenty-five new titles a year. The list of
both fiction and nonfiction is eclectic and focuses
on publishing commercial and literary books and
discovering and nurturing talent.